BEAUTIFUL RUIN

AMY OLLE

Copyright © 2015 by Amy Olle

Editing: Hot Tree Editing and Em Petrova Editing
Cover Design: Michele Catalano Creative
Cover Photography: Wander Aguilar
Cover Model: Andrew Biernat

ISBN: 978-1-944180-01-0

For my dad. I miss you.

ina Winslow's gaze journeyed across the once-grand room inside the old, abandoned home, over the range of rubble, rot, and ruin buried underneath layers of dust and dirt. It was a crumbling, dilapidated mess.

And it was all hers now.

"Well?" A niggle of panic closed the back of her throat. She inhaled a deep, steadying breath, only to choke on the mildew and decay in the air. "What do you think?"

At her side, her contractor, Sam, toed the bottom stair of the once-grand curved staircase in the one-hundred-and-fifty-year-old Winslow mansion.

The floorboard crumbled beneath his booted foot. "Congratulations. It's a shithole."

Her abrupt laugh kicked up a puff of dust in front of her face. "It's a fixer upper, for sure. It has potential though, right?"

Years of neglect had caused extreme damage to Mina's ancestral home. The summer before she was supposed to head off to college, her grandmother, Rose, had become ill and the massive house had fallen into disrepair. Since Rose's passing over ten years ago, the brutal north Michigan weather had lashed at the home with ferocious fury.

Now, Mina was determined to rescue the only home she'd ever known from the ravages of ruin.

Sam gave the banister a soft nudge, and the railing shook. "If I take on this project, I won't see my wife again until Christmas."

"I'll buy Sarah a fruit basket."

"We've got to rip out the plaster walls to get at the mold and upgrade all the electrical and plumbing." Sam ran his palm across a swath of peeling wallpaper. "We'll need a new roof to stop these leaks, and we'll have to deal with that crack in the foundation…. God knows what else we'll find once we start poking around her dark places. We're gonna have to tear her apart before we can put her back together again."

Mina gulped down a fresh surge of panic. "How much is all that gonna cost?"

He bent his head over his clipboard. "Her damage is… extensive."

Fear drummed in her chest. "We can save her, can't we?"

"Sure, but it won't be easy." His eyes swung to her face. "Or cheap."

"Right," she said around the lump in her throat. "How much?"

His long, lean face screwed into a grimace while he tallied the home's list of imperfections with small slashes of his pen.

The silence stretched out until the flow of oxygen to Mina's lungs rasped to a halt.

His hand dropped to his side. "You're looking at damn near six figures."

What little air she had in her lungs wheezed from her.

"That's only to keep her standing," he rushed to add. "To make her livable, it's gonna be upwards of that by a lot."

Busy running her own calculations, Mina's brain tripped over the massive numbers.

The house's poor condition had knocked the sale price down to a manageable five figures, for which she intended to pay cash with a portion of her unused college tuition. She'd also created a detailed spreadsheet with rough cost estimates for all the renovations she expected to need, offset by the paycheck she earned from her day job and the potential income she expected to bring in when she opened her doors as a bed and breakfast next summer.

Sam's estimate meant she wouldn't turn a profit for...a very long time.

"You're going to buy it, aren't you?" Sam asked.

She managed a weak smile. "I already did."

His critical gaze swept around the room once more. "You sure she's worth it?"

When she surveyed the space, she didn't see the flaws drawing Sam's trained eye. Through the wall of murky glass doors running across the back of the house, a lush green lawn gave way to sand and sea stretching to the horizon. The sun hung low over Lake Michigan and chased the chill from the room with pink, orange, and lavender swirls. It was a million-dollar view for a money-pit house.

But having lived in the house as a teenager, Mina remembered the grand estate before its slide into disrepair. She'd been happy here.

Happy and *safe*.

She shook off the memories.

For the second time in her life, this house was her fresh start. And after the year she'd just had, she was ready for a change.

"She's worth it." It was the only thing she knew for certain. "Will you help me save her?"

Sam gnawed on his lip for a moment, then shrugged.

"Sure," he said. "Why the hell not?" A cheeky grin brightened his face. "It's not my money we're throwing away."

~

WHEN SHE'D BOUGHT the house two months ago, Mina had wanted a home. Someplace she could call her own. A sanctuary away from the world. Free from cheating ex-boyfriends and all the other duplicitous jerks out there.

Because honestly, putting her heart into a ramshackle old house seemed infinitely safer than trusting it to a man.

Any man.

But to her disgruntled dismay, overseeing a massive home renovation meant, most days, she had a house full of strangers.

A house full of strange men.

Large, virile males greeted her at every turn. When their earsplitting power tools weren't shattering the quiet, their shouted commands and bickering, which contained more colorful language than she'd heard in her entire lifetime, echoed through the house.

She'd never realized it before, but men, especially men she didn't know and who she kept finding herself trapped alone with inside a house miles away from the nearest neighbor, made her nervous.

Sometimes, the anxiety became too much for her. On those days, she'd escape to an empty room and work alone.

Which is why, when Sam found her one afternoon in the library at the back of the house, he appeared exasperated. "There you are. We've got an issue."

She continued to peer at the two dozen paint chips taped to the wall. "I'm getting tired of hearing you say that."

"I'm tired of saying it, believe me."

First, a family of raccoons living in the fireplace had

required her to hire both an animal control specialist and a chimney repairman. Not large expenses, but ones not accounted for on her spreadsheet.

When the spring rains arrived, the basement flooded. Three times. After the final deluge, she'd paid for an extensive, *expensive* re-grade of the land around the house to funnel water away from the home or risk further damaging the home's foundational structure by letting it sit in a swamp six months out of the year.

Next, upgrades to the home's outdated plumbing system revealed that the well placement was no longer up to code and needed to be moved. With her heart in her throat, Mina had waited for the cost estimate to drill a new well.

She must've blacked out, because all she remembered was hearing the massive dollar amount spoken in her own uncharacteristically shrill voice. "Twenty thousand dollars?"

At that point, her spreadsheet had required a complete overhaul, and the next time she'd gone to the bank, she'd had to request an application to apply for a home equity loan.

Now, she risked a glance at Sam. "What is it this time?"

He ran a hand through his sun-kissed brown hair and scratched his scalp. "It's the well. Again."

"What? No. How?"

"They're pulling out."

"What?" Her heart lurched. "Why?"

"They found... something...."

She blinked at him.

He held out a small hunk of rust. "At first, they thought it was just a broken piece of metal or scrap."

He dropped the crusty object into her palm. Only two or three inches long, it held surprising heft. "What is it?"

"An arrowhead."

She frowned. "Okay... So...?"

Sam stuck something under her nose. "We need to

contact the state archaeology office and ask them to send someone out to inspect the area."

Reluctantly, Mina took the business card and glanced at the tiny black typeface.

"The crew won't resume installation of the well without their written approval."

Frustration gathered in the back of her throat as a growl. "Because of a broken arrowhead?"

"They say it might mean the site has some historic significance."

She shot Sam a pointed look. "What do *you* think?"

Wrinkles formed between Sam's eyebrows. "I suppose it's possible."

Her boss at the university, Walter, had been a faculty member in the anthropology department before he'd accepted the promotion to dean five years ago. Maybe he could give her some advice or help her find someone to check out her back yard right away. She couldn't afford another delay.

She squinted down at the dirt-covered barb in her hand. A tiny morsel of hope implanted in her chest and drove out the creeping hysteria. "It could end up being a good thing."

"Oh?" Skepticism drenched Sam's measured tone. "How so?"

"What if it's something super cool, like an old fort or a settlement? It might attract visitors to the island." Visitors who might turn into guests at her bed and breakfast.

"Maybe..." He attempted to hide the doubt in his voice. "But while we wait, your renovation is on hold."

The blunted tip of the arrowhead pressed into her palm when she fisted her hand into a tight ball. "The entire renovation?"

"Unless we can reshuffle some contractors to work around the fact that there's no water..."

"Can't we move the well someplace else?"

Sam was shaking his head before she'd even completed the question. "Code requires we put it on the east side of the house, opposite the septic system. We can't push it farther out than it is now without running into tree roots from the grove. We can't come north because of buried power lines, and there's not enough firm ground between the house and the beach sands."

Panic threatened to overcome her, but she gave her head a hard shake and pushed it aside. "Okay," she said. "It's okay. I'll think of something."

First thing in the morning, she'd talk to her boss and consult her spreadsheet. Her simple plan had become a little more complicated, but her goals were still within reach.

As long as no more unexpected expenses cropped up. Neither she nor her spreadsheet could handle any more surprises.

~

NOAH NOLAN GAPED at the man across from him. "You're offering me a job?"

Walter Ambrose peered over the top of his wire-rimmed glasses. "Are you interested?"

Not even a little, Noah thought.

"Classes start at the end of this month and run through mid-May," Walter said.

No way in hell Noah would stay on the Island until next May. He pushed a hand through his hair and considered his next words.

Walter must've mistaken his hesitation for actual deliberation because he launched into a sales pitch. "We're a small school, but we have a lot to offer our faculty."

When Noah shifted in his seat, the wooden chair groaned beneath him. "I'm sure you do—"

"The student body is mostly in-state kids," Walter explained. "They're hardworking and bright enough—when they choose to apply themselves."

Noah bit back a sharp reply. "I'm flattered, but I'm not looking for a job. I'm on sabbatical."

The word tasted like failure on Noah's tongue.

Sabbatical.

His department chair had first uttered the offensive term last spring. At first, Noah had thought she was joking, but then she'd expressed her belief that he'd lost his fire. Burnout, she'd called it, then she'd suggested he take some time off from teaching at the university to recharge. To reawaken the passion that had driven him to the top of his field.

Her accusation had pissed Noah off.

Mostly because he knew she was right.

So he'd taken a year-long sabbatical, and for the first month of his "rest from work," he'd sat around his flat in Dublin with nothing to do except reflect on his life.

And drink.

As he'd teetered at the edge of an existential crisis, the letter had arrived from the States.

Noah pushed to his feet. "I thank you for the offer." That much was true, at least. "But I can't commit to anything long-term at the moment."

So that one was a lie. He was on sabbatical for the next several months and could do whatever the hell he wanted. He had no job, no family or friends holding him back. No wife or girlfriend to bother him. He was free.

So what if half the residents of this small, remote island preferred he stayed away and never came back? That truth hadn't factored into his decision-making process. Not at all.

He hadn't spent the last thirteen years worrying about what they thought of him, and he wouldn't start doing so now.

A disheartened smile fought its way across Walter's grizzled face. "I understand. I appreciate you hearing me out anyhow."

With an odd pang of regret, Noah accepted Walter's extended hand and gave a firm shake. "Thanks for letting me use your library while I'm in town."

"Sure, sure."

But Walter's attention had already shifted to the blanket of paperwork strewn across his desktop. His fluffy white eyebrows pulled together when he rescued the arrowhead fragment from amidst the clutter of papers.

Noah had noticed the relic while they'd talked. Late eighteenth century, if he had to guess.

Suddenly, Walter held up the arrowhead cradled between his fingers and his blue-gray eyes fastened on Noah's face. "You wouldn't be interested in something short-term, would you? Just a side project that's come up."

Noah resisted the surge of curiosity that prickled, but the words popped out of his mouth before he could restrain them. "What kind of project?"

CHAPTER 2

Mina crumpled the printed copy of her spreadsheet into a ball, and with an aimless flick of the wrist, sent it skittering across the across the cool wood floors of the shabby ballroom.

The hold on the new well had set off a domino effect of delays that had populated her spreadsheet with more bright red dollar signs than a department store closeout sale.

She lifted a wine bottle to her lips, tipped her head back, and drained a long swallow of cheap merlot. The alcohol didn't drown her anxiety, but the chilled liquid sliding down her throat fended off the oppressive, late-summer heat that invaded the room through the patio doors. Her limbs grew heavy, and the ballroom, where she sat on the floor with her legs outstretched, took on a cozy glow.

She lowered the glass and licked the sticky sweetness from her lips. The knot of fear tightening her shoulders remained.

Outside, soft rain fell. She plucked the flimsy fabric of her T-shirt away from her body as a breeze wafted in through the French doors to kiss her heated skin. A sigh of relief eased from her.

Then her gaze slipped to the cruel violence of upturned earth slashing across the pristine landscape of her back yard. Her stomach gave a little wrench.

Two weeks had passed since she'd shown the arrowhead to Walter, who'd declared it authentic, then promised to send someone to her house to assess the situation and give her crew permission to continue their work.

But no one had shown up.

Mina drowned the rising panic with another nip from the bottle.

With a start, she realized she was no longer alone. A presence infused the air. She turned her head to find a man standing beneath the archway.

The fading light threw shadows across the room and obscured his features. She could only tell that he was tall and broad-shouldered, strongly lean.

One of Sam's guys returned to retrieve a forgotten tool or misplaced hardhat. With her bad ear turned toward him, she hadn't heard his approach.

She climbed to her feet. "Let me guess. You forgot your favorite drill?"

The newcomer moved toward her with the smooth, fluid grace of someone comfortable with his body. "The door was open."

At the man's deep Irish brogue, she stilled. Her smile faltered and her heart tripped over in her chest.

How many times over the years had she thought she'd glimpsed him only to realize it was some other dark-haired man, someone else's schoolgirl crush?

He stepped from the shadows, and she found herself ensnared by dark, deep-set eyes, which might be brown or black but with traces of amber glinting throughout. Sort of like molasses.

Her stomach dropped with a dizzying swoop. She swayed. "Noah?"

For several long seconds, he stared, pinning her in place with those eyes.

"Hello, Mina." His voice was deeper, his accent more pronounced than she remembered.

His gaze slipped down the length of her body and wandered back up without hurry. She felt the perusal like seeking hands before his eyes gripped hers from beneath the sweep of black lashes.

Despite the muggy heat, a shiver raised gooseflesh across her skin.

"It's been a long time." His softly lilting accent tipped her world. "How are you?"

Her thoughts scrambled. *Lonely. Lost. Drunk.*

"Good," she lied. "You?"

He shoved his hand into the pockets of his blue jeans. "Good."

She wanted to thread her fingers through his dark hair. The soft strands, shot through with streaks of caramel and golden honey, curled at the ends and teased the tips of his ears and his nape.

Caramel, honey, molasses....

She realized then she shouldn't have skipped dinner in preference to the bottle of wine.

Noah's gaze dropped to the bottle in her hand. He gifted her with a lopsided grin. "Drinking alone?"

She held out the wine bottle to him.

With a quirked eyebrow, he drew nearer. His large hand closed around the bottle's thin neck, then he raised the wine to his lips. When he drank, the long column of his throat worked.

At the sight of him, his head thrown back and mouth pressed to the place where hers had been only moments before, an unfamiliar hum of sensation chased through her body.

A worn T-shirt hugged his broad shoulders and sinewy biceps and exposed a portion of the Celtic cross tattooed in black ink on his right arm. Beneath the collar of his shirt, a flash of silver glinted in the fading sunlight.

Mina's heart gave a little pinch. He still wore the St. Nicholas pendant.

She stared, trying to calibrate her fantasies—uh, memories—to the flesh-and-bone reality.

With a choked cough, Noah wrenched the bottle away. With his soft, full lips stained ruby red, he shot her a hard look of indignation. "This tastes like shit."

She lifted one shoulder. "They were buy one, get one free."

His low, throaty chuckle moved through her, transporting her to a fall night half a lifetime ago when they'd laughed together.

Hours later, he'd gasped in her ear when she'd taken him inside her body.

The memories dissolved when the tip of his tongue appeared to lap at the moisture on his lips. As if in echo of the disturbance inside her, a low rumble of thunder rippled across the distant sky.

Mina faked a calmness she didn't feel. "What are you doing here?"

He rolled his shoulders, as if to shake off the shadows that clung to him. But it was no use. The darkness lingered at the edges of his striking features. "Nothing but chasing ghosts, I fear."

At the soft sorrow in his voice, a pang struck her in the chest. "I'm sorry about your dad."

"Don't be." The light in his dark eyes took on a dangerous gleam. "He doesn't deserve your sympathy."

Her breath caught. "I'm sorry. I didn't mean to…"

"I know you didn't." With a sharp motion, his arm shot out, and he thrust the wine bottle at her. "It doesn't matter."

The air in the room grew thick with the heavy silence. Even the chorus of crickets outside had quieted.

The moment she closed her fingers around the smooth glass, he shoved his hands into his pockets. Turning his head and broad shoulders, he glanced around the room. His dark eyes were alert, exacting, and suddenly, she felt naked, exposed by his probing gaze.

When he discovered the faded frescos of impish cherubs floating across the ceiling overhead, a curious smile touched his lips.

"So," he began, "what brought you here tonight?"

"I live here."

Dark eyes swung to her face. "You live here? In this house?"

"Actually, I'm living in the carriage house out back while I do some renovations."

With a cold swiftness, his expression closed. "You own it?"

He continued his study of her home, this time with an alert, exacting gaze that took in every detail, from the dulled marble fireplaces at either end of the massive room to the crumbling plaster and tired hardwood floors, their poor condition visible even beneath the scattered array of power tools and sawdust.

When his gaze returned to her face, a rush of alarm chased through her as, for one terrifying, irrational moment, she feared he saw too much.

Heat warmed her cheeks, and she scrambled to erect barriers. To fight off the invasion. To keep hidden those parts of her no one should see. Even she did not inspect those places.

His smile lingered. "I love what you've done with the place."

A nervous laugh escaped her. "I know it's a mess." Then, because the wine had loosened her lips, more words tumbled out. "The previous owners couldn't keep up with the repairs. They walked away, and the house sat empty for years. Until I bought it from the bank three months ago, but everything's gone wrong and… well, you can see. It's a disaster."

For one aching heartbeat, his smile reappeared. "It's a great house."

Her heart struck against her breastbone with painful wallops. "It could be beautiful. One day."

"It's beautiful now." His voice was soft. "It just needs someone to see that. Someone like you."

Through the patio doors, raindrops plopped to the earth in a steady patter. The ceaseless rhythm lulled her, and in that moment of captivation, her barriers started to crumble.

She stared at him. A part of her wanted to hate him. Not only for leaving, but for leaving her, and for taking with him all that she'd ever wanted. But just then, she couldn't muster any anger. She felt only sorrow. Regret for the young girl who'd dreamed of his easy smile and longed for his gentle touched.

So many years between then and now.

So very many dreams never realized.

Before her eyes, his face swam.

When he swallowed, his Adam's apple bobbed in his throat. "What is it?"

"I can't believe you're here." Even knowing the wine made her weak, she couldn't crush the question of her heart. "Where have you been?"

He made a bitter sound, like a laugh but without a trace of

humor. Only a pained loneliness she recognized all too well. "Everywhere. Nowhere."

The emotion shimmering in his dark eyes drew her nearer to him.

His scent, a tormenting mix of soap and citrus and man, pulled her closer.

He stilled.

She might've shrunk back if not for the naked vulnerability playing across his features.

Slowly, she rose on her tiptoes.

Then she touched her lips to his.

With her mouth against his, he held himself immobile. Rigid.

Her heart stuttered to a stop. She pulled back so that she could see his face. "You're not married, are you?"

"No. Are you—?"

She gave a small shake of her head, cutting off his next words. "No. There's no one."

At her waist, he slipped his hand to the curve of her lower back. His palm splayed, and he bent his head low.

She tipped her chin.

But he didn't kiss her. At the last possible moment, he flinched. A tiny movement, which might as well have been a slap across her cheek.

As she watched, his well-shaped features hardened to stone. "Be careful, Mina. You're not slumming it with the Nolan bastard this time."

HOT FURY ERUPTED in her sapphire eyes. She opened her mouth, ready to lash out at him, but at the last, she swallowed it down with a ruthless resolve. Falling back, she put several feet between them.

She regarded him with huge, earnest eyes. "It wasn't like that."

She spoke of the past, but the present had gripped him by the balls and blinded him to all else.

Her youthful attractiveness had fallen away to reveal a goddess. Her features were sharper, clearer. Like a blurry photograph snapped into focus. Her large blue eyes seemed brighter. Her small, straight nose was more flawless.

Her kissable, over-plump mouth was exactly as he remembered. Except hotter.

High school was a distant memory as he gaped at the woman she'd become. All soft curves and gentle roundness offset by small, tantalizing dips and hollows. With her baby-doll face and cut-off blue jeans, she might've stepped straight off the pages of an X-rated fairy tale.

The effort to shake off the cobwebs of lust cost him much of his composure. "What was it like then?"

"I don't know, but whatever you're thinking, it wasn't like *that*."

"If you say so." He injected boredom into his tone to mask the bitterness.

Hectic color stained her cheeks pink. "You're the one who left."

She was right, of course. Except, "You didn't want me to stay."

"That's not true."

He couldn't let the lie go. "I came to see you, to tell you—to talk to you. You just smiled and said, 'Have a nice life.'"

Incredulous disbelief stared back at him. "I was supposed to beg you not to leave?"

"If that's what you wanted, yes."

She snorted. Actually snorted. "I wasn't that naïve. I understood what was between us."

Anger lashed at him. "What the hell does that mean?"

"We were young and having some fun. A wild, random hookup." She tugged on the hem of her sleeve, a self-conscious gesture he recalled from high school. When she did so, he saw her hands trembled. "It was nothing more than that."

His ire faded as quickly as it'd spiked.

He made a lazy, deliberate show of folding his arms in front of him. "So, you were just using me?"

She gave a firm nod. "Exactly."

"I feel so cheap."

Her eyes narrowed. "I'm glad you find this funny."

"I'm not laughing." His arms fell to his sides, and he took one cautious step toward her. "It was more than a random hookup, Mina. Wild, yes, but not random." As he spoke, he prowled nearer to her.

"Of course it was random. It was a one-night stand. That's the definition of random." Exasperation amplified her voice, and she stumbled back. "You might've been the best I've ever had, but it was still just a random one-night stand."

"It was none of those things. We'd been building up to it for months. Long before that night."

She waved off his words. "Technicality."

"Fact," he countered, pressing close.

She gaped at him as if he'd sprouted another head. He might have, for all the crazy shit coming out of his mouth. But it'd lived like a splinter under the surface of his skin for too long, and he wasn't about to walk away at his first real chance to extract the irritant.

"Fine." She planted her feet and lifted her chin in challenge. "What would you call it?"

Though he hadn't thought of their hookup in years, it all came rushing back to him, the memories so vivid they might've been imprinted on his brain.

It'd been fall of their senior year. The mingled scent of

damp soil, decaying leaves, and campfire smoke clung to him as he wound his way through a sea of costumed high school and college kids. That was when he saw her. All crazy-sexy curves and dark, wavy hair of an indeterminate color.

His feet carried him to her without his conscious consent. As he approached, she looked up and the heat from her smile warmed his belly.

He took in her dirt-stained white dress, torn at the shoulder and the thigh. A pair of feathered wings hung off her back at a cockeyed tilt, and her hair lay in artful disarray, a crooked halo buried in the riotous curls. A well-placed dirt smudge lived high on one softly rounded cheek.

His balls tightened. "Don't tell me. A fallen angel?"

"Yes! Thank you." Laughing, she shook her head. "Everyone keeps asking me if I'm okay. Like they think I fell or something." Her smile turned rueful. "I look ridiculous."

They drank keg beer and talked for hours, until lust and hunger drove them into the woods behind the house, where he helped her out of her wings and dragged the tattered hem of her costume up her thighs. Over her waist.

He remembered the feel of her legs wrapped tight around him. The rush of moving inside her. The heart of her clenching his cock while her soft moans echoed in his ear.

An angel, indeed.

Afterward, she acted as though he didn't exist.

The dark ocher of bitterness stained his memories of their night together. What would he call that night they'd spent making sweet, passionate love in the woods? A hookup? A moment of abandon?

A mistake.

His lips curled into a cold smirk. "I'm fond of your other description for it—what was it you said? 'Best you ever had,' I think it was? I can live with that."

The heightened color on her cheeks deepened to a

furious blush. "I said, 'might have been.' As in, you might have been the best I'd ever had, and it still wouldn't have changed anything."

"You don't just throw something like that out there unless you mean it."

The fire on her cheeks reached her eyes. "I was trying to make a point, not a statement of fact."

"Right."

She trained those doe eyes on him then. "Well, I didn't expect a marriage proposal."

A bark of laughter burst from him. The thought of Mina Winslow, the darling daughter of one of the wealthiest, most powerful political families in the state marrying one of the Nolan boys was too goddamn funny.

"Yeah, that would never happen." Not until the words left his mouth to sit in the air between them did he hear them as they must've sounded to her ears.

An awful, despairing look slashed across her delicate features. "I know that." She spoke with a quiet dignity that squeezed a spot in the center of his chest.

A flash of lightning streaked across the sky, followed by a crack of thunder that rattled the windowpanes.

The storm should've compelled his attention, but eyes the color of sapphires had captured him. In the darkening light, they gleamed, their vividness striking him like an electrical current. Vulnerable and imploring, yet somehow guarded.

Suddenly, he realized the danger he was in. "Look, I didn't come to do this."

"Why did you come?"

He shifted his weight. "I heard they found some artifacts." With a shrug, he spit out a lame lie. "I was curious."

He wasn't sure why he didn't tell her the truth. That they had asked him to assess the site and consider its suitability for excavation. Maybe a part of him wanted to know how she'd treat him if she still believed he was a high school dropout.

"It's too muddy to go back there right now." Turning her back to him, she moved toward the French doors overlooking the back yard. "You'll have to come back later."

Having dismissed him, her gaze searched the horizon like a seasick sailor seeking a stable reference point.

A rush of angry words rose in his throat. He wanted to tell her she was wrong about him. Wrong about them and what had happened between them all those years ago.

He opened his mouth, then snapped it shut again, biting down so hard his teeth made a loud clack.

What the hell was he doing? He couldn't argue with her. He couldn't dispute her claims and break down all the ways she was wrong.

Because she wasn't wrong.

And even if she was, it didn't matter. They were ancient history, and this was one historical event he had no desire to dig in to.

He turned to leave. Each step that carried him farther away from her seemed like another rung added to the ladder of his regrets.

He gave himself a mental shake.

The past was the past, no matter what they'd once had. No matter what they could have had. He and Mina Winslow had no future together. Unless he couldn't get to the site, there was nothing for him here.

CHAPTER 3

$\mathcal{N}$oah darted through the rain and ducked inside the black Chevy Colorado. The truck awoke with a growl, and—knuckles white on the steering wheel—he navigated down Mina's driveway and onto the winding coastal road leading back to town.

He pushed back a hank of wet hair from his face and peered through the whirring windshield wipers. Dark clouds loomed while whitecaps churned and battered the shore. Gray and violent, remote and forbidding. It summed up everything he remembered about the small island nestled off the western coast of northern Michigan.

Everything except her.

Less than eight miles long and three miles wide, the island's only connection to the mainland was a car ferry that made four trips per day. When he and his brothers came to live on the island from Ireland when Noah was just ten years old, they'd viewed the isolated community much as one would a prison sentence.

Until he'd met Mina. She'd been the singular bright spot

in his dreary existence. All these years, he'd assumed he was alone in that thinking. Now he knew otherwise.

Now, he knew he was the best she'd ever had.

A smug smile worked its way across his mouth, only to dissolve as he passed by the closed-up factory where his dad, Daniel, had sometimes worked. When he stayed sober long enough to remember to show up.

The icy rage that'd once leapt to life in Noah's chest when he thought of his dad didn't come. Something else had replaced it. Something new. Still heavy but less rigid.

Grief.

Exhaustion pulled at him, and he scrubbed a hand over his face.

On Main Street, he drove over the stone bridge and rolled into downtown. As the turn-of-the-century brick and mortar buildings drifted by, more haunted memories arose from the shadows in his mind. With an annoyed scowl, he shoved them back into their dark corners.

The thought of returning to a dingy motel room didn't appeal to him, so, on impulse, he whipped the truck into an empty parking space and killed the engine.

When he climbed from the cab, a wall of humidity hit him. Scents both familiar and foreign assailed him, but he resisted the pull to a time and place he'd rather not go and homed in on the only bar he hadn't once had to drag his drunk dad out of—Lucky's Irish Pub. The pub, which hadn't existed when he'd lived on the island, might be the best improvement made to this tired old town since he'd left.

With a quick glance, he crossed the street and bounded onto the sidewalk. He yanked the pub door open and stepped inside.

The dim interior enveloped him. When his eyes adjusted to the light, he scanned the room, taking in warm woods and exposed brick. As it was too early for the dinner rush, most tables sat empty.

He headed for the bar, where a line of locals dotted the barstools. As he approached, Noah admired the bar. Massive and solid, the large mahogany structure was well-worn with use. It was a stunning piece, as immovable as the brother staring him down from the other side.

Noah pulled up suddenly. He remained frozen in place while his mind worked the puzzle before him. The man possessed Shea's chiseled features and vivid blue eyes, but his dark brown hair had lightened. At thirty-five, his smooth skin and lean, well-muscled physique stood in stark contrast to the lightly grayed strands in his hair.

Alerted by Shea's fierce regard, the row of men sitting on stools turned as one.

Shit.

The last thing Noah needed was a freaking family reunion. With reluctance churning in his stomach, he forced his feet to move.

Wood scraped against the slate tile flooring as one man stood. Father John was in his mid-fifties now. He was tall and slender, with an athletic build, and his clean-shaven face and head provided a stark canvas for his bright blue eyes. The same hue as Noah's mother's.

Ensnared by that direct blue gaze, Noah fought the urge to squirm like the ten-year-old little shit he'd been the first time he'd met his uncle. With damning eyes, John peered into Noah's face until Noah's heart thumped in his chest and echoed in his ears.

He couldn't move. He wanted to shout. To bare and gnash his teeth. To demand answers and understanding.

To beg forgiveness and give none in return.

But those were the impulses of his youth, long ago tamed.

Without warning, a wide smile split John's lean face,

revealing one front tooth set a tad forward. "Welcome home, son."

A snort of laughter from Jack punctured the tension. "Cut the Holy crap, Uncle John. You're retired."

"Resigned," John corrected as he retook his barstool. "There's a difference, ye know."

"About time you showed your face around here." A scar cut through Jack's left brow, the result of an incident with a hockey stick when Jack was ten and Noah was thirteen years old.

The bitter swill of swallowed-back resentment clogged in Noah's throat.

"How long are you in town?" Jack asked.

Noah hesitated, uncertain.

"'Cause I'm gonna be straight with you." Jack studied Noah with steely green-gold eyes. "I need a fourth."

Noah blinked. "A what?"

"A fourth man. So we can enter the Gordie Howe tournament next month."

"The Gordie Howe...?" Noah gaped at his little brother. "We're talking about playing hockey?"

"Of course we're talking about hockey. Luke's in goal, so you'll be the left forward."

The fourth of five boys, Jack had a notorious competitive streak. One that had led him to multi-year career as a professional hockey player in the NHL.

"I haven't skated in years," Noah said.

"And I guaran-goddamn-tee you're still faster than either of these two." Jack thumbed his hand toward Shea and the man still perched on his barstool. "If we're gonna win this thing, we need more speed up front and someone who isn't afraid to hurt people."

Noah narrowed his eyes at Jack. "Are you even allowed to play in amateur games?"

Jack's expression darkened. "We're locked out again. I can do whatever I want."

The last dark-haired man slipped off the barstool. He came to stand beside his brothers, and Noah looked into a face remarkably similar to his own.

Luke. The last time Noah had seen him, he'd been a gangly teenager with purple hair and guy-liner.

Noah swallowed hard.

"They throw a tournament together every time Jack's in town." A lazy grin tipped up one corner of Luke's mouth. "Seems grown men love little more than getting their asses kicked by a pro athlete."

Noah returned the sly grin on Luke's uncommonly handsome face. "You look good, little brother. Not so damn ugly."

Luke's smile flashed wide and bright. "Wish I could say the same."

A laugh startled from Noah and some of the tightness drained from his shoulders.

Luke grasped Noah's hand and tugged him close. "It's good to see you."

"We were talking 'bout taking *The Irish Fart* out in the morning." Jack reclaimed his barstool next to John. "You should come."

Noah lifted one eyebrow. "*The Irish Fart?*"

"It's my boat." John's bright eyes lit up. "She's a real beauty. A thirty-five-footer."

Noah couldn't stop himself from asking. "You named your boat *The Irish Fart?*"

John's smile vanished, and he shot a withering glance at the others. "No. I named it *The Gaelic Wind,* but some *eedjits* can't seem to remember that."

Snickers carried around the trio of brothers. Proof of a shared history Noah knew nothing about.

Noah rubbed the nape of his neck and stepped up to the bar. "I'm in."

He risked a glance at Shea, the oldest of the five brothers and at one time Noah's closest friend in the world. "You work here or something?"

Shea folded his arms across his chest. "I own it."

"You own it." A sardonic smile twisted Noah's lips. "Of course you do."

"What are you doing here?" Shea's deep, raspy voice cut through the small group.

With that, their cozy family reunion succumbed to the inevitable.

Unease moved through Noah, and he shoved his hand into his hair. "I heard about Dad."

Shea's gaze sliced to Father John.

John held Shea's gaze steady. "He had a right to know."

A beat passed between them, then Shea dropped his head and turned his back.

"Came to pay your respects, did ya?" John said.

Respect had little to do with the alcohol-fueled reasoning that brought Noah to this place. "How did he die?"

"Heart attack." Luke sipped from his pint.

Shea picked up another glass. "If you bothered to tell someone where you were, we would've sent word he was sick."

"John found me." Noah couldn't banish the accusatory tone from his voice. "But let's not kid ourselves. Daniel wouldn't have wanted me to come."

"His opinion wasn't the only one that mattered," Luke opined from behind his pint.

"Don't waste your breath." Shea's accusing gaze locked on Noah. "He isn't staying."

Noah bared his teeth. "Of all people, you should know better, Shea."

Shea tossed the towel aside and placed his palms on the bar top. "That was a long time ago, brother."

"And yet here we are." Noah barely won the battle to keep his voice even.

"Ah, I miss this." Luke tipped his glass. "To good times."

He drank alone.

Noah took a measured step back. "I should go."

Shea made a derisive noise.

Noah's body coiled, ready to strike. He'd thought all this was behind him, but the intensity of anger and resentment swirling through him told a different story. He dragged in a deep, steadying breath, then turned and made for the door.

"Meet at the dock at seven," John called after him.

With no other outlet for his frustration, Noah smacked his palm against the pub door, flinging it open with enough force to bang against the outside wall.

He dodged a passing car and crossed the street. At his truck, he slid behind the wheel.

He wasn't the fuckup they thought he was. Last they knew, he was a pissed off nineteen-year-old with a criminal record and all the makings of a drinking problem. But he wasn't that angry kid any longer.

Reassured, he turned the key in the ignition.

He'd wanted to tell them he wasn't a delinquent loser anymore, but his damnable pride wouldn't let him. Why would they believe him? He had to show them he'd changed. Prove it past the point where they could doubt him or deny him.

He plucked his cell phone from the pocket of his blue jeans and scrolled through his log until he found the number.

He hit the call button. The interior lining of his gut churned while the strident ringing buzzed in his ear.

"Walter, it's Noah Nolan," he said when the other man picked up the call. "Does the job offer still stand?"

A beat of silence crackled over the line. "Of course it stands."

"I'm sorry, I can't commit to the entire academic year, but I can teach a couple of classes fall semester while I complete the dig at the Winslow property."

Walter sputtered with surprise. "Dr. Nolan, I'll take you any way I can get you."

"In that case, I'd like to accept the position."

"This is excellent news. Most excellent." Though a nervous waver edged Walter's voice.

Noah heard papers shuffling, followed by another round of anxious grunts and noises. Unease prickled up his spine.

"I'll have an office cleared out for you by, uh, Monday—T-Tuesday." The last two words erupted as an almost shout through the phone's speaker. Walter coughed. "The end of the day on Tuesday."

"I can make do without an office for a few—"

"That won't be necessary." Determination filled Walter's voice. "We'll be ready for you on Tuesday."

Noah disconnected. He ignored the rumblings of disquiet his impulsiveness had caused and backed out of the parking spot.

As he steered the vehicle in the motel's direction, unease clung to him.

He shifted in his seat. He should feel calmer. Now he had work, and work was the only thing that'd ever calmed him.

Except, if he were going to stay on the island, he was going to need a semi-permanent living situation.

He scratched at the back of his neck. Words like "permanent" and "home" always made him break out in hives. All his life, he'd avoided putting down roots. What good was a home? It was nothing but a place they could throw him out of.

Screw it. He could stay in the motel for a while. How bad could it be?

In a matter of days, he'd be back in a classroom. And if he were lucky, he'd soon be too busy with Walter's little side project to care where he laid his head at night. Could he be so fortunate as to have stumbled onto a legit excavation? One he could lose himself in for several weeks?

That depended on what lay buried in the dirt behind Mina's house. To learn the answer to that mystery, he needed to inspect the site. And to do that, he had to go through Mina.

An image of wounded blue eyes in a heart-shaped face floated through his mind. Suppressing a groan, he scrubbed a hand over his face.

The woman he'd thoroughly pissed off less than an hour ago was now the one woman who could ruin his plan.

A curse formed on his tongue. To contain it, he bit down on his bottom lip, and the lingering tang of cheap wine teased his tastebuds.

He had one shot to prove himself, and one woman stood between him and success. One woman with a plump, ripe mouth, perfect for kissing.

CHAPTER 4

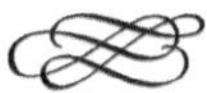

Mina gaped at her boss across the desk while his words knocked around inside her brain. Her face went hot, her cheeks burning as though she'd been slapped.

"You're firing me?"

Walter dragged a handkerchief across his damp forehead. "It's only a layoff. With time, the financial picture might change. This isn't a reflection upon you, personally."

Protests piled in her throat. Not personal?

Humiliation.

Failure.

Poverty, starvation, homelessness...

How could it not be personal?

"The budget is tight," he went on. "I had to make some choices. Tough choices." His lamentations rang hollow, echoing around the untidy office.

Tendrils of dread coiled in the pit of her stomach. Budget cuts? Tough choices? It was the professional equivalent of "it's not you, it's me."

"Enrollment's been flat for two years, and our graduation

rates have dropped off. I had to take extreme measures." A brightness glittered in his cloudy blue eyes, and his chest puffed up. "I've hired a new professor. He's incredible, a genius, and he wants to work *here*. For me. I couldn't pass up the opportunity."

Her heart plummeted, crashing somewhere near her navel. In the five years she'd worked for him, she'd never seen Walter Ambrose glow. He rattled off a list of credentials, each one like a blow to her aching head.

"He's young, but is already one of the best in his field. World-renowned. A veritable rock star."

She didn't quite stifle a snort. An academic rock star? Was such a thing even possible?

Walter frowned. "We're a mid-major university. We're never going to be a top student's first choice unless we make some big changes. He'll bring instant credibility to the department. With his name, we'll stand out and could become a destination program, attracting the brightest minds. We can turn ESU into one of the best mid-majors in the country."

Mina's dread turned to panic. "Wow. This one guy is going to do all that?"

Walter's weary sigh sent a ripple across the papers spread out on his desk, and a touch of pity softened his weathered features. "He gives us the best chance to turn this program around. I'm sorry, but I have to try. I wish you the best."

MINA STARED, open-mouthed and mute. She bent her head back to gawk. All the way up the seventeen-foot-high wall. Out of the corner of her eye, she glimpsed Pete, her painter.

A wide grin split his face. "You like?"

"It's purple."

To keep the renovation proceeding, she'd tackled some tasks out of sequence. Like painting the library, one of few rooms they hadn't taken down to the studs.

"It's a bold color. I'm surprised you picked it." Pete plunked the paint roller into the tray at his feet and straightened. "I thought you'd pick beige. But this?" His chest expanded, and he planted his hands on his hips. "*This* is a nice color."

"Beige is a nice color," she felt compelled to point out.

"Of course." He swept her words away with a wave of his hand. "It's plain. Like you."

With her annoyance, she frowned.

"This is a man's room." Pete puffed out his chest. "It needs a powerful color."

"It's *purple*."

"It's masculine, no?"

"No."

"No?"

"No," Mina ground out. "This is not the paint I picked."

His eyebrows pulled together. "What do you mean?"

"The color I picked was red." A deep scarlet red that had taken her weeks to match to the original paint in the room. It was historical, dammit. Definitely not plain. Or purple.

Pete bent down and flipped over the lid to the paint can. "Eggplant Dream."

Misery settled on her shoulders. "No, the color I picked is called Cinnamon Stick."

In silence, they stared at the expanse of purple wall. Pete consulted the lid once more, and the clipboard hanging from his ladder.

With a heavy sigh, his shoulders slumped. "But we're almost done."

Seriously? Nausea unfurled in her stomach. She abhorred confrontations. "It's *purple*."

Pete rubbed the back of his neck. "It's not that bad."

Behind them, a throat cleared. "It's pretty bad."

At the sound of Noah's voice, Mina's heart tripped into an erratic rhythm.

When she turned, he stood in a stream of golden sunlight that slanted across the room and played with the golden-honey streaks in his dark hair.

For a brief, aching moment, they were back in high school, and she was that troubled teenager looking for someone to rescue her. Before she'd realized boys like Noah Nolan didn't date shy, chubby girls like Mina Winslow.

His eyes shimmered with a mischievous light. "Not a purple girl?"

"If you're here to check out the... whatever it is out there… you'll have to fend for yourself. I'm busy." She faced the wall once more.

"You don't sound too thrilled to see me."

She wished that were true. Her heart beat a rapid rhythm that left her lightheaded, and her breaths came quick and shallow.

Because of all the purple, she told herself.

She pivoted back toward Noah. "Don't I? And to think I had such fun the other night."

White teeth flashed in Noah's tanned face. "Me, too. We should do it again soon."

"No, thanks. I don't enjoy arguing with someone when I don't understand what we're arguing about."

"Were we arguing?"

She narrowed her eyes at him. "Yes."

His brow wrinkled. "Interesting, but that wasn't what I was talking about. I was talking about the kissing. We should do more of that."

She snorted. "Liked that, did ya?"

Dark eyes bored into her. "What do you think?"

She lifted one shoulder. "Could've fooled me."

"Then let me make myself clear. I enjoyed kissing you, Mina." His voice deepened. "Immensely."

Mina's cheeks warmed, and her gaze darted to Pete, whose head had snapped up from his clipboard during their exchange. He startled and ducked his chin.

Noah leaned close. "For what it's worth, Cinnamon Stick sounds like a much better color. Tastier too."

She narrowed her eyes at him. "Stop trying to butter me up."

"Why?"

"Because it won't work."

"How do you know?" A molasses smile touched his lips. "I'm pretty good at it."

"Is that right?" Doubt thickened her voice.

Noah raised a fist over his mouth and made a production of clearing his throat. "Ready?"

Her attempt to bite back a smile flopped. "Ready."

"If the purple in this room didn't make my eyes bleed, your beauty would've blinded me."

Crouched at her feet, Pete snorted. He continued pouring paint from the tray back into the can, so she frowned at the top of his head.

Suddenly aware of Noah taking it all in, she lifted her chin and attempted to sweep from the room. Instead, the toe of her sneaker caught on the drop cloth and she stumbled to a stop. With a series of short yanks, she shook her foot loose, then darted through the door.

In the hallway, Noah fell in step beside her.

While she pretended to ignore him, his delicious scent grasped and grabbed at her.

At one time, she'd have given anything to feel the slow lick of heat slipping through her body at a man's nearness. She should be relieved that she wasn't as arid and frigid as an arctic winter. Now, she just wished Noah wasn't the cause of her arousal.

It was bad enough she'd thrown herself at him only to have him reject her, but even more horrifying was the fact he'd made an appearance her as the star of her lurid sex dream last night.

A sex dream? Her? Seriously?

Seriously.

Vivid, erotic fantasies of Noah had mingled with stress-induced nightmares about the house, until she'd dreamed of him making love to her on the cool ballroom floor while overhead, chubby cherubs had tittered and taunted her. She'd jolted awake as the dream orgasm had gripped her.

She waved him through the back door. "Enjoy your tour. It's the enormous mud puddle in the back yard. You can't miss it."

He twisted to face her. "You're not coming with me? Don't you want to make sure I don't steal anything?"

She didn't bother to quell a derisive smirk. "I don't think you'll find anything here worth stealing."

Dark eyes took a slow journey over her features. "I'm not so sure about *that*."

Then he brushed past her, stepping back inside the house.

At the closest doorway, he leaned into the room. "What's in here?"

"Uh, it was a conservatory." While his gaze devoured the room, she kept her focus on him. "Right now, it's just another storage space."

"The light in here is incredible." His sharp gaze swiveled to her. "Will you keep it as a conservatory?"

Somehow, his scrutiny frayed her nerves, like a pulled thread unraveling a knit sweater, and words started tumbling out. "Wherever possible, I want to restore the house to its original configuration."

With the languid sidle of a lazy sunrise, warmth from his slow smile washed over her. "Is that so?"

Basking in the heated glow of his lazy smile, she nodded.

He left the conservatory behind and moved down the hall, pushing deeper inside the house. "When was the home built?"

"They built the primary structure in 1864." She trailed after him. "This wing was added twenty-some years later."

"Do we know who built it?"

"My four-times-great-grandpa, Henry Winslow."

"The governor?"

"No, that was his son, James. Henry started the logging empire."

As she followed him through the formal dining room and foyer, he continued peppering her with questions about the home's history or commenting on something that'd captured his interest, which was pretty much everything.

She found herself drawn in by his curiosity, and soon she confessed her plan to convert the house into a bed and breakfast.

Brown-black eyes swung to her, and she only just stopped herself from stumbling back. "A bed and breakfast? Here on the island?"

"Yeah, well... I'm still thinking about it." More like trying to figure out how to finish the house with all the delays and losing her job. She poked her toe at a clump of dirt on the floorboards.

"You should do it," he said.

Her head snapped up.

"This town needs a decent place for visitors to stay." His tone softened. "And this house deserves to be filled with people who'll appreciate it."

The warmth spread to her chest, and the icy knot gripping her insides eased a bit. "Do you, uh, want to see the rest?"

With the swift appearance of his full-blown smile, her breath hitched.

"Absolutely," he said.

They climbed one of the rickety twin staircases to the second floor, which housed six bedrooms in various states of disarray and rehab. Each bedroom boasted crown molding and ten-foot ceilings, but also yellowed wallpaper, leaky windows, and scarred hardwood floors.

At the end of the hall, she tossed a conspiratorial smile over her shoulder. "This is the best part."

One of Noah's dark eyebrows climbed upward as she pulled on the doorknob.

She motioned for him to go ahead of her and followed him up a steep staircase. At the top, a small landing and wall-to-wall windows provided a panoramic view of the island.

Shards of sunlight danced and shimmered across Lake Michigan while, far out, merry waves peaked and gamboled toward shore. Here, at the northernmost tip of the island, the view expanded in every direction. The neat roads and rolling hills of Thief Island lay to the south.

"Holy shit," he breathed. "You can see the entire island from up here."

She smiled and sank down on the top stair. She'd spent countless hours on this exact stair, looking out over the world.

He turned and held out his hand to her. "C'mon up."

She shook her head. "I'm good."

"You can't see from that spot."

"I've seen it before. Hundreds of times."

His gaze ate up the scenery. "You can't possibly see this view enough times."

She stayed glued to her spot on the stair.

His dark eyes remained on her, intent and assessing. She bent her head and inspected a chipped fingernail.

"You're afraid of heights."

"I'm not afraid." She sputtered the denial. "They make me dizzy."

He made a noise.

She scowled up at him. "What?"

"Nothing. Just... that's interesting."

"Why is that interesting?"

He shrugged. "I never figured you for a coward."

She rolled her eyes. "Nice try. You're not getting me to come up there."

His eyes shone with the quick mischief that gave his face such a charming aspect and he shrugged. "Worth a shot." Then his attention swiveled back to the bank of windows. "Is that the site?"

"Big pile of dirt? Yep, that's it."

"How was it discovered?"

"The work crew that came to put in a new well found it when they started digging. My boss—my *former* boss—thinks an excavation will have to be done."

Noah's eyebrows knitted together. "Your boss knows about archaeological excavations?"

"He's a professor at ESU."

Shimmery brown eyes clamped on her face. "You work at ESU?"

Crimson heat swept over her face and neck. "I did. Until Friday."

"What happened Friday?"

The Phenom of Higher Education had happened. Darts of self-doubt pierced and wounded.

"I lost my job." She swallowed the distasteful bitterness on her tongue. "They fired me."

"I'm sorry." His voice, gentle and full of concern, tried to wrap itself around her.

She shoved to her feet. "You can't really see it from up here. You want to get a closer look?"

Without waiting for his reply, she scrambled down the stairwell. Back on the first floor, she inhaled a deep, steadying breath, her first since ascending to the highest stair of the widow's walk.

Outside, the passing storm forced out the stifling heat and a cooler breeze kicked up off the lake to lick her skin and set the ends of her hair dancing. Noah pulled a crumpled baseball hat from his back pocket and tugged it over his head.

The treetops rustled and the lake's rhythmic churn accompanied them as they headed toward the section of the property that jutted out into Lake Michigan. The terrain sloped upward, and the grade grew steeper the farther they moved from the house.

Noah's pace quickened the higher they climbed while she huffed along behind him, dragging oxygen into her lungs and pushing on despite the burning in her thighs as she tried to keep up with him. At last, she achieved the top, where a blast of wind skipped off the lake to greet her.

She shielded her eyes to the brilliant shards of sunlight reflecting off the water and gulped a large lungful of air.

As he stood poised at the edge of the cliff, Noah's hungry gaze devoured the landscape. He turned, taking in the view from every direction. "They would've been hidden up here, but able to see everything for miles."

She pulled her hair into one hand, securing it against the wind, and squinted up at him. "They? Who's they?"

He stooped, gathered a fistful of dirt in his hand, and let it fall between his fingers. "It's the perfect location."

"The perfect location for what?"

Standing, he brushed his hand on his shorts. "A fort, or maybe a trading outpost."

He walked the perimeter of the upturned earth, squatting occasionally to study something for a moment before moving on.

She grew a little lost in watching him, noticing the way the little commas of his curls stuck out from under his hat and bobbed with the wind gusts.

So when he abruptly looked up and right at her, she jolted.

"Check this out."

She forced her eyes to the ground where he pointed. "What is it?"

"Another arrowhead."

She leaned closer, but all she saw was dirt and mud.

"The Potomac Indians lived in this part of Michigan. Maybe it's one of theirs." He reached out and filched something from the earth.

"Another arrowhead?"

He shook his head and held up a chipped, cylinder-shaped object. "A bullet casing, I think. Thief Island had a bit of a reputation as a pirate hideout at one point, didn't it?"

"Didn't you hear?" She nearly had to shout to be heard above the gusty breeze. "My five-times-great-grandfather drove the thieves and ruffians off the island when he settled here."

He shot her a meaningful look. "Uh-huh."

"My family's entire political legacy is based on that story," she said. "So it must be true."

His deep laughter rang out, and her heart took notice of the sound. When he returned his attention to the ground, the playfulness slowly faded from his features.

Head bent, he prowled the area. Then suddenly, he crouched. Reaching out, pulled another small clump from the earth. With the pad of his thumb, he brushed aside dirt and debris to reveal the long-obscured object.

He cradled the piece in his strong, tanned hands, turning it with a gentleness that snatched the breath from her lungs. She couldn't fathom what it was. A hunk of metal or a broken garden tool? He held it up, and a small, fascinated smile curved his mouth.

Everything inside her stilled.

She stood immobile, caught in the web spun by the rapt expression on his face. Seagulls screeched overhead, but she could barely hear their shrill squawks over the thrashing of her heart.

What was he doing? Why was he so enthralled with something lost so many years ago? Something tossed aside and forgotten? Why did he care so much about…junk?

She wanted to tell him to leave it alone. Whatever it was, it was dirty and ugly and better left buried below ground.

But he gazed upon that pathetic thing as though it were worthy of his reverence. As if it deserved to be uncovered and brought forth for all the world to see and adore. It was almost as though, despite its severe and irreversible flaws, that piece of trash was precious to him. That knowing and protecting it were vitally important to him. Almost as if his life depended on it.

Or his livelihood.

Jagged breaths rattled in her lungs. Concrete blocks cemented her feet to the ground, and a rapid-fire assault of disturbing thoughts pelted her brain.

The truth slammed into her.

"Omigod," she whispered. "You're the rock star."

oah's head came up, the smile lingering on his face. "What did you say?"

"You're an archaeologist." She made it sound like an accusation of murder, and he straightened to his full height.

"A good one," she rushed on. "You've written b-books, and-and you taught at Cambridge. You found a k-king." She pointed a condemning finger at his chest. "You were on the BBC."

His fingers worried the smooth surface of the artifact he held. "What do you want me to say?"

"Am I right?"

He held his arms out at his sides. "He was a prince, not a king."

She gasped her horror. "You stole my job."

Her horror became his, curling through his gut like a slow-acting poison. "No."

"They fired *me* to hire *you*."

"I didn't know." He took a step toward her. She stumbled back, and he froze. "I swear to you, if I'd known they were going to fire anyone, I never would've accepted the position."

She twisted away blindly, only to whirl on him a split second later. "You work for ESU now?"

"I do."

"And you're here because of this?" One of her small hands sliced through the air, sweeping over the area of upturned earth.

He inclined his head. "I am."

"You're here to…to…" Her hands moved about her head in frustrated whirls. "…to what?"

"To give you my professional opinion."

She dropped her arms heavily to her sides. "Which is?"

"I think an exploratory dig is necessary to determine whether the site is archaeologically significant."

With a scowl, she folded her arms over her stomach, as if she might contain all the pieces of herself. "What does that mean?"

"It means we need to excavate."

"How long is that going to take?" Panic crept into her voice.

He scanned the area, assessing the size of the area involved. "Depends what we find."

"You're the expert." Each word dripped with her scorn. "What do you think you'll find?"

"More arrowheads, bullet casings, that sort of thing." He resisted the urge to launch into a long list of all the potential evidence he could find. "Give me a couple of weeks and I'll be able to tell you more. A couple of months, at most."

"A couple of *months*?" The words erupted from her. "All I need is a freaking well."

"Can you put the well someplace else?" Turning his head, he tracked her movements as she paced back and forth in front of him. "That way, you get your well and I can complete the excavation without bothering you."

She tripped to a stop and swiveled to face him. "Wait.

You're going to do the excavation? You're not sending someone else out here to do it?"

"That's right."

"But that means…?" Ripples of confusion rolled across her features. "You're staying?"

"I'm staying." Defiance rode at the edge of his tone.

"For how long? You said…" she gulped, "months?"

"Until I'm done." He rolled his shoulders, attempting to shake off the weight of his hasty decision. "Or until the money runs out."

The color leeched from her cheeks. "Money? What money?"

"The money to pay for the cost of an excavation."

"Will the state pay for it?" she asked, her complexion colorless. "Or ESU?"

"ESU has made some funds available. But they'll only scratch the surface. Literally. I'll have to apply for grants for the rest."

"But that will take months."

He conceded her point with a nod. "Maybe I can convince Walter to cough up some more money."

"And if he can't, or won't?"

"Then it's going to take longer. The project can't move forward without funding." From beneath the bill of his baseball hat, he shot her a pointed look. "And your work cannot move forward until the site is secured."

Her jaw dropped, but no words came out and she paced several feet away before she whipped back around and pinned him with a fierce glare. "So my entire renovation is on hold, indefinitely, until you find enough money to pay for an excavation?"

With a shrug, he shoved his hands into his pockets. "Or you could pay for it."

A gust of wind off the lake knocked into and she weaved slightly on her feet. "Me?"

"As the property owner, legally, it falls on you to protect the site. The fastest way to get the site secured and an excavation completed is to pay for it yourself. I can start today."

"How much are we talking?"

"It's a small site. Equipment, permits, lab fees—"

"How much?" Her voice pitched toward hysteria.

"You're looking at around ten thousand. If everything goes according to plan—"

A strangled noise sounding suspiciously like a sob escaped her. "When do things ever go according to the plan?"

Why the hell was she so upset? She was a *Winslow*. She had access to more money, and friends with money, than she could likely spend in her lifetime. Hell, she had enough money to buy a dilapidated mansion that, from the looks of it, needed to be rebuilt from the ground up, to attend a prestigious Ivy League school, and to purchase the sleek BMW parked in her driveway.

"That's not a problem for you, is it?" he asked.

It was the wrong thing to say. The cloud of panic gathering around her evaporated, and she trained her big blue eyes on him. For a long moment, she stared, assessing.

"No, of course not," she said coolly. "It's no problem at all."

He'd disappointed her, and knowing that displeased him. More than it should.

"Why don't I just go grab my magical Winslow checkbook and write you a big fat check?" Whirling, she scrambled down the hill.

"Mina, wait—"

She spun to face him. "Shall I make it thirty thousand? No, wait, let's do fifty. That's a nice round number."

He yanked his baseball hat from his head and cursed.

With a shocked gasp, she reared back.

Noah froze, one hand buried in his hair. "What?"

"Did you just call me a bitch?"

"*What?* No!"

"Oh." Her puffy mouth screwed into a frown. "Then what did you say?"

"'Son of a bitch.' I said 'son of a bitch.'" With long strides, he stalked toward her and pressed into her space. "Do not assume the worst about me. I don't deserve that, and whether or not you believe me, I regret if anything I did caused you to lose your job. That's not what I wanted."

Standing so close to her, he caught the sharp hitch in her breathing.

Cruel satisfaction kicked in his chest. So, she wasn't as composed as she'd like him to believe.

"I'm sorry if my being here complicates your life." His gaze prowled over her delicate features, then crept lower, to the spot at the base of her throat where her pulse fluttered. "If it makes you feel any better, you're one hell of a complication for me, too."

Her hand flitted to her neck. "Is that what we're calling each other now? A complication?" She lifted her small shoulders. "I guess that's better than a mistake."

He tore his gaze away from her mouth. "Ah, so this is about us? About our past?"

She scoffed. "I don't think what we have counts as a past."

"It counts."

"Well, it has no bearing on the present situation."

"You sure about that?" He brushed aside her trembling fingers to reveal the thrumming pulse point on the side of her neck. "The best sex of your life. I mean, you don't forget something like that, do you?" Her light scent teased his senses, and he dipped his head closer. "Every time you're with another man, can you stop yourself from comparing him to your best ever?"

Color rushed into her cheeks.

"Every time you're face-to-face with the man who gave you the best sex of your life..." He inhaled softly. "You can't help but remember your time together, can you? Every vivid, arousing detail must go through your mind, over and over, again and again, wouldn't it?"

The flush from her cheeks crept down her neck to the creamy expanse of skin across her chest. "Speaking from experience?"

A slow smile lifted one corner of his mouth. "We should compare notes."

She rolled her eyes. "This is pointless."

"Sex is never pointless. Meaningless, maybe, but there's always a point to it."

"Focus," she snapped.

All he could focus on was her over-plump mouth.

"It's been a long time." He dropped his voice to a low timbre. "I've gotten better, you know."

She swept her critical gaze over him. "I should hope so."

"Is that a challenge?"

"Sorry, no." Turning, she set off toward the house. "I don't consort with academics."

"Oh?" He fell into step at her side. "Why is that?"

"Huge but fragile egos. I simply don't have the time or inclination to deal with it."

He ate his smile. "Too bad. Might've been fun. I mean, I *am* the best you've ever had—"

An exasperated sound burst from her. "That's not what I was saying."

"But it's what you said." God, she was fun. "Admit it."

"Fine, I admit it." She threw up her hands in surrender. "But what the hell did I know? You were the first guy I ever had sex with. You might've been awful, and I still would've thought it was earth-shattering."

When his brain tripped, his steps slowed, then stopped. He was her first? Had he known that? His mind made a frantic search through his memories. No, he definitely did not recall ever learning that small, critical detail.

How had he *not* known that?

When she realized he'd fallen behind, she stopped and turned. The wind nipped at her hair and the sun picked out the golden and auburn strands buried in amongst the darker ones.

"I was your first?" Still absorbing this new information, his words slipped out, poorly considered. "Is that why you refused to talk to me afterward?"

She gave her head a small shake. "I don't know what you're talking about."

"After that night, you acted like I didn't exist." The old resentment chafed.

"That's not true," she finally said. "You left."

"Not right away. I was in town another month, at least."

For a moment, her mouth moved wordlessly, then just hung open.

He stared dumbly back at her. Was it possible she didn't remember?

"The week after Halloween, we were on midterm break, and when we came back, you wouldn't talk to me." He searched her face for signs of comprehension but saw none. "You wouldn't even acknowledge me."

Her expression, open and bright one moment, slowly closed. While he watched, her pupils dilated to swallow all the light, until her eyes appeared enormous, almost black.

"Mina? What is it? What's wrong?"

He reached for her, but she jerked back and stumbled over the uneven terrain. He cursed and caught her arm.

"I have to go." When she tipped her chin and gazed up at him, she appeared stricken. "Please," she whispered. "Let me go."

The instant he eased his grip, she spun and scrambled down the hillside.

"We're not finished talking," he called after her.

"You can s-start the excavation," she said over her shoulder. "I'll—I'll find you the money."

"That's not what I—"

Her feet slipped more than once, but each time, she caught herself before she fell. Noah's muscles bunched, but he remained on the hill, wondering what the hell had just happened?

As he watched her pick her way across the rutted ground, an odd prickle raced up his spine, and he rubbed the back of his neck.

The sensation wasn't unfamiliar. He felt it almost every day. At work. It was the thrill of the chase. The quest for discovery. The hunt for the story yet untold.

A mystery lured him every time.

But he'd never experienced the telltale prickle when he considered a woman.

Until now.

CHAPTER 6

She needed to get rid of Noah.

Moments after deserting him on the hillside, Mina realized what an awful, terrible thing she had done. She'd given him permission to do an excavation. Permission to come to her house every day for the foreseeable future. Permission to dig and prod, and to expose any secrets buried in her yard. Why had she done that? What had she been thinking?

Maybe that was the problem. She hadn't been thinking. If she had, she never would've relented. Instead, his strange questions had set off an avalanche of panic inside her, and in her desperate need to get out from under his damning gaze, she'd blurted out the first words that'd popped into her head that might've given her a chance to flee.

Now she was stuck with him.

She snatched her cell phone off the kitchen counter and punched in the number to her old office phone. With her thumb over the call button, she hesitated. If she fired him now, how much longer would it take to get this stupid excavation underway and over with so that she could continue her renovation?

A frustrated growl vibrated in her throat, and she abandoned her phone to the countertop. At the table, she slid into a chair and switched on her laptop. What if she could find someone else to conduct the excavation? Her fingers flew over the keyboard as she jumped down the rabbit hole of an internet search.

An hour later, she'd learned no list of archaeologists existed from which she could pick someone to replace Noah. Nor could she skip completing the excavation altogether. What he'd told her about the law had been the truth. Not only was she responsible for protecting the site, but failure to safeguard it could cause massive fines or even imprisonment.

Freaking prison? Seriously?

But the fact was, until she proved she'd safeguarded the area, she could not install the well.

With a harsh slap, she closed the laptop. She stabbed two fingers at her temples and rubbed the ache forming there. Everything he'd said was true, except for the estimated timeline, which he may have undersold by a month or more.

She was really, truly stuck with him. Until she came up with the money to pay for his excavation, she couldn't get rid of him. Without that money, all she had was a big, beautiful, gutted mansion with no running water.

She pressed her fingers against her brow and massaged with furious tiny circles. Where was she going to find the money?

Defeated, she folded her arms on the table in front of her and dropped her head into the crook of her elbow. When would this nightmare end?

I suppose that depends. The sound of her grandmother's voice floated through Mina's mind. *When are you going to finish it?*

Slowly, Mina lifted her head. She'd already sunk everything she had into this renovation. It was too late to turn back now. The only way out of this mess was to get through it.

There had to be a way to come up with a chunk of cash fast. Preferably, one that didn't involve committing any crimes.

What would her grandmother, Rose, have done to save her home?

In Mina's memories, Rose had been a sophisticated, virtuous woman, but also a tough broad who had zero tolerance for people she'd deemed foolish. And she'd been wholly unimpressed by the Winslow family fortune, often reminding Mina's grandfather he had no right acting like a rich man given that he'd done nothing to earn the immense wealth he'd inherited.

Once, Rose had joked that the rich got rich by persuading other rich people to give them money.

"And how do you persuade these rich people to give you money?" Mina had asked, laughing.

"You convince them you don't need it," Rose had replied with a wink.

The memory struck Mina with a jolt, straightening her spine. Maybe that was it. She could borrow the money. All she had to do was convince someone to loan it to her.

Mina pushed up from the table and scooped her cell phone off the counter. Desperation clawing at her, she ignored the icky feeling it gave her to rely on her Winslow name and forced herself to make the call to Mr. Renshaw, the bank manager at Winslow Sterling Bank, to arrange a meeting. She might as well benefit from the perks that came with belonging to a powerful, well-connected family.

Lord knew she'd paid the price tenfold.

With the meeting scheduled, she disconnected the call

and returned to her laptop to complete the online loan application per the service representative's instructions. Once done, she passed through the cramped living room of her small apartment and flipped on the overhead light in her bedroom. It was time to test Rose's theory.

She donned black slacks, a neat ivory twinset, and the diamond stud earrings her ex-fiancé had given her less than a month before he'd slept with another woman. Then she secured her wavy hair in a tidy bun, hoping she'd make it through her meeting with Mr. Renshaw before the humidity coaxed free the curlicues at her nape and temples.

Next, she flung open her closest door and rummaged for the Coach purse her mom had given her last Christmas. A robust hunt finally turned up the designer bag on the floor in the far corner, underneath the disheveled pile of size-four secondhand designer clothing. Another "gift" from her mom, who was not ignorant to the fact that Mina hadn't been able to wear a size four since that one week in fifth grade following a bout of the flu.

Mina understood the purpose of the too-small clothes was to encourage her to lose weight. They had the opposite effect, however, as every time she thought about them, she either poured a glass of wine or stuffed food into her mouth to stop herself from screaming.

She crammed her feet into a pair of overpriced heels—thank you, Mom—and fastened a string of Rose's pearls around her neck before surveying herself in the mirror.

A spoiled rich girl stared back at her. Just as planned.

But within moments of entering the bank, Mina's plan backfired with a concussion blast loud enough to shatter her one remaining eardrum.

"Mr. Renshaw sends his apologies, but he isn't available to meet with you today." The receptionist at the front desk was all sugary sweetness. "He's given your application to the Assistant Manager. She'll be right with you."

An office door opened, and Mina turned as Phoebe Taylor appeared on a cloud of spite and cruelty. Clad in a sexy-secretary skirt and form-fitting suit jacket, her dark hair cascaded down her back in lush waves.

Mina swallowed back bile.

In grade school, the other kids had teased Phoebe mercilessly because she'd often come to school dressed in their donated clothing, and because her mother had had a penchant for sleeping with their fathers. Appalled by the vicious attacks, once or twice Mina had found the courage to defend Phoebe against their cruel taunts.

But by high school, Phoebe had become the biggest bully of them all, and Mina was one of her favorite targets.

Brutal memories bubbled up of an incident in junior year. With their school lockers assigned alphabetically, only one locker separated Phoebe Taylor from Mina Winslow, that belonging to the cute and popular Josh Vanderwall.

Josh and his entourage often hung out at his locker between classes, while Mina tried to blend into the scenery. On this day, as Mina gathered the books she needed for her next class, Phoebe basked in the spotlight of the boys' undivided attention.

Phoebe's voice carried over the clamor of noise in the crowded hallway. "Who would you say is the prettiest girl in school?"

The boys all agreed Phoebe was. Of course.

Mina rolled her eyes.

"Who do you want to have sex with the most?" Phoebe's question elicited a few snickers and excited murmurs, and she plunged on. "What about Mina Winslow? Would any of you sleep with her?"

"Who?" Mark Sadler had asked.

"The redhead with the big tits," Josh said.

The crude description whipped color into Mina's cheeks.

A dark smile curled Mark's lips. "Sex with a chub has its advantages."

"Oh, yeah?" someone had asked.

"Yeah. They're so desperate for affection they try harder."

Male laughter erupted. Sick and humiliated, Mina fled while Phoebe's cruel laugh hounded her down the hallway.

And that wasn't even Mina's worst memory of Phoebe. The worst would be four months ago, when Phoebe had slept with Mina's then-fiancé.

Needless to say, Mina realized she wasn't getting the loan, even before Phoebe called her into the corner office, perched on the oversized mahogany desk, and leveled Mina with a dead-eyed stare that didn't quite conceal her barely contained glee.

"I'll keep this brief." Phoebe crossed her long, slender legs. "We won't be able to approve your application."

Her grip tight on her purse strap, Mina sank into a chair. "Was that Mr. Renshaw's decision, or yours?"

"That'd be the decision of any sane person." Phoebe filched a stapled pack of papers off the desk. "You have no income, pitiful savings, and your only real asset is thirty percent ownership in an old house," she said, flipping through the pages. "Do you honestly believe any bank would give you this loan? With or without your last name?"

Warmth flushed Mina's cheeks. "The beachfront property alone is valued at nearly half a million dollars."

An exaggerated sigh pushed through Phoebe's heavily painted lips. "It's a rundown old house. You'd be lucky to sell it for half that."

"Hence the need for the loan," Mina ground out. "With a few repairs—"

Phoebe held up a manicured hand. "The answer is no."

Waves of anger poured through Mina, washing away any

clever words or parting shots. Her fingernails dug into the soft flesh of her palms as she rose.

At the door, Phoebe's sarcastic drawl stopped her. "You might reconsider your spending habits. All those designer labels can't be cheap, even if they are last year's collection."

NOAH FOUND the carriage house tucked away in a copse of oak trees. Oblivious to the sun warming his back and the birds chirping away in the shrubberies, he crossed Mina's side lawn, a mix of unease and expectation whirring through his body.

In the three days since he'd last seen her, she hadn't been far from his mind. That pissed him off. He didn't want to spend his time thinking about Mina Winslow, deliberating all the ways he wanted to explore the curves of her body.

Nor did he wish to ponder the cause of her strange behavior on the hill. He didn't care if she'd forgotten the way she'd treated him all those years ago. It didn't change a goddamned thing.

A narrow porch attached to the west end of the carriage house led him up to the second story. At the door, he lifted a hand to knock, but when he spotted her through the screen, he froze. Her back was to him, her head bent over a mass of papers spread out across the kitchen table, her cutoff blue jeans hugging her heart-shaped ass.

The punch of lust hit him in the gut. Too absorbed in her task, she hadn't heard him approach.

A scowl pulled at his features. This time, he needed to stay focused. At least long enough to get her damn signature. Since accepting the position at the university, he'd designed an entire course curriculum around the Winslow property excavation, and classes started in two weeks. If he blew this, he'd have to face thirty hypercritical, attention-span deficient undergrads empty-handed.

He rapped on the wood doorframe, and she whirled toward him. Her T-shirt, loose at the waist, strained heroically across her glorious breasts.

The blood left his brain and surged to his groin. Christ, but her body was built for sex, and Noah's body well knew it.

She tugged at the jumble of papers behind her, as if to hide them. Charmed by her tits, he almost missed the interesting behavior.

With effort, he dragged his gaze to her face, where deep blue eyes brimmed with apprehension.

He showed his palms. "I come in peace."

A small smile peeked through the wariness. "Where's your flag?"

"No flag." He stepped through the screen door, which closed behind him with a soft *thwack*. "Only paperwork."

The soft edges of her features pinched. "You're not helping your cause."

He reached back and pulled the folded document from the back pocket of his blue jeans. "Nothing scary. Just a formality."

She accepted the paperwork from him with caution. "What kind of formality?"

"A disclosure form." Her scent teased his nostrils. Fresh and flowery, it reminded him of the white jasmine his mom had planted in their garden in Ireland when he was a kid. "I'm required to provide you with a list of project objectives and a timeline for the work."

"That's all it is?" Unfolding the papers, she snuck a cursory glance at the cover page.

"I need your signature. I can't conduct an excavation without your written consent."

She refolded the form. "Mind if I read it over first?"

"Of course not. Let me leave you with my cell phone number, in case you have questions."

Visibly relieved, she stretched across the table to fumble for a pen that lay on the far side. The desire to palm her rounded bottom surged, and he tamped down his lust with vicious resolve.

Twisting around, she stuck the pen and the form under his nose.

He scrawled his number across the folded paper, then handed it with the pen back to her. The light brush of her fingers against his hand ripped through him like an electric shock and his brain short-circuited with fragmented memories of her lying naked on the forest floor, her legs parted for him.

Her soft gasp told him she'd felt the jolt, too.

Beneath his gaze, her cheeks flushed a furious shade of pink, and he feared his lustful thoughts showed on his face. She fidgeted from one foot to the other, and her chest rose and fell with her suddenly shallow breathing.

She was so fucking hot, the way she lit up around him. The way she tried to hide her reaction to him, but couldn't. His cock pressed against the fly of his jeans.

Focus, Nolan.

"Do you use that shed out back?" His voice sounded as tight, like his balls.

"The white one?" She shook her head. "I was going to have it torn down. Why?"

"Can I use it? I need some temporary storage."

"Sure." Her brow crinkled. "I think there's a key around here somewhere."

She moved past him, and he turned to follow, getting his first full look at the interior of her home.

It was small, not over six hundred square feet, he'd guess, and open-concept. The area where they stood inside the door fitted a round white table, and tucked into the corner, a small kitchen with white cupboards and wainscoting. The space melted into the living room, where the exposed brick walls stood in sharp contrast to the overstuffed furniture drowned by floral pillows. Taken together, the room was rustic with a whole bunch of girly-girl thrown on top.

He followed her as she moved toward one of the two doors split off from the main room, then disappeared through the doorway. Beneath the archway, he faltered.

Her bedroom.

The wide-plank hardwood floors in the rest of the apartment extended into the bedroom. Above her cast-iron bed, a small chandelier dripping with teardrop crystals hovered.

His focus shattered, and he was powerless to stop the visions of Mina lying naked, not on the forest bed, but among the creamy sheets, her thighs parted in welcome.

"Aha!" Her hand shot up, a key pinched between her fingers.

The swing of her hip when she used it to shove the dresser drawer closed knocked into him. As she walked back to him, lust and need whipped through him. His hungry gaze devoured the soft sway of her hips and breasts.

When she offered him the key, he saw that her hand trembled.

She saw that he saw, and alarm flashed in her eyes.

He only just caught the cool metal key when she dropped it into his palm and pushed past him.

It both thrilled and destroyed him to know he disturbed her as much as she disturbed him.

"Thanks for the paperwork," she said as she bolted across the room. "I'll get them back to you right away."

At the table by the door, she returned to her mysterious papers, studying them with renewed interest.

He'd been dismissed.

Slowly, he retraced his path to the table. But he didn't leave. Instead, he moved to stand beside her.

He waited until her wary gaze found his face.

"You don't like me," he said.

The statement seemed to surprise her. "I don't *not* like you." As soon as she said the words, alarm stole across her face. "I don't like you, either. I mean, I don't like or dislike you. I don't think about you at all. Like that. I have no feelings one way or another about you."

Rather than feel offended, he relished her tongue-tied rambling. "I suppose it's not essential that we like one another."

With a sigh, she conceded, "I like you. It's just..." Her tongue darted out to lick her lips.

His eyes fastened on her mouth. "It's just what?"

Her throat worked when she swallowed.

Then the realization struck him. "I make you nervous."

Her eyelashes fluttered as she tried to avoid looking at him. "That's ridiculous."

"Is it something I said? The other day, on the hill—"

"No." The word burst out, and she sucked her bottom lip between her teeth, as if to pull the denial back. "There's nothing. It was nothing."

She took a small step back, and her hip bumped hard into the table. When she risked a peek at his face, ripples of vulnerability disturbed the twin pools of her blue eyes.

Drowning in cobalt, he floundered, only to find his fingers ensnared by a wayward curl at her temple. He hooked the lock around his finger, then toyed lightly with the silky softness. Everything about her fascinated him, even the unusual shade of her hair. With strands of auburn and gold, chestnut and russet, the unique mix defied classification.

"What color do you call it?" he murmured.

"My hair?" The tip of her pink tongue slipped out to wet her lips. "B-brown."

"No, that's not it." He pushed the curled lock off her forehead. "It's more than that."

His hand fell away, his fingers tracing along the delicate line of her collarbone. "Your heart's racing."

While she stared up at him with huge, round eyes, her head moved with an infinitesimal shake.

"Tell me why I make you nervous, Mina." The question slipped out, even though he shouldn't care why. He *didn't* care. "Is it because of what happened in high school?"

Dark shadows swept across her face, and his chest constricted with sharp regret at having invited them. But before he could find the words to chase them away, she slid her bottom onto the table and pressed her hands to the tabletop behind her. Her breasts heaved upward toward him.

His balls tightened.

"I don't want to talk about high school, Noah. Or anything else." The soft heartbreak in her eyes reached her voice. "I can't explain how I feel when I'm with you, but I can show you."

Then she parted her thighs, just the tiniest fraction, and ruined him.

No matter that he should, there was no way he could refuse her invitation.

CHAPTER 7

$\mathcal{A}$ stirring growl vibrated in his throat, as though he'd lost a long-fought battle.

Uncertainty swamped her. She'd never tried using sex to distract a man before, but she had no answers for the questions in his eyes. So she offered him her body instead.

But would he want her?

The soles of his boots scuffed against the wood floors when he stepped between her legs. Then his warm palms touched her bare thighs and the smoldering fire low in her belly ignited.

"Are you sure about this?" A rough rasp shredded his voice. "It won't be a repeat of high school."

She couldn't attend to the wounded hitch in his words. "High school has nothing to do with this."

He smoothed his large hands across her sensitive skin, sliding downward. With his fingers, he traced tiny circles behind her knees while his sharp gaze searched her face.

"I'm not lying to you, Noah." She pressed her hand against his flat abdomen, then lightly explored the solid muscles through the gray Henley he wore. "I want you."

She'd wanted him for as long as she could remember. Long before the night they had snuck into the woods and made love under the stars. Though awkward—the way sex between young, first-time lovers often is—it'd been the most special experience of her life up to that point. He'd been tender and gentle in all the ways that mattered.

It was the only time a man's touch hadn't turned her stomach. With him, she'd enjoyed the physical intimacy. She'd relished it.

She wanted to feel that again, now, after living so long without.

Her fingers found the waistband of his blue jeans. When she popped the button, the outrageous copper of his eyes sparked and ignited a fire low in her belly.

With the fire came a lick of fear, but she pushed it away. If they surrendered to their bodies' desires, slackening their physical aches, there was no reason to involve their hearts. It was better this way. Safer.

His hunger clear on his face, he gave a soft yank on her legs, and his erection came up hard against her core.

She gasped with shock and pleasure. Proof of his arousal fed the fiery need building inside her and she shifted her hips to feel him more fully.

Sensation surged between her legs. She'd never been so hungry, so wanton, so bold. She'd never wanted anyone as much as she wanted Noah. She wanted him to touch her, to soothe her.

She wanted him to fix her.

And then she wanted him to leave. Before the questions returned to his lips.

Just when she expected him to give in to his lust, he shifted his stance, putting a little space between their bodies. Leaning over her, he bent his head low. His mouth brushed her forehead, her temple, and the fingers of one hand danced up the column of her throat and along her jawline. He whispered her name as a thick, husky plea.

When his mouth hovered above hers, the fluttering in her stomach became furious. She didn't possess the courage to meet his eyes, so she focused on his mouth as he drew closer and closer. His full, puffy lips parted, then flesh met flesh in a whisper-soft kiss.

He took several light, tormenting nibbles from her lips, then delved deeper, exploring her with his mouth. He gently pressed the tips of his fingers against her chin, lifting her face up for his pleasure-taking and, with his tongue, stole soft, succulent tastes of her. The sweet tenderness with which he touched her squeezed her heart. Emotion clenched her throat and threatened to overwhelm her.

Frantic with the fear of her feelings, she tore at his shirt and waistband.

But he was undeterred from his slow, indulgent exploration of her mouth.

Each light brush of his lips blazed a scorching path over her mouth. Just when she worried the heat might become too intense, his tongue slipped out to soothe the burning pleasure-pain.

The soft lick sent a lush wave of sensation spiraling through her and dragged a moan from her throat.

He was right. All these years later, he was better. More experienced and refined. Even more tender and worshipping.

His masculine scent and magical mouth wrapped her in a sensual cocoon until she became dizzy with desire.

With a single, simple kiss, Noah had accomplished what no other man had ever done. He'd reawakened her dormant libido.

Need consumed her. She snuck her hands beneath the hem of his Henley and smoothed her palms up and over his heated skin. The well-defined muscles of his torso rippled beneath her fingers.

On a groan, Noah dragged his mouth down the side of her neck, burning a trail to her collarbone. Her head fell back to grant him unfettered access and his fingers took the same path his mouth took to the V-neck opening of her low-cut T-shirt. He grappled at the thin fabric, then, with a gentle tug on her shirt and bra cup, freed her breast.

Driven by lust, she arched up into his touch. He swept his thumb across her pebbled nipple, then cupped her, lifting the heavy swell of her breast. When he drew her into his mouth, a greedy moan escaped her.

She threaded her fingers through his thick, dark hair and held him to her. Thrilled to touch him, finally, she slid her hands to the sides of his face. The skin over his sharp cheekbones was taut and smooth. Along his jawline, the soft stubble where he'd shaved that morning scraped beneath her fingers.

He gripped her wrist and pressed his mouth to the heart of her palm.

Abruptly, he pulled up, and with his fingers still clamped around her wrist, inspected her hand. He smoothed the pad of his thumb over the sore spot where a blister had recently formed. His eyes on her face were hot molasses melting into tenderness as he lifted her palm to his mouth once more.

When his lips lightly grazed the pink welt, her heart tripped over in her chest. Her heart, which she willed to remain unmoved, thundered with the power of a thousand galloping horses.

She balled her hand into a tight fist and tucked it behind her back. With her other hand, she pulled his head down and claimed his mouth. Talent and skill gave way to a raw intensity that lashed her luscious waves of arousal.

While he kissed her, the pads of his thumbs brushed over the delicate skin of her inner thighs, then nudged under the frayed hem of her shorts. She clutched at his shirt, gathering fistfuls of fabric in both hands.

His thumbs inched higher, to the edge of her panties, and her stomach clenched with want. The tip of one thumb slipped beneath the cotton and stroked her aching core. Jolts of sensation ricocheted through her, and she almost leaped off the table.

His intimate touch was foreign and shocking, and so exquisitely perfect.

With dark eyes, he watched her face as he massaged her wet heat. Her flesh swelled and tingled, and she strained toward him. He eased a finger inside her, and her legs fell farther apart, unabashedly begging for more. Her awareness narrowed until she registered only heat and hunger. Hers, his, theirs.

"Noah." His name on her lips sounded too full and thick, too desperate to her own ears. She hugged him to her and rocked against his clever hand. "Please. Oh, please, Noah. Please. Please."

Color burst behind her eyelids as her orgasm crested. Voluptuous waves rolled over her, one on top of the other, with tortuous pleasure.

When the last tremors shuddered through her, he nipped at the corner of her mouth, then eased his fingers from her body. While her breathing slowed, he brushed a wayward strand of hair off her forehead and peered down into her face.

His stunned expression mirrored her own dazed surprise. One moment, he'd been on his way out the door, and the next, she'd orgasmed. On her kitchen table.

Behind her, a male voice punctured the air. "I hope I'm interrupting."

~

AT THE SOUND of the man's voice, Mina's complexion blanched, and by slow, painful rungs, her open, unguarded expression closed.

Still reeling from those moments of lust and loss of control, he stumbled from between her thighs on weakened legs.

Mina slid off the table. "What are you doing here?"

The newcomer let himself in, and the screen door banged shut behind him. He was in his mid-to-late-thirties, and with a well-cut suit draping his tall, lean frame, dirty-blond hair, and light eyes, Noah supposed some might consider him good-looking.

In a punk-ass, pretty-boy kind of way.

"I wanted to check in on you." His almost translucent gaze slid from Mina to Noah and back again. "Find out how you're doing."

"That isn't necessary." She held her body rigid.

Pretty Boy's belittling smile revealed a fortune in dental work. "It's the least I can do after everything we've been through together."

Sensing the tension that vibrated off her, Noah stepped forward and positioned himself between Mina and the man. "We appreciate your concern, but as you can see, Mina is doing well."

"Oh, uh, Drew, this is Noah. Noah, Drew Alexander."

"Nolan, isn't it?" Drew's tone carried the unmistakable tang of distaste as he sized up Noah for admittance into a club Noah had zero interest in joining.

"Reputations," Noah said. "Pesky things, aren't they?"

Drew's practiced smile rang hollow, but his shoulders relaxed. "I played football with your brother, Shea, in high school."

"If he plays football the way he plays hockey, then I'm sorry for you."

"It's impressive what he's done with the pub in only a year," Drew said. "After your dad's first heart attack, I thought he'd close the pub down for good."

The pub? First heart attack? Noah slid a mask of ease over his face, preferring not to show Drew Alexander anything he could interpret as weakness.

Rather than reveal his lack of knowledge about his own damn family, Noah remained silent.

"Your brother's business has been a welcome surprise for the island," Drew added.

What he meant without saying it was that he, along with everyone else on the island, had assumed Daniel Nolan's five rowdy sons would grow up to be clones of their father.

Alcoholic. Deadbeat. Convicted felon.

"Guess you didn't know Shea all that well," Noah said.

With a smirk, Drew's pale gaze slid back to Mina. "How's the renovation going?"

"Great." With a guilt-ridden glance at Noah, she shifted from one foot to the other. "The renovation's going great."

"I still can't believe you bought this old place." Drew gave his head a condescending shake. "I thought I'd talked you out of it years ago."

"Not at all." She lifted her chin with a defiant tilt. "I just stopped discussing it with you."

"I see." Drew's cool eyes turned glacial.

Mina sidled closer to Noah.

Drew slipped both hands into the pockets of his black

dress pants. "Your latest round of permits should be approved this week."

"That was fast." Blatant mistrust attached to her words.

Drew shrugged. "I called in a favor."

"You didn't need to do that."

"What's the point of being mayor if you can't pull some strings once in a while?"

In the awkward silence that followed, Drew regarded Mina with an odd expression.

The hairs lifted on the back of Noah's neck.

"You look good." Drew's casual tone could not mask the strange undercurrent beneath his words. "Have you been talking to Dr. Smallwood?"

Doctor? Noah's heart lurched. Was Mina sick? He peered closely at her.

Two bright spots of color stained her cheeks. Emotions flitted across her face so quickly, Noah couldn't distinguish one from the next.

The asshole mayor pressed on. "I hear she's an excellent therapist. You should call her."

Mina's eyes met Noah's briefly, then darted away.

The urge to plant his fist in the bastard's mouth expanded inside Noah. He curled his fingers into a ball, but one look at Mina stopped him.

She appeared trapped, panicked even, and he feared his anger would only upset her more.

"I don't mean to embarrass you." The faux-concern in Drew's voice was faker than an artificial sweetener. "I'm worried about you. We all are."

Noah hated the look on Mina's face. He eased his weight onto one foot so that his body blocked Drew's view when he reached out and brushed his hand against her icy fingers.

The phantom touch seemed to send a jolt of strength through her body. Her spine snapped straight, and the rosy color returned to her face. "It's really none of your business."

Drew's expression showed all the wounded affront of a kicked puppy. "I was only trying to help."

"I don't want your help." She drew up to her full height. "I want you to leave."

Drew flung an accusatory glare at Noah.

"It's been a great talk," Noah lied. "But Mina and I are busy catching up."

"Catching up? Is that what the kids are calling it these days?" the smug asshole quipped.

"That's it." Mina pushed between the men and held open the screen door. "Drew, it's time for you to go."

Drew seemed more amused than offended as he ambled toward the door. He stopped before her. "Call me if you need anything."

She shoved him the rest of the way through the threshold and let the door snap shut with a resounding thud. She seemed to hold her breath while Drew's footsteps faded.

Noah leaned back against the table and folded his arms across his chest. "Charming fellow."

"I'll get those papers to you as soon as possible. Thanks for dropping them off."

He frowned. "You're kicking me out, too?"

"It's not like that." Her hands twisted in front of her. "It's just... it's getting late and I need to get over to the house and get some work done."

"And we need to talk about what happened before the mayor showed up."

Alarm flickered across her face. "I don't think that's necessary."

"I do."

"Why?" Desperation added an extra syllable to the word.

Noah gaped at her. *Why?* Because he'd almost fucked her

on her kitchen table. Would have done so if Mayor Frosted Tips hadn't intruded when he had.

"Let's not ruin it by talking." Mina shuffled toward the kitchen. "What does it mean? Where do we go from here? Blah, blah, blah." She placed the kitchen island between them. "It was fun, right? Can't we leave it at that?"

"In case you've forgotten, I'm the guy in this relationship. Those are my lines."

That earned him a smile.

A genuine smile.

At the sight, he felt suddenly, slightly winded, like he'd sprinted a half mile or taken a kick to the nuts.

"Nothing philosophical." His voice sounded faint to his own ears. "I promise."

She nodded. "All right, but not right now, okay?"

He wanted to push it, to push her, but given the chaos in her eyes, he suspected any conversation they had now would be to disastrous effect.

"I can wait," he said easily. "Until you're ready."

"Thank you."

He waited for one heartbeat, and then another. "When will that be?"

Her mouth quirked with a small, crooked smile. "Tomorrow." One of her small hands flitted through the air. "I'll call you tomorrow."

He crossed to her, and as he drew nearer, the now-familiar heat sparked between them. Her lashes swept down to hide her eyes from him, but her body hummed with tension. Not the tight, annoying kind of tension, but the other, rather pleasant sort.

Like expectation, but better.

Anticipation.

His cock pressed against the fly of his blue jeans.

He didn't understand his reaction to her, but nor could he

deny it. And now that he'd had a good, long taste of her, he wanted more.

"Until tomorrow then." Unable to stop himself, he reached out and traced the curve of her rounded cheek. "And Mina?"

Big blue eyes clamped on his face.

"Next time, I won't be distracted."

CHAPTER 8

The next morning, as she rubbed sleep from her eyes and padded into the kitchen to make coffee, Noah's paperwork shouted at her from the kitchen table where it'd laid, untouched, since he left.

Heat flushed her skin at the memory of what had happened on that table only a few hours before. The aftershocks of her orgasm still reverberated through her and she fumbled with the buttons on the coffeepot.

She'd never done anything like that. She'd never used sex to change the subject. To be honest, she was surprised that it'd worked so well.

On both of them.

While the coffee brewed, she distracted herself by washing the small stack of dishes in the sink. Memories of the way she'd begged him to touch her flooded her mind. She nearly dropped the wet dish in her hands.

Oh, god. She *had* begged him. Loudly. With words and moans.

Mortification burned her cheeks, and she scrubbed the dish with frenzied motion.

How long had Drew been standing at her door before she and Noah had noticed him? It was bad enough knowing Noah had heard her cacophony of lusty noises, but had Drew overheard her too?

Humiliation and resentment twisted around her throat and squeezed. Which, where her ex was involved, was nothing new.

Her engagement to the son of her uncle's political enemy had caught the attention of a local media outlet, which had painted her relationship with Drew as a star-crossed lovers fairy tale. True love against all odds. The story had gone national, and when the jerk cheated on her, a tabloid picked up that story as well. Their piece included photo evidence and a side-by-side comparison of Mina and the slim, long-legged Phoebe Taylor.

Mina had found out about the affair on Facebook, after which she'd instituted a self-imposed lifelong ban on all social media.

When she'd confronted Drew about his infidelity, he'd blamed her sexual deficiencies for driving him to sleep with another woman. He'd called her cold and withdrawn. He'd said she was bent.

She'd believed him.

She'd believed him because, by then, they'd been together for two years. Two years with a handsome, successful man. A man she had too little desire to sleep with. Clearly, something was wrong with her.

She'd tried everything she could think of to spark her interest. Dirty books and movies. New positions. Props and toys. Each thing had worked for a while, but nothing had changed her. Nothing had made her better. More. The numbness always returned, and with it, the disinterest. She didn't want to have sex. Not with her ex. Not with herself. Not with anyone.

She wasn't just bent. She was broken.

But then, with one meaningless orgasm, Noah had blasted through her wall of indifference. Was it possible she wouldn't have to live a sexless existence for the rest of her life?

A part of her, a tiny, vindictive, vain part, hoped Drew knew just how loud and heartily she'd screamed out with the ecstasy Noah's talented fingers coaxed from her.

With a secret smile playing on her lips, she approached the table and rescued his papers from the scattered stacks. The first page laid out the steps for conducting a survey and excavation of the area, and following page contained everything else he'd told her on the hill. Last, an itemized price list of necessary supplies and equipment included brushes, sifting tables, nylon rope, and costs for lab analyses.

Air wheezed through her lungs when she read the number totaled at the bottom of the page. Though the estimate came in a little below the figure he'd cited the other day, a choking fear wrapped around her heart.

The papers fluttered to the tabletop. What was she going to do? The fear spiraled, so she swiveled toward her laptop and stabbed the power button. When the screen lit up, she clicked to her spreadsheet and spent the next hour combing through the file, looking for places to cut and scrimp costs so she could shift the money to pay for the excavation. Anything at all she could justify eliminating, she did.

When she calculated that it'd save her several thousand dollars, she resolved to fire the painters and cut the lawn maintenance crew. She'd have to do that work herself. So what if she'd never painted in her life or kept a houseplant alive through a cold, gray winter?

She liked to learn new things. Growing up in a privileged political family, she'd never lifted a finger to do chores or tasks that were deemed menial or that might ruffle her appearance—you could never be certain a media hound wouldn't jump out of the bushes and snap an unflattering photo.

She hadn't known how much she didn't know until after high school, when she'd foregone college and discovered in just how many ways she was lacking. She had no skills, no talent, no ambitions. Not a single thing or attribute she could point to with pride to show her worth in the world.

Until she'd bought this house.

She stared at her spreadsheet, awash in bright red and negative dollar amounts, but soon, she needed to turn away from the dismal math. There was no magic to be discovered in her spreadsheet. The money had to be found somewhere else.

She had to save this house.

An hour later, she'd canceled her cable TV subscription, dropped the insurance coverage on her car to the bare minimum allowed, and traded in her smartphone for the dumbest one on the market. Then she brewed more coffee and spent the rest of the morning preparing a half-dozen job applications to go with the batch she'd sent out the previous week.

Still, the problem remained of finding a quick infusion of cash for the excavation.

Lost in her troubling thoughts, she reached blindly for her coffee mug, and her hand bumped against her purse, which she'd dropped on the table, per her usual habit. With the brush of her hand against the handbag, a fragment of an idea formed in her mind. Slowly, she rubbed the smooth leather strap between her fingers while the fragment expanded into a partial plan.

Without signing Noah's papers, she bounded up from the chair.

In her bedroom, she flung open the closet door and, with

a wide sweep of her arm, shoved aside the clothes draped on hangers. The heaping pile of designer label clothing from her mom loomed. Mina dropped to her hands and knees and began chucking clothing, shoes, and handbags out into the room.

From the ground level storage space beneath her second-story apartment, she fetched several moving boxes and filled them all to overflowing with size single-digit designer castoffs and the overpriced men's dress shirts Drew had left behind when she'd kicked him out of their downtown apartment.

She hauled the boxes downstairs, crammed them into her mom's hand-me-down BMW, then hopped on the car ferry to the mainland and drove her booty to a secondhand shop in an upscale part of Traverse City.

When the store clerk complimented Mina's Coach purse, Mina emptied it and sold it along with the rest of her loot.

She tossed the contents of her purse into a plastic shopping bag and made the trip back to Thief Island, nearly a thousand dollars richer. By the time the ferry docked in the harbor, the sun had slipped beyond the horizon.

But the small thrill she experienced by having cash in her pocket wore off as she drew closer to home, where Noah's paperwork awaited. There was no way around signing the document. She knew that, and yet, she dreaded the moment when she'd hand him the papers. He'd tuck them away some place safe. Then, he'd want to have The Talk.

She wasn't ready for The Talk. If she couldn't answer his questions *before* he'd finger-fucked her on her dining table, she certainly couldn't provide any logical responses afterward.

So she delayed just a little while longer, stopping by the main house to check on things there. Though she knew full well nothing had changed since she'd last walked through the property. When she finally returned to the carriage house, the time had long passed for her and Noah to have a serious or lengthy conversation.

Feeling secure in that knowledge, she snatched up her cell phone to call him, but when she tried punching in his digits, her hands shook so badly that she wound up fumbling with the small device.

Come to think of it, it was probably too late to call him, anyway.

Of course it was. She should've realized that fact sooner.

With light, steady fingers, she typed a quick text message and sent it to his number. *I have your papers. Where should I mail them?*

There. Done. That wasn't so hard.

Feeling buoyant, she flipped off the kitchen light and headed to her bedroom. It might be hours before he responded—

Her cell jangled with the chime of an incoming text.

She twisted toward the sound, then scooped up her phone and opened the new text message.

Coward.

That was all.

She waited, but no other texts came. Not that night or the next morning. She went through the entire next day wondering if he'd follow up on that one stupid word, but her phone remained silent.

What the hell was that? Was that his way of accusing her of running scared? Which she was. Still, the accusation stung.

A tangle of emotions curled through her, but she couldn't tease them apart.

Why was she running scared? What was she afraid of?

Everything.

No, not everything. That'd be ridiculous.

That was it. She was afraid she was ridiculous.

Again.

Still.

Whatever.

What if it was a game to him? His interest in the house? The kiss? The orgasm? What if it'd all been a ploy to, uh, ease his access to her land?

What if he'd planned the whole thing from the start? Beginning when she'd thrown herself at him that first night in the ballroom and continuing right on through to the previous day, when she'd served herself up to him on her own dining table?

Did he believe one little orgasm—no matter how soul-stirring—was all it'd take?

Damn.

Maybe that *was* all it took.

Maybe she was still the idiot who couldn't tell the difference between a man who liked her and one who would use her, even sleeping with her, or proposing marriage, only to advance his career.

BITTER MEMORIES CURDLED in Noah's gut as he walked up the front path of the ramshackle old house. The place had been a shithole fourteen years ago and he couldn't imagine it was fit for human habitation now.

He pushed aside his unease and lifted a hand to bang on the front door with the soft side of his fist.

A few moments passed, then the unmistakable beat of footsteps sounded, and the door swung open.

"What do you know about Drew Alexander?"

Shea's surprise at seeing Noah lingered on his face when he asked, "The mayor? Not much. Why?"

Jack hadn't been able to tell him much of anything about

the man that'd so thoroughly unsettled Mina, and Luke was nowhere to be found. So that left Shea, who, for some godforsaken reason, was now living in the rundown two-story where the brothers had spent much of their youth.

"Our paths crossed a few days ago." Noah scratched his unshaven jaw. "I couldn't get a good read on him."

"And?"

"And…" Noah rolled one shoulder, then the other. "I want to know what you think about him."

Shea considered Noah for a moment, then wedged open the door a crack wider. "You, uh, wanna come in?"

Not even a little.

But then Noah reminded himself Daniel Nolan was dead and buried, not passed out in his stained brown recliner, so he ducked inside after all.

"He comes into the pub once in a while." Shea kicked a laundry basket full of folded clothes aside and bent to scoop up the spread of fast-food wrappers on the coffee table. "Likes the hard stuff. Bit of a pretty boy."

"He has money?"

"Yeah, he has money."

A wry smile twisted Noah's mouth. Some things never changed.

"His high-profile engagement ended badly last year." Shea crumpled the food wrappers into tight balls and stuffed them in the paper bag. "And that's pretty much all I can tell you about him. He and I don't exactly run in the same circles."

"What does your gut say?"

"He's a politician. I assume the worst and hope to be proven wrong."

Noah planned to do just that.

A crack of noise from the kitchen shattered the quiet in the house. The back door banged shut. The thunder of footsteps followed, and then—

"Dada!" A child's squeal rang out, and a two-foot blur launched into Shea's arms.

The lines etching his brother's face smoothed away in an instant.

"How you doing, buddy?" Shea buried his face in the little boy's dark hair.

Perhaps two or three years old, he sported a tiny Red Wings jersey and a pink tutu. Noah's gaze clashed with Shea's over the child's head, where a sparkly butterfly captured a hank of his hair.

Even as he bit the insides of his cheeks to keep from smiling, the scene tore at something in his chest, like an old wound ripping open.

"Give me a second?" Shea moved toward the kitchen. "I'll be right back."

Shea slipped through the doorway, leaving Noah alone with the ghost of their dead father. Daniel's memory lived in the space, and Noah twisted away from the room. At the sliding glass door, he stared past his own reflection and into the small back yard.

The old oak tree, once small and sickly, had grown to twice its size. He recalled the last time he'd scrambled up the massive tree, fear and anger pumping through him. Threatening to tear the sobs from his throat, even against his will. He'd climbed as high as he could and huddled on a too-thin branch, his back pressed to the tree's solid trunk.

With everything in him, he'd prayed. Prayed that his mom was still alive and that he might stop making his dad so angry. That his youngest brother, Leo, would start talking again.

Noah turned from the window and the memories. He found a pair of round, vivid blue eyes pinned on him.

Shea's eyes, except they belonged to the little girl. She hovered in the doorway, one miniature pink croc stacked on top of the other, and regarded Noah with a mixture of fascination and alarm.

"Hey there," he said. "What's your name?"

She fixed him with a dark look of mistrust and ducked her chin, showing him the crown of her head. Her hair was dark, like her mother's.

As if summoned by his thoughts, Isobel poked her head through the doorway. "Omigod, it's really you."

Genuine affection warmed his smile. "Good to see you, Isobel."

"I can't believe you're here." She approached with caution, as though she feared he might startle and bolt. "How long are you staying?"

"A few months, it seems."

"Good." Her smile brightened the bleak room. "That's good."

Noah tipped his chin at the little girl standing between them. "How old is she?"

"Three." Isobel laid her hand on top of the girl's head. "This is Maisie."

At mention of her name, Maisie clamored up into Isobel's arms. She laid her head on her mother's shoulder and regarded Noah with suspicion.

Shea stepped into the room, still cradling the little boy in his arms. "What are you all doing here?"

"It's your weekend." A crispness Noah couldn't recall ever hearing crept into Isobel's tone.

"I'm working tonight." Shea shifted the boy's weight to his other arm. "The bartender called in. I have to cover for him."

In Isobel's arms, Maisie whimpered.

"It's okay, pumpkin," Isobel soothed.

"I just have to stay through the dinner rush." With one finger, Shea playfully booped Maisie on the nose.

"I told you about this last week. We're doing inventory

tonight." Isobel rocked back and forth, trying to soothe the toddler in her arms. "I have to be there by six. I can't call in again, Shea—"

"Stop." Shea's eyes darkened with pain. "I'm not out to sabotage you. I just forgot."

"Of course you did." Isobel shifted Maisie to her other hip.

"Where's Finn? Can't he sit with them for a few hours?"

Isobel shook her head. "He's staying at a friend's house."

The little one in Shea's arms, too small to understand his parents' tense exchange, clamped his tiny mouth shut while his wide brown eyes took it all in.

"I'll call Luke." Shea moved toward the cell phone lying on the coffee table.

Isobel hoisted Maisie higher on her hip. "He's on duty tonight."

Noah straightened. "Duty?"

Shea's gaze swiveled to Noah. "Luke's a cop."

Noah cringed. He and his brothers had spent a fair portion of their youths ducking and dodging the island's old, tyrannical police chief. "You're kidding me, right?"

"Afraid not."

Noah bit back a curse.

"What about John?" Isobel asked.

"He took the boat up the coast for the weekend." Shea shoved a hand through his hair. "It's the busiest night of the week. I can't leave the place short-staffed."

"My job is important to me, too."

"Dammit, Isobel—"

"I'll do it." Noah didn't realize he'd spoken the words until two heads swiveled in his direction. "I can do it." He injected as much confidence into his voice as he could manage. "What time should I be here?"

Shea gaped at him for a moment, then shook his head. "Not a chance in Hell."

Isobel gasped. "Seamus Michael!"

"We haven't seen him in fifteen years."

Isobel's smoke-gray eyes blazed with fury. "As hard as it must be for you, try not to be so pigheaded."

A muscle ticked along Shea's jawline. "We don't know if we can trust him."

The words sliced a gash in Noah's chest.

"He's your brother," Isobel said, a space between each word. "I trust him. Without him there to help after Finn was born, I might've lost my mind."

Intense astonishment siphoned the color from Shea's face. "What are you talking about?"

"It doesn't matter." She shifted Maisie back to her other hip. "When I needed him, he was there for me."

Noah seldom allowed himself to think about those few short years when he'd lived with Shea, his new wife, and their newborn baby. It was the only stability he'd known since his mother's death, and Noah had loved everything about living with Shea and his family. Even the chaos, disruption, and ball-busting challenge of a newborn.

"Why didn't you tell me you were struggling?" A swirl of emotions radiated off Shea, and for one moment, Noah experienced a stab of pity for his brother.

"You were working at the firm. I couldn't add to your stress level." The unwelcome tension stretched tight while Isobel swung Maisie back to the original hip. "I want our children to know their uncle. All of their uncles."

Shea's shoulders slumped. "Can you be here by five?"

"No problem," Noah said.

"Actually, I need to head out now." Isobel stepped forward, rose on her tiptoes, and pressed a kiss to Noah's cheek. Then she dumped Maisie into his arms. "Thank you."

Shea's eyes narrowed. "Don't mess this up."

Noah looked at the kid in his arms. She stared back at him, her expression filled with all the alarm he felt.

"Take care of your brother for me," Isobel said to the little girl.

Good advice, Noah thought, since he knew less than nothing about taking care of kids.

CHAPTER 9

In his first hour of babysitting, Noah learned three things.

First, when choosing which apple to eat, a two-year-old needed to sample each apple piled in the bowl.

Second, Umizoomi was an actual thing.

And finally, Shea's kids, at two and three years old, knew far too little about hockey.

The littlest one, Connor, twisted around on Noah's lap. "Unca Noah, what he doing?"

"Trying to score a goal," Noah said.

"Why?" Connor somehow gave the word two syllables.

"Because that's how you win." Did Shea teach them nothing?

A whistle trilled.

From her position tucked into his side on the couch, Maisie gazed up at him with enormous blue eyes. "What happen?"

"Chicago just got called for a penalty," Noah said.

Her forehead puckered. "What?"

"You see that guy right there?" Noah pointed at the TV

screen. "He slashed a defenseman, so now he has to sit in the penalty box for two minutes."

Crickets.

Noah shifted Connor on his lap and tried a new tactic. "He was naughty. He hit another player with his stick and has to go to time-out."

Maisie's mouth formed a perfect O, and her enormous blue eyes filled with distress.

Noah froze. "What?"

"He got in trouble," she whispered. "Is he gonna cry?"

Her dismay struck Noah, a direct hit to the center of his chest, and he reared back. "Is he—? Ack, no. There's no crying in the penalty box. Never, ever. There, see?" The TV camera cut to the player sitting inside the walled Plexiglas jail and Noah tilted his chin at the screen. "He's not crying, is he?"

A row of itty-bitty teeth flashed with her smile. Her tiny shoulders almost touched her ears, and she shook her head.

His cell chimed with an incoming text, cutting off his laugh. He straightened his leg, dug his phone from his hip pocket, and retrieved the message.

Do you want these papers or not? it read.

His smile fell. Two days had passed since he'd lost himself in her sweet heat. She was a hot, needy woman, and he ached to fuck her properly.

But for two days, she'd avoided him while his hunger for her had only grown. If he were less secure in his manhood, he'd be worried he was a chump.

He typed a reply and hit send. *I can't start the work without them.*

He'd meant to tell her that part, but she'd chewed him up and kicked him out before he'd gotten the chance.

Her reply came straight away. *Where are you? We need to talk.*

That's what he'd said. Four days ago! He hammered out a response, his agitation causing careless thought. *At my dad's old place.*

The words jolted him. This wasn't his dad's place anymore. His dad was dead.

An uncomfortable tension formed in his chest and burned a path to his gut. Heartburn.

Except it didn't feel like heartburn, and it tasted like regret. Regret…and a sorrow so old he'd forgotten the flavor of it on his tongue.

In his arms, Connor's head dropped to Noah's shoulder and a contented sigh shuddered through his tiny body. Moving as little as possible, Noah stretched out his arm and, snagging the remote, lowered the volume of the hockey game.

It was beyond too late for regret and sorrow.

When, twenty minutes later, headlights crawled across the living room wall, he welcomed the distraction. He flipped back to the cartoon with the zooming tykes and moved to the front hall, a slumbering two-year-old slung over his shoulder.

At first, he didn't recognize the prim princess standing on the other side of Shea's door. Not so much because of the neat slacks and frumpy blouse, but because of the cold, composed way she held herself, with her shoulders high and tight and her spine rigid. She felt near, but far away. Remote. Untouchable.

Heartburn congealed into an angsty ball in the pit of his stomach. Where was the fiery woman he would've fucked on the kitchen table if they'd hadn't been interrupted?

Her gaze touched on the child in his arms, and she softened, just a little. "You could've mentioned the other day things were on hold until I signed your papers."

Noah shifted Connor, his human shield, to the opposite shoulder. "I was distracted, remember?"

Hectic color washed over her face and neck. "You couldn't find anywhere in the conversation to slip it in?"

"The mayor interrupted before I got the chance."

Blueberry thunderbolts flashed in her eyes. "Is this a game to you? Am—am I a game to you?"

The cold she'd brought with her inched through his veins. "Are you serious?"

She stared up at him with large, solemn eyes.

"Tell me." His tone took on a dangerous edge, "What kind of game do you imagine I'm playing?"

Her lashes swept down, shutting him out. "I don't know. It's just..." She shook her head. "Forget it."

Connor whimpered and lifted his head, but he only turned to lay his other cheek on Noah's shoulder. "Just so you know, I haven't been sitting around all week waiting for you to sign the release. I've applied for a permit and gathered some supplies."

A soft pucker appeared between her eyebrows. "A permit?" She smoothed a hand over Connor's small back and he relaxed more deeply in Noah's arms. "Let me guess. You can't start work without it?"

"That's right."

"How long will that take?" The sharp bite of her impatience couldn't hide the ring of defeat in her voice.

He hated the sound. "A couple of weeks."

She stabbed at her temples and rubbed.

"Honestly, I can't do much else until I have more money."

Her spine snapped ramrod straight. "I've got your money. Almost. I'll, uh, get it to you... soon."

"Then I'll continue with preparations."

"Great." Her orthodontia-perfect white teeth bit down on her bottom lip with brutal force.

"I found a grant opportunity I'm applying to." He didn't know why he even mentioned it. "It'll take a few months, but if we're successful, you'll recuperate some of the costs."

"Really?" A slash of hope cut across her features. "That'd be great."

He eyed her with suspicion. "If you don't have the money, we can wait—"

"I don't want to wait," she burst out. Then, with a glance at Connor, she lowered her voice. "Will you send me an invoice, or should I mail a check somewhere?"

"I'll get you something."

Her arm shot out, and his now-rumpled papers poked him in the biceps.

He took them from her trembling hand. "I'm not the enemy here. You know that, don't you?"

She hesitated a moment longer than he liked. "I do."

"Good. Because we need each other."

The color leached from her face, and as he watched, the slow beat of fear marched across her features. "What I need is a well, and for this excavation to be finished. As soon as possible."

He couldn't bear the panic in her eyes. "I'll do everything I can to make that happen. Trust me. Please."

Slowly, she shook her head. She fell back a step and nearly tripped off the front porch stoop. "Sorry, but I can't do that."

His gut twisted around her words with a sickening wrench. Helpless to the pain, he stood inside the front door, mute and unable to move, as she whirled and shot down the walkway. After ducking behind the wheel of the BMW, she cranked the engine.

Connor startled in his arms, and Noah bit back a curse. He crooned something nonsensical until Connor's head dropped back down.

He could only watch as the taillights of Mina's Beemer faded into the blackness of the night's shadows.

She couldn't trust him. That was what she'd said. Bitter anger lashed at him.

What the hell had he expected? His own brother didn't trust him. Why the hell would she?

Noah turned from the door, closing it behind him. He hadn't expected them to welcome him back with open arms, but neither had he expected such profound mistrust.

They mistrusted *him*.

Damn, but it hurt.

He laid Connor gently across the sofa cushions and brushed his hand across the boy's forehead until he settled. With Maisie curled up at the other end of the couch, Noah moved to the only other available spot in the room—his dad's old chair.

When he sank down into the threadbare recliner, years of heavy baggage dropped on top of him.

He didn't need this. The crushing load on his shoulders, dragging him down. He had a job to do, then he needed to get the hell off this bloody island before their toxic view of him poisoned his belief in himself.

MINA'S LUNGS burned and her muscles ached as she wrestled a massive, rolled-up old carpet through the front door. When the large roll wedged in the doorframe, she cursed.

Just then, the crunch of gravel snapped and popped, and she looked up to see Noah's truck rambling up her winding driveway. Near the house, he parked among the other vehicles scattered round the lawn.

Stuck between the carpet roll and the doorjamb, she could only watch as he climbed from the cab. His baseball cap and mirrored sunglasses obscured his eyes, and his full mouth pulled into a tight line as he yanked a backpack from the truck bed and slung it over his shoulder.

With long strides, he strolled toward her side yard. As he passed by, he spared her a brief glance.

"The permit is in."

That was all he said. There was no mischief. No teasing her about her present predicament. Nothing, before he rounded the corner of the house and disappeared from her view.

She sagged back against the jamb. It'd been a week since they'd last spoke, and the memory of his wounded expression as she'd dashed from Shea's front porch stoop had hounded her. No matter how many times she replayed their conversation in her head, she couldn't pinpoint the exact words that'd put that injured look on his face.

Indeed, she'd said a lot of hurtful things. Any of them might've caused him pain and trying to isolate the precise cut that'd delivered the fatal gash proved impossible. It sucked, knowing she'd messed up but not understanding exactly how.

For the rest of the day, she snuck peeks outdoors, careful not to get too close to the windows and glass doors where he might spot her. Once, she grew a little lost in watching him as he picked his way around the site, measuring and making notes.

The next day, he arrived early and stayed late. While he worked, the sun teased out the caramel highlights from his dark hair and the light breeze ruffled the wavy locks. By the time he left, he'd staked out large, square sections and delineated them with bright yellow rope tied to two-foot-tall wooden spikes.

The following day, he crouched in the dirt, spending

hours within one squared-off section before moving to the next. He followed the same pattern the next day as well.

The day after that, he arrived with two other vehicles in tow. Eight people filed out of the cars, and the group chattered excitedly while they walked with him out to the site. Given their ages, Mina surmised they were his students from ESU.

Before the students, Noah talked for a long while, gesturing with his hands and moving through the roped-off area to point and signal at various things. Then they broke off into groups of three, with each trio working in a different square while Noah wandered the site.

He stopped occasionally to give instruction or to hunch over something a student pointed to in the ground, but mostly, he hung back and observed.

Fascinated, she watched him.

After the students left hours later, he worked alone for several more hours.

When the sun hovered at the horizon and he returned to his truck, she thought that, finally, he'd reached the end of his workday. Instead, he drove his truck over the rough terrain of her yard and angled it so that the headlights' bright beams shone across the site. In the streams of light, he continued working.

Did he always work such long hours? Other than the granola bar he'd filched from his backpack, she wasn't aware of him stopping to eat or take a break from the physical work or the scorching sun.

That night, just before she crawled into bed, she peeked outside one last time. He still crouched in the dirt, working beneath the glow of his car's headlights.

CHAPTER 10

*H*e was her last thought as she drifted into sleep and the first to pop into her head when she awoke. Throughout the night, he wove in and out of her dreams.

The hazy glow of daylight squeezed in around her closed curtains when she climbed from the bed and shuffled over to the window. She drew open the window coverings and squinted against the sudden flood of sunlight even as her gaze cut the quickest path to the site of upturned earth.

There, kneeling in the dirt beneath the first rays of sunlight, was Noah.

In her chest, her heart squeezed. Had he even slept? Could he have been out there all night?

Past the point of admiring his work ethic, Mina worried he wasn't well. He was working eighteen hours days, outdoors, and skipping meals. Why? Whatever he recovered from the ground had laid there undisturbed for decades. Why the mad rush to retrieve it? What was so important that he had to forego sleep and food?

On the nightstand, her cell phone jangled, jolting her

from her thoughts. She snatched up the device and accepted the call from an unfamiliar number.

The woman on the other end of the connection introduced herself as Marianne, the office manager at the accounting firm where Mina had applied for a secretarial position. Still in her pajamas, Mina smoothed a hand over her tousled hair, as though Marianne might view her through the phone.

When Marianne asked if Mina would like to interview for the position, Mina nearly shouted her emphatic "yes!"

That week marked her first payday with no paycheck. At the prospect of draining her bank account to zero, a slow, icy terror crept through her veins. She needed a job. Desperately.

In her eagerness, Mina scheduled the interview for Marianne's first available opening later that afternoon. After disconnecting the call, she spent the rest of the morning preparing for mock interview questions, then she donned her spoiled rich girl getup and made the short drive to the accounting office downtown.

Throughout the interview, a swarm of butterflies banged around in her stomach, but her talk with Marianne seemed to go well, and Mina left the small, tidy office building feeling relieved and optimistic.

As she started toward home, her thoughts returned to Noah. Was he still at the site, working as he had been when she'd left? Had he factored in his long workdays when he'd estimated the time it'd take him to finish the project? Or was there some other reason he worked at such a backbreaking pace? When was he going to ask her for the money?

An upcoming traffic light flipped to yellow, then red, and she slowed the Beemer to a stop.

She pulled her bottom lip between her teeth and worried the soft flesh.

Between selling her clothes and making cuts to her renovation costs, she'd cobbled together enough cash to pay for one-third of the total excavation. The weight of her worry sat heavy on her shoulders. Where would she find the rest of the money? If she didn't come up with it soon, did she risk another delay?

So far, Noah hadn't asked her for a single penny, and she wondered, who had paid his expenses up till now?

Through the car's windshield, a large blue-and-white sign screamed for her attention.

Al's Autos, it read. *Now buying and selling new and used cars!*

Why hadn't he asked her for the money? She knew he needed it, so what was stopping him from coming to her to get it?

The memory of his dark, troubled eyes when she'd left Shea's house throbbed in her chest. Not only had he not asked her for the money, he hadn't spoken to her at all since he'd started the dig.

Because she'd hurt him?

A car horn honked, and her startled gaze shot up to the bright green traffic light. She eased through the intersection, but at the last possible moment, she flicked on her turn signal and swerved into the car dealership's parking lot.

After thirty minutes and a less-painful-than-expected barter with Al, Mina drove from the lot, not in her four-year-old mint-condition BMW but in a twelve-year-old pickup truck with rusted-out floorboards and a broken air conditioner. Any doubts she might've had dissolved with the large check she'd netted in the exchange. Enough to complete the excavation.

At the house, she discovered Noah was not at the site. A pinch of disappointment nicked her beneath the breastbone, and a frown pulled at her features when she realized her disappointment had little to do with the fact no work was being done.

She freed her hair to the humidity and fumbled through her grocery bag purse for her cell phone. Her fingers tapped the keypad.

I have your money. Her thumbs stilled. *Want me to bring it to you?*

In the bedroom, she stripped out of her interview outfit and pulled on a work shirt.

From the bed, her phone winked at her. Retrieving it from her rumpled bedsheets, she opened the text from Noah.

I will never refuse an offer of money, his reply read.

She laughed. *Where are you?*

His instructions came amidst her frantic search for her favorite blue jeans.

My office— 404 Hannah Hall.

When she read the address, she stumbled over the edge of the throw rug. She stared down at the phone cradled in her hand as the adrenaline zinging through her body slackened and clogged in her veins.

She suppressed a groan. Then, shaking off her dread, she continued her hunt for her pants. She was too desperate—er, eager—to care about his precise location.

Forty-five minutes later, she had taken the ferry to the mainland and driven the remaining distance to arrive on campus. She parked in the lot outside Hannah Hall and hustled inside the nineteenth-century campus building. Hastening down the long corridor, the soles of her sneakers padded against the concrete floor and echoed off the familiar cement block walls. She ran a clammy palm down her jean-clad thigh and fussed with her unruly hair.

As she rounded the corner, Noah's lilting accent drifted out to her through his opened office door. She peeked inside to find him sitting behind his desk, talking with a youthful-looking girl in the chair across from him.

He immediately spotted her. "Mina!"

When his bellow rang out, she jerked in surprise.

He sprang from his chair and swooped down on her. "Come in, come in."

She hung back. "I can wait—"

"Sit," he barked. "Lindsay, I'm afraid we'll have to pick this up another time. I'm late for a meeting."

Lindsay gave Mina a quick once-over and retrieved the backpack at her feet. She slung her bag over one shoulder, and the motion caused the scrap of material stretched across her breasts to shift and twist in scandalous ways.

A sympathetic shiver passed through Mina. The poor girl must be freezing.

"Thanks, Dr. Nolan. See you in class Wednesday." Lindsay's singsong farewell elicited a grunt from Noah.

Mina averted her eyes from Lindsay's perky breasts only to behold her shorts. Shorts so short, the curve of each firm butt cheek peeked out from beneath the hems. Despite a familiar envy at never having been able to pull off such an outfit—even at eighteen—Mina had to admire the girl for her courage.

Mina snuck a glance at Noah, expecting to find his male attention riveted to the girl's impressive assets. Instead, he stood with his arms folded over his chest, his focus pinned to the far wall over Mina's shoulder.

Alone, Mina leaned close. "Will that be all?"

He scowled. "She's been here every damn day this week," he hissed. "She's incapable of understanding the most basic concepts."

"I suspect she understands just fine."

Noah's eyebrows slammed together, his confusion clear.

"Something tells me you're pretty popular with your students, Professor Nolan."

"Yeah, so?"

"Your *female* students."

She saw the moment comprehension struck.

He recoiled, revulsion contorting his features. "That's disgusting. She's a child, for fuck's sake."

"Hardly," Mina muttered.

"I'm her *teacher*." He was sputtering now. "She's my *student*." His protests ceased, and he fixed her with a narrow-eyed stare. "Don't you dare laugh at me."

"I wouldn't think of it." She couldn't repress a small, private smile.

She'd worked in academia long enough to know sleeping with their barely legal, power-disadvantaged students did not repulse every professor.

Noah's dark gaze clamped on her face and thoughts of skeezy student-professor relationships scattered like college kids at a keg party with no beer. His gaze journeyed the length of her body, lingering at a few key destinations, and a punch of heat blossomed in her belly, then spread through her veins with a delicious warmth.

How did he do it? How did he make her feel so sexy? She never felt sexy. Her hips were too wide, her legs too short, but somehow, when Noah looked at her, she couldn't seem to remember those facts. She wanted to give herself over to him, allowing him to do whatever he wanted with her body.

To hell with the eighteen-year-old.

The window air conditioner kicked on and emitted a whiff of mildew into the stale office air. Mina endeavored to rein in her lust-filled thoughts and pulled the check from the dealership out of her back pocket.

She filched a pen off Noah's desk and scrawled her name on the back before handing over the slip of paper.

While he read the check, creases formed between his eyebrows, then his head snapped up. "You sold your car?"

With a flick of her wrist, she waved her hand. "Do you have any idea how much furniture it takes to fill a seven-thousand-square-foot house?"

The lines of concern on his forehead deepened. "Not in the slightest."

"Neither do I," she admitted. "But I'm guessing it's a lot." She shoved both hands in the butt pocket of her jeans. "A girl needs a truck if she's going to do any proper shopping."

Slowly, his expression smoothed, and an easy laugh rumbled in his chest.

He rounded the desk and pulled open a drawer. "We've finished surveying and will start excavating a few days early." He tucked the check away and walked out from behind the desk. "The well is still an issue, though. I need a little more time. I'm sorry."

Fatigue settled in puffy bags under his eyes, and a faint sunburn painted color high on his cheekbones and across the bridge of his straight nose. The image of brash headlights slashing through the darkening night sky rose to mind.

Was it possible he'd been working such long hours…for her?

Her throat constricted. "Don't be sorry." She forced out the lame reply. "It's not your fault."

He leaned back against the desk and folded his arms across his chest. "Did you have any trouble finding me?"

"Not at all." She half-turned, surveying the small space. "This used to be my office."

The furniture was the same, but he'd added an area rug and a bookshelf, which sat mostly empty. A box sat on the floor, opened but packed to the brim with books. Several framed documents propped against the wood shelves, and she noticed he'd hung one like them on the wall behind his desk.

Beneath his tanned skin, he'd paled. "Please tell me you're joking."

"I wish I were."

He pushed away from the desk. With a distressed wrench, he shoved a hand through his hair, which caused a large swath on top of his head to stand on end. "I swear, I didn't know."

"It's okay." It surprised her to realize it was true. "I don't think any of this is your fault."

Her misfortunes weren't of his making. Not by design, at least.

Though he remained standing as he was, his eyes blazed with a sudden intensity, as though he needed something from her and feared she would withhold it.

"I...I..." She swallowed past the lump forming in her throat. "Thank you. You've been working so hard and...I... well...I just wanted to say thank you."

The heat from his gaze warmed her cheeks. Soon, his laser beam stare spread a blistering warmth through her body and she slipped around behind his desk to escape it. A framed document hung on the wall and she squinted up at it.

Then she tossed a glance back at him over her shoulder. "You studied at Oxford?"

"I suppose it's not every day a high school dropout gets into Oxford." The faint tinge of bitterness attached to his words.

"It's not every day *anyone* gets into Oxford."

Mischief glinted in his dark eyes. "I had an in."

"You had an in?" She arched one eyebrow. "At Oxford?"

His easy smile curved his soft mouth. "I was tending bar at a pub outside London, and one summer, a group came to town to excavate some Roman ruins in the area. They came to the pub almost every night, and they talked incessantly about the excavation." The smile turned sheepish, and he scratched the scruff on one cheek. "I started asking questions and soon enough, I was on my knees in the dirt with nothing but a couple of garden tools and instructions not to fuck it up."

Their laughter met and mingled.

When the sound faded, he went on. "The professor overseeing the project took me under his wing. He encouraged me to apply to the program and even lined me up with a few scholarship opportunities, so I had no real reason not to attend once they accepted me."

"So you went back to school?"

"I came back here, took the GED, and enrolled at Oxford the following spring."

She twisted around, facing him fully. "You were here? On Thief Island? When?" And why did it hurt to know he'd returned but hadn't come to see her?

"A long time ago." His quiet words rumbled through her like thunder.

Afraid her expression revealed too much, she stooped before the framed diplomas leaning against the bookcase and tipped through the short stack. Besides the PhD from Oxford, he held two bachelor's degrees and a master's.

She gave her head a baffled shake and stood. "It's incredible. *You're* incredible."

Too late, she wished to pull back the sappy words. Heat burned her cheeks, and sweet embarrassment hung in the air between them.

"I quit high school. There's nothing incredible about that." Beneath the derision, an ember of vulnerability flickered across his face.

"You were bored, not stupid," she snapped, the words lashing with the heat of her agitation.

His dark eyebrows crept upward.

"I'm sorry." She expelled a calming breath. "I didn't mean to snap at you. It's just... You weren't stupid."

In the hall, a door banged open. Voices poured into the corridor as a class let out.

She inched toward the noise. "I should go."

"I'll walk you out."

She couldn't suppress a wry smile. "I know the way."

He winced. "Right."

When she neared the door, his deep brogue reached out to her.

"And Mina?"

When she turned, his dark eyes glittered. "You're welcome."

Her heart tripped over in her chest and fluttered wildly as she pushed through the crowded hallway. A smile fought its way to her lips, but she banished it with a ruthless bite. She couldn't let her heart run away with its hopes and dreams again. The stupid thing had no chill.

Faces of college-aged students weaved before her, and she over-focused on each one, crowding out a certain dreamy, dark-eyed gaze from her mind.

He hadn't arrived early and stayed late every day for the past week for her. At least, that's what she tried telling herself. He was only doing his job. She couldn't forget that.

A life-altering orgasm on the kitchen table was one thing, but she'd given up the rescue fantasies long ago.

CHAPTER 11

For two weeks, he'd busted his balls so he could finish Mina's excavation and escape the island for good. If no one wanted him here, he'd rather be anyplace else. That was the plan. For two solid weeks.

Then she gazed up at him with big, earnest eyes, and *thanked* him, and he no longer cared if he hadn't slept more than a few hours a night going on fourteen days in a row.

Even now, as her house filled his view, its buttery yellow limestone exterior glowing in the afternoon sun, his blood pressure dropped. Not, he feared, because the work that he loved awaited him there. But because she did.

He drove up the tree-lined drive and parked off to the side amidst the crush of trucks littering the driveway and front lawn.

When he climbed from the cab and hauled his bag from the bed of the truck, a steady whir of activity emanated from inside the house. He slung the pack over his shoulder for the long trek.

Since he had begun the excavation, he'd grown accustomed to the rhythms of her life. He knew it'd be a few more hours before the crew packed up and headed home for the day, and that afterward, she'd take a walk along the beach before returning to the house alone to work late into the night.

He couldn't help but admire how hard she worked, and how much she seemed to love that old house. Though he couldn't understand her longing for a home she could call her own, he found her desperate search for one somehow endearing.

He'd seen no signs of girlfriends stopping by or family dropping in on her. No late-night visitors, or early morning departures, to make him suspect she had a lover.

At the site, the sun pushed through the clouds to give him suitable light to work. He should still be in Hannah Hall, grading the stack of papers he'd collected from his students earlier that day. But he was here instead, using his passion project as an excuse to catch a mere glimpse of her.

Because apparently, he was a glutton for punishment. So what if she'd recognized his hard work and had thanked him for it? It changed nothing.

Still, what was the harm if he could leave this place with some pleasant memories to replace the dark, bitter ones?

He shut down the clashing voices in his head and tossed his backpack to the ground. A steady wind blew in from the southwest, so pulled a bandana from his backpack and tied it in a tight knot at the back of his head. Then he kneeled in the dirt before a four-square-foot section of earth, one of fifty such sections, and removed a trowel and brush from his bag.

Probably the same thing that drove him to turn to the past for answers. If you couldn't connect with the living, why not try the dead?

For the next few hours, he lost himself in working the earth, trying to convince her to give up the mysteries of the past.

Sometime later, he pulled an arrowhead from the ground and placed it beside the shard of porcelain he'd extracted moments before. He placed a few handfuls of soil on a sifting table, and dirt fell away to reveal more porcelain fragments.

He smoothed away the caked-on mud and laid the pieces along the table's edge. The shards all contained the blue-and-white pattern, and soon, he'd fitted some of the broken pieces together. With a little more digging and fitting together the fragmented shapes, he reassembled one-third of a dinner plate.

He couldn't wait to show Mina.

The thought blindsided him.

He kept doing that, thinking about her when he wanted to talk about work or share a clever thought or a joke. It'd only gotten worse since that day in his office when she saw his diplomas and her eyes brightened with pride and admiration. Admiration for him.

Noah could not remember a time in his life when anyone gave a good goddamn what he did or didn't do. Not since his mom had died. Aside from the professional interest of a boss or mentor, no one cared what he had or hadn't accomplished. No one, that is, until Mina.

He climbed to his feet and stretched the kinks out of his neck. With the hem of his T-shirt, he wiped a layer of dust from his face. The sun waned toward the horizon and, still needing to attack those essays before the next day's class, Noah packed up before darkness settled in.

Besides, he'd tortured himself enough for one day, being near her, but wanting to be closer, and hating himself for the wanting.

Engrossed in the ritual of securing the site, he didn't at first register the far-off keening cry, until the siren howl grew louder and the screeching wail was upon him. He glanced up as an ambulance turned into the drive and ambled up the winding gravel path. The vehicle disappeared around the front of the house, then the siren fell silent.

He hoped this wasn't a repeat of last week's nail gun incident, which had earned one pitiable crewmember a trip to the hospital. Still, a prickle of unease skittered up his spine, and he started toward the house.

Moments later, a Thief Island Police vehicle rolled up the drive and Noah's normal gait turned to long strides, his apprehension propelling him across the lawn.

By the time he reached Mina's sprawling front porch, his lungs burned and his heart pounded in his chest. He took the stone steps two at a time and burst through the door.

But once inside, his resolve deserted him.

Men milled about in somber silence, foreboding a tangible thing in the charged air. He scanned the room, skimming over all vertical bodies. Like a slow-motion heat-seeking missile, his gaze zigzagged through the foyer, to the open door of the library.

His stomach lurched.

A splatter of thick red droplets sprayed down the wall and across the floor. He gripped the doorjamb and searched out the source of all that blood.

A voice crackled over the paramedic's radio, and a cluster of male bodies parted. At their feet, a still form lay crumpled in a heap.

Mina.

His insides clenched. Blood soaked her white shirt and stained her smooth skin.

So much blood.

Heart in his mouth, Noah moved forward on shaky legs. Over the roaring din of his own blood rushing past his temples, his scientific mind began cataloging the facts of her appearance. Her chest rose and fell with deep, even breaths, if a little rapid.

But there was so much blood.

He stopped.

No, wait. Not blood. The shade of red was a touch darker, with a hint of brown.

Cinnamon Stick.

Air flooded his lungs on a near-painful gasp.

Paint. It was only paint.

Mina's enormous blue eyes popped open and stared up at the cluster of men standing over her. Then her gaze found Noah.

He searched her face. Alert but stunned, annoyance held sway over the fear and pain.

She tried to sit, and he moved to help her. Once she sat propped against the wall, he crouched to peer into her face.

"What happened here?" His voice sounded rusty with emotions he didn't care to acknowledge or even name.

"I fell off the ladder," she said through white, trembling lips.

The ladder now lay on its side on the floor. Near the ceiling, red paint gave way to the purple nightmare.

"You were at the top when you fell?"

She nodded.

He flicked a wayward curl off her forehead. Her pupils were dilated, but evenly sized. "You're afraid of heights."

She shifted, then winced. "Now you know why."

Her teasing went a long way to calming his racing heart. "Did you get dizzy?"

"A little. Then the paint can tipped, and I tried to catch it..." Her voice was weak and held a slight tremor. "The next thing I knew, I was on my ass on the floor."

A smattering of laughter stirred from the men within earshot.

"How we doing over here?" Luke squatted next to Noah.

Mina's gaze slid from Noah to Luke and back again. "I think I'm seeing double."

Laughing along with the others, Luke squatted next to Noah. "Are you light-headed?"

"Yes. All the male beauty is making me woozy."

"I've been known to have that effect on women." Luke's magnetic smile erased any arrogance his words might've carried.

Noah wanted to punch his brother. Was he seriously flirting right now?

"Anything else hurting?" Luke asked.

"Only my pride."

Luke took her hand and placed two fingers on the inside of her wrist while Noah moved to sit beside her.

After finishing the count, Luke rose to his full height. "I think the paramedics want to take you to the hospital. Make sure you don't have a concussion. I'll go check on your ride."

Without thinking, Noah reached for her small hand, lying limp in her lap. Her fingers were ice cold, and he wrapped her hand tight in his. She dropped her head to his shoulder.

It made little sense, but his spirits soared.

He laid his head on top of hers. "If you wanted some attention, all you had to do was ask."

Her head popped up, knocking him in the chin. "What did you say?"

"Nothing." Noah rubbed his chin and pulled her head back down to rest on his shoulder.

Soon, two paramedics appeared and loaded Mina into the ambulance. Noah followed close behind in his truck, traveling the short distance to the island's small hospital.

Once there, things progressed smoothly, albeit slowly. After a brief wait in a curtained cubicle, a nurse questioned Mina about her medical history. Nothing too interesting, until Mina mentioned something about a shattered eardrum and hearing loss. The nurse didn't pursue the topic, and the ER doctor's arrival thwarted Noah's plan to do so.

He examined Mina and ordered a range of tests, including an X-ray of her wrist, which had grown swollen and sore. An hour later, a technician showed up to take her for the scans and, a half hour after that, returned her to her cubicle.

Then they waited.

A nurse appeared and checked a chirping gadget hooked to Mina's finger. A short time later, a different nurse showed up with an ice pack and a splint.

"You have a torn ligament in your wrist," she explained. "Twenty minutes of ice and then we'll wrap it up for you. You're not lefthanded, by any chance?"

Mina shook her head and motioned toward the splint lying on the end of the bed. "How long should I wear that?"

"A few weeks at least. Until the sprain heals up."

The nurse disappeared behind the curtain wall, and another chunk of time passed before the doctor reappeared to explain Mina was, in fact, concussed and he wanted to observe her for a bit before sending her home.

So again, they waited.

Mina ate ice chips while Noah snacked on potato chips and candy bars from a vending machine. They watched a chick flick, which was actually kind of funny, and the second half of a college football game that went into double-over-time and was totally badass.

When five hours passed with no puking and no memory lapses, they set Mina free.

With the screech of metal grating against metal, the discharge nurse swept open the curtained wall. The nurse was a round, middle-aged woman with short, salt-n-pepper hair and permanent scowl lines etched around her mouth and eyes. "Ready to go?"

Mina bolted upright in the hospital bed. "Yes, ma'am."

The nurse pushed the glasses up her nose and referred to a clipboard she propped on the shelf of her stomach. "We've filled your script for a painkiller at the pharmacy on the first floor. You can pick it up when you leave."

Though she addressed Mina, she handed Noah a sheet of paper. "Here are her aftercare instructions. For the next seven days," the nurse's stubby index finger popped up, "drink plenty of fluids, take your meds, and get lots of rest." A second and third finger joined the first as she spoke. Then her head swiveled to Noah and her mouth pulled into a stern line. "You'll need to monitor her overnight. We want her to sleep, but wake her up every three to four hours and talk to her. Make sure she's lucid and not in too much pain."

Mina raised her hand, like a student in class. "Oh, he's not—"

The nurse's chin pressed into her chest, and she peered at Mina over the rim of her eyeglasses.

Mina shrunk back under the nurse's gaze. "Just that, uh, he's not my boyfriend."

"You have someone staying with you tonight?"

"She won't be alone." The statement rolled easily off Noah's tongue.

The nurse tapped the paper in his hand. "Our number is here. Call if you experience a headache that the meds won't take care of, loss of consciousness, confusion, or changes to your vision. Understood?"

"Yes." Noah and Mina spoke together.

The nurse directed Mina to follow up with her primary care physician in the next couple of days and disappeared behind the curtain.

With a frown, Mina scooted closer to the edge of the bed. "Why are you smiling?"

"I love sleepovers." Standing, he moved to help her. "Can we share secrets and have a pillow fight?"

"No." Her legs tangled in the blankets and she kicked to free them. "You are *not* spending the night."

Noah feigned a gasp of horror. "You're not going to disobey that woman, are you?"

"No, but…." Exhaustion clouded her features while she tugged up one shoulder of the oversized hospital gown they'd given her.

The pang that pinched his chest sent a scowl to his face. "Don't be reckless with your health. I can stay."

Her cheeks flushed an attractive shade of pink. "I don't think it's a good idea."

He didn't bother trying to hide his roguish smile when he handed her a clean T-shirt from his truck. "Here, put this on."

"Where's my shirt?"

"Covered in paint." He lifted a plastic bag off the floor. "You have nothing to worry about. I'll be good, I promise."

She took his shirt and rose on unsteady legs. "Have you been good a day in your life?"

"That's debatable," he admitted. "But give me some credit. You're infirm. It wouldn't even be a challenge."

"You're not the one I'm worried about." She clutched the T-shirt and shot him a pointed look. "Do you mind?"

Noah turned his back to her. "Afraid you can't keep your hands off me?"

"You know how irresistible you are." Her voice sounded muffled through the fabric. "It's disgusting."

"First, I'm the best you ever had and now I'm irresistible." He shook his head. "Be careful. You're going to inflate my ego."

"You can turn around." She pulled her hair through the shirt's neck hole. "I can't change the facts, and I can't let you set foot in my house while I'm weakened by a head trauma."

His witty rejoinder died on his lips when she rubbed her forehead and sank onto the bed. She'd gone pale again, and her features were drawn and pinched.

"All right, fine. I won't fight you. This time." He held out the cup with ice chips to her. "But I am going to call you."

"You'll what?" She dug out an ice cube and crunched it between her teeth.

"Every three to four hours, I'll call and wake you up."

With a heavy gulp, she swallowed. "You don't have to—"

"It's that or I'm staying."

Her soft smile sidled up next to his heart. "Fine. You win. This time."

With nightfall descending, they left the hospital and rolled along the country roads back to her house. In the passenger's seat, Mina dozed, and over the sound of her soft snores, Noah thought he heard her stomach growl.

He phoned the pub and placed an order for takeout. When he parked in front of Lucky's and killed the engine, Mina stirred.

He brushed her cheek with the backs of his fingers.

Her eyes fluttered open, and when her gaze landed on him, the trace of a smile touched her lips.

"Meat or no meat?"

A pucker formed between her eyebrows. "What are we talking about? Food or sex?"

His soft chuckle rumbled in his chest. "I already know your preference regarding sex. We're talking about food." He swept his finger down the tip of her small nose.

Her nose crinkled adorably. "No meat."

"I'll be right back."

She murmured something unintelligible.

"Rest, *a chuisle*." With the tips of his fingers, he traced the curve of her cheek. "I won't be long."

When he returned to his truck, she slept once more, so he

drove the rest of the way to her place in silence. She stirred when he cut off the truck's engine, and he strode around to her door to help her climb from the vehicle in the dark.

With his hand pressed to the small of her back, they crossed the wet lawn and moved toward the dark silhouette of the carriage house. At the door to her second-floor apartment, he took the keys from her shaking hands and let them inside.

While she shuffled toward the couch, he flipped on the lights and rummaged around the kitchen for plates and utensils. He carried everything, along with the takeout, to the living room.

He eased onto the couch next to her and pushed the magazines and paperbacks aside to make room for her dinner on the coffee table. "Do you think you can eat?"

She cracked open one eye.

Her stomach released a deep grumble, and she moaned. "Oh, no. You bought nachos."

He froze, a scoop of fully loaded nachos suspended above a plate. "You don't like nachos?"

"I *love* them." She fought her way to a sitting position on the overstuffed sofa.

Dropping the warm food onto the plate, he smiled, pleased with himself.

"Okay, here's the deal." He handed her a plate and napkin. "If you don't answer in four rings or fewer, I'm coming over."

"Yes, sir." She managed a mock salute.

He struck her with a dark scowl. "Test me, and watch what happens."

"I wouldn't dare think of it," she said around a mouthful of chip and beans.

"Good girl." He pushed to his feet. "Call me if you need anything."

She nodded. Wrapped in a pile of blankets, her makeup

mostly worn away, she appeared young and vulnerable. She rubbed her eyes with her knuckles, and a sudden, fierce surge of protectiveness rose from somewhere deep in his chest.

Regret and defiance twisted through him. He never should've agreed to leave her. He didn't want to leave. He wanted to stay, and eat nachos with her, and be close by in case she needed something, anything. Or even if she didn't.

He wanted to stay.

Unable to push words past the lump in his throat, he moved silently toward the door. It was just as well he couldn't speak, for he couldn't very well tell her the truth—that he would not be able to keep the promise he'd made to her at the hospital.

CHAPTER 12

Mina crawled through the hazy fog, clawing her way back to the surface of consciousness. Incessant, shrill chimes cycled through her dulled awareness until, with a jolt, she recognized the noise as her cell phone's ringtone.

She fumbled for the device. "Hello."

"Dreaming of me?"

The pounding ache in her head pulled a groan from her. "I'm concussed, not hallucinating."

Noah's deep rumble of laughter lured her further from sleep.

"What time is it?" she asked.

"Two o'clock. How many fingers am I holding up?"

"One?"

"So close. Five."

She snuggled deeper into her quilted cotton bedspread.

"Did I tell you how much I like your choice of paint color?" His voice carried through the phone and reached inside her, feathering out to touch all those hidden, lonely places.

"It took me forever to match it to the original color." She wanted to sit beside him and tell him all about the house and her plans. But her head throbbed and all she could manage was a deep sigh.

"You did good." He spoke as softly as a fleece blanket.

"Thanks."

"Too bad you suck at painting."

She laughed, then winced as pain pulsated inside her skull. "I suck at ladders. It's yet to be seen if I can paint."

"Maybe start on the ground floor. Work your way up."

"Good idea," she said through a yawn.

"All right, go back to sleep. I'll talk to ya soon."

"Okay."

As she pulled the phone away from her ear, the warmth in his deep voice reached out to her. "Goodnight, Mina."

"Goodnight, Noah."

"HELLO?" Dryness seared her throat.

"What are you wearing?"

"Pajamas."

"What color are they?"

"Black leather with lace."

"I'll be over in five minutes."

Mina chuckled, which hurt her head. She moaned.

"Head hurt?"

"Mm-hmm."

"I set your meds on the nightstand. Take two now."

Mina found the prescription bottle next to a glass of water. She fumbled with the cap, dumped some pills on the end table, and popped two in her mouth. The water soothed her throat, and she took several greedy gulps before returning the glass to the nightstand.

She fell back against the pillows.

"Close your eyes." His low voice soothed all her aches. "Are they closed?"

"Mm-hmm."

"Sweet dreams, *a mhuirnín.*"

~

"Good morning, sunshine." Noah kept his voice low. "Congratulations, you're still alive."

She groaned.

Her misery carried over the phone, and he clenched his teeth against the urge to bang through her front door. "How are you feeling?"

"Are you sure I'm not dead? I mean, it's possible, isn't it?"

"Well, let's see." He rubbed at the ache in his neck. "Does your head hurt?"

"God, yes."

"Then you're not dead." He punched a button on the truck's dashboard and the clock light winked on. "Time to take your meds."

Through the phone, he heard a soft clatter. Then she cursed.

"Everything okay?"

"Who designs these bottles?" she mumbled. "They're impossible to open."

"Did you take your medicine?"

"I will in a minute."

"I'm coming over—"

Another curse tickled his ear. "I'm up, I'm up. Geez. Nurse Ratched was a pansy-ass compared to you."

But he'd already climbed from his vehicle and had strode halfway across her side lawn.

"Too late," he said. "I'm already here."

"Wha—? How did you…?"

Sunlight danced on the raucous waves when he bounded up the stairs to the apartment. "You gonna let me in?"

"I… Yeah, okay. Hold on."

The rustle of bedsheets carried through the phone.

"How long have you been here?" she called through the door.

"Oh, you know. A bit."

As his words still hung in the air, footsteps sounded, then the door swung open wide. "Don't you ever sleep?"

He slid his cell phone into his pocket and stepped around her. "Here and there."

Without breaking stride, he beat a direct path to her bedroom and retrieved her medication from the nightstand. On his way back to the kitchen, he popped the lid.

She slouched in a chair at the kitchen table and cradled her chin in her palm. He spilled two of the small white pills from the bottle and they skittered across the table's surface before sliding to a stop in front of her.

In the kitchen, he poked around in the cupboards until he found a glass. He filled it halfway with water from the faucet and delivered it to her.

"Thank you." She settled into a chair, and as she swallowed each pill one by one, he took a quiet inventory of her.

Dark circles smudged the hollows beneath her eyes.

The kick of protectiveness echoed in his chest. "What are you doing today?"

"I don't know…" She pushed a hank of her wild hair behind one ear. "What time is it?"

"Nine a.m."

"I might go back to bed."

"I think that's a brilliant idea." Though every muscle in his body screamed at the thought of leaving her, he pushed to his feet and moved toward the door. "You know how to reach to me if you need me."

"What about you? What are you doing today?" Her eyes journeyed over him. "Wait, why are you wearing the same clothes you had on yesterday? How did you get here so fast? Did you…? Did you stay here last night?"

The spot between his shoulder blades ached, and he rolled his shoulders. "I stayed."

"But…not here." Her fingertips hit the tabletop. "Where did you sleep?"

His throat was dry, and he coughed to clear it. "In my truck."

Her eyes melted with a softness that made the kink in his neck worth the persistent stab of pain.

"You didn't have to do that."

"I know." The chair leg scraped against the wood floors when he stood. "I'm headed out to grab a shower and get some work done. I'll call you later." Halfway through the door, he turned back. "And Mina?"

"Yeah?"

"Stay off the damn ladder."

MINA TOOK Noah's advice and stayed off the ladder. She attempted something far more perilous instead.

A visit with her mother.

The trip to the emergency room, inclusive of an ambulance escort, would command a hefty price tag. All the heftier because of her unemployed, and thus uninsured, status. So she swallowed her tattered pride and prepared to ask her mom for a loan.

The petite, beautiful Vivian Powers Winslow Thornton was prone to temper tantrums and shouting matches, and collected diamond jewelry, vacation homes, and ex-husbands.

Mina was Vivian's polar opposite.

Vivian's husband, Jake, joined them for lunch on the patio by the pool. Vivian dressed in white slacks and a gauzy tunic cinched at her tiny waist with a chain belt. The day was warm, and the sun dominated a cerulean sky full of puffy white clouds, though a crispness on the air foretold summer's end.

"Why don't you stay here while we're in Martinique?" The gold bangles on Vivian's wrist jangled as she gestured to the mansion behind her.

"I have a house, Mom."

Vivian sighed. "Honestly, Wilhelmina. You sleep in a barn."

"It's not a barn anymore," Mina said. "You should come see it."

Vivian scoffed and sipped her wine.

"We'd like that," Jake said, his brown eyes soft and warm. "When we get back next month."

Mina lobbed a grateful smile at her stepdad.

An easygoing man, Jake was the perfect crosswind to Hurricane Vivian.

Mina endeavored to change the subject. "Guess what?"

Her mother feigned interest.

"Emily is coming to visit."

Mina's cousin, Emily, was the daughter of Vivian's sister. Born a few months apart, Mina and Emily had become steadfast friends as children during Audrey and Emily's brief visits. But by the time the girls reached their teens, the visits had stopped.

Over the years, they'd stayed in touch with sporadic emails and texts, so when she heard Emily planned to visit, Mina was thrilled.

Vivian's dainty features pulled into a frown. "Oh? Too bad we'll be away when she's here."

"She's flying in today. We're having dinner later. You're welcome to join us."

Vivian frowned into her glass. "Unfortunately, we can't. We need to finish packing."

Lunch progressed with more awkward conversation, including one reference to Mina's foolish quest with "that house" and two remarks about her weight.

Mina wanted to tell Vivian not to bother with her put-downs. Her criticisms already played in an incessant loop inside Mina's head.

Instead, the pounding inside her skull gave way to nausea, and rather than make a request for money, she only wanted to get home to her pain meds. Soon, she stood at the front door, making her goodbyes.

"Where's the BMW?" Vivian asked.

Mina cringed inwardly. "I sold it."

Shock turned to annoyance on Vivian's face. "Why on earth did you do that?"

"I needed the money." Unable to think up a lie through the haze of her headache, Mina blurted the truth.

"For what?" From the look on Vivian's face, a foul stench hovered above her head. "For that house?"

"Yes, for the house."

"Honestly, Wilhelmina, that place is more trouble than it's worth."

To think, Mina had once thought the renovation would make her mother happy, considering the house was the focal point of the Winslow family legacy. A legacy Vivian had adored being a part of, even after Mina's father had died. But in buying the house, as with all things, Mina had only disappointed her mother.

"I gotta get going." Mina descended the front steps. "Have a safe trip."

As she hurried toward the red pickup, she spotted movement at the neighbors' house. Glancing over, she slowed her footsteps. Two men hauled a floral sofa through the front door. They stumbled across the front lawn and dropped it on the curb with a careless plunk.

A crack of sound jerked Mina's attention to the side lawn, where another man heaved large hunks of broken wood into a truck-sized dumpster, then retreated inside the house.

With a couple of quick glances over her shoulder, she sidled closer to the massive dumpster. On her tiptoes, she tried to peek over the top, but she didn't quite have the height. She placed one foot on the wheel well, grabbed a hold of the dumpster's edge with her good arm, and hoisted herself up.

When she saw what lay inside, she gasped. Among scraps of linoleum and drywall, oak cabinetry packed the large bin. Though the wood finish appeared dated and tired, she could find no evidence of irreparable damage. With a little paint or stain, the cabinets would be perfectly functional, possibly even cute.

The men reemerged from the neighbors' house with an elegant buffet that sent Mina's heart racing and staggered toward the curb.

She chased them down and, after a quick conversation with the homeowner, learned all about the massive remodel they had undertaken. Having no use for the old stuff, they'd planned to throw it out, but agreed to let Mina take anything she wished to haul away.

Adrenaline gave her strength as she lugged a kitchen cabinet across the neighbors' lawn. It was an awkward task with her gimpy wrist.

Through the front window, Vivian spotted her daughter

looting the neighbors' home and sent her henchman, Jake, out to put a stop to the unseemly ransacking. But rather than scold her, Jake lifted the heavy cabinet from Mina's arms and carried it the rest of the way to his garage.

Together, they pilfered the oversized dumpster and crammed as much stuff as they could fit into the back of Mina's pickup truck. Then they stowed the rest of the booty in the garage for safekeeping until she could return to retrieve it.

As she plunked another load onto the cement floor, Vivian appeared at the door leading inside the house from the garage.

"Mina, honestly," she hissed. "Have you no shame?"

Mina was so ecstatic about her good fortune she couldn't erase the smile from her face. "No. None."

At one time, digging through someone's trash would have mortified Mina, too. But not now. Not when the scavenging yielded roomfuls of furniture. Free furniture. Furniture she desperately needed and, at present, had little to no means of buying. Even when she'd still had a job, the expense of furnishing a nearly seven-thousand-square-foot home was daunting.

By the time she returned to the island, every muscle in her body screamed with exhaustion, and she dreamed of a warm bath before heading out to meet Emily for dinner.

She recited another silent thank you that Sam had figured out how to keep the water running at the carriage house while they worked out the issue with the well.

Noah's Colorado sat parked under the massive oak tree. A shiver rippled through her, caused by the cool north wind kicking up off the lake. At least, that's what she told herself as she escaped into the carriage house.

She flipped through the small stack of mail she'd snagged from the box. At an envelope from the accounting office, she paused, then tossed the other mail aside and ripped it open. Before hope even took flight, she'd finished reading the curt note informing her they'd chosen another candidate to fill the secretary position.

Dejection weighing her down, she dropped the letter into the trash and plucked a wineglass from the kitchen cupboard. The box of wine sat on the counter, and she twisted the nozzle, but a thin trickle of blush-colored liquid dribbled into the glass. She rocked the box forward and backward, trying to dredge more liquid from the bottom.

When her efforts produced less than half a glass, she plopped down hard on a stool at the counter and raised the glass to her lips.

Just then, the thunder of footsteps sounded on her porch stairs, and a moment later, Noah burst into view. His chest heaved, and his dark eyes glittered, even through the screen door.

Her heart stuttered its welcome. Indeed, her whole body hummed with awareness of him.

But he only stood there, breathing hard and not speaking, while a puzzling mix of shock and wonder swirled across his face.

Her hammering heart plunged to her toes. "Oh, no. Now what's wrong?"

"Nothing's wrong." He tugged open the screen door and slipped inside. "How are you feeling? You okay? How's your head?"

A bubble of laughter tickled her throat at his rapid-fire questioning. "I'm okay. A little tired, but I feel fine."

"Any headaches? Blurred vision?"

"Nope."

"Great." Light flickered in his dark eyes and a smile softened the curves of his mouth.

"What's gotten into you?" she demanded. "You're beaming."

"I found something."

"What, like, at the site?"

He nodded. "It's big."

She frowned. "Can you rent a bulldozer or something?"

"Not big, big. *Important* big. Huge."

The weight of expectation grew heavy. "Well? What is it?"

"Come." Noah held out his hand. "I'll show you."

$\mathcal{M}$ina stared at Noah's hand, as if he offered something dangerous. Dangerous and thrilling.

But before she could stop herself, she'd placed her hand in his, and his long, warm fingers clamped around hers. Before she fully registered his heat and the feel of his work-roughened skin, he was pulling her outside and down the porch stairs.

As they sprinted across the yard, dew kissed her sandal-clad feet, while overhead, bloated gray clouds blocked out the sun's heat. He tugged her along, and as they stumbled along, hand-in-hand, laughter tumbled from her.

Together, they scrambled up the embankment to the site. He crossed to the clapboard storage shed. Breathless, her sides aching, Mina stood panting as he worked the lock.

When he pulled the doors open wide, she followed him into the dark interior. He vanished from her side, and a moment later, soft lights winked on above her head.

Three rows of tables ran the length of the room, and as he

led her down one aisle, she craned her neck to peer at the objects littering the tabletops.

"You found all this stuff out here?"

He drew to a stop in front of an assortment of mud-covered debris and, still looking over her shoulder, Mina crashed into him.

"This is it." His voice was rough with emotion.

She squinted down at the odd jumble of junk. "Is that…a shoe?"

"It is." He laid his hand atop a small wooden box. "But this is what I wanted to show you."

With extreme gentleness, he tipped the box on its side. His fingers danced over the surface, questing, until a small sliver of wood slid away to reveal a hidden compartment. He inserted a finger inside the dark nook, and out popped a skeleton key.

Her breaths came quickly as he guided the key into the tiny lock and twisted until the latch clicked. The hinges creaked when he raised the lid and revealed the contents inside the box.

A gasp slipped from her. There, amidst a handful of silver and gold coins, lay an array of jeweled trinkets and ornate hairpins.

His eyes gleamed like gems. "I found it when I stuck my hand into a muddy, mucky pit."

"What exactly is it?"

"I'm not sure, but it appears to be some kind of treasure hoard." A trickle of laughter escaped him.

"Are you serious?"

"I swear, I'm serious. Maybe someone hid all this stuff during a raid or stowed it here for lack of a safer place." Shadow cut across his face but couldn't dim the light in his eyes. "Or it's possible the rumors are true, and Thief Island was, in fact, a pirate hideout with a booming criminal underground."

"That's a joke, right?" Laughter started low in her belly. "Pirates? In Michigan? On the island?"

Noah shrugged. "Why not? It's isolated. Remote. Surrounded by water. It's not a bad spot if you want to disappear for a while."

"And don't forget the arctic winters. What's not to love?" Mina wiped a tear of mirth from her eye. "Who comes to northern Michigan and finds pirate booty? Professor Nolan, you are one lucky bastard."

He rubbed the back of his neck. "Ah, technically…it's yours."

Her laughter died on her lips.

The line of his mouth tightened a fraction when he regarded her with suddenly serious eyes. "You're the property owner. It's your call what happens to anything we find out here. Within the bounds of the law."

She heard his words, but they refused to fall into order inside her head. "I don't understand."

"After we're done, we'll need to find a permanent home for all the artifacts."

"Won't they go to a museum?"

"Only if you decide to sell or donate them to one."

Mina dragged her gaze from Noah to the muddied hodgepodge of treasure. "What else would I do with them?"

"You could sell to a private collector."

"Oh, sure. I must know a half-dozen people looking to buy an old shoe and—what's that?—a jar of red... gunk."

"Makeup, and you don't need to know anyone. *They'll* find you." An edge crept into his tone.

"They?" She gaped at him. "Who? Who buys something like this?"

"History junkies. Treasure hunters. Hawkers might sell it

in parts and pieces. The market for artifacts like this is large, active, and difficult to regulate."

"So all this would…?"

"Some pieces may end up in a museum. Eventually."

She studied his expression. "But probably not."

A heavy sigh rattled through him. "Most of it would disappear into private collections where things often get lost, broken, stolen." He shut the lid. "There's time to think about it. It'll take me a while to figure out what all this is. When you decide what you want to do, I can help you find the right people to talk to."

"I already know what I want to do." She touched the box, feeling its solid wood, and tried to imagine how something so old and ordinary-looking could be so significant. "It should go to a museum, so people can see it. One in Michigan, if possible."

When she looked up, he was watching her, a soft smile on his face. "I think that can be arranged."

She got the sense that she'd pleased him, and a blush of pleasure warmed her cheeks. Continuing down the row, she inspected the range of artifacts.

"I meant to bring you out here before now." He trailed behind her.

"Why didn't you?" She glanced at him over her shoulder.

His brow creased. "Oh, you know…"

She had no idea, and she told him so.

"I know you're not exactly thrilled I'm here." There was no heat in words, only that soft shimmer of vulnerability in his eyes.

At the sight, her heart pinched. "Aside from the money, and the mess you've made of my landscaping, and the whole not being able to flush a toilet in my house, it hasn't been so bad."

A smile touched his puffy lips, but didn't banish the disquiet from his dark eyes.

She arched one eyebrow. "Is that the only reason?"

He pondered her for a moment, then sighed. "I'll have to get back to you on that."

Another small object caught her notice, and she bent over it.

"Pick it up." From behind her, he spoke low, next to her ear. "It's okay."

The black stone was cool beneath her fingers. Little more than the size of a silver dollar, the figurine fit into her palm.

"It's made of obsidian. Most likely French."

The carving of a man, his arms outstretched, palms facing upward, made him instantly recognizable.

"He came with the first settlers." Noah was at her side. "Together, they survived harsh winters, war with the Indians, the Brits. Bears, too, I imagine."

A bubbly laugh accompanied her wide smile.

"He was the source of their resolve." Noah reached past her and filched another artifact from the table. "Here, check out this one."

He launched into an explanation about the object cradled between his fingers, describing interesting tidbits and details about the piece that made it special. He did the same for the next artifact, and the next one, too.

While he talked, she noted the way his expression changed, softening with his wonder, and how his accent thickened with the heightening of his passion. Her heart filled as he shared that passion with her. She couldn't help but compare the animated, impassioned man to the aloof, uninterested teenager he'd been in high school.

She stared at him in amazement.

He cut himself off midsentence, and the soft smile reappeared on his lips. "What?"

"You're a dork."

The sexiest, most incredible dork.

His grin, wide and unrestrained, lit up his entire face. "Don't tell anyone. You'll ruin my street cred."

"Not a word," she promised.

His laughter tickled a spot beneath her breastbone, and she experienced a moment of buoyant happiness, the sensation lighter and headier for the fact she'd lived so long under the weight of fear and worry.

How could she not fall in love with him again?

The warm fuzzy feeling burst like a popped balloon.

"Have dinner with me."

On a gasp, she reeled back. "What? No. Absolutely not."

He placed a hand over his heart. "Ouch."

She winced. "Sorry. That was emphatic. But, really, I can't."

"Can't? Or won't?"

"Both?" She pulled her bottom lip between her teeth.

His eyes narrowed. "Explain."

"I made plans. So I can't. Not tonight." He appeared unconvinced, so she pressed on. "Even if I could, I shouldn't."

He moved a fraction closer. "Shouldn't is not the same as wouldn't. Why *shouldn't* you have dinner with me?"

"Probably the same reason you haven't brought me out here before now. Why is that again?"

His gaze tracked to the V of her sweater. "Because if you thrust those beautiful tits in my face one more time, I'm going to throw you to the ground and bury myself inside you."

Heat rushed over her skin. "Oh, that's a d-different reason than I was thinking."

His fingertips swept across her cheekbone to push back a lock of her hair. "Cancel your plans. Come with me instead."

"I can't?" Her words sounded faint, breathless.

The warm molasses in his eyes turned cool. "Who is he?"

"*She* is my cousin, visiting from out of state."

His expression cleared. "Excellent. Family reunions are the best. Shall we ride together or meet up?"

"Oh, no—"

"Your cousin won't mind, will she? What's her name?"

"Emily, and it doesn't matter if she'll mind. I will."

"Listen, I didn't want to do this, but you've left me no choice. I insist you and your cousin come to dinner with me. I need backup."

"Backup?"

"I'll settle for a buffer."

"What in the world are you talking about?"

"Leo's supposed to be in town, Shea wants to kick my ass and Luke—did you know he's a cop? What the hell am I supposed to do with that?"

Shock clouded her mind, and she shook her head slowly to clear the haze. "You want me to have dinner with you and your brothers?"

"I don't know them anymore." The shimmer of vulnerability in his eyes had returned. "We've talked a couple times, emailed here and there, but we haven't all been in the same room together in—Christ, I don't know—fifteen years."

"Oh, Noah," she whispered.

"Come with me. You're all I have." His hand found hers. "I need you."

She released a sigh of defeat. How could she possibly say no to that?

It'd taken a saint's patience and a Nolan's stubbornness, but Noah had gotten his way.

Satisfaction turned up the corners of his mouth and he placed a hand on the small of Mina's back as they navigated through the packed weekend crowd.

After stopping by his apartment to shower, he'd picked Mina up, and they had headed to Lucky's together. The dinner rush was in full swing, and the occasional clink of glasses rose above the constant hum of voices and Irish music playing overhead.

Her light scent wafted over him while heat from her body seeped into his skin. He fought the urge to let his hand roam and explore the interesting curve of her hip or, better yet, her luscious, heart-shaped ass.

He balled his hand into a tight fist and pulled it away from her body.

They found an empty booth in the back near the fireplace and slid in on opposite sides. When Mina slipped off her coat, her green sweater pulled tight across her ample breasts, and he struggled to keep his gaze from riveting to her glorious cleavage.

She gave the room a thorough scan. "I don't see Emily. Any sign of your brothers?"

Noah spotted only Shea, who tended the bar that was currently under siege by a crush of bodies.

"Looks like Shea will be busy for a while." He checked his cell phone. "Nothing from the others yet, but I imagine they'll be here soon."

"Are you nervous?"

He slid his phone back into this pocket. "Nervous about what?"

"About dinner."

He shot her a dead-eyed stare. "I don't get nervous."

"Sorry." She chewed the smile from her lips. "Are you, uh, excited? Happy? Worried? Angry? What feelings can you have?"

"I'm ready."

"You're ready?" Her smile broke through. "That's not a feeling."

"Exactly."

With a soft, thoughtful frown, she studied him for a moment. "They've missed you."

A small flicker of hope sparked in his chest, which his battered heart quickly snuffed out. "Your head's not quite healed up yet?"

"I'm serious. Every time I run into one of your brothers, they somehow find a way to work you into the conversation. It used to freak me out. I thought they knew I had a crush on you."

She'd had a crush on him? He sat stunned, trying to digest that piece of information when she hurled another grenade at him.

"Then I realized it wasn't just me. They talked about you to anyone who would listen."

Her words conjured the memories...

Of Leo, not yet five years old, perched on Noah's hip while Jack engaged him with a game of peek-a-boo in a ploy to distract them all from their growling bellies while Luke stood on a chair at the stove, trying to scrounge something edible from the meager, stale foodstuffs in the sparse kitchen cupboards. No matter how little they had, Luke always created a meal out of it somehow.

More than likely, Daniel was passed out, hungover, or chasing the intoxication that would lead to both, and Shea was at whatever shit job a thirteen-year-old kid could find, working to bring home whatever little money he could earn for them.

It was a common enough evening.

"They love to tell stories about you growing up," she said. "Funny stories."

"I didn't know that." Surprise stole the power from his voice.

"Of course, none of them bothered to mention you're a famous archaeologist."

He rubbed the tension-filled spot at his nape.

Her eyes narrowed to tiny, suspicious slits. "They do know, don't they?" Her eyes widened. "Noah!"

"What?"

"You haven't told them?"

He dropped his gaze. "It's too much to explain."

"What is there to explain? You only have to tell them."

"They'd probably think I was making it up."

"Are you kidding?" She was incredulous. "We all knew you'd be wildly successful."

He lobbed a pointed look at her. "That's not true."

"Yes, it is. You're a genius."

Shock drove him back into his seat. "No, I am not."

She tipped her head to one side. "You never came to class. You never studied or finished your homework assignments. Yet somehow, you aced every test. Every time. If you're not a genius, how did you do that?"

He shifted his weight on the hard bench. "Maybe I cheated."

"Off of who? You were smarter than everyone else. Even the teachers. Remember how you used to freak out Sister Margaret?"

He remembered. It hadn't been the first time his thinking had overtaken the nun's. Indeed, the only adults not bothered by Noah's sharp mind had been his mother, before she died, and Father John.

About the time Noah's boredom with school led to a penchant for finding trouble, John started bringing him books, giving him assignments and indulging him in conversations well beyond the level of his peers. Books on religion and philosophy, geography and science. History, art, and mathematics, too. Noah had devoured them all. For a while, he'd even preferred them to booze and petty crime. The man had saved his life.

In more ways than one.

A server appeared at the table, red-faced and breathless. "Hi, guys. Sorry about the wait. What can I get you?"

They placed their order, a Guinness for Noah and a light beer for Mina, and the waitress shuffled away again.

Mina leaned forward. "So, tell me, why archaeology? Was it the money and fame? The promise of glory?"

Her teasing smile tugged at his groin. "There is no money or fame, and I was unaware there'd be such glory." He mirrored her posture, leaning with his elbows on the table. "You will not believe this, but I liked the discipline."

One of her arched eyebrows inched upward. "You? Discipline?"

"It's the truth, I swear." A soft chuckle knocked around inside his chest. "It was a novel experience for me, and a welcome change."

"And now?"

"Hell if I know." Caught in the web spun by her smile, the confession slipped out. "The work is tedious and solitary. It's downright boring most of the time."

Her eyes, the color of deepest sapphire, sparkled in the soft lighting. "But you love it, anyway."

"I do." He nudged her foot under the table. "How about you? Why a massive old crumbling house?"

A twinge of unease stole into her eyes. "It's a great house."

"It is, but it's also a huge financial risk and a ton of work."

She folded her napkin into a tight, tiny square. "I guess... I had a rough year—a rough decade, and I needed a change. A challenge." Big blue eyes caressed his face. "I needed something all my own, if that makes any sense."

His heart thrummed with the pulse of the music. "It makes perfect sense."

"My dad grew up in that house, and I think...I don't know. Being there makes me feel closer to him."

He searched the file of his memories, but came up empty. "I don't remember your dad."

"He died when I was five."

The thought of her as a little girl having just lost her dad kicked him in the ribcage. "I'm sorry. How did he die?"

"He drowned in a boating accident on Lake Michigan." She tortured the napkin some more. "I don't remember much about him. My mom never talked about him and I've wondered what he was like. Was he kind or serious or wild or goofy?" Her sudden smile lit up her pretty face. "I like to think he's haunting the place."

A startled laugh burst from him as the waitress reappeared with their drinks.

Mina thanked the dark-haired woman. "It's so busy tonight. I don't know how you're keeping up."

The waitress exhaled a long breath. "We're getting slammed. Can I get you anything else?"

"Actually, we're waiting for some others to join us." Mina's words held a ring of apologetic regret.

"Should I come back in a bit?"

"That'd be great."

When the waitress had gone, he stretched his legs out under the table. "You said it's been a rough decade, huh? Tell me more about that."

"Why?" Mina sank back into the booth. "Did you want to ruin your appetite?"

"How bad can it be?" Her delays only made him more curious. "Married? Divorced? Secret babies, boyfriends?" He arched one eyebrow at her. "Girlfriends?"

"That's, like, eight questions," she protested. "Besides, I just went. It's your turn."

"I didn't realize we were keeping score."

"Bullshit. You've been keeping score since day one."

He didn't deny it. "Fine. What's your question?"

She sat up straighter in her seat. "Okay, let me see… Oh, I got it. Why did you come back?"

He took a moment, choosing his words. "I think it's safe to say I have daddy issues. I thought seeing him buried would close the book for me. For good."

Her features softened. "Did it?"

"Uh, you'll have to get back to me on that one." He reached for his pint. When he took a long drink, she pressed her advantage.

"Why did you stay?"

His heart pounded in his chest. "To do the excavation."

She narrowed her eyes at him. "Were there no other archaeologists who could excavate my property?"

He scratched his jawline. "None as good as me."

"Why did you take the job at ESU?"

"I was on sabbatical and bored out of my freaking skull. I needed something to do."

She let his words hang over the table for a moment. "Is that all?"

Was it? He studied the liquid in his glass, as though the answer floated in his beer. At one time in his life, he'd searched for answers at the bottom of every bottle of liquor he drank.

But the answers weren't there then, and they weren't there now.

He met her knowing gaze. "You're good at this."

"Thank you."

"It wasn't a compliment."

Her mouth hooked up at one corner. "You're not going to answer, are you?"

He fended off the enchantment of the deep blue sea in her eyes. "We're here to celebrate. How about we skip the sad stories?"

She searched his face, and for one unguarded moment, he let her glimpse what lay there.

After a beat, she tipped her head. "Fair enough."

Relief flooded him, and he pulled another long swallow from his pint. Settling into the booth, he went on the offensive. "Okay, Winslow, it's your turn. I showed you mine, now you show me yours."

"Sorry to disappoint you, but there have been no girlfriends."

"A man can dream, can't he?"

Her soft laughter knocked his own smile loose. "No marriages and no babies, either."

"Boyfriends?"

With a groan, she lifted the beer bottle to her lips.

"Too painful to talk about?"

A grimace pulled down the corners of her sexy mouth. "Too pathetic. I'll spare you the details of my pitiful relationships."

"A hot chick with self-esteem issues. My favorite type of woman."

Her throaty laughter gripped him by the balls. "You're shameless."

"Thank you."

"It wasn't a compliment."

A swirl of emotions chased across her face, and Noah begrudged Shea his decorating sense, for the dark woods and dim lighting obscured his study of her.

She leaned forward in the booth. "Truth?"

He leaned in too. "Truth."

"I don't think I've ever loved any of them. I think... I'm incapable of love or something."

Her words stilled him. "Incapable?"

"I'm thirty-three years old, and I've never been in love. That's weird, right?"

He'd asked himself that same question countless times, always assuming his fucked-up relationship with his dad or his mom's untimely death when he was only ten had somehow damaged him, leaving scars too deep to heal over. "I don't think it's weird."

"You don't?" She worried her plump bottom lip.

Noah's gaze lingered on her mouth. "No, I don't. I can't say I've ever been in love, either."

She waved off his confession. "You're a guy. It's okay for you to be emotionally unavailable. But I'm a girl. We're supposed to be in touch with our feelings. We're supposed to fall in love and dream about proposals and big weddings, and babies."

"I hate those girls."

Her bright smile lit up the entire pub. "Yeah, me, too."

He wanted to make her smile all the time. "Maybe you're just cautious."

He could see her mind latch on to the thought. She sat up a little straighter. "There's nothing wrong with being cautious."

"It's smart." He tipped his pint at her. "Mature."

"Did I mention how good I am at rationalizing my issues?" She hit him again with a genuine, full-blown smile.

He hid his reaction to her behind his pint when he drank.

"I mean, it's not like I haven't been enjoying all the sex."

The swig of Guinness nearly shot out of his nose. He wiped the back of his hand across his mouth—and then he caught the playful gleam in her eyes.

She was fucking with him.

His laugh erupted in a whoosh of relieved breath. "So, you're using men for sex while you wait for The One?"

She blinked at him innocently. "Is that wrong?"

"Not at all. Being used as a sex object is every man's life goal. Myself included."

Pleased with herself, she sipped her beer.

Damn, but she was a gorgeous woman. Pretty and smart, and able to give as good as she got.

"So, in all these years, Mr. Right never crossed your path?"

She blasted him with a get-back smile. "No sad stories, remember?"

Damn. "Fair enough. I'm content with the subject of sex." *For now.*

She toyed with the label on the neck of her beer bottle. "We could do more than talk."

But for the twinge of vulnerability in her voice, it might've been the hottest thing a woman had ever said to him.

With ruthless resolve, he reined in the desire swirling through his veins. "As I recall, you still owe me an explanation about what happened the last time we did more than talk."

Her nose scrunched up. "I thought you'd forgotten about that."

He gave his head a small shake. "Not a chance in hell I've forgotten about that."

She wiggled in her seat. "So here's the thing."

"There's a thing?"

"It's been a long time since I... since I wanted... since the sex was good, and I know with you it's good. *Really* good. So I want to do it again, as often as possible, while you're here."

Okay, *that* was the hottest thing a woman had ever said to him.

"While I'm here..." An unsteady waver invaded his voice when he repeated her words. "So it doesn't bother you I won't be staying?"

"Not at all. I prefer it, actually."

"Oh? And why is that?"

Large, grave eyes gripped him by the balls and squeezed. "I don't want your future, Noah. Just your right now."

He shifted, trying to adjust so his stiff cock wasn't so painful. "So, it'd only be sex between us, then?"

She hesitated for a beat. "And friendship."

"We're both carrying a little baggage. What do we do about that?"

"Why don't we just agree not to talk about the past?"

Every one of her clarifications only left him with more questions. "*Our* past? Or *the* past, more generally?"

"Our past. The other stuff…. We're friends. We can share if we want, but we don't have to," she rushed to add. "And none of the… emotional stuff."

She was the perfect woman. His dream girl. Every man's dream girl, most likely.

"Emotional stuff?"

"You know, no tears or tantrums." A small shudder passed through her. "Who has time for that kind of drama?"

His lips curled with his disgust. "Agreed."

"And no fighting."

"Define fighting. Can I correct you when you're wrong? Who's going to keep you in line?"

She shot him a stern scowl, then rolled her eyes at him. "Disagreeing is okay. Yelling and throwing things is not. Oh, and no name-calling."

"Agreed." Darkly, he wondered about her past relationships. "Anything else?"

Her fingers fidgeted with the napkin a moment, then she pushed it away with a firm shove. "Fidelity. If you want a break, or some space, or you're ready to move on, just say so. But no sleeping with other people. At least not while we're…"

"Fucking?"

Pink stained her cheeks, but she inclined her head.

The heat from her blush shot straight to his groin. "I can live with that."

With a slight catch of her breath, a smile touched her lips.

His erection pressed against the fly of blue jeans and scrambled his mind. "So to recap, we don't talk about the past, don't expect a future, and no emotional stuff. Do I have that right?"

She dragged her plump bottom lip between her teeth and nodded.

His gaze riveted to her mouth and his body tensed. With a desperation bordering on needy, he wanted to give her what she wanted. He couldn't get inside her soon enough.

"When did you become so naughty?" He teased her mostly to distract himself from his raging hard on. "What happened to the sweet, innocent girl I once knew?"

Rather than pick up his barb and lob it right back at him, as he expected her to do, the color slowly seeped from her face. "I was never that girl."

He opened his mouth to tell her he knew for a fact she tasted as sweet as a peach and came with the abandon of an innocent virgin, but something in her pained expression stayed him.

Looking deeper, he spotted the shadows in her eyes. His gaze dropped to the table where her fingers once again tortured the shredded napkin. Her hands trembled even as she negotiated with him about the parameters of a full-blown, no-strings-attached sexual affair.

Damn, but she grew more fascinating by the moment.

Just then, movement over Mina's shoulder caught his notice.

"Brace yourself. My brothers are here."

CHAPTER 15

$\mathcal{A}$s Luke and Jack filed into the booth across from them, Mina scooted closer to the wall and Noah settled in at her side.

Luke plopped his elbows on the table. "They released the schedule this morning. We play Friday night at ten," he said. "I can't remember who we play first."

Jack clapped his hands together and rubbed. "Doesn't matter. They're toast."

"Hockey," Noah leaned close to her to say. "We joined an amateur league."

"Ah," Mina said. "How long has it been since you all played together?"

A trio of thoughtful frowns popped up around the table.

"We've never played together, have we?" Jack asked.

Luke made a gesture to include Jack and Noah. "Didn't you two play on the same traveling team?"

"We were on opposing teams." Jack's eyes danced and his gaze locked on Noah. "You remember the brawl in Pentwater?"

Luke snorted. "What's this?"

Jack pointed an accusatory finger at Noah. "He cross-checked me."

"It was a clean hit," Noah insisted.

"Bullshit," Jack said. "The refs swallowed their whistles."

"So we discussed it with our fists," Noah said with a smile.

Jack's smile matched his brother's. "Naturally."

"There was a long history of bad blood between the teams," Noah said. "When we started going at it, the benches cleared. Then that bastard, Murphy, sucker-punched you."

With a frown, Mina asked, "Sucker-punched?"

"Kid hit him when Jack wasn't looking," Luke explained.

Noah released a beleaguered sigh. "I couldn't stand for that."

"He was your teammate," Jack pointed out.

"Yeah, well, you fight like a punk, you get your ass kicked like one." Noah's dark eyes gleamed in the soft lighting. "Soon, it was Jack and me fighting against everyone else on both teams."

"Did a pretty good job on them, too." Shea, carrying an overburdened tray, appeared at the head of the table along with the waitress. "Sorry I couldn't get away sooner." He helped unload two platters of food, two pitchers of beer, and many pint glasses onto the table. "We've been getting killed all night."

Luke reached for a glass and a pitcher. "Have you hired anyone yet?"

A harried scowl pulled at Shea's wide mouth as he swung a chair around from the nearby table and straddled it. "No, and another one just quit."

The news shot through Mina like an electrical charge. Her spine straightened. "You have a job opening?"

Shea's striking blue eyes landed on her. "Yeah, I need a server. Know anyone who might be interested?"

"I might be interested." Fear and excitement heated her

face. "But I don't have any experience working in a restaurant."

"I'll take anyone who'll show up for their shift. On time, if it isn't too much to ask." The taut lines around Shea's mouth and eyes smoothed with his lopsided smile. "Can you do that?"

Mina's smile knocked loose. "I can do that."

Shea looked up at the waitress. "When are you working next?"

"Tuesday night." The waitress tucked the tray under her arm.

"You mind if Mina tags along?"

"Not at all." A smile brightened the woman's pretty face. "Hi, I'm Heather. Meet me here around seven?"

And like that, Mina had a job. An actual *paying* job. She had doubted she'd ever find another one of those. "See you Tuesday."

"Now, was that so hard?" Luke slid a glass over to Shea.

Aware of Noah's gaze on her, she risked a glance at him to find he studied her as though she were one of the dirt-covered hunks of junk he'd fetched from the ground. What was he thinking? He was probably wondering why someone with the last name Winslow would moonlight as a waitress. Didn't she have a pile of money somewhere that needed spending?

Jack lifted his pint. "A toast—"

With his pint suspended in midair, Jack's gaze zeroed in on something behind Noah. Luke's gaze quickly followed Jack's and, as a group, the others twisted in their seats to find a woman hovering at the edge of the group.

"Emily!" Mina shoved Noah out of the booth and motioned for Emily to sit. "When did you get here? I didn't hear my phone."

Emily tucked a strand of her strawberry-blonde hair

behind one ear and slid in next to Mina. "I can't get any r-r-reception on m-m-my cell out here."

Their communications over the years had been sporadic, and typically via text and email, so Mina had forgotten Emily stuttered.

"I'm so glad you found us," Mina said as Noah squeezed in at the end of the bench. "Everyone, this is my cousin, Emily."

Mina introduced each brother by name, starting with Luke, who studied Emily over the rim of his pint with sea-green eyes. While Mina continued with the introductions, she noticed Emily's gaze kept stealing back to Luke.

Introductions complete, Jack pointed to Emily. "She needs a drink. Someone get the woman a drink."

Luke reached for a pitcher and filled an empty glass, then slid it across the table to a flushed Emily.

Jack raised his pint. "To family and—get yer glass up, Shea —fresh starts."

Glasses clinked, and the group fell quiet as they drank.

Lowering his glass, Noah swallowed. "Speaking of family, where's Leo?"

Tension whipped around the table, moving from one brother to the next like a cascade of dominos.

Until it reached Noah. "All right, that's enough," he barked. "What the hell is going on?"

Jack's gaze dropped to the ring of condensation his glass created on the table.

Finally, Luke said, "He's not coming."

Shea cursed. "You talk to him?"

"He texted about an hour ago. Didn't give any details."

Shea turned somber eyes on Noah. "He's been MIA for the better part of a year now. Ever since he was discharged."

"Discharged?"

Shea's shoulders sagged. "Leo joined the military right out of high school."

Noah's dead-eyed stare pierced Shea. "You're shitting me, right? First a cop and now this? What happened to you guys?"

Noah's questions seemed to amuse his brothers.

"I'm sure he's fine." But worry tightened Jack's voice. "He probably met a girl and hasn't come up for air yet."

"I hope you're right." Shea trailed off as Heather reappeared over his shoulder.

"Hey guys, you playing tonight? We're getting a lot of requests."

Jack smacked the flat of his hands against the wood table, and his gaze swung to Noah. "You still play?"

"Of course I still play. I'm still Irish, aren't I?"

With that, a flash of movement erupted around the table. Shea stood and swung his chair back around to an adjacent table.

Luke bounded from the booth behind Jack. "Who's got the drum?"

Dark, questioning eyes clamped on Mina's face. "Do you mind?" Noah asked, his voice low and clandestine.

Gooseflesh rippled over her arms. "How could I deprive the public of the Nolan Brothers' reunion concert?"

As the foursome disbanded to head off in different directions, Emily sagged in her seat and fanned herself with her napkin. "Wow."

Mina's laughter rang out. "Sorry. I hope you don't mind."

"Mind?" Emily's smile coaxed a dimple to her cheek. "Not w-when they're so pretty."

"Isn't it annoying?" Mina hissed, secretly relieved she wasn't the only one disconcerted by the Nolan brothers' obvious charms. "It's so good to see you. How long are you in town?"

The line of Emily's mouth pulled taut, and a deep, aching

sorrow slashed across her face. "Only a few days." She snatched up her glass and drank several long gulps.

"What brings you all this way?" Mina nudged.

Emily's lips trembled, and she pushed a hard puff of air through her lips. "I'm here to... to... to bury m-my m-m-mom."

A shocked gasp burst from Mina. "What? Oh, Emily. What happened?"

Emily's hands twisted in her lap. "She was sick for a long time. Several years."

"I'm so sorry. I didn't know. When did she die?"

"Three weeks ago yesterday."

A heavy silence hung over them.

"She wanted to be buried here?" Mina asked finally.

"W-we haven't visited since I was a kid, b-b-but that was her w-wish so...." Emily scrubbed her forehead, as though trying to snuff out an ache. "The priest is going to say a prayer for her at the cemetery later this week."

Mina's heart wrenched for her cousin. "Would you mind if I come?"

Emily's throat worked, and her brown eyes glistened. "I'd like that."

When applause broke out, they turned as the brothers took the small stage.

"Good evenin'." Shea's deep voice boomed through the pub, and a cheer went up. He slung a guitar over his back and took a long drink from the pint on the barstool at his side. "Welcome to Lucky's. If ye'd all be obliging, my brothers and I'd like to play you a couple o' tunes."

A watery laugh escaped Emily at Shea's obvious attempt to ham it up, and the crowd, in an obliging mood after all, sent up another cheer.

With a guitar in one hand and a violin in the other, Noah stepped onto the stage and moved behind the microphone next to Luke, who pulled a banjo from its case. At the back, Jack settled in with an Irish drum.

For the next twenty minutes, the brothers played a compilation of raucous Irish tunes. With each song, the crowd grew more animated, singing along, shouting requests, and dancing in small groups between tables. They stomped and clapped with the beat Jack drove, and hung on every word Shea sang, his deep, gravelly voice mesmerizing the audience with tales of love and loss, loneliness and longing.

Their set ended to chants for an encore. Seemingly unaware of the crowd, Noah and his brothers sipped on their pints and chatted amongst themselves until the calls grew louder and longer. Shrill catcalls and whistles joined the robust foot stomps and reached a deafening, fevered pitch before the brothers retook their places behind the microphones.

Noah strummed the first chords of a somber ballad, and the crowd quieted. He played a few more notes of the opening refrain, and a ripple of laughter ran through the crowd as they recognized the tune. For their encore, they'd chosen a Top 40 pop song crooned by a heartbroken teenage girl on every radio station every hour of every day.

This time, Luke sang the lead vocal. He leaned in, bringing his mouth close to the mike, and when he sang, his clear, smooth voice held a teardrop quiver that cast a mesmerizing spell over the room. The brothers had stripped the tune of all the synthesized electronic sounds and distilled the familiar hit song down to an acoustic ballad. In their rendition, the silly pop ditty became a soul-baring, gut-wrenching lament and their show-stealing performance was hilarious and moving at once.

Luke reached the crescendo, and Emily lurched to her feet.

Mina's surprise turned to concern when she looked into her cousin's face. "Emily? Are you okay?"

"I'm tired and—" The song ended, and applause drowned out her next words.

Mina found herself wrapped in Emily's warm, flowery embrace, and then she was gone, disappearing into the mob of people faster than Mina could say "boy band."

Mina blinked after her for a moment, confused.

Then she scooted from the booth and jumped up to follow her cousin. She'd made it only a few steps when she realized she'd forgotten her purse, so she twisted back around to grab it.

And bumped hard into a solid male chest.

She tipped her head back and looked up at the last person she wished to see.

Her ex.

$\mathcal{M}$ina repressed a groan and locked her attention on Drew. "What do you want?"

The pale blue Fendi dress shirt he wore turned his light eyes brilliant. "You're making a fool of yourself."

There was a time she'd worried about his opinion of her. Now, she couldn't care less what he thought.

"More foolish than a woman whose fiancé was caught cheating on her by a national tabloid a month before their wedding?"

Drew's expression morphed from annoyed to pitying so fast Mina felt dizzy. "You're enamored with him."

He always knew the best way to poke at her insecurities.

Her face heated. "Who are we talking about?"

"You're aware he's only using you, right?"

"Oh, Drew, you're such a charmer."

"Believe it or not, I'm trying to help you."

She sighed, and then, because she wanted to hear how ridiculous her own doubts sounded when spoken aloud, said, "Okay, I'll play. What could he possibly be using me for?"

He gaped at her as though she were dumb. "You're a Winslow."

"God save me," she muttered and plucked her drink off the table.

"Some people think the Winslows are still influential." Scorn dripped from Drew's tongue. "Attaching himself to one would be a real coup."

Beer bottle poised at her lips, Mina paused. "Speaking from experience?"

He didn't even bother to feign insult. "You didn't want to marry me, either."

He was right, of course. If only she'd realized that sooner. She'd let herself forget that, to Drew, she was a business arrangement. A political merger of the Winslows and the Alexanders, two decades in the making. Practical and economical. Even the sex had been... mercantile.

Though that was probably her fault as much as Drew's.

"Do you honestly believe the Winslow's name means anything to him?" She set the beer on the table with a hard thud. "He isn't a politician. He's a scholar. A *world-renowned* scholar. The Winslows and this town are nothing to him. Myself included." A pang sliced through her heart to realize her statement was likely true.

Drew's expression turned derisive, as if he'd caught her, a silly schoolgirl, dreamily doodling Noah Nolan's name on her Trapper Keeper.

"Are you okay?" he asked. "You're not acting like yourself."

"I might say the same to you. *You're making a fool of yourself.*" She mocked his tone and manner. "You sound like a mobster."

"I'm the mayor."

"Close enough."

"Be careful with him."

Drew's dark warning sent a ripple of suspicion prickling up her spine. "Why do you care so much about it?"

He threw back a swallow of his whiskey. A piece of ice crunched between his teeth. "I guess you'll find out soon enough. I'm running for Congress."

"Congratulations. You'll fit right in. But what does that have to do with me?"

"The media will be creeping around. I thought we could try not to write the headlines for them this time."

"Is that what you think happened? That *we* caused head-lines?" Last she checked, *he* was the one only who'd had an affair, and the one who'd gotten caught.

"You know what I mean."

"You want my help to make sure *you* don't make an ass of yourself? Again." She tapped her index finger against her chin. "Let me think. What can you do? What can you do? Gosh, I can't think of a thing."

Drew released a martyred sigh and dragged a hand through his blond-streaked hair. "We've been through a lot together. I'd hoped we could remain friends."

The reference to their past stunned her for a moment and she ducked her chin, hiding her face while she fought to regain her composure.

"How are you doing?" he asked when she didn't respond. "How's the house?"

"I'm fine." She snatched up her drink. "The house is fine."

"You need anything?"

"Got fifty thousand dollars?" She took a long drink from her beer.

A light of interest danced in his eyes. "I heard you were in a tough spot. Why don't you let me help?"

She'd only been kidding. The mere suggestion coming from him made her skin crawl. "Your girlfriend is okay with that?"

"Phoebe has no say in this."

"Why not? She's had plenty of say up to now." Mina glanced over her shoulder, searching for the emergency exit. "And, no, I don't want your money."

"It's not a handout, but a loan. I'll even charge you interest if it'll make you happy."

Mina's reply died on her lips when a heavy shadow fell over the table. A shiver chased through her body, even before she slowly lifted her gaze and found Noah standing there, the features of his handsome face set in a hard glower.

Her heart sank.

"Mr. Mayor." Noah's polite greeting didn't match the brutal edge of his voice.

"Dr. Nolan." Drew eased back in his seat. "You have a way with the fiddle."

"You should see what I can do with a flute."

Their gazes locked and held until a smirk curled Drew's lips and his pale eyes shifted to Mina. "Take care of yourself." Then he slipped from the booth.

When Drew had disappeared into the crowd, Noah slid into the spot he'd vacated.

His dark gaze fastened on her. "Why is Drew Alexander offering you money?"

Words clogged in her throat. "I...uh...."

She scanned the pub and pinpointed Shea behind the bar, pouring drinks, while across the room, Luke and Jack had joined a table of women.

Under the table, Noah's knee bounced. "Are you sleeping with him?"

"No."

"Then what is he to you?"

She swallowed convulsively. "My ex."

Revulsion twisted his features. "Why did you ask your ex-boyfriend for money?"

"Fiancé."

His knee halted.

"And I didn't ask."

"Fiancé?" The word sounded foul on his lips.

"*Ex*-fiancé."

Revulsion turned to disgust, and a curse slipped from him. "Why didn't you tell me?"

"There's nothing to tell."

"You were going to marry him," he bit out. "That's not nothing."

"It was a mistake, and we're both well aware of that fact now. It's over. Way, *way* over."

"Then why does he believe you'd take his money?"

"I don't know. I don't even know how he found out I need money…" she trailed off as the puzzle pieces snapped together.

Phoebe Taylor. She'd told him about the loan request. So much for client confidentiality.

Noah's scowl deepened. "How he found out what?"

She fumbled for a moment, trying to find the words, but it was hopeless. With a small shrug, she admitted the truth. "I don't have any money."

He showed no reaction, but only stared at her, as if he awaited the punchline. After a beat of silence, a choked laugh burst from him. "You're kidding, right?"

She should be used to such reactions from people by now, and she was. Except she didn't want to believe Noah was like all those others who judged her without bothering to learn the truth.

Her heart ached with the knowledge. "I'm not kidding. It's true. I'm broke."

Stunned to speechlessness, he gaped at her.

"Shocking, I know." Years of bitterness bubbled up and over. "A Winslow without money. It's like a Kardashian without a TV camera."

Noah sighed, and some of the tension drained from his shoulders.

"It's okay if you find it funny. Most people do."

"Mina—"

"I would never take his money." Her words came out in a rush. "Even though I could really, really use it for the well, and the excavation, and my hospital bill—"

"Mina—"

"I went to the bank and tried to increase the amount on my home equity loan, but they refused to even consider it now that I'm unemployed."

With a frustrated jerk of his arm, he shoved a hand through his hair. "What about your family?"

"It's only my mom and me, and she isn't... able... to help me."

His expression softened. "I wish you had told me."

Inexplicably, tears pushed to the surface, but she turned them back. "Why would I do that?"

"Because maybe I could've helped." His jaw clamped tight, except for a small twitch at the jawline. "We could've delayed the excavation—"

"I didn't want to delay. The sooner I finish the house, the sooner I stop hemorrhaging money."

With no words left to say, they stared at each other.

Then his shoulders slumped, heavy with whatever thought had visited him.

The soft heat she'd grown enamored with seeing in his dark eyes was long gone, replaced with a chill hardness. "I wish you'd trusted me enough to tell me the truth."

Cold misery swept through her. Once again, she'd disappointed him.

"Look, I'm going to be out of town for a few days." He spoke with a businesslike indifference that left her feeling empty and alone. "But don't worry. I built the time away into the schedule, so I won't set you back."

"Where are you going?" She couldn't stop herself from asking.

"To a conference." He slid toward the edge of the booth.

"Noah...."

"C'mon," he said as he climbed to his feet. "I'll take you home."

~

WITH NOAH'S COOL PARTING, a chill breeze swept over the island and into Mina's heart.

Just when she thought they'd finally buried their past, something else popped up. She couldn't help but wonder what might've happened when he'd brought her home if Drew hadn't ruined their evening. Would he have kissed her goodnight? Or come inside for another drink? Would he have stayed?

Bitter regret chased through her, and she shivered.

It seemed all they ever had was what could have been.

By Tuesday night, she was thankful to start her training with Heather, where she had to push aside her troubled thoughts about Noah in order to focus on learning all the varied details of her new job.

On Wednesday, her injured wrist ached from carrying the heavy trays, and by the end of her shift, she struggled to keep the evidence of her pain hidden from the customers.

As she approached one couple with their order, her wrist gave out, and she dropped the tray on their table with an indelicate thud.

A pint teetered.

She leapt to steady it, but only hastened its fall. Amber liquid splashed across the tabletop and rolled into their laps.

Gushing apologies, she used a towel to sop up the spillage, then slunk away.

On Thursday, she stood beside Emily at the cemetery as they buried Emily's mother. Father John said a prayer, and Emily laid a bloom of lavender atop the casket before they lowered Audrey Rutherford Cole into the ground.

The melancholy of the day had stayed with Mina that night throughout her shift at the pub.

A packed crowd and live band made hearing the customers difficult for her. The men with deep baritone voices caused her the most trouble, and she got several orders wrong. For one especially perturbed guest, she had to ask Shea to comp the meal.

Her pride stinging, she ducked behind the bar and worked at filling drink orders for the table of five just seated in her section.

She missed her desk job.

She missed the half-dozen fingernails she'd broken in the last week alone.

Worse yet, she missed Noah.

The longer the week wore on without hearing from him, the more she agonized over their last conversation and the look of betrayal and disappointment on his face when he'd learned she'd almost married Drew.

Who was he to judge her? He didn't know what it'd been like for her.

Because you didn't tell him.

Well, why would she?

A long, woeful sigh pushed through her lips, and she rotated her sore wrist in every direction, searching for a position that might ease the ache in the ligaments.

No matter how convincingly she argued her case inside her head, she couldn't shake the notion she'd let him down.

She was a devout people pleaser, and no amount of self-righteousness was going to convert her now.

"Oh. My. God." A piercing cackle carried above the pub noise and grated along Mina's spinal cord. "You're a waitress?"

Weary dread stole over Mina. She ignored Phoebe Taylor and the snickers of the other women with her at the bar, but their cruel laughter drew the attention of others seated nearby.

Mina ignored her and placed the last pint on the tray.

"Excuse me, waitress." Phoebe smacked her hand on the bar top until Mina acknowledged her. Then she lifted her tumbler and jiggled the empty glass so the ice rattled. "I need a drink."

Mina hefted the bulky tray and shot Phoebe a disinterested look. "I'm not *your* waitress."

Phoebe's face screwed into a murderous scowl as Mina turned away. She ate her satisfied smile and delivered the drinks to her table.

Somehow, Mina made it through the long night, only to be woken at seven a.m. to loud noises from the crew arriving for work.

She crawled from bed and changed into her work clothes. With a restorative cup of coffee in hand, she entered the main house through the kitchen door.

Within minutes, Sam found her in the hall, staring down at three small patches of stain she'd rubbed onto the hardwood floor the previous day.

"Which one do you like?" she asked him.

"What color is going on the walls?"

"Something light." She hid her face behind her coffee mug when she sipped. "Probably beige-ish."

"Then I vote for the dark one."

She smiled. "Good choice."

"You got a minute?" Sam asked.

A jolt of dread shot through her. "Not if there's an issue, I don't."

Sam's smile softened his long, angular face. "No issues, for once. I wanted to give you a heads-up that I'll be off on vacation for a couple of weeks."

"Oh?" She swallowed an expletive. "How nice. Does that mean you'll need to pause your work here?"

"Nope. I'm leaving Eddie in charge while I'm gone. He'll keep things on track and deal with the subcontractors. He knows what he's doing and shouldn't give you any trouble." With a covert glance left and right, Sam dropped his voice. "But he's new at this."

"New to renovating?"

"New to supervising. I need you to help him keep an eye on the others. Sometimes, they need to be... motivated."

"Motivated. Got it."

He frowned at her. "*Do not* let them take advantage of you."

"All right..." The words leaked out slowly as dread congealed in her veins.

"I'm serious." Sam pinned her with a hard stare. "You give 'em an inch, they'll take a mile. You need to be firm. Let them know who's in charge."

"Who's in charge?" she squeaked.

"That'd be you," he said. "Your money, your rules."

"My money, my rules," she repeated. "Right. Of course."

He gave her a smack on the back, which sent her lurching forward. "Good luck, and have fun."

"Oh, you, too," she muttered at his retreating back.

Trepidation tasted sour in her mouth, and she took a swig of coffee to wash it down. Just what she needed—more stress and work and worry. At least the week was almost over.

She received an answer to that cursed question a few

hours later. As she worked in the living room at the front of house peeling tattered wallpaper off the plaster walls, the crunch of gravel sounded in the driveway. She moved to the front window just as Noah's truck pulled off the drive and into the grass beneath the ancient oak tree.

Her heart jumped. What was he doing here? He wasn't supposed to return for another two days.

He bounded from the truck's cab, slamming the door shut behind him even as he twisted toward the house. With long, ground-eating strides, he cut a direct path toward her door.

Her stuttering heart climbed into her throat.

Then suddenly, he pulled up, and his gaze swept across her lawn, taking in the full range of trucks and cars scattered about the property. The hard set of his features became severe, and he stood in the cheerful sunlight scowling at her house, as if considering whether to charge the front gate or send a flurry of fiery arrows over the ramparts.

In the end, he turned away. He hauled open his truck's door and plunged inside the cab. The engine fired, and he backed the vehicle out from under the tree and careened down her driveway with enough zip to leave a cloud of dust spiraling in his wake.

Her heart sank to her toes as she stared after him. Why had he come all this way, even approaching her door, only to walk away without talking to her? What had he come to say? And why had he decided against saying it to her now?

Given his stormy expression, he was still upset, but if that were the case, why hadn't he called her that week to talk to her about it? Or come inside the house just now?

Unless he'd decided, right then and there, that she simply wasn't worth the trouble.

Fall had descended on the island in the days Noah had spent away. The world had caught fire in his absence, torching the treetops in crimson and orange, amber and ochre.

When he climbed from his truck, the crisp, sweet perfume of falling leaves teased his nostrils. Mist kissed his skin as he gazed up at Mina's mansion.

Unlike earlier in the day, her house was quiet now, so he bypassed the front door and strode along the hedgerow. As he rounded the corner, a gust of wind burst off the lake and he ducked his head against the stinging gale.

He stalked toward the carriage house. After the brief trip away, it was odd being back. Already, the place felt familiar to him.

Like home.

Though he'd made plans to attend the prestigious academic conference more than a year ago, he might as well have skipped the stupid event. The entire week, thoughts of Mina had coiled through his brain, pushing out everything else to the point he couldn't concentrate during sessions and couldn't focus long enough to strike up any meaningful discussions with other scholars in his field.

In his head, it'd been all Mina Winslow all the time.

Mina Winslow and Drew Alexander.

Mina Winslow, naked and open, for Drew Alexander.

Apart from murder or intoxication, Noah knew of no way to drive the images from his mind. So he'd left the conference early and driven straight from the airport to the northernmost coast of the island.

Back to her.

Only to discover, as usual, she had a house full of men.

But what he needed to say couldn't be said with an audience, so he'd bit down hard on the impulse that'd propelled him to her doorstep and forced himself to leave her property. If he stayed, there was no telling what insanity might overcome him.

So he'd left, and he'd waited. All day he'd stewed, simmering in his agitation while anticipating the moment when the last crew member's vehicle would pull out of her driveway and he could finally get her alone.

Now, as he marched across her side lawn, the war he'd been fighting in his own head all week raged on.

I hate that he touched her. I hate that she let him. It should've been me.

But you weren't here.

So what? She should have told me.

Why? You left fifteen years ago and never so much as sent a postcard.

And when she had told him, what had he done? He'd stomped off to pout.

Absorbed with this inner brawl, he failed to notice her among the hedges until a crack of sound split the air.

He whipped around, then blinked at the spectacle before him.

Up to her ankles in mud, she wielded an ax overhead and brought it down with brute violence on a helpless rosebush. *Whack!*

Her ponytail hung limply to one side, and auburn ringlets sprung loose in all directions when she raised the ax above her head once more.

But at just that moment, her gaze swung in his direction and cobalt-blue eyes latched onto him. She dropped her arms and the ax blade sank harmlessly into the mud.

"You're back." It was an accurate statement, delivered with a large dose of *who gives a shit?*

So, she was mad at him. Fair enough, he supposed. Though he could barely attend to her annoyance, stunned as he was by the sight of her standing in mud and wielding an ax.

His chest tight, he stared. She was unbearably beautiful. A wood nymph. An earth goddess amongst the moss green grass and burnt orange leaves. Lost in mist and fog. In her presence, his body hummed, electrified.

He wanted her.

There was no denying the uncomfortable fact. He only wished he didn't want her so much.

Unable to recall what he'd come here to say, he flashed a smooth grin, the one that always whipped color into her cheeks. "Miss me?"

Nothing. Not even one of her polite, fake-ass smiles. Instead, her blue eyes swirled with emotion.

He peered closer, and that's when he saw it—the pain and anger. The fear.

Taken aback, he searched for the source of her distress.

"Stop it," she snapped.

"Stop what?"

"Looking at me like—like—" Her hand flitted through the air. "Like *that.*"

The tightness in his chest squeezed. "Something happened while I was away."

Her face fell, then screwed into a dark scowl. "You're really annoying, you know that?"

"I know. Will you tell me what happened?"

She ran a hand through her hair, and her fingers caught on the sagging ponytail. With a vicious tug, she yanked the rubber band from her head, and her auburn hair fell about her shoulders in tousled disarray.

Then ax blade met rosebush with a ruthless *whack!* "They're all laughing at me."

The anguish in her voice constricted his chest yet more. "Who's laughing at you?"

Whack!

"They don't even try to hide it." *Whack!* "They hear my last name and think they know me." *Whack!* "My life is a joke to them." *Whack!* "I'm a joke to them. To all of you."

She hoisted the ax again. He stepped forward and seized the handle midair.

Without a struggle, she surrendered the blade and staggered from the hedges, her exit from the mud punctuated by the undignified sucking sound of her rubber boots releasing from the thick sludge.

In the grass, she spun to face him and her big, blueberry gumdrop eyes hit him like a punch to the gut. Her chest rose and fell with each deep, desperate breath she dragged into her lungs.

"I'm an awful waitress."

He cast the ax aside. "I'm sure that's not true—"

"I can't remember the drink orders and I keep m-mixing them up." Her voice sounded suspiciously watery. "God forbid anyone wants to eat something not *exactly* as it's listed on the menu, because I'll screw that up, too, and why are the trays so freaking heavy? It's like they want us to drop them."

"It's your first week. Give yourself a break."

She pinned him with a look. "I spilled an entire Coke *inside* a woman's purse."

He only just stopped himself from wincing.

"It was a big purse. Huge." She motioned with her hands. "And jam-packed with... sticky... wet... stuff."

He did wince then. "Okay, that's unfortunate, but no one can expect you to be mistake-free while you're still learning. Waiting tables is a hard job, and you're brand new. You'll get the hang of it."

She wiped her cheek with the back of one hand, smearing a dirt stain across her rosy skin. "Stop being so reasonable."

"I'm sorry," he said. And he was sorry—truly, desperately sorry for every hurt and setback she'd ever experienced to put that quiver of vulnerability in her voice.

She sniffed and wiped her nose. "It makes them happy to see me fail."

"No one is happy—"

"They are." Confusion crinkled her brow. "I don't remember high school all that well. Was I a terrible person?"

He swallowed the sudden lump lodged in his throat.

Had she been a terrible person?

The memories rushed forward to crowd his mind. He remembered...

She'd been painfully shy and sweet.

They'd met junior year, when he was assigned the seat behind hers in English Lit. Three weeks into the semester, which was also the first day he'd bothered to show up for class, she'd turned in her chair, smiled her crooked smile, and shyly offered to share her notes with him.

Her smile was infectious, and he couldn't help but smile back. Of course, he'd been drunk that day.

She was studious and serious.

He wasn't.

She'd scold him when he skipped class, and then give him her notes anyway when he asked for them. He showed up on test days, and when his scores still rivaled hers, her annoyance warred with her admiration.

A competition of sorts had grown between them that semester, with Mina eking out the win. Though it'd taken a whole grade deduction for poor attendance to drop Noah's A beneath her A minus.

Senior year, the subject was math, and Noah attended more classes in those first few weeks than he had the entire previous school year.

At Halloween, they'd hooked up, but when classes had reconvened after the midterm break, she hadn't been there.

He'd forgotten about that…

Then she'd returned, but she wouldn't talk to him. She wouldn't even look at him.

A few weeks later, his life had blown up in his face, and soon after, he'd fled the island. They wouldn't see each other again for fifteen years.

Through the haze of memories, her dirt-splattered face materialized. Torment clung to her as she watched him with devastated eyes.

His heart hammered a bruising beat in his chest. "You weren't a terrible person. And if anyone is going to judge you based on high school, they're complete fools."

Himself included.

A fragile hope poked through her misery. "Really?"

"Once they get to know you, they're going to love you." He wiped a splotch of mud from one curved cheek. "How could they not?"

Her eyes grew wide, and he was so relieved to supplant that wounded look from their deep blue depths that he didn't even care he might've revealed too much.

He stroked the soft hollow below her ear, then let his

fingers trail down the side of her neck. Her pulse leapt beneath his touch.

The wind kicked up to bite at her hair and the shirttail of her flannel shirt. A throng of dried leaves skittered across the lawn.

Pulse thrumming, his name fell from her lips.

"What is it, sweetheart?"

"Are you still mad at me?"

"I was never mad at you."

"But—"

"I was disappointed."

Her face crumpled, and she moved as if to pull away, but he gripped a handful of her shirt over her stomach and dragged her back to him.

"Disappointed that I know so little about you." He slipped his hand beneath the curtain of her hair. "And jealous that that bastard received even one speck of your affection."

She licked her lips, a nervous gesture that riveted his gaze to her over-plump mouth.

His cock jumped.

He dipped his head, and his mouth hovered above hers while their ragged, needy breaths mingled as white puffs of air between them.

With everything inside him, he wanted to taste, to take, but he hadn't flown home and charged to her house for sex. There were reasons—good reasons—he shouldn't fall into her bed. For one, he had a few pointed questions about her relationship with Drew Alexander. And there was something about secrets and entanglements, but he couldn't recall exactly what those things were or why they mattered.

Mostly, she was vulnerable and hurting, and he'd be the lowest kind of pervert to exploit that to his advantage.

Despite the many reasons he shouldn't kiss her, a calming sense of rightness washed over him at the thought.

Then he looked into her eyes, and his resolve shattered.

He swooped down at the same moment she rose up and their mouths met in a soft clash of heat and hunger. The flavor of her sweetness wrenched a groan from him. He craved more, so he took a small nip from her puffy bottom lip and, with his tongue, licked at the corner of her mouth.

She opened for him, easily. Eagerly.

Triumph roared through him, flanked by want and need. At the small of her back, he clenched fistfuls of her shirt and held her against his body.

Her warm mouth felt like home. The brush of her fingertips on his face soothed the wild, restless part of him that'd trekked across three continents and North Africa rather than stand still. She was fire in his arms, fierce and bright. Dangerous and essential. And he wanted her more than he wanted his next breath.

Suddenly, she broke the kiss, and on a gasp, she fell back.

Heart pounding, cock straining, he reached for her as though she were the light in the darkness.

Both her hands clasped around his, and for just a moment, dread twisted through his gut with the certainty that she was going to send him away.

Instead, she took another small step back, toward the carriage house, and tugged on his hand.

The invitation, shyly delivered, pierced him. A welcome arrow through the heart.

Accepting would be wrong. He couldn't allow himself to do it. But he needed to find the words to turn her down without hurting her more than he'd already had.

He needed to find the words—some words, *any* words—to refuse her, when everything inside him screamed to take what she offered.

All he had to do was say no…

CHAPTER 18

*H*e didn't say no.

His heart battered his ribcage, thrashing along to the warning siren going off inside his skull. With his hand still clasped inside both of hers, she took another small step backward and tugged.

Desire swelled his cock and, as if drawn by her magnetic pull, he moved toward her.

She stole another step, and another, and then they were stumbling across the side lawn and tripping up the carriage house stairs.

At the top, she fumbled through the front pocket of her jeans and he glimpsed the flash of metal before she reached for the doorknob.

Her hands trembled badly, and when she tried to insert the key into the lock, it slipped between her fingers, clattered to the floorboards at her feet, and disappeared through a gap in the wood planks.

On a dismayed gasp, she dropped to her knees, as though she would follow the key down into the underbrush beneath the porch.

"Leave it," he growled.

He caught her by the elbow and hauled her to her feet, pressing her back against the door even as his mouth took hers with demanding possession. Sparks flared behind his eyes, ignited by the tiny, tentative licks of her tongue. A throaty moan escaped her, and he swallowed it.

When the need coursing through him became too painful, he broke the kiss. The sharp pants of their breathing echoed in his ears while he worked the buttons of her flannel. At the last fastening, he shoved the fabric past her shoulders and the shirt fell to the porch floor.

The tantalizing swells of her breasts strained against the binding of her bra, and with shaking hands, he banished the cruel garment to the porch floor as well.

Exposed to the cool air, her nipples puckered. A curse slipped between his lips and he cupped her. The weight and feel of her heavy roundness sent a jolt straight to his groin and dragged another pleading obscenity from him.

He grazed over one pebbled peak with the pad of his thumb, then he bent his head and lapped his tongue across the perfect, pink bud.

The moan that vibrated in her throat reminded him of a cat's satisfied purr. Her head fell back against the door in surrender, and he seized upon the access she offered him. He slipped his arm around her waist and explored with his mouth the incredible fullness of her breasts, the silky smoothness of her delicate skin, the slender column of her throat, and the secret spots behind both her ears.

When he took one earlobe between his teeth, she shivered, then hauled up the hem of his T-shirt. As her small hands rushed over the heated skin of his chest and torso, he reached behind his head to grasp a handful of the cotton and yanked. With the shirt still over his eyes, blinding him, she worked open his fly and snuck a hand inside his boxer briefs.

A sharp intake of breath hissed between his teeth when she gripped him. Her touch buckled his knees and his palm smacked hard against the door behind her head when he braced for balance. His T-shirt slipped from his fingers and landed at their feet beside her flannel.

She started to pump him, and the blood rushed from his head to swell his rigid shaft. With awkward, uneven strokes that nonetheless delivered an agonizing pleasure he couldn't recall ever experiencing before, she worked him, pumping until he hurtled toward the brink of climax.

He caught her wrist and pulled her hand away. "Enough," he croaked.

"Tell me what to do." Her voice shook with her urgent plea. "I want to please you, too, this time."

He couldn't speak past the lump that suddenly lodged in his throat, so he trailed the tips of his fingers along the waistband of her jeans and popped the button free.

"All I want is you." He dragged down the zipper.

With a rush of movement, she wriggled out of her jeans, a seductive display of artless sensuality that left her standing before him, bathed in the warm glow of fading sunlight and clad only in white cotton panties.

His breath hitched. At his sides, he curled his hands into tight fists and drank in his fill of her until he became intoxicated. Like a starving man at an all-you-can-eat buffet, he devoured the sight of her, gorging himself on every abundant curve. Each lush swell and provocative dip. The voluptuous splendor of her figure and also the small, secret places that promised pleasures both carnal and pure.

Her body, like the woman herself, was generous and soft, and so fucking sweet.

Emotions he could not name snatched the air from his lungs.

After a battle that cost him much in the way of his

composure, he dragged his gaze back to her face to find she watched him with grave, lucid eyes, as uncertain as a doe. Her skin flushed a soft shade of dusty pink and she lifted her arms to cover her breasts.

The twinge in his chest was a physical ache. "No, wait." He clasped both her hands and pulled them away from her body. Then he laced his fingers through hers. "Please. Don't hide from me. I can't bear it."

On her face, her struggle with his words played out, then slowly, her arms relaxed. The uncertainty in her eyes didn't fade completely, but she banished the slight slouch from her shoulders and raised her chin a notch higher.

In that moment, at least, she decided to trust him. Her deliberate display of that trust had the effect of lifting her glorious breasts to his ravenous gaze.

His heart swelled along with his cock.

He drew close, skin to skin, and pressed his lips to her bare shoulder. "Thank you," he murmured as he grazed one beaded nipple with the backs of his fingers.

The soft cadence of her breathing turned ragged and rushed past his ear with short, uneven puffs. He pulled back far enough to see her face. Tension hummed through her body as she gazed up at him with enormous eyes darkened with her arousal, but her expression caught him up.

Though the obvious signs of her surging desire showed in her flushed skin, heavy eyelids, and the small parting between her lips, beyond the hunger, something more swirled. She'd never looked at him in exactly this way before now and he peered closely, inspecting the divergences.

If he weren't stupid with lust, he would've sworn the difference was in her eyes. In the way that she looked at him. Like he mattered to her. Deeply. As though he were her anchor. Someone she relied on to let her bob and roll in the dangerous waters yet keep her tethered through the coming storm.

Someone she believed would see her safe.

The rush of emotion threatened to drown him. Unnerved but unable to sort through his reaction while captive to the need that drove him, he gripped her hips and turned her away from him.

From behind, he slid an arm around her waist and drew her body snug against his. She sank back, and he cupped her, then watched over her shoulder as his large, tanned hands massaged her full, pale breasts. Between his thumbs and forefingers, he fondled her sensitive nipples.

His erection strained against the confines of his clothing and he skimmed his hands down her body, over her small ribcage and waist, and the erotic flare of her generous hips, to the edge of her panties. One thumb hooked the elastic waistband while, with his other hand, he slid over the flimsy cotton to stroke between her thighs.

At the first feathery caress of his fingers, her head dropped back to lie on his shoulder. Lightly, he teased her, and she raised the heel of her foot to allow his hand more room to explore her.

So he did.

With featherlike strokes and soft, swirling rubs, he toyed with her until the cotton dampened beneath his fingers. She arched her back and swiveled her hips, chasing his touch. Her moans became greedy, and her breasts rose and fell with the increasingly roughened passage of heavy breaths.

When he could resist no more, he slipped his hand inside her panties and pushed through the springy curls to her heated core. A groan rumbled deep in the back of his throat when he found her body open and eager for his touch.

Foreplay over, he rubbed her wet slit with long, even strokes until her hips rocked in time to the rhythm he set.

She rose on her tiptoes and he massaged deeper. When he brushed against a sensitive spot, she gasped, and moisture drenched his fingers.

Holy fuck, but she was hot. Fire scorched his veins and his rigid shaft hardened with painful stiffness. He hadn't even gotten inside her yet.

He'd wanted to take it slow with her this first time, but the blaze of his desire raged. Soon, he would be beyond the point of self-control.

Mina's moans morphed into whimpers of need which grew lustier and louder with his relentless pleasure-giving. She circled her hips, her motions expanding wider and faster.

Though hidden among the treetops, anyone who peeked through the gaps in the leaves or arrived at Mina's doorstep might see them. Might see her, fully exposed, and him with his hand tucked inside her underwear, moving with obvious purpose. It was carnal and thrilling, and he was harder and hotter than he could ever remember being in his life.

His blood roared with the impulse to spread her thighs where they stood and drive himself home. Just barely, he conquered it.

With a soft cry, Mina pitched forward and grabbed on to the porch railing in front of her. She threw her head back and ground against his hand. Her body clenched around his fingers.

But Noah was nowhere near ready for this to end. He wanted more.

When he withdrew from her body, she whimpered. He spun her around, and cupping her face in both his hands, he claimed her mouth with his own, nipping at her puffy bottom lip with his teeth, then licking the swollen spot.

She tore at the open fly of his blue jeans, and soon he stood naked before her.

Her eyes ate him up, and beneath her hungry gaze, his cock jumped. Need swelled.

A warm sensation arose in the center of his chest and he rubbed the spot a moment before he realized it didn't ache, as it had done since the day his mom died. With her passing, his world had fallen apart and a painful, rotting wound had opened up inside him. The hole had never closed and even now, years later, the throbbing tenderness had persisted.

Until now. Right as he was about to bury his aching cock inside Mina Winslow.

He didn't know what was happening to him. Sex with her that first time had been hauntingly memorable. But the second time…?

It wasn't what he'd expected. It was hotter, sweeter, and so much better than he could've imagined. He didn't know it could be like this.

This.

What was *this*? So far, it was only a hurried tryst on a rickety old porch. He hadn't even experienced the sensation of her body wrapped around him.

Even so, it'd already surpassed every one of his prior sexual encounters.

"Noah?" His thoughts scattered when she touched his cheek. "Are you all right?"

Her fingertips traced a path of fire along his jawline that rocketed straight to his groin. The punch of lust knocked the wind out of him.

"I need you." His voice shredded with the force of his need. "I…I need to touch you. To get inside you… Mina…please."

She reached for him, but he caught her hand before she seared him with her touch.

"Please," he whispered. "I need you to say yes."

His words appeared to confuse her, and she searched his face while the moment stretched out.

Then a soft tenderness filled her blue eyes. "Yes, Noah." Like his, her words trembled. "I want you too."

He wished to argue with her use of the word "want." What he felt went beyond mere wanting. It was elemental. Essential. He had to have her.

Overcome with need, he dragged down her panties. Then he seized her bottom in both his hands and lifted her hips so that her damp slit brushed against the long length of his erection. When he plunked her down hard on a rickety wooden table, a small potted plant crashed to the floorboards.

She hadn't yet regained her balance when he stepped between her legs and smoothed his palms up her inner thighs. With both hands, she gripped his shoulders to steady herself, then she pressed her back against the porch pillar and parted her knees, exposing her sweet core fully to him.

The urge to plunge deep tugged at his cock, but he forced himself to slow down. Too soon, this moment with her would end.

He wasn't yet ready for that desolate inevitably.

While he watched her face, he stroked the impossibly soft skin on the inside of her thighs with his thumbs. When he ruffled her moist curls, arousal flared in her eyes.

He dipped his thumb into her honeyed heat, then brought his hand to his mouth. Her eyes widened, then bulged with shock as he licked the moisture from the pad of his thumb.

Slowly, he lowered to his knees before her. His broad shoulders pressed her thighs wide when he dipped his head and deposited a kiss onto her stomach. The intoxicating musk of her arousal teased his nostrils.

His eyes captured hers. An aching tenderness touched her features, and she threaded her fingers through his hair.

Without letting go of her gaze, he teased her with light, questing touches. Then he nuzzled closer. For one tiny taste.

She gasped his name.

A smile hanging inside his heart, he licked deeper. With the next sweep of his tongue, her gasp rolled into a moan. Her sweet, heady scent intoxicated him. He nibbled and ate until her grip tightened in his hair and her hips gyrated with the pleasure she took from his mouth.

Beyond the boundary of their secretive sex hideout, the sound of the turbulent lake provided the harmony to her greedy moans.

Her stomach muscles trembled as she begged him for more. "Noah, please. Oh please oh please. *Noah….*"

Her breathless pleas pulled a droplet of come from his shaft. "Tell me what you want."

"I n-need you," she panted. "Inside me."

Satisfaction roared through him. There it was.

Need.

She needed him, too.

He filched a condom from the wallet in his discarded jeans and as he rose to his feet, she plucked it from his hand and tore open the package. With gentle pressure, she rolled the sheath down his hard length while she squeezed his balls with gentle pressure.

The pleasure was excruciating.

The joy, unbearable.

His heart tried to thrash its way out of his chest. How did he get so lucky to be in this moment with this woman?

Fully sheathed, he stepped between her thighs. The head of his penis poised at her entrance, her tightness clutched at him, and he trembled with the effort to keep from slamming into her, hard and deep.

He nudged a fraction inside her, then retreated to tease at her opening with his glistening tip.

She wrapped her legs around his waist and shifted her hips, trying to lure him further into her wet hollow.

He obliged, but when he'd reached only midway to the base of his shaft, the first ripples of release quivered, and he withdrew.

Her protest tightened his balls.

"Tell me again what you want," he rasped.

"You." She wriggled beneath him. "Noah, I want you."

"What do you want from me?"

Between her eyebrows, a small pucker formed, and a frown pulled at the corners of her plump mouth.

He slid his hand under her chin and dragged his thumb across her bottom lip, as though he might wipe the scowl from her pretty mouth. Then he dropped his head and tried to kiss it away instead.

When his lips touched hers, she opened for him. He groaned and licked inside.

She rocked against him and broke the kiss on a gasp. With the surge of sensation, her worry vanished.

Large, guileless eyes undid him when she looked into his eyes and said, "I want you to fuck me, Noah. *Please.*"

In one long, smooth thrust, he burrowed all the way inside, his passage made easy by her slickness. Her humid hollow clamped tight around him and a guttural groan escaped him.

Beneath his feet, the world shifted, and he pressed his forehead to her shoulder. His awareness narrowed to that one blessedly glorious point of contact.

Though he had not yet come, he felt completion.

He set a languid rhythm, sliding all the way inside and pulling all the way out, savoring every inch of contact with her luscious body. Over and over, he pushed inside, then pulled back, again and again. Colors swirled behind his eyelids.

He increased their pace.

Mina met each of his thrusts with eager abandon, even raising her arms above her head to grasp the porch pillar at her back.

His soul sang.

Wild, desperate desire drove through him, and he plunged deeper, faster. The table rocked beneath them, so he slipped his arms under her knees and gripped the table's edge to steady it. The position spread her wide, and he pushed into her sweet heat with urgent, savage thrusts.

The sounds of their joining filled the tiny porch enclosure. The rush of their ragged breaths.... The soft slap of skin smacking against skin.... The slippery slurp of her arousal....

Still, it wasn't enough. He needed more.

With her knees hooked over his elbows and her legs pressed wide, he seized her hips, holding her in place while he sank into her. The motion made her ample breasts sway and bounce.

More. Faster. Deeper.

He dropped his head and sucked a pink puckered nipple between his teeth. She cried out.

More.

He wanted to go deeper, longer and harder, until he became a part of her. He wanted to take her pleasure and give her his in return, making them one.

Sweat glistened on their skin as their bodies collided, relentless in desperation and greed.

He couldn't last much longer, so he reached between them and brushed his thumb over her swollen sex.

A cry of painful pleasure broke from her, and her sweet pussy quivered around his cock. With a growl against her throat, he roared over the edge with her.

Tremors continued to roll through him for many

moments afterward. Their breathing slowed and their skin cooled.

Still, neither of them moved. He stayed inside her as the last remnants of sunlight faded and a chill infused the darkening night air around them.

With his face pressed to the side of her neck, he inhaled. Usually, sex satiated him. It relaxed him. But now, the gnawing hunger remained. Along with that troubling need to slack something other than his lust.

He'd agreed to only sex between them, but suddenly, it wasn't enough.

Now, he knew "only sex" was the lie he'd told themself. The lie that'd allowed him to take what he wanted without having to think about what it meant.

"Only sex" wasn't possible for them.

But how was he going to convince her of that?

He ran a hand up her spine. "I'm afraid you're going to be picking splinters out o' your back for a week."

Her smile appeared stiff when she slipped out from under him and silently began collecting the pieces of her clothing scattered about the porch.

Unsteady on his feet, he joined in the search. As he pulled his blue jeans over his hips, he noticed she wouldn't meet his gaze.

A ripple of unease disturbed him. "You're not having post-orgasm regret, are you?"

Straightening, she clutched her rumpled clothes to her chest like a shield. "No, of course not."

But he detected the rigid set of her shoulders as she tugged on her clothing and the way she kept her chin ducked as she focused on buttoning her shirt.

The lash of his anger was swift and vicious.

Damn it all, she was going to shut him out again. Just as she had in high school.

He'd warned that wasn't an option this time.

This time would be different, he'd told her.

They'd talked about it. They'd made fucking rules about it. Despite that, she thought she could throw him away? Even after—

She tugged on the hem of the sleeve.

His racing thoughts seized, and the hand he'd been shoving through his hair froze. He watched.

Then she did it again.

It was a small thing, just a self-conscious gesture she used to make in high school, usually right before she disappeared from the lunchroom or the hallway where they'd gathered with their classmates.

And that's when it hit him. She was uneasy. Uncomfortable.

Maybe even a little scared.

Not of him, or of the sex. She'd made it clear she wanted both.

But something had her spooked.

Maybe, like him, she felt shaken? Unnerved by what had just happened between them?

The sex didn't scare her.

The way she felt about it did.

She knew as well as him it hadn't been a quick, meaningless fuck between them.

So she wanted to get away. She wanted to run. But she wasn't running from him.

She was running from herself.

"Good." A soft *zzziiippp* sounded when he dragged shut the fly of his jeans. "Because I'm not letting you kick me out this time."

CHAPTER 19

She abandoned the hunt for her panties. "I didn't kick you out."

"You did." The playfulness of his tilted mouth didn't make the journey to his eyes.

Abruptly, she ducked her chin and resumed her search.

"I had work to do." Her fingers clamped around the white scrap of material. "Actually, I *have* work to do now—"

Slowly, he reached out and pressed a finger to her lips. "I'm staying."

"But—"

"I warned you, Mina. This isn't high school." He scraped his finger across her bottom lip. "Things are different now."

The blood left her head in a dizzying rush. Blindly, she twisted toward the door to her loft, only to recall with a groan of distress the fumbled key in the grass beneath the porch.

Beneath the porch, she embarked on a frantic, disjointed search through the grass in the fading sunlight while Noah took a calm, methodical approach that finally turned up the missing key after a fifteen-minute hunt.

Back upstairs, her shaking hands made fitting the key into the lock more difficult. When the lock at last released, she burst into the carriage house and tossed the keys on the table. Without breaking stride, shot across the living room.

"I'm going to grab a quick shower." At the bedroom door, she glanced back over her shoulder. "I won't be long."

Noah rounded the table with slow, cautious movements. His features remained impassive, but the distinct ember of concern burned in his dark eyes.

"I have mud in my hair." It was her only defense.

"I'll be here."

She barricaded herself in the bathroom.

The shower nozzle creaked when she cranked it. Water beat against the tub basin as she stripped out of her flannel shirt once more before stepping under the warm spray. The hot, pounding stream rushed over her skin and the pleasant burn soothed her aching muscles.

What had just happened? One minute she was lost in the misery of humiliation and failure, and the next she was…naked.

With Noah.

Having sex.

With Noah.

On her front porch.

She pressed her forehead against the shower wall.

She'd never been so bold and reckless. So lost in the moment.

Tell me what you want.

The words had sent her hurtling into his arms without a thought to consequences, or even the circumstance of their surroundings. Not only had he wanted to please her, he'd wanted her to be in control of her own pleasure. He wanted her guidance.

He wanted her permission.

He wanted her ecstasy as much as he wanted his own.

She had never slept with a man like that. So deliberate and protective. His care only fed her arousal. It caused her heart to pound painfully in her chest and the blood to whir in her ears.

She squirted shampoo into her palm and rubbed the flowery scented salve into her scalp with vigorous strokes.

In all the years since she and Noah had indulged in clandestine sex in the woods, other men had rarely tempted her. The ones she had slept with hadn't affected her the way Noah had, wringing everything out of her, until she had nothing left to give.

It horrified her to realize that was because none of them had been *him*.

It'd always been him.

Damn, damn, damn, damn, damn.

With another sputter of curses, she squeezed body wash onto her loofa, then attached the caked-on mud splatters on her arms and neck.

When he'd appeared out of nowhere and asked what was troubling her, the deep timbre of his lilting voice had smoothed over her like a balm, and the words had come pouring out of her.

In that moment, she might have told him every secret she carried. Laid every burden at his feet. She'd have revealed every scar and imperfection if he'd asked her to.

The water ran cold, and she twisted the faucet to stop the flow. Wrapped in an oversized towel, she wiped the fog from the mirror. As she raked a brush through her tangled hair, she refused to look too closely at the rumpled, overwrought woman reflected at her.

When she'd dressed in leggings and an oversized college sweatshirt, she emerged from the bedroom.

Noah stood behind the kitchen counter, pouring a glass

of milk. He glanced up as her feet padded against the wood floors.

"Pizza's on its way. I hope you like veggies." His sharp gaze betrayed his casual tone.

"I love them." In the tiny kitchen, she tried to slip past him, but he shifted to give her room at the exact moment she moved to sidestep him, and their bodies collided.

They ducked out of the way, only to bump against each other again.

With a soft laugh, his large hand found her hip and held as he scooped his milk off the counter. He crossed to the table and dropped into a chair while she went to the cupboard and pulled down a wineglass.

She splashed a hefty dollop of the blush liquid into the empty glass and downed it. As she refilled, she risked a glance at Noah. A dark scowl touched his features and beneath the table, his knee bounced in a staccato rhythm.

Surprised by the tension radiating off him, she stared for a moment, catching herself only when wine nearly flowed over the rim of the wineglass.

Her mind scrambling, she set down the bottle. Was it possible he'd only been faking calmness when, in reality, he felt as awkward and unsteady as she did? Why was he so tense? Was he unhappy? Uncomfortable? Did he feel trapped?

Did he want to leave, but feel obliged to stay?

Relief swept through her.

At the table, she plopped into a chair across from him. "Noah, it's all right. You don't have to stay. If you want to leave, please go."

His knee stilled, and his eyebrows slammed together. A dangerous spark flashed in his eyes and arced between them.

With a shiver of unease, she shifted in her seat. "I meant it when I said I'm okay with whatever you want out of... uh... our arrangement. Even if it's only sex and pizza."

The crease vanished from his forehead, and he leaned back in his chair. "Is that right?"

She mirrored his posture. "No matter what, I promise not to cry or pout or beg you to stay."

"Well, that's a relief. Because I meant it when I said I'm staying." Leaning forward, he pressed his elbows to the tabletop. "I want to talk with you about some things."

The sip of wine she'd taken caught in her throat, and she coughed.

He smacked her on the back until she waved him off. "Oh? Like what?"

"Your ex-fiancé."

Her stomach gave a little wrench of misery. "You said you weren't mad."

"I'm not mad. What I feel is far worse than anger." Disgust curled his upper lip. "I'm jealous."

An inelegant sound escaped her. "Jealous of what?"

"Of Drew."

She rolled her eyes. "Can you be serious for five minutes?"

He held her gaze, not a hint of humor on his face.

She choked down the laughter bubbling in her throat. "You have no reason to be jealous of Drew Alexander. Believe me."

"No? He's wealthy. Powerful. Good-looking. And he had you in his bed for... how long did you say?"

"First off, he didn't earn any of those things. His money and power are nothing but the luck of his birth, and what people mistake for confidence isn't. He's conceited, not confident, and there's an enormous difference."

"And yet you were going to marry him."

Her cheeks heated.

"How long were you together?" His voice dropped with the heavy weight of his somberness.

"Two years."

"Why did it end?"

Her fingers fiddled with the stem of the wineglass. "It's... complicated."

"Try to explain it to me. Please."

While she floundered for the words to explain how she'd almost made the biggest mistake of her life, she gulped down a large swallow of her wine. No words were adequate for the task, so she took a deep breath and stated the facts.

"Our families were long-standing political rivals, until my uncle and his father, who were both up for re-election and losing badly, decided a marriage was the quickest way to align forces and give themselves a bump in the polls."

"How romantic."

"They pushed the relationship for months before we gave in and went on a date. Eventually, I agreed to marry him to make them happy." She searched the contours of his face and found no judgment there. "I failed."

His dark eyes glittered with emotion, liquid and deep. "Did you love him?"

"I thought I did. I tried to." Memories of their disastrous relationship replayed in her mind. "But, no, I didn't love him. Not as a man. I loved the idea of him, but nothing more."

"Was he good to you?"

Surprised by the question, she fumbled to answer. "Yes, and no. He was a friend to me, once. A long time ago. But as a boyfriend and fiancé, he sucked."

"Is he a friend to you now?"

"I don't think I'd consider him my friend, no." That truth depressed her.

"How long ago did you break up?"

"All this poking and prodding is starting to hurt." She hid

her lack of a smile behind her glass. "Don't you have any failed engagements or unstable former lovers we can discuss?"

"Nope." He took a long drink of milk.

Her eyes narrowed, and she pondered the tightness that appeared around his mouth. "Too many lovers to remember?"

His smile vanished, replaced by a fierce scowl. "Absolutely not."

"More than a hundred?"

He laid a hand over his heart, feigning offense. "That's only seven women a year. Do you think so little of me and my sexual prowess?"

She thought quite a lot about his sexual prowess.

"Over ten?" she ventured.

"Per year?"

"Grand total."

"Not so many as that, no," he murmured.

"What about the love of your life?" As she spoke the words, her heart kicked in her chest. "Was she in there somewhere?"

A peculiar expression slipped across his face, quickly replaced with a roguish grin. "They were all the love of my life. In that moment."

Yes, she could imagine they were. A rush of heat warmed her body as she recalled the front porch. Drew's aim in bed, as in life, had been strictly goal-oriented, while in contrast, Noah's focus centered on the process.

The difference was everything. Rather than feeling lonely or hollow with Noah, she felt special. Cherished. She might believe she was the love of his life. If only in the moment.

"I have no doubt they felt well loved." Her lighthearted humor faded. "Were you?"

His wicked smile evaporated. A frown appeared on his

face, and just when she thought he wouldn't answer her, he did. "I've been lonely as long as I can remember."

The confession knocked the breath from her body.

"And no." A soft light flickered in his eyes. "I wasn't in love with any of them."

She had difficulty swallowing, as if a hand had closed around her throat. "So you never married, either?"

"Not even an engagement." His foot nudged hers under the table. "Ill-advised or otherwise."

A knock at the door announced the arrival of their pizza and while Noah paid, Mina fetched plates and napkins from the kitchen.

The pizza's aroma filled the small loft, and her stomach let loose with an angry growl. Or maybe it was the relief that rumbled through her at having escaped his pointed questioning.

Back at the table, he opened the box and steam rolled out. He dished a warm, heaping slice onto a plate and slid it her way.

"Are you going to avoid my questions, then?" He scooped another piece from the box.

She stifled a groan. "There've been, like, seventy questions. Which one are you referring to?"

His lips twitched. "When did your engagement end?"

"March."

The pizza slice landed on the plate with a thud. "This March? As in seven months ago March?"

Her appetite fizzling, she stared down at her plate. "That's the one."

"That's not very long ago." He reclined in the chair and folded his arms across his abdomen. "What happened?"

"He cheated on me." She snuck a peek at him.

Dark shadows clouded his face. "I really don't like that guy."

"The cheating was the deal breaker." She picked a black olive off her pizza. "But I knew before that I couldn't marry him. I just hadn't found the courage to break it off yet."

"Why didn't you tell me this before?"

"Because it's humiliating." She flicked another olive aside. "It's not exactly something I enjoy telling everyone about."

"I didn't ask you to tell everyone. I asked you to tell me."

Her stomach gave a little flip. "You're the last person I wanted to find out."

"Why?"

Beneath his scowl, she squirmed. "Well, until…a few days ago, you hated me."

"I didn't hate you." The denial shot from him.

She sliced him with a look.

He opened his mouth, as if to argue, but then he snapped it shut again. "I didn't hate you," he finally said. "I was… I felt a lot of things. But I never hated you."

"A lot of things?"

His eyes narrowed. "You're trying to change the subject."

"I am not."

"You are." Straightening in the chair, he studied her with interest. "Why don't you want me talking about your cheating ex?"

She pretended immense interest in her pizza slice.

A soft curse dropped from his lips. "You think it's your fault, don't you?"

The accusation sounded ridiculous, and she winced.

It *was* ridiculous. Ridiculous, and yet true.

"*He* is the asshole." Noah ground out the words through clenched teeth.

"Yeah, and I'm the stupid woman who almost married him." Because she'd been too weak to stand up for herself.

"It's always the sweet ones," he grumbled, shaking his head. "You blame yourselves for their bad behavior."

She wanted to defend herself, but he cut in before she got the chance.

"Pricks like him seek your type out, you know. They seek you out and they ruin you for the rest of us."

Soft laughter bubbled in her throat. "He is a prick, isn't he?"

He plucked the slice of pizza off his plate. "You're way out of his league."

Pleasant warmth replaced the knot in her chest. He was probably just saying that, but the idea held such appeal she indulged it, recalling the little hurts and sorrows he'd caused her. And the big ones, too.

"He didn't want me to buy the house."

"Yeah, I gathered as much."

"It sat abandoned for years." She tore a bubble of burnt cheese off her crust. "Most of the damage occurred then. I bought it a month after I found out he was sleeping with someone else."

"Nicely done." The warmth from Noah's smile spread through her. "Did he also blame you for his infidelity?"

Her heart tripped over in her chest. "Wh-what?"

"Did he tell you that you didn't please him? That you forced him to seek other woman?"

It was as if he'd peered inside her heart, found her greatest insecurities, and shined a spotlight on them.

For a long, painful moment, she sat speechless, gaping at him. How did he know that? Was it obvious from their encounter on the porch she left her lovers disappointed?

Air rattled through her tight lungs. "Wo-women."

Mid-chew, he froze, then swallowed with a hard gulp.

"Not one woman." Her heart thumped in her ears. "But lots of women."

Noah discarded his pizza onto his plate and slid to the edge of his seat so that her legs nestled between his hard thighs. His dark gaze seized hers and held. "I'm sorry to be the one to tell you, but your ex is a bastard."

She tried to hide her mortification behind a smile, but her chest ached. "How did you know Drew said those things?"

"I've known guys like him." When his fingers brushed her hand, she turned her palm, chasing the feel of his warmth. "It's always someone else's fault. Never their own."

She stared down at his large, warm hand clamped tight around her cold fingers. "Some of what he said is... a little true."

Patient and watchful, he waited.

Until the words started to pour from her. "I didn't... I don't... I'm not very adventurous. In bed. I didn't want to do some of the things he liked."

Noah's eyebrows inched upward. "Like what? Sex on the kitchen table? Or, say, the front porch?"

Her cheeks burned.

"Listen to me," his voice gentled even as his hand gripped hers tight. "He was a selfish prick, and selfish pricks make the worst lovers. I seriously doubt your relationship dissolved because of some defect in you."

She wanted so badly for that to be true. To know she wasn't broken or flawed beyond redemption.

Ruined.

"Isn't it possible he was simply the wrong guy for you?" he asked.

"Oh, he was definitely the wrong guy for me." Just as she was wrong for him.

"But...?"

No words would come to explain the numbness she sometimes battled, or the suffocating self-doubt. So again, she settled for the facts. "I don't... I didn't... sometimes..." She gulped. "I can't or-orgasm. Very often. Ever."

Fire sparked in his dark eyes. "I made you come. Twice."

Twice.

With that one numerical word, heat spiraled through her body.

Slowly, he unfolded his lean body from the chair.

Her gaze tracked up his tall frame, past the broad expanse of his chest and shoulders, to his throat, and sensuous mouth, before colliding with those penetrating eyes. A flurry of soft flutters tickled her stomach.

With her hand still cradled in his, he tugged her to her feet so that she came up hard against the full length of his body.

His other hand stole around her waist, then slipped lower. "Shall we try for three?"

Sleep dragged at her. After Noah had given her another orgasm and she'd help him find one of his own, they'd collapsed into an exhausted heap in her bed, dozing in the buttery soft glow of light spilling from the lamp they'd left on in the corner.

Through the haze of her slumber, a sound intruded, and she realized he'd whispered something near her ear, too quietly for her to hear.

Rousing, she turned her head. "What did you say?"

A gentle sadness came into his eyes. "I asked how you lost your hearing in this ear."

The smile froze on her face. Her heart stuttered while her mind struggled with the question.

She rolled to her side, facing the wall. "It was so long ago I hardly remember."

"Tell me what you do remember."

With that, the memories emerged from the darkness.

"After my dad died, his brother sort of adopted my mom and me."

"The senator?"

"He wasn't the senator then." Even through her fatigue, the old bitterness remained. "His dead brother's widow and young daughter made a great prop on the campaign trail."

Noah's hand moved to her hip.

"We lived with Uncle Preston until I was seventeen. His son, Jeremy, and Drew were friends."

She felt him stiffen beside her.

"One night, they got into a fight, which I walked into the middle of. Jeremy had Drew by the throat, and Drew was turning this horrible shade of purple. Like an idiot, I tried to break them up, but Jeremy.... He turned on me."

His hand on her hip squeezed. "He hit you?"

"I think so. I just remember there was this awful pain, and I was on the ground. When I fell, my head hit the floor, and I shattered my eardrum."

His warm mouth found the spot below her ear, and her eyes fluttered shut.

"The doctors couldn't help?"

"They thought it might heal, but it became infected. My hearing never came back. After that, my mom sent me here to live with my grandma."

"To protect you?"

"Yeah, I guess." The lie dropped easily from her tongue.

He toyed with the hair at her temple. "It must've been hard for you, not living with your mom."

"I was so happy not to have to campaign with Uncle Preston anymore. I didn't care if I only saw my mom once every few months."

In the quiet, Mina's eyelids grew heavy. She stifled a yawn.

Sleep beckoned once more when Noah's soft voice

reached out to her. "I don't remember anyone named Jeremy Winslow."

Her eyes shot open.

"Did he go to Sacred Heart?"

She nodded. "He was four years older than us."

"What does he do now?"

"He died."

Noah pressed a kiss to her temple. "I'm sorry."

"It was a long time ago."

Into the silence, he asked, "Did he ever put his hands on you again?"

She stared at the far wall, at the spot where light gave way to shadow.

"No," she whispered into the dark. "Never."

One night with Mina stretched into two, then three, and before he realized it, more than a week had passed. She was like a drug. The more he had, the more he wanted, and the more he feared her running out. So he refused to give her the option.

Because, as it turned out, *she* was the best *he'd* ever had.

After a quick, late-night shower, he rubbed a towel through his hair as he emerged from the bathroom. She lay beneath the sheets in her oversized bed, watching him through heavy eyelids.

Every morning, she headed off to meet with the crew at the house while he worked at the site or made the trek into campus, and the last three nights, she'd worked the late shift at Lucky's as well, returning to the carriage house after midnight.

Despite her obvious exhaustion now, her gaze swept over his bare chest, and a small, secret smile curved her soft mouth. A contented sigh that sounded like a purr vibrated in her throat.

Laughing, he fell into bed beside her and pulled her

plump bottom lip between his teeth. Then he proved to her, yet again, that she was anything but orgasmically challenged.

Afterward, lying in the dark, he dozed when the mattress dipped and bounced as she rolled to her side.

As he drifted into sleep again, she rolled to her stomach, jostling him. The movement aroused a hint of white jasmine to tease his nostrils and he realized that, with the hockey bag full of clothes and other belongings he'd hauled into her loft, his own unique scent now mingled with hers. It'd taken only a few short days for hers and his to become theirs.

That pulled a satisfied smile from him, and soon, he slipped toward oblivion.

When she heaved a sigh into the air and twisted onto her back, her elbow caught his shoulder.

With a grunt, he rolled to his side and slipped an arm around her waist. "Woman, go to sleep."

"Sorry," she huffed, then turned onto her side so that his larger body cradled her smaller form.

His hand slid over the delicious curve of her hip. "Need me to distract you from your thoughts?"

"I'm still sore from the two times you distracted me already today."

"Man, you're easy."

Her soft chuckle held a distinct ring of delight.

He stretched out his arm and laid his head on his biceps. "Am I going to have to tell you a bedtime story?"

"Maybe one with a happy ending this time?"

"Hmmm…." He dipped his head, bringing his mouth to the side of her neck. "There aren't too many of those."

"So I've noticed," she said dryly. "Why is everyone always dead in the end?"

"Okay, I've got one." He slanted onto his back and tucked his hand under his head. "This story is a classic tale," he began. "A poor boy falls in love with a beautiful girl. It's an impossible love, you see, for she's the daughter of the king, and her family would never accept him. He's a hoodlum and street rat and isn't good enough for their beloved daughter. But the girl is charmed by his handsome face and good manners, and, miracles of miracles, she falls in love with him, too."

"Is this a Disney movie?"

"Ack, no. All my stories are R rated. As I was saying, her family would never allow the match, but the daughter is obstinate, and she defies them. From her father's palace, she gathers all the valuables she can carry and goes in search of her one true love. She gives all her riches to him and begs him to take her to see the world.

"The boy refuses her gift, as he desires her, not her abundant riches. They agree to marry, and in anticipation of their vows, they consummate their love for one another beneath the stars."

Beneath the bedcovers, his foot found hers.

"Afterwards, they go in search of the priest, but on their way, the king's men catch them. They drag her away, screaming and with tears in her eyes, and lock her in the dungeon beneath her father's palace, a place so horrible it was called *La Fosse Noire*—The Black Pit."

"The Black Pit? You're making this up, right?"

"No. Be quiet. In his misery, the boy banishes himself to the desert to live out his days. He will not eat or drink, and soon he becomes emaciated. His heart full of grief and his body malnourished, he loses his mind and comes to be known as Madman, or *Fear Buile*."

At her silence, he paused, wondering if she'd dozed off.

"Then what happened?" she asked, her voice taut with anticipation.

"One day, a peasant happens upon him. Having no use for the bread in his pocket, the *Fear Buile* gives it to the peasant.

In gratitude, the peasant insists on handing over his only possession in the world, a tarnished silver cup." With his fingers, he fondled her hair and the fine bones of her ear. "But it's no ordinary cup, mind you. It's a magical vessel, and with it, the poor boy amasses great wealth. He gathers an army and sets out to free his love from her father's dungeon, but when he arrives, the pit is empty. For many days and nights, he searches the land until he finds his love living alone in a cottage in the woods. He kisses her, and she weeps with joy at his longed-for return."

Unable to resist, he rolled to his side and pressed his lips to the spot where her neck and shoulder met before picking up the story.

"They stay in bed for days and are loath to ever be apart again." He nipped her earlobe and smiled when the shudder chased through her lush body.

"Their time is limited, for she had recently escaped the pit and run away to the woods rather than be married to the man her father picked for her, and her father's warriors are hunting her. The king's men find them, and a battle ensues. The fighting is so fierce and bloody, its legend lives on even today."

"I've never heard of—"

He cut her off. "In the end, the poor boy is triumphant. He marries his girl and takes her away from the people who would do her harm. They live out their lives, traveling from village to village, seeing all the places she dreamed of while confined to *La Fosse Noire*, and he is happy, for she is by his side."

He toyed with the hair at her temple. "The end."

She rolled over and when they lay facing each other, she used the tip of her finger to trace a tiny circle on his bare chest, above his heart. "That's an interesting story."

"It's a classic tale."

More tiny circles fell from her fingertips.

"He banished himself?"

"Yep."

"Because of her?"

The spot over his heart grew warm beneath her touch. "He had some other stuff going on."

"What other stuff?"

"Family stuff."

The heart circles stopped. "How young were they?"

"Teenagers."

"That is young. Did you say he loved her?"

He tucked a strand of her hair behind one ear. "She was hot and looking at her made him hard, so, yeah, he loved her. I mean, that's love, right? At least, to a teenage boy, it is."

She pinched his side. "That's so romantic."

In one fluid motion, he pinned her beneath him and held her wrists above her head. His face near to hers, he inhaled deeply so her heady scent filled his senses. "She was a smar-tass, though, so he had to take command early on."

He covered her mouth with his to cut off any protests, but he swallowed only her yielding giggle. He gentled the kiss, taking his time to lick and savor, until finally, out of breath, he pulled back.

Earnest blue eyes gazed up at him. "Why did you tell me that story?"

"I guess...I wish things had gone differently for us, and I wanted you to know that." He dropped a kiss on the tip of her nose and rolled off her.

She rolled with him and, resting her chin on his chest, peered up at him. "Are you saying you broke the rules?"

"Technically, no. I never mentioned our past. Not until you brought it up."

"Technically?" Her chin poked his sternum as spoke. "So you cheated."

"I exploited a loophole."

"That's cheating."

"I'm hoping you're going to punish me for my insolence."

The flash of her smile was brief. "You never told me what happened. Why did you quit school?"

"My dad and I didn't get along." The air squeezed from his lungs with the memories. "I needed to leave town for a while."

After a long silence, she asked, "Did he hit you?"

Noah stared at the ceiling, though darkness obscured the contours. "Only when I pushed him too far."

She pushed herself upright in the bed and swung to face him, sitting with her legs crossed in front of her. "What does that mean?"

"It means I pissed him off a lot."

"He had a temper?"

"He did."

She chewed on his words for a moment, then said, "You did it on purpose, didn't you? You made him angry on purpose?"

His mouth suddenly dry, he swallowed thickly. "I did."

"But…why?"

Unsure how to explain the reasoning of a child, he struggled to fetch the words. "At first, I just wanted to get a reaction out of him. To put something other than that blank look in his eyes."

The darkness set loose the memories of peacefulness erupting into chaos, of sleep exploding into pain when his head slammed against a wall or his dad's fist crashed into his face.

"But he took to it." A bitter smile ghosted his lips. "So then I did it just to keep his focus off the little ones."

"Oh, Noah." He felt the break in her voice inside his heart. "I'm so sorry."

He wished to banish her hurt, so he tried to shrug, but the bed pillows got in his way. "The hitting stopped about the time Shea turned sixteen and started fighting back."

"I knew you and your brothers didn't get along with your dad very well, but…I didn't know…I'm so sorry…"

He didn't know why or how it happened, but he began to speak of things he'd never spoken of before. "My mom's death changed him. Before she got sick, he was more like a normal dad. He went to work and came home for dinner. We played ball in the back yard, did fun stuff together."

Noah scratched a phantom itch on his shoulder. "But after her death… He stopped coming home. Or he'd drop us at a friend's house or leave us with someone we'd never met, and disappear. He might be gone for a few days, or a few months. When he did show up, he wasn't our dad. He was angry. Mean."

The brush of her skin against his pushed back the storm building inside him.

"One day, after being away for almost two months, he suddenly showed up. He was sober and well dressed, and he took Shea and me for a walk, just the three of us. He bought us a Coke."

A stupid fucking pop and, like the child he'd been at the time, Noah had foolishly thought everything was going to go back to the way it had been before.

"I was standing there, drinking my Coke and feeling like a fucking king, when the storefront across the street exploded."

Her soft gasp sent shock waves ricocheting through him. "What do you mean it 'exploded'?"

"It was a bomb."

Her sharp intake of breath seemed to suck the air out of the room.

"Bombs and assassinations…those kinds of things were a

part of life there for a while, so it wasn't all that unusual." He tried to explain the unexplainable. "The building was on fire, and people were running in every direction. Screaming. It was like a nightmare, except I couldn't wake up."

Mina's small hand squeezed his. When had she taken his hand in hers?

"There was so much blood," he heard himself say. "I just stood there. I couldn't move or yell. So I...watched. And I remember...there was this kid. He was about my age and his face was covered in dirt and blood."

Her warm lips pressed to the heart of palm.

"He was sitting in the street, next to a woman's body. She was dead." His throat parched, Noah swallowed painfully. "He didn't cry or call for help. He just sat there holding her hand, with this awful expression on his face." Noah untangled his hand from hers and smoothed it over the soft skin of her calf. When he reached her ankle, he grasped it tight. "It wasn't fear or anguish, like I'd felt after my mom died. All I saw on that kid's face was...hate."

Noah had turned to his dad, certain he'd see on Daniel's face the revulsion he felt, but there was nothing, and Noah recalled thinking how peculiar that was.

Absently, he swept his thumb over Mina's anklebone, back and forth, back and forth.

"Fourteen people died that day." The words held a hollow ring. "Ordinary people, families, going about their lives...."

"Noah, I'm so sorry." Her watery voice preceded the teardrop that hit his hand.

In the living room, the antique clock on Mina's mantel chimed three times.

"He didn't flinch."

Her silence filled the space of several fractured heartbeats. "Who?"

"My dad. When that bomb went off, he didn't flinch. He

took us there and waited. He knew what was going to happen, and he took Shea and I to see it."

She dropped her head and her hand moved to cover her mouth, as if to hold back the horror.

But there was no holding it back. He remembered the horror, and the way it turned the soda to chalk in his mouth, choking him with panic and grief. The way it'd gutted him, hollowing him out with the certainty that nothing would ever be right again.

"For five days I lived with it." The old horror choked him even now, stealing the strength from his voice. "I understood my dad sympathized with the Catholics in their fight against the British, but I don't remember him being a zealot. Maybe it was just convenience. He was mad at the world and lost without my mom, and he wanted an outlet to vent his pain. I don't know…"

For several long, quiet moments, he listened to the soft whoosh of Mina's breathing. The steady rhythm gave him strength. He'd come this far. He might as well finish it.

She might as well know the truth about him.

He couldn't quite keep the waver from his voice when he said, "On the sixth day, I skipped school and went to my uncle's house."

He'd circled the block four times before ringing the bell.

"He was a retired cop, and I told him what I saw. I told him I thought my dad might be involved in the attack on that store."

They'd come for Daniel that night, and soon after, Noah and his brothers were ripped away from their home, the last remaining fragment of their old life before their mom had died, and sent to the States to live with their mother's brother, Father John.

"I turned traitor to The Cause."

The mattress swayed when she leaned over him and pressed her palm to the spot above his heart. "No."

"I violated the Irish code of silence."

"No," she said again.

"I don't know if my dad ever found out I was the one who squealed, but he knew I didn't approve, and he never forgave me for that."

All these years, the shame had tormented him. Even as he realized and reminded himself, repeatedly, that his dad had been sick, his twisted mind unable to distinguish right from wrong, good from evil, love from hate.

For so long, Noah had tried to let go of the shame, but the shame refused to release him.

"Sometimes, I wish I'd kept my mouth shut. Because of me, my dad was sent to prison, my brothers were orphaned and shipped off in disgrace to live an ocean away from their home."

"It's not your fault. Your dad did those things to himself, and to you and your brothers. Noah, you have to know that."

Daniel had served only three years before a ceasefire agreement had led to his pardon. As an ex-con with nothing and no one but a few "friends" still active in the fight, he'd followed his sons to a new life overseas.

And picked up where he'd left off. Distraught and adrift, living just to breathe, and spread misery.

She touched the side of his face. He flinched, not knowing her intention in the dark, but relaxed under her feather-light touch. "You're amazing," she whispered.

I'm a traitor. A shudder passed through him with the effort to bite back the words.

"How old were you?" she asked.

"Ten."

"Omigod," she murmured as she pressed her forehead against his. "A baby."

A wave of longing gripped him. He wanted to stay in the moment forever, where forgiveness washed over him with a whiff of white jasmine and a soft kiss on his forehead.

He wanted to stay.

With the realization, his pulse thrummed a frantic beat. She tempted him with more than honeyed kisses and the best sex of his life. But he couldn't let himself forget how things had ended between them last time, or that even now, she would never consider him suitable for anything more than a physical relationship.

Because she didn't trust him. She'd said as much right to his face.

Which meant he couldn't trust her, or any absurd thoughts that had him contemplating them as anything other than two consenting adults who liked to fuck each other.

She laid her small hand over the center of his chest. "You have such a good heart."

"Oh, man, you are such a sucker." He rose to his knees, grasped her ankle, and tugged. She slid onto her back and he moved over her. "A hussy and a sucker. How did I get so lucky?"

"You are good." The defiant ring in her voice echoed through him.

He used his knees to part her thighs and nuzzled that sweet spot below her ear, where her scent was strongest.

It wasn't true, of course. Just ask the brothers he'd betrayed.

"Your dad was wrong." Just as her legs clamped around his waist, her words tried to clutch his heart. "He was lost and confused, and you deserved so much better than that."

Hands shaking, he fumbled for a condom and clumsily sheathed his rigid shaft. Her body easily surrendered to his when he pushed inside her. Lost in her warm, wet heat, her voice sounded far away.

"You are good, Noah. So good."

He pumped his hips.

"You are good," she said again, and again.

His arousal climbing, his hips pumped faster. He drove deeper.

She kept saying those words, over and over, and he kept trying to destroy the pain and anger with the fire of his agonizing pleasure.

A guttural groan ripped from his throat as her body clenched around his cock and swallowed his shame.

Buried in her sweet pussy, he could believe what she said was true.

Almost.

But when the throbbing ache for release subsided, and the passion waned, he'd remember the truth about who he was.

And so would she.

CHAPTER 21

$\mathcal{M}$ina stole across the side lawn, making her escape from the apartment for the main house while Noah still slept.

She'd awakened to the rhythmic sound of his deep breathing and had slowly blinked open her eyes to find him lying naked, spent, and satiated beside her. In sleep, his long eyelashes had dropped shadows onto his high cheekbones and the taut cast of his features had smoothed into soft peacefulness. Her heart had skipped clumsily in her chest and she'd smiled.

It was a singular experience for her, sharing a bed with a man without her stomach hurting. He wasn't drunk, and neither was she, and she was almost certain he wasn't thinking about how fat her thighs were. She never wanted to leave their warm cocoon.

Her thoughts had drifted to the previous night, to what he had told her about his childhood, and her chest had grown tight with the rush of emotion. For a moment, she feared her heart might burst with love for that little boy who'd tried so hard to remain loyal to his family, but was too honorable to stay silent.

A shuddering breath rattled through her. If she woke up to Noah's face every morning for the rest of her life, it wouldn't be enough.

The truth ricocheted through her with the impact of a nuclear explosion. Inwardly, she cringed. What was she doing? Falling in love with him? After only a week spent together, had she already given him her heart?

The same heart she'd vowed never to give to another man who had no interest in possessing it?

The same man who'd made it one thousand percent clear he didn't want forever, but only the present, sex-filled moment with her?

Though exhaustion had pulled at her heavy limbs, she crawled from the bed and dressed in the darkened room to avoid waking him. She seriously needed to get a grip, and she didn't know how to do that with him nearby, tempting her the way no other man ever had.

At the house, most of the crew had arrived, and she spent several minutes looking for Sam before she remembered he was on vacation. She shifted her target to Eddie and followed the sound of male voices to the foyer where a large group of men had gathered around Ethan as he setup a raunchy joke about a big-breasted barmaid.

Overtired and under-caffeinated, she experienced a flash of irritation, and right as he launched into the crude punchline, she burst out with a bright, "Good morning."

Ethan choked back his climatic ending, and with an array of shamefaced expressions, the men scattered like cockroaches exposed to the sudden glare of light. Even Eddie grunted and shouldered a straight path in the opposite direction.

Mina cursed under her breath and considered running

after Eddie so she could talk to him about the schedule, but after years of working a desk job, the switch to balancing a home renovation with a waitressing gig and taking on a hot-blooded, enthusiastic lover had her muscles protesting every quick or strenuous movement. So she skipped the mad dash and went about making her daily rounds through the house, checking on the progress of various ongoing projects while also keeping an eye out for Eddie.

At the point when she typically became absorbed in her plans and dreams for the house, Noah intruded on her thoughts. Was he still asleep in her bed? If she returned to him now, as she wished to do, would he make love to her the way he had last night? With sweet urgency and dark beauty?

With the pang that squeezed her heart, she tried to banish him from her mind, but the exile lasted only a few moments before his next invasion breached her walls.

As though she might outrun her thoughts, she absconded to the second-floor bedroom where she'd been working the previous day. But in the room, Joe and Ethan were engaged in a heated exchanged as they worked to repair a broken length of crown molding.

"You cannot be that stupid," Joe spat. "You can't miter the corners in a house this old. It'll look like shit. You have to cope them, dumbass."

"Fine." Ethan pitched the hefty wood molding onto the hardwood floors. "I didn't know you were a fucking expert. Why don't you do it then?"

Her stomach wrenched with queasiness. The last time she'd stepped between two men who were fighting, she'd been the one to take the brunt of their hostility. So she grabbed the putty knife and container of spackle and fled.

In one of the other, blissfully empty bedrooms, she set to work spreading the gooey spackle mixture over the holes and cracks in the plaster walls to prep them for fresh paint.

The mindless work allowed space for her thoughts to wander, and of course, they went straight back to Noah.

How long had he carried alone the burden he shared with her last night? Other than his brothers, was she the first person he told? It'd obviously cost him much to tell her the entire story, and she doubted he would've told many others something so personal.

But…had he? And if so, who did he tell? One of the less than ten other women he'd been with? All of them?

A housefly buzzed around her, and she swatted it away with the putty knife. As the nights grew colder, the pests sought the warmth inside the house and squeezed in through every crack and crevice they could find, which were plentiful in the drafty old home.

From the other room, Joe continued to bark and snarl, and each stinging rebuke had Mina clenching her teeth with agitation. She didn't recall hearing such verbal abuse when Sam was in charge. Where the hell was Eddie, anyway?

She rubbed her neck to loosen the knot forming there, then renewed her efforts with the putty knife.

An image of a Noah, naked and fully erect as he moved over her, popped into her head just as another fly buzzed her, and she struck out with one hand to shoo it away along with her troublesome thoughts.

"Hey, Tyler," came Joe's obnoxious bellow. "How's your sister?"

Aggravation tinged Tyler's reply, even muffled as it was through the walls.

"Oh, yeah?" Joe called. "That's what *she* said."

She rolled her eyes as a growl of annoyance vibrated in her throat. Did Noah ever behave like that? In all the years she'd known him, she couldn't remember a time when he'd ever acted so uncouth. Never once had she witnessed him bullying anyone.

The pesky fly bounced off her cheek as if to remind her she was doing it again. She was thinking about Noah. She was obsessing over him in a way that far exceeded the purely physical nature of their relationship.

She was allowing her heart to expand to accommodate his presence in her life.

A thread of panic wove through her, and she dropped her forehead into her palm. Head bent, she watched a fly land on her forearm and crawl across her skin. With a flash of motion, she smacked at it.

Pain radiated up her arm, and she scrubbed at the stinging spot while the annoying monster flitted away unharmed.

For lunch, she returned to the carriage house for a quick bite, but when she discovered Noah was gone, a surge of disappointment overcame her.

Followed by a swift kick of frustration. What the hell was wrong with her? A few nights with the guy had turned her into a lovesick teenager. It was pathetic. *She* was pathetic. She was tired and cranky, and now also disgusted with herself.

The effort to reclaim all the reckless pieces of her heart started now.

Before returning to the main house to resume working, she hunted up a flyswatter. She gripped the metal wire in a tight fist as she entered the house through the kitchen door.

Within moments, she'd made her first kill. A small ripple of satisfaction rolled through her when she flicked the bug's carcass into a trash bin. She could do this, she thought as she prowled toward the dining room in search of another flying pest. She was a cold-hearted killer. Not a love-struck fool.

She tracked another housefly across the hall and into the front room, where Ethan and Ben measured the window openings for replacements and Joe and Tyler pried up the floor trim ahead of refinishing the hardwoods.

"Get your head out of your ass," Joe snapped at Tyler. "You can't do it like that or it won't be flush." He yanked a length of trim from Tyler's hand and crouched on the floor.

While Joe showed the correct technique to Tyler, a flood of negative putdowns poured from his mouth, and soon Ben and Ethan abandoned their work and wandered off, no doubt escaping the tension in the room.

Mina, who'd sighted another fly, swung, and missed. She squeezed the flyswatter handle and stood stock still, waiting until she spotted the little beast.

Finally, he landed on the wall above Joe's head. She crept closer.

"You think you can handle it?" Joe said, climbing to his feet. The heel of his boot caught on Tyler's toe and he stumbled a step before righting himself.

"I got it," Tyler muttered.

"You sure about that?" Joe said. "Because I think you might be too stupid to do this, too."

Whack!

With a curse, Joe twisted around. He glared at her and rubbed the spot on his arm where she'd struck him. "What the hell was that for?"

"That was for being a jerk to Tyler. Now can you please be quiet for, like, two minutes? You're giving us all a headache."

Joe opened his mouth.

She raised the flyswatter, and his jaw snapped shut.

Her arm relaxed.

"But he—"

She cut him off. "I saw him try to trip you." She turned to Tyler. "Do not encourage him. Please."

Fighting a smile, Tyler ducked his head. "Yes, ma'am."

With a sulky frown on his face, Joe kicked Tyler's foot. "Asshole."

Whack!

He gaped at her in disbelief. "What was that for?"

"I said two minutes. No talking."

The fly buzzed by her, and she chased the pest into the hall.

Beneath the archway into the dining, Ethan and Ben stood with wide grins on both their faces.

Ben offered her a mock salute. "Best two minutes of the whole day."

"Remind me not to piss you off." Ethan tipped his chin at the flyswatter in her hand. "You're lethal with that thing."

A small smile touched her lips before she chewed it away. Amused, but also bewildered, she twirled the flyswatter between her fingers and resumed her hunt. Is that what Sam had meant when he told her to let them know who's in charge? Was a flyswatter all it took?

She studied the flimsy plastic weapon in her hand, pondering its power. It may have helped her today with this weird group of guys, but she didn't see how it could help her with a man like Noah.

She couldn't see how it might help her take control of her own rebellious heart.

As NOAH REACHED for the coffeepot, a yawn racked his body and made his eyes water. Another night spent in Mina's bed had done little to allow him to catch up on sleep. He'd also neglected his work at the university, and when he'd logged in a few minutes earlier, a throng of emails had filled his inbox.

But he had no regrets. Indeed, while a stream of coffee poured from the carafe into the white mug covered with pink lips he'd filched from her kitchen cupboard, the thought struck him that when he was back in Ireland, he'd miss this cramped, girly-girl apartment.

He would have to return to Ireland, eventually.

Coffee mug in hand, he settled with his laptop at the kitchen table and scrolled through the long list of new emails. When he spotted an email from his department chair in Ireland, he clicked on it and read her brief note informing him the Irish consulate had approved his request to perform an excavation in western Ireland. Three other times, he'd applied for this same permit, only to be turned down. He could begin as early as February.

Noah shoved both hands through his hair and reclined in the chair. While he pondered his response, he chewed the side of his thumb.

Eventually, Mina would decide she'd finished with him, or the situation with his brothers would finally implode. One thing he knew for certain—he would need to depart the island in the not too decent future.

When the time came, he would be ready to leave.

He leaned forward and typed a quick reply.

Just as he hit Send, her bedroom door opened, and a disheveled, half-clothed sexpot appeared. In nothing but an oversized T-shirt, she padded across the room.

As she approached, he peered closely into her face, searching for clues about her mental state. Dark shadows bruised the hollows under her eyes and the blueberry-colored irises shimmered with worry. The long hours were catching up with her, too.

That, or she'd come to her senses about him.

"How did you sleep?" he asked.

"Terrible," she said, even as a coy smile touched her lips. "I had an insomniac sex fiend in my bed."

His feet carried him to her. "Sorry about that." He slipped his hands around her waist, then lower, seeking warm skin.

She sagged against him. "I forgive you."

His fingertips found the hem of her sleep shirt and slipped beneath. And just like that, his train of thought derailed. "You're not wearing any underwear."

"I thought you'd already left."

His hands circled round to smooth over her bare behind. "Do me a favor—never put *on* underwear for my benefit." He drew her snug against his body and backed her toward the sofa.

She tumbled over the armrest, and he followed her down, covering her with his body even as he worked to rid her of the scanty sleep shirt. She was bared to him in an instant.

He rose on his knees and parted her thighs. Hunger threatened to overtake him, intensified by the fact she'd told him she was on the pill and he'd only just gotten his first full feel of her.

He pressed his palm to the soft swell of her stomach. Huge doe eyes, guarded and uncertain, grabbed at his insides.

He watched her fight through her shyness, and then she offered her breasts to him. With a tremor in his fingers, he cupped her. His mouth followed the path forged by his hand, over the dips and valleys of her body.

He nestled between her thighs and licked inside her.

Lost in her scent and sounds, the outside world faded away. So it took a moment for the distant noise to penetrate his sex-crazed skull.

He lifted his head. "Did you hear that?"

"Wh-what?" Her gasp held the agony of suspended grati-fication.

He cocked his head.

A series of sharp knocks reverberated through the carriage house.

Someone was at the door. Noah dropped his head to rest on Mina's stomach.

Muted through the door, a woman's voice called out. "Mina, are you in there?"

"Oh. My. God." Her face drained of color. "It's my mother."

She squirmed out from under him and rolled to the floor in front of the couch. After a brief pause, she lurched to her feet, stumbled over a jumble of throw pillows, and dashed to the bedroom.

Noah pushed slowly to his feet.

He entered the bedroom as Mina stepped into a pair of jeans. Sans underwear.

She cast aside the sleep shirt and, arms crossed in front of her breasts, stalked the room until she found a bra. "You have to leave. Now."

"I don't think that's an option."

Another knock sounded at the door, and Mina jumped. "It's my *mom*. I'm-I'm-I'm naked. And you're—" Her eyes raked over his half-clothed body. "Oh, God." She fumbled with the fastenings of the bra.

He pulled a T-shirt over his head and pushed his arms through the sleeves. He double-checked the zipper on his jeans and headed toward the bedroom door. "Get dressed. I'll handle your mom."

"No!" The panic in her voice reached a level of shrillness only dogs could pick up.

"Mina, I can't leave without her seeing me."

"Then... stay in here. I'll get rid of her."

"You're half-dressed and she's about to beat down the front door."

She gaped at him, her mouth opening and closing without a sound.

"Hyperventilating won't help." He pulled open the door. "Come out when you're ready."

"Wait!"

Noah waited, but she only stared up at him with panic-filled eyes.

Cold slithered up his spine as the truth crept over him. She was still too ashamed to let the world know she was in a relationship with Noah Nolan.

"Why?" He regretted the snap in his tone. "What are you waiting for, Mina?"

Her big blue eyes darted frantically around the room, as though searching for an escape route. "I…I…um…"

"Are you embarrassed by me?"

With a blink of shock, her panic evaporated. "What? No. Never. Not even a little. It's just—"

She startled when her mother pounded on the door.

Undeterred, he remained planted in the bedroom doorway. "It's just what?"

"It's her." Mina's voice wavered over the words. "I'm embarrassed by *her*."

His anger dissipated like dew beneath a dawning sun. The tightness in his chest eased.

"She's…" Mina licked her lips. "She's…pretty intense."

"Intense how?"

"Well… she's… small."

A frown tugged at his features with his confusion.

"And fussy."

He let loose with a cocky smile. "Small, fussy women are my specialty."

The panic had stolen into her eyes again, so crossed to her and dropped a kiss on her forehead. "We got this." He turned toward the door.

"No!" She lunged and grabbed his arm. "Don't go out there. Maybe she'll go away."

Another muffled plea from her mother sounded through the walls. "Honestly, Wilhelmina, I can hear you. Open the door."

His head snapped around, and he slowly lifted one eyebrow. "Wilhelmina?"

"Shut up." With a soft shove, she flung his arm away.

He ate his smile as he strode toward the door. "Come out when you're ready."

He pulled the bedroom door shut behind him and crossed the small living space.

Amidst another series of thundering knocks, he swung open the front door.

And came face-to-face with Mina's mother.

CHAPTER 22

She was small, that much was true, attaining a scrap above five feet and with dark hair cut in a trendy, chin-length style that swung elegantly about her angelic face. She wore the cold-weather uniform of the posh and beautiful —fur and supple leather, with enough large pieces of jewelry to showcase her wealth.

She regarded him with cold eyes. One expertly arched eyebrow lifted as she took in his unkempt hair and bare feet. "Where is my daughter?"

Noah fixed a smile on his face. "Mina is on her way out. I wanted to introduce myself." He held out a hand to her. "Hi, I'm Noah. I've been working with Mina on a project."

She eyed his hand as if inspecting for germs. "I heard about you."

Noah balled his hand into a fist and slipped it into his pocket. "Good things, I hope."

Her tiny chin lifted. "Sorry to disappoint."

His smile turned rueful. That was his cue to leave. He sidled closer to the counter and reached for his wallet and keys.

Behind him, the bedroom door opened, and Noah turned as Mina appeared.

Not Mina, exactly, but the prim princess who'd shown up at Shea's house with his signed contract.

She'd pinned back her auburn hair and strung a pearl necklace around her slim neck, though her hot little body made blue jeans and a buttoned-up cardigan appear scandalously provocative.

Then he took one look at the pained, panicked expression on her face and knew he couldn't leave. Not yet.

He dropped into a chair at the table and settled in to take advantage of the opportunity to be near her, and to observe. His two favorite things.

"Look who's here." His tone dripped with mock delight.

"Tell me it's not true." The small, fussy woman lifted a hand to her throat. "Are you"—she gulped—"a waitress?"

"It's true." Mina's smile was tight.

"She's not half-bad, either." Noah gave Mina a reassuring nod.

In return, she flung him a dark scowl. "Mom, this is Noah. Noah, my mom, Vivian."

Noah gestured with his hand. "Oh, we're well acquainted."

Vivian's gaze could freeze Lake Michigan in July. "Drew told me all about the archaeologist sniffing around my daughter's door."

"Did he?" Noah bared his teeth. "That Drew is a real stand-up bloke, isn't he?"

That elicited a genuine smile from Vivian. "Yes, he is." She aimed a stern frown at her daughter. "You need to patch things up with him before it's too late."

"I don't want to patch things up." Mina sidestepped Vivian, who hefted a grocery bag off the floor at her feet and plunked the heavy load onto the counter.

"Don't be ridiculous," Vivian said. "It's not like you have

any better prospects." Catlike hazel-green eyes full of suspicion alighted on Noah.

A sound of exasperation emanated from Mina's direction. "Mom, what are you doing here?"

"I texted you last night and told you I'd be by today for lunch." Stiletto heels clicked over wood as Vivian moved into the kitchen.

"My phone battery must've died," Mina mumbled, shooting Noah a guilt-ridden look.

"I brought salad." Vivian pulled a wedge of cheese and a large ripe tomato from the bag. Her critical gaze swept over Mina. "Light, frequent meals will do wonders for you."

Mina arranged her features into a placid expression, though there was no concealing the heat that burned her cheeks. "You came back from Florida to bring me a salad?"

"I was tired of waiting for you to call me."

"Um...what were you waiting to hear?"

"Drew called me two weeks ago." Vivian sliced open the bag of lettuce with a manicured fingernail. "I expected a call, a text, *something* from you."

"Drew called you?" Annoyed disbelief filled Mina's voice. "Why in the world is he calling you at all?"

Her mother shrugged. "We talk almost every day. He's practically my son-in-law."

"No, he's not." Mina laid her palms on the kitchen counter and pinned Vivian beneath her hard stare. "Mom, he's my ex. We're not getting married."

One of Vivian's delicate hands swept aside Mina's words. "You're missing the point."

"Which is?"

Vivian withdrew a knife from the drawer and sliced into a red onion. "Drew's wedding. There's still time if we act quickly."

A heavy beat of silence hung over the room before Mina finally spoke. "Drew's getting married?"

Without pausing in her attack on the onion, Vivian snuck a glance at Mina. "I thought you might not know. No need to worry. Yet. This girl he's picked is all wrong for him."

Big blue eyes darted to him, then away. "Maybe we can talk about this later?"

Vivian's gaze followed Mina's.

Settling deeper into the chair, Noah smiled. "Don't mind me. Pretend I'm not even here."

"Done," Vivian chirped.

"*Mom.*"

Vivian blinked innocently at Mina. "What?"

"Be nice, please."

"I'm always nice."

The snort that escaped Mina elicited a frown from her mother.

"Do you want my help or not?" Vivian asked.

"Definitely not," Mina said.

"You don't mean that." Vivian's nose wrinkled as if she'd swallowed a bug. "She's a Howard. I think her name is Francine. Drew gains nothing from the match. She's not very attractive, the poor girl, and she's downright heavy." Vivian executed a flourish with the knife. "She's even heavier than you."

Mina took the verbal blow without flinching. Indeed, she gave no sign that she registered the assault. Which told him she'd grown accustomed to such put-downs long ago.

His jaw clenched too tightly to allow him to speak.

Mina traced little lines into the kitchen countertops. "Mom, there's something I need to tell you. Drew cheated on me, and the woman is not his fiancée now."

"I know he did." Vivian opened a cupboard and closed it without selecting anything.

"You know?" Mina gaped at her mother. "Then why are you pushing me to get back together with him?"

"Because you two make sense." Vivian opened another cupboard and withdrew a glass mixing bowl. "Honestly, how long are you going to punish him for his mistakes?"

Noah's gut gave a nauseating wrench.

"Oh, geez, let me see…," Mina said with a bite of sarcasm. "I was thinking, like, forever."

"You have to understand something about Drew." Vivian dumped the bag of lettuce into the mixing bowl. "Jeremy's death hit him hard. He struggles with it still."

The color leached from Mina's face with such swiftness, Noah straightened in his chair.

Clueless to her daughter's upset, Vivian continued, "It's true he made a mistake with you, but he's not a bad guy. He's hurting."

Shadows chased the enchanting animation from Mina's face. "Jeremy's been dead more than a decade."

"You never get over something like that." Vivian tilted her head to one side, studying Mina, then reached out and touched her daughter's chin. "You need to stop holding these grudges, dear. Bitterness ages you."

Mina jerked her chin away.

After that, lunch preparations resumed in silence. That was, until Vivian sniped at Mina about her cheap knives and cramped, odd living quarters.

While Mina finished preparing the salad, Vivian prepped the chicken Noah knew Mina wouldn't eat while educating Mina that the lack of animal protein in her diet depleted her energy reserves, which caused her to overindulge in carbs and prevented her from losing the weight.

Noah wanted to stab out his right eye rather than listen to another word of wisdom from Vivian.

His temper, which had ignited as a tiny spark at the first

lash of Vivian's sharp tongue, grew to a quiet burn as the warm, witty woman he'd been sharing a bed with for the last week vanished before his eyes.

Replaced by someone he didn't recognize.

Noah tried to capture Mina's attention, to shoot her an encouraging smile or a knowing, conspiratorial eye roll, hoping to lighten her mood, but he never connected, and Mina continued to withdraw by degrees. The more Vivian quibbled, the more Mina retreated into herself.

By the time the chicken was cooked, Mina was distant and uncommunicative.

Vivian cut into a wedge of cheese. "Has Audrey's daughter left town?"

"Yes. She only stayed for a few days." Mina pulled a small stack of plates from the cupboard. "She said she might be back soon."

"Did she say how her mother is doing? I haven't heard a peep from Audrey in years."

Noah might've pointed out bitterness had aged Vivian as well, but he decided staying silent was the best course of action.

Arms suspended in midair, Mina froze a moment. Then she continued in her movements and withdrew three glasses.

Several seconds ticked by before she managed a response. "Mom, Audrey died."

The only sound was the soft clip of the knife as it sliced through cheese and struck the butcher-block cutting board.

"How?" Vivian asked.

"Cancer."

A neat pile of thinly cut slices materialized. "When?"

"A couple of months ago."

Vivian meticulously transferred the cheese slices to a platter and added an assortment of crackers and fruit to the arrangement. She tinkered with the hors d'oeuvre a moment before she carried the platter to the table and set it calmly down. Then, with a flash of movement, she plucked her purse off the counter and careened toward the front door.

"Mom...?" Mina took a step forward and then stopped.

The wood-framed chair creaked under Noah's weight as he stood, but Vivian passed through the door and traveled halfway down the porch stairs before he could pull it open for her.

Mina stood immobile, as if caught in a web. Then she was in motion.

She plucked the salad and glasses off the table and dumped everything on the kitchen counter with careless regard. Noah collected their plates, but before he could deliver them to the kitchen, she breezed past him in retreat to the bedroom.

He found her sitting at the end of her bed, bent over to lace up her sneakers. Her hair hung in unruly waves about her shoulders, and she wore one of her men's dress shirts.

"I warned you," she said without looking up.

"You were right. Your mother is small."

She flashed him that damn fake smile. The one hiding a wounded heart. Then she risked eye contact, but her nerve quickly deserted her and her gaze slid away.

She surged to her feet. "I'm behind schedule. I need to spend the day working on the house."

At the doorway, she tried to push past him, but he held his ground. "Was it hard growing up without your dad?"

A small shrug lifted her shoulders. "I lived in a mansion—two mansions—and went to the best schools. I was given everything I could want. What's not to like?"

That was what he'd always thought. He'd seen the money and the prestige and made assumptions, but now he wondered about the reality of life inside those mansion walls.

"Does she always talk to you like that?"

Pink stained her cheeks. "I've learned to ignore her."

Disappointment slashed through him. She fought so hard not to share her inner world with him. With anyone, he suspected. He tried to tell himself he understood. He wasn't exactly an open book.

But he couldn't let it go. "Some of that stuff is hard to ignore."

When she lifted her gaze to his, the sad, quiet defiance in her eyes tore at him. "I know what I am. Her saying it doesn't change anything."

The pounding in his chest reached his skull. "What the hell does that mean?"

A weary sigh shuddered through her. "Nothing. It means nothing." She pushed past him.

He touched her elbow.

She whirled on him. "I'm know she's not perfect, but she's my mom. She was twenty-five years old when my dad died. She had a five-year-old, no job, and no place to live. I can't imagine what it was like for her."

He tried to swallow, but his throat wouldn't work.

"I don't blame her." All the emotion seemed to drain from her at once. "I just wish things had been different."

He'd always thought their lives were so different. She, the daughter of wealth and privilege. He, the son of misfortune. But they were both children of dysfunction, and while he'd turned rebellious and defiant, she endeavored to appease, and to please.

She was so much stronger than he was.

With a soft tug, she freed her arm from his grip. "I have a ton of work to do and don't know when I'll finish up for the day. I understand if you don't want to wait around."

Her words slashed at him. "Are you telling me to leave?"

He didn't want to leave. Not now. Not yet. He wanted to

stay and banish the haunted shadows from her face. Her happiness mattered to him. A lot. Which sucked, because that meant he was vulnerable. The one thing he didn't want to be.

The spot in the center of his chest ached, and he rubbed at it.

From the doorway, her cool expression didn't quite mask the panic in her eyes. "Do whatever you want. No pressure, remember?"

With that, she disappeared through the carriage house door.

CHAPTER 23

$\mathcal{M}$ina entered the house through the back door to a trail of muddy footprints stalking across her newly refinished, pristine hardwood floors.

With a defeated sigh, she snagged a bucket off the back stoop and retraced her steps across the lawn.

The mess inside her house might as well have been a metaphor for her love life.

Correction: her *sex* life. It was supposed to by just sex between her and Noah. That's what they'd agreed to.

So why was she constantly scrubbing her thoughts of him and wiping away the soft, fluttery feelings from her heart?

At the spigot that tapped into the carriage house's water source, she filled the bucket. As she lugged the pail back to the house, the contents sloshed while her breathing grew labored from exertion.

She struggled to maneuver the door with her heavy load. When her grip on the handle slipped, the bucket landed with a hard bang and cold water slopped over the rim to soak her sneaker.

With her hip, she propped the door open and stretched to drag the sloshing container closer.

"Need some help with that?" a male voice asked.

Ass in the air, Mina bolted upright. "Oh, hey, Tyler. I think I got it now."

He bit into an apple and held the door while she wrestled the bucket over the doorjamb.

"What's that for?"

Hands on her knees, Mina wheezed for air. "Just getting some water so I can clean up the mud."

"Why don't you just use the faucet?"

She straightened. "What?"

He crossed to the sink in the mudroom and cranked the nozzle. Water—glorious water—streamed from the tap.

A choked sob wrenched from Mina, and her hands flew to her mouth. "But when—? How—?"

"The well guys were here yesterday." He crunched on another bite of apple.

She'd worked a double shift at the pub and, apparently, missed the well installation. "But there's an injunction."

He waved the apple in front of her face. "That professor guy said it was okay."

"Noah? He didn't say anything to me."

"Yeah, that's him. I overheard him talking to Eddie about it."

Unease rippled through her like the still-trembling water at her feet. "When did they talk?"

"Uh, a couple of weeks ago. I think."

"Noah talked to Eddie two weeks ago? While Sam was on vacation?"

Tyler scratched his chin. "Yeah, I think he was, actually."

Noah had lifted the injunction.

Right after he'd fucked her on her front porch.

Icy dread snaked its way through her veins. Why hadn't he told her? Was it her reward for sleeping with him? Or had he been punishing her for not doing so all along?

With a mental shake, she discarded the thought. No, it wasn't like that. Noah wasn't manipulative, and he wasn't malicious.

She was being paranoid. The quality of her thinking often plummeted after a visit with her mother.

She set to work wiping up the now-caked-on footprints. Soon she discovered they tracked through the entire house and she followed their path, scouring and scrubbing until her muscles grew stiff and exhaustion pulled at her.

Though every cell in her body cried out for a reprieve, she kept cleaning, even after the crew packed up and headed home. With a feverish pace, she removed layers of drywall dust and dirt that'd been building up for months, as though she might clear away the debris Hurricane Vivian had whipped up inside her.

Outside, the sun slipped into the lake and cloaked the landscape in darkness, and shortly after, Noah appeared.

He didn't press her to talk or call her out for snapping at him and then running away, but simply picked up a cloth rag and silently worked alongside her.

It wasn't the first time he'd helped her by doing work on the house. After long days on campus and digging in her back yard, he often spent another hour or more inside the house doing little things to move her closer to her goal.

He was a hard worker and a good friend.

Or a ruthless career man manipulating her to some ambiguous, but no doubt wicked, end.

The thought came unbidden. It was ridiculous, of course, and ultimately irrelevant. They were both getting what they wanted from each other—a smooth-running, timely excavation...and sex.

He dunked the dirty rag he was using into the bucket. "They lifted the injunction on your well installation."

"They just told me." She scrubbed hard on a brand new, crystal clear window the crew had installed the previous day. "It happened a couple of weeks ago…?"

"You were at work when the paperwork came through," he said, wringing water from the towel. "But I let your contractor know right away."

With each swipe of her cloth towel across the glass, short, high-pitched squeaks punctured the air.

"I'm sorry I forgot to tell you," he said. "That was the day I came back from the conference and a gorgeous woman distracted me."

The rapid fluttering of her heart whipped heat into her cheeks. "Things have been hectic lately."

"Still, I should've remembered to tell you. I know how important it is to you." The gravity in his tone drew her gaze to him. "I'm sorry."

The apology wrenched a pang from her chest and the shame spiraling through her coiled tighter. She'd been wrong to doubt him. He was too honorable a man to play games with her livelihood. She'd been right the other night when she'd told him he was a good man.

A good man, who was only interested in her for sex, she quickly reminded herself. She flung her rag into the bucket and squeezed the excess water from it with several ferocious twists.

He was using her.

She was using *him*.

They were using each other.

Her heart had no place in their relationship.

She fled upstairs, as though putting some distance between her heart and its obsession might make even one iota of difference, and holed up in the bedroom she'd been using to store the few antique furniture pieces she'd inherited from Rose.

There, she approached one of the room's two oversized, arched windows and picked at the manufacturer's label, still stuck to the paned glass. When she peeled the corner, the sticker ripped, so she retrieved a razor and a wet rag to scrap off the adhesive.

Engrossed in her task, she didn't realize he stood in the doorway until she caught sight of his reflection in the window.

He leaned with one shoulder against the doorframe, watching her. At his silent inventory, a chill chased through her, for in that moment, she spotted no heat or lustful yearning in his expression, but only a cool, keen assessment, and the knowledge that he was very dangerous stole over her.

She picked at the sticker with her fingernail. "I can't understand why they use so much glue on these things." Her voice sounded strained. "It's going to take forever to get them off."

"You've been at it a long time." His casual tone belied the intense perusal he'd been giving her. "Can I make you some dinner?"

"I just want to finish up in here if I can."

He pushed off the doorframe and moved into the room.

She renewed her attack on the stickers.

Slowly, he picked his way between the pieces of furniture and came to stand behind her.

In the window's reflection, his dark eyes appeared as smudgy pools of liquid. "Are you okay?"

"I'm fine."

"Does it upset you so much? Hearing about Drew's engagement?"

She snuck a quick glance at him and caught the worried frown that marred his beautiful face.

That face. She used to dream of it often. When she was young and foolish, and again, when she'd agreed to marry Drew.

Like an unwelcome phantom, he'd returned to haunt her at the exact moment she'd determined to move on with her life.

Even before now, his ghost had hounded her, appearing at the most inconvenient times. Such as when Drew kissed her, and she'd close her eyes and pretend he was Noah. Or when Drew touched her, and she'd imagined it was Noah's hands on her body.

Guilt and shame had tormented her, and the old horror returned now, crashing over her and sending her back to the darkest days of their relationship, when she'd thought she might die with the loneliness of it all.

Before she'd learned to close off her heart.

She swung her gaze back to the stubborn sticker. "I feel sorry for his fiancée. The last thing Drew Alexander wants is a wife."

"It'd make your mom happy if you went back to him."

"My mom? Happy?" A bitter laugh stuck in her throat. "Nothing I do will make her happy. Not really. But it doesn't matter what she wants. I don't want Drew. I never did. All I wanted was someone to... someone who...." Tiny pieces of herself cracked, crumbled, and her whole body shook with the effort to keep from falling apart. "Someone who'd make me forget about you."

A ripple of shock disturbed his features. "You mean...?"

"Drew never made me happy." Her cheeks warmed, and she wiped her forehead with the back of her hand. "In two years, we never laughed together. We never did anything silly or fun." The bitter laugh broke from her then. "My god, I never had an orgasm with him. And I thought that was my fault."

Now she knew better. She'd done all those things with Noah, though their affair was still new.

"You went without for two years?" he asked.

Heat burned across her face and neck. "I didn't go without. Not…exactly."

His dark eyebrows lifted. "You were with other men?"

"I…" Her skin was on fire. "I learned to take care of myself. While Drew found his pleasure with other women, I found mine alone. While thinking of you."

The confession fell from her lips and seemed to turn him to stone. He stared at her, frozen and mute.

"I was supposed to be in love with another man." Her own reflection through the glass harried her, and she had to turn her face away. "But all I could think about was you. Being with you. Which makes me just as bad as Drew, doesn't it?"

Behind her, his shoes softly scuffed the wood floors as he drew closer, close enough that she could feel the warmth from his body.

"Mina." The rasp in his voice abraded down her spine. "Look at me."

Shame stole her courage, so she lifted her gaze to his mirror image.

Naked hunger blazed in his dark eyes. The intense heat seared through her, and with the slow lick of her arousal, her breath snagged.

He laid a hand on her shoulder and used his fingers to draw her hair away from her neck, then drag down the collar of her T-shirt. His warm mouth seared her bare skin at the spot where her shoulder and neck met.

Her stomach clenched tight with tenderness and need.

His eyes found hers in the window. "If I brought you any amount of pleasure, I'm glad."

"It wasn't just the pleasure," she whispered.

His mouth brushed next to her ear. "What was it then?"

The old anguish lashed. "Thinking of you...remembering... You made me feel less alone."

He plucked the rag and razor from her grasp and tossed them aside, then he laced his fingers through hers.

"I'm here now." He pressed their clasped hands against the window on either side of their reflection and leaned so that the length of his body cradled hers. "And I want you too. Mina, please say I can have you."

Gazing at him through the window's reflection, she could almost believe she'd stepped into one of her daydreams. The one where he'd never left, and she hadn't spent half her life longing for a man she could never have.

In this dream, the hope inside her heart didn't flit and flutter in defiance of all rationality, but only did exactly what it was meant to do—beat for Noah Nolan.

Words jammed in her throat, so she nodded, then twisted toward him.

But as she moved, his body tensed, blocking her from turning around.

He nibbled a path down the side of her neck, and she tilted her head to ease his sensual journey.

With her hand still entwined in his, he reached between her body and the window, and popped the button on her jeans. Slowly, he dragged down the zipper.

He returned her hand to the windowpane and spread her fingers wide as he disentangled his grip so that her palm lay flat against the glass. Then he released her other hand in the same way and, with her hands anchored to the window, he tugged her jeans over her hips, sweeping her underwear down along with them.

When she was exposed, his calloused palms smoothed over her bare bottom. Fire licked low in her belly in anticipation of his touch.

His warm, work-roughened skin burned a path across her backside, over her waist and hips, to the softly curved swell of her lower abdomen. He slid his blue jean-clad leg between her naked thighs and gently nudged until she stood with her feet shoulder-width apart.

Heat pooled between her thighs.

At her back, he gathered a fistful of her T-shirt and twisted it until the fabric pulled high and tight over her breasts, baring the plane of her stomach and the soft fuzz between her parted legs.

In the window, his dark molasses eyes feasted on her body.

Her heart quit.

The column of his throat worked when he swallowed hard. "You are so beautiful."

She swallowed a startled laugh. No one had ever called her beautiful. "You don't have to say that."

"I know." From behind, the feather-light stroke of his fingers brushed along her slit. "I would never lie to you about something like that."

Her sharp hiss of breath rolled into a deep moan as sweet sensation spiraled through her body.

"You are beautiful." His voice rasped in her ear while he rubbed in tight, tiny circles. "And so fucking hot."

Never before. Only with him.

Her body yielded to his touch, giving him all of her. With one hand, he caressed her from behind while with the other, he pushed through her damp curls to tease her swollen sex. Her moans morphed into desperate whimpers and her legs trembled.

When he withdrew his touch, she protested, but a whoosh of air ruffled her hair when he whipped off his T-shirt and his knuckles grazed her backside as he fumbled with his fly, then his hot skin and rigid erection pressed against her.

She rose on her tiptoes and arched her back as he skimmed both his hands up her body, dragging her T-shirt off over her head. Before her bra hit the floor, he'd slid inside her with one prolonged, silky stroke.

Buried deep, a groan vibrated in his chest, and he dropped his forehead to her shoulder.

For many long moments, he didn't move.

Then he clamped his arm tight around her waist and pumped his hips. He pushed deep, then pulled all the way back to the edge of her entrance. Again, he plunged and retreated, then again.

Her body swallowed every inch of him, but even with his thick shaft stretching her wide, she ached for him. He filled her heart and the delicious pain of it all squeezed the back of her throat. She let her head fall forward.

"Don't you dare close your eyes, *mo chroí*." He tangled his fingers in her hair and tugged gently, lifting her face to the glass. "Look how beautiful you are when I fuck you."

With the words, her core clenched. Helpless to the aching need, she obeyed his command and peered into the window at their reflection.

His large hands gripped her hips, and his eyes as he watched her burned with a dark intensity that stoked the fire between her legs. Her cheeks flushed pink and her tousled hair fell across her forehead as he rocked into her. With every thrust of his hard length, her breasts swayed, and her hands pushed flat against the glass.

The desire that'd been building inside her suddenly

expanded, filling the space between every breath, every heartbeat. Sweet relief was upon her.

But just as the cry of ecstasy piled in her throat, he pulled out. A broken sob tore from her, and she twisted around.

He cupped her face in both his hands and soothed her with soft, slow, drugging kisses. When she'd calmed, he took her hand in his and led her through the maze of boxes and furniture to the far side of the room, where she'd propped a bed against the wall.

He kicked boxes out of the way with his foot, then pulled the mattress down onto the floor and guided her to it.

She eased onto her back and he moved over her, suckling one of her pebbled nipples into the wet heat of his mouth.

Sensations pelted her. His body was heavy on top of hers and his warm skin against hers fired every one of her sensitive nerve endings even as his hot mouth burned a trail across her breasts to the side of her neck.

Near her ear, he whispered her name.

He lifted his head, and intense dark eyes bore into hers. "Mina, I need you to do something for me."

In that moment, she'd have given him the world if he'd asked her for it.

Raising up, she stole a taste from the corner of his mouth. "Okay."

"I need you to show me." Emotion shredded his voice.

But she didn't understand his words, so she gave her head a small shake.

"When you would think of me..." Capturing one of her hands in his, he brought it between their bodies. "I need you to show me."

Heat rushed to the surface of her skin, and she snatched her hand back. "Wh-what?"

With gentle tenderness, he reclaimed her hand. He

scraped the pad of his thumb across her palm and slowly pushed open her curled fingers, then delivered a soft kiss to each tip. His mouth brushed the heart of her palm and the throbbing pulse point on the inside of her wrist.

Then he guided her hand lower.

When he lifted his body off her and sat back on his haunches, his rigid shaft pressed against the flat plane of his stomach. "Show me how you touched yourself."

Her heart stuttered.

"Please." His soft plea held a desperate ring that stirred some buried part of her. "I have to know."

Their fingers grazed the puckered peaks of her hypersensitive nipples and the soft skin of her near her naval, then pushed into her springy curls.

Together, they stroked.

The first light flicks of their fingers reawakened her arousal. Her heart banging against her breastbone, she closed her eyes and gave herself over to the moment. To the possibility that she might please him in a way no one ever had.

The moan that filled her throat fractured when his hand fell away.

She managed only a few tingling lashes on her own before her eyes flew open.

He'd eased back to sit at the end of the mattress, and his heated gaze had locked on the juncture of her thighs.

When she teased her swollen lips, his cock jumped. When she pushed one finger into her honeyed slickness, his breathing changed.

Addicted to the control she had over his reaction, she swiveled her hips beneath her hand. His tongue slipped out to lick his bottom lip.

Her touch, along with his rapt attention, fed her hunger and her knees fell farther apart. Sensation rippled from her core outward to the ends of her limbs and her eyes fluttered shut.

Noah's fingers clamped around her ankle, as if to keep her from floating away. His thumb circled her anklebone with feverish swirls.

Still, he watched her hand.

Her stomach muscles clenched, and her head came up off the mattress. "Noah."

In a flash of movement, he pushed her hand away and covered her body with his. She clamped her legs around his lean waist as he gripped the edge of the mattress above her head and thrust into her.

With him buried deep, finally, she couldn't escape the feeling that he'd reached inside her and touched some secret, sacred place. A place that only the two of them belonged.

While he fucked her, a lock of his dark hair fell across his forehead and the St. Nicholas pendant he wore danced and swayed before her eyes.

Once, a long time ago, she'd asked him about the necklace, and he'd told her his mother had given it to him before she'd died, explaining that St. Nicholas, the patron saint of children, would protect him in her absence.

At the memory, Mina's heart constricted. She clung to him as years of loneliness and regret burned away.

She'd never experienced sex like this. She'd known awkward and ugly, and the sex that left her feeling lost and lonely. With Noah, it was intense and lusty, but also gentle. And so tender.

It was soul-searing.

She squeezed her eyes shut and clenched her jaw to quell the sob rising in her throat.

"Fuck me." His gruff command delivered a lick of fire to her core. "Not because you're scared or sad or lonely, but because you want me."

Her sob broke free. He was trying to steal her soul, and she was helpless to stop him.

"Noah…" She tried to close her heart to him, but he took it anyhow. "Please…"

"Tell me what you want."

"You." She gasped when the first ripples of her climax unfurled. "Only you. I love you."

He tensed above her.

She *loved* him.

Fear shot through her, but the orgasm gripped her, and she lifted her hips to take him deeper.

On a groan, he plunged.

She'd thought she loved him back in high school, but truly, she hadn't known him then. She hadn't known he slept little, or that he chewed the side of his thumb when his mind worked on a problem. She hadn't known he drank milk by the gallon, or that he sought the love of his family with a desperate urgency that broke her heart.

She loved *him*.

"I still don't want anything from you," she whispered in his ear.

He pushed to his knees. With both hands, he pressed her thighs wider. Unrelenting, his hips pumped. The color rose high on his cheeks and his dark eyes blazed when he peered down into her face.

"Say it again," he demanded in a low voice.

She gasped when he grew bigger, harder inside her.

"I love you, Noah."

With a harsh cry and one last savage thrust, he shuddered and emptied himself inside her.

As the last voluptuous waves of pleasure faded away, a tight dread settled over Mina.

She'd told him she loved him.

With the silly, foolish confession, she'd not only broken

their rules, but he knew she had. Would he be angry? Would he laugh at her?

Worse than the fear of what he might do or say was the terror of her own reaction. She was in love with a man she could never keep. Not for long.

What the hell was she going to do now?

CHAPTER 24

She'd sucker-punched him.

The chill night air bit at his skin as he stumbled across the lawn on shaken legs. At his side, Mina remained quiet at his side as they climbed the rickety porch stairs and ducked inside the carriage house. She disappeared into the bedroom.

For once, Noah didn't mind her avoidance. He sank into the sofa cushions.

When the sound of running water came from the shower, he laid his head on the sofa back and stared at the ceiling. His thoughts careened out of control.

She loved him?

There was no way. She couldn't have meant it.

Could she?

No, of course not. It was the heat of the moment that'd brought the words to her lips. The passion.

They kept doing that—getting consumed by the flames of their fiery lovemaking. They were hot together. He couldn't deny that.

Love? Was it possible?

No. Definitely not. Not for him.

Not for him. Not with a woman like her.

Still, she'd said the words. She said she loved him. He hadn't been able to say the words back to her. That she hadn't expected him to rankled a bit. Even knowing it couldn't be true, he'd made her repeat the words. He was a bastard for doing it, but he didn't regret it.

No one had said those words to him in so long he'd forgotten how it felt to hear them. His mom was the last to utter them to him, and she'd been dead for over twenty years.

Since then, a few women had gotten it into their heads that they'd loved him, but they didn't count. They couldn't love him. They didn't even know him, and he knew they didn't know him because he'd made damn sure of it.

That wasn't the case with Mina.

But was it love?

He stared with an unfocused gaze at the ceiling.

He wanted her. He wanted to spend time with her. Coax that infectious laugh out of her and talk to her about his work and travels. Bury himself inside her and never pull out.

Most of all, he wanted her. All of her. For as long as possible. But love?

He loved the tiny mole not three fingers' width from the honey-brown fuzz at the juncture of Mina's thighs. He'd discovered the secret mark when he'd kissed her there just that morning.

He loved her smile. The real one.

And when she came... *Oh, God.*

He'd seen the sunrise over Jerusalem, touched the walls of the Hagia Sophia, and smelled the air inside the Sistine Chapel, but none of it compared to Mina in that moment of trust and freedom. She broke his heart.

But the sad fact was, at thirty-four years old, he'd never been in love, nor had he known the love of a good woman.

He released a slow breath from deep in his chest.

What the hell was happening between them?

It was full-on darkness when he woke her sometime later. He moved over her and took her mouth in a soft kiss. He licked the small hollow beneath her damaged ear. She opened for him and he thrust inside her.

He made love to her that way, with an underlying urgency he didn't understand.

He didn't need to understand. At least, that's what he told himself before getting lost in her soft, wet sex.

In three months, he'd be in Ireland, working on his next excavation.

And Mina Winslow would be nothing but a part of his past once more.

THE FOLLOWING FRIDAY NIGHT, a boisterous crowd packed the pub.

Mina checked in on a table of college-aged men who'd ordered several rounds, and one guy wanted to order some food. She leaned close so she could hear him over the loud music, then stretched across the table to retrieve the stack of menus she'd left with the group.

Just as she snagged them, she looked up and caught the guy leering down her blouse.

She jerked upright.

When the guy realized he'd been found out, a slow smirk twisted his ugly mouth.

Clutching the menus to her chest, she hurried away.

At the kitchen window, she put in the order and tried to shake off the sickening churn in the pit of her stomach. It was a bar. These kinds of things happened. Heck, if she worked it, she might even increase her tips.

But the thought repulsed her. She lacked the talent for innocent flirtation, let alone seduction.

Another large group arrived and piled in around a table in Mina's section, and soon she was too busy to spare another thought for the frat boy with the brazen gaze. She filled drink orders and fetched food, squeezing in and around the intermingling customers that packed the pub.

She delivered an overburdened tray of nachos and burgers to the newcomers and refilled their beers from the pitcher she'd brought with her. As she backed away, she tripped over someone's foot and bumped up hard against a big body.

Hands reached out to steady her. Her mind was slow to recognize the nature of the touch. Not chivalrous or courteous. Not the innocent outcome of an overcrowded barroom.

This touch was intimate.

Questing.

And wholly unwanted.

Mina whipped around, holding the tray and pitcher of beer between herself and the groper like a shield.

A part of her mind recognized him as the leering frat boy even before she turned. She may not have been surprised to see him, but the glint in his eyes lifted the hairs on the back of her neck.

His aim was not to flirt or tease. His intent was dark. Cruel.

When his fingers bit into the flesh of her behind, she gasped.

Icy talons clamped around her heart, freezing her from the inside out. Her vocal chords iced over, and a meek "Don't" was all she squeaked out.

When his seeking hand slid between her legs, rough and forceful, terror gripped her. She couldn't move. Couldn't defend against or deflect him. He peered into her face, and a cruel smile curled his lips.

He saw her fear, and he liked it.

Someone jostled him, and he pitched forward, bumping hard into her. She used the moment of chaos to shove the tray at him, and he stumbled back. Then his heel caught on a chair leg.

The scene unfolded as if in slow motion. As he started falling, and he flailed his arms wide in frantic circles, like large windmills blindly grappling for balance.

Horror froze her in place as bodies dodged the area and heads around the room began turning in their direction.

Then Shea appeared to grasp the groper by his shoulders and steady him.

Vivid blue eyes locked on Mina, and Shea jerked his head at her. "My office. Now."

Still struggling to recover from those moments when the past had seemed to repeat itself, she stood cemented to the spot while Shea hauled the groper bodily toward the pub's front entrance.

By slow increments, she became aware of the curious gazes of patrons on her. Had they seen the way he'd touched her? Revulsion ripped through her. She backed away from the crowd, then turned to flee.

On weak legs, she made her way toward Shea's office.

Suddenly, a man bounded out of the men's restroom and crashed into her.

She fell back with enough force to smack into the wall, and a jolt of pain exploded in her shoulder.

"Sorry, darling." Hands gripped her waist.

Her stomach heaved. She stumbled down the hall and burst through the door, slamming it shut behind her and sagging against the solid wood.

The muffled thump of music leaked through the walls.

She understood the shame and revulsion she felt was disproportionate to the incident. The guy was a jerk—a drunken jerk—and he'd copped a feel. So what? It happened every night, in bars in every city. It was not a big deal.

Yet her skin crawled, and her throat clogged with fear and helplessness.

She pushed off the door and sank into a chair at Shea's desk.

Was he going to fire her?

Of course he was. She had just *shoved* a customer.

Rather than panic, an overwhelming surge of relief swept over her with the possibility.

When Shea opened the door, noise from the bar flooded the small office, then quieted again when he swung it shut behind him.

Each one of his heavy footsteps as he crossed to her sent ripples of tension vibrating through her. He collapsed into the chair next to hers and ran a hand over his head. The same way Noah did when he was tense or frustrated.

"I'm sorry," she said.

Fierce blue eyes fixed on her face. "Don't you dare feel sorry."

"I won't make you fire me. I should've quit weeks ago."

He dropped his hand into his lap. "I'm not firing you. I wanted to get you away from that guy and give you a few minutes to yourself." His concern deepened. "You want to quit?"

The palms of her hands grew clammy, and she rubbed them over the denim on her thighs. "I'm a terrible waitress."

A dimple popped out in Shea's left cheek with the smile he tried to hide. "I wouldn't say terrible."

Unbelievably, she laughed. The fact he was so nice only intensified her guilt.

Shea shifted forward in his seat and propped his elbows

on his knees. "If you're worrying about that guy, don't. No one may touch my staff. Ever. He will not be back."

The trembling in her hands eased at that, though the weight of shame pressing on her chest squeezed tighter.

She pointed at the ledger lying open on his desk. "You should use a spreadsheet."

Shea looked at the ledger crammed with handwritten numbers and notes scratched between the lines and in the margins. "Can I have my fingernails yanked out instead?"

They shared a smile.

"We've only got another hour before closing," he said. "You wanna call it a night?"

She did, desperately so, but she pushed to her feet. "No, I'm okay."

"You sure?"

"I'm sure."

"So, you're not quitting?"

She shook her head, but when she opened her mouth, a "Maybe?" slipped out instead.

The lines of worry around Shea's eyes deepened, and his hand swept over his hair once more. Then suddenly, he stilled.

When his head snapped up, his electric-blue eyes gleamed with a bright light. "You don't want to quit, but you don't want to waitress anymore, is that right?"

She frowned, confused by the question. "Yeah..."

"Great." His palms smacked together with a crack of sound. "I have an idea."

CHAPTER 25

*W*inter settled over northern Michigan like a mantle, shrouding the earth in a thin layer of pristine snow that littered the earth with shards of diamonds.

As Noah steered his truck into the gravel parking lot of the little stone church on the southernmost tip of the island, he marveled at the picturesque scene. He'd forgotten so much about this place. But now that his boss had emailed to let him know the project in Ireland was a go, and he knew his time on the island had an end date, he couldn't stop noticing such things.

Snow crunched beneath his work boots as he hustled up the walkway to the double door entrance. Built in the early 1800s, the Catholic church perched atop the hill overlooking the frothy sea and he hoped to keep his visit somewhat short so that he could get back to the carriage house to meet Mina for dinner.

Several weeks had passed since she'd told him she loved him, and there had been little time for him to grapple with the information, as they'd both been working nonstop, giving as many hours as possible to their projects before the harsh, frigid winter weather set in. Some nights they were too exhausted to do anything more than lie in the dark, talking, until they drifted off to sleep.

He enjoyed their routine, and a contentment that'd eluded him all his life was suddenly, simply, present. For so long, he'd been discontent and alone—*lonely*—and he hadn't known why. It'd been a riddle even his overactive mind couldn't solve.

But with Mina, the questions stopped.

Is that why he hadn't told her about his plans to leave?

He needed to tell her. A couple of nights ago, he'd tried to tell her, cutting his class short so he could be sure to catch her before she headed to work at the pub or at the main house. But when he'd arrived at the carriage house, he found her in the kitchen eating a slice of cold pizza, and on the counter, next to the box, was a key sitting on top of a bright yellow Post-It note.

Leaning close, he read the note written in her neat script.

In case you need it.

It was a key to her apartment. A key to her private sanctuary. A key he hadn't asked her for, but she offered nonetheless.

So casual. So simple. So *trusting*.

He'd stared down at her key for many long moments, his heart thundering in his ears, before he picked it up and slipped it into his pocket. His plans to tell her he would soon leave dissolved like that morning's light dusting of snow beneath the sunlight.

Inside the church vestibule, he stomped the snow and slush from his boots, then tread quietly into the nave.

Memories rushed forward to greet him, but he beat them back when he realized he wasn't alone inside the church. In a pew near the front, a man kneeled with his head bent.

Noah wavered a moment, but then walked up the aisle toward the altar. At the occupied pew, he slid in beside his uncle.

John's head remained bowed in prayer, but Noah caught the side-eyed glance his uncle cast his way.

They sat in silence while John finished his prayers. Over the years, they'd spent many hours sitting together in these pews, pondering and praying.

Noah recalled one of those times, a year after he'd arrived on the island. His mom was dead, his dad was in prison, and he and his brothers banished from their home. Near to tears, he'd confessed to his uncle, then the Church's Father, that he feared he'd lost his faith.

Rather than react with anger or worry, John remained calm. "What makes you say so?"

Noah had shrugged his skinny shoulders. "I don't know."

"Try to explain it."

"No, that's it. That's my answer. I don't know."

A soft glow had entered John's eyes, and he'd nodded. "You have questions."

Noah shook his head. "I've asked my questions, but the answers make little sense."

"Anything in particular?"

Angry and defiant, Noah had scowled up at the altar. "Sister Anne said Mom's in Hell because she disassociated with the Church."

"That's a bunch of crap." John had crossed his arms over his black clergy shirt. "What does Sister Anne know about your mother's personal relationship with God? Unless your mother told her. Did your mother tell Sister Anne?"

Again, Noah shook his head. "No."

"No, she didn't, so there's your answer. Don't listen to Sister Anne's opinions about your mom. What else?"

"Well..." Swinging his feet beneath the pew, Noah had

hedged.

"Go ahead," John had nudged. "What else?"

"It's just…every time I ask Sister Anne or one of the other nuns a question, they tell me to stop thinking so much and pray to God that He'll restore my faith."

John's soft chuckle elicited a jolt of surprise from Noah.

"There's more than one way to believe. Sadly, not all who follow Him understand that." Then John had lifted his gaze to the altar, and his expression slowly transformed into something Noah could only have described as love. "To wonder and seek truth is to walk the path of true faith. Without questions, and even doubt, faith becomes a static, lifeless thing. It becomes self-serving. Always doubt, Noah, for doubt is sacred."

It'd become their parting salutation. *"Take care. Always doubt."*

Now, Noah looked at the man he respected above all others. Light lines etched the skin around John's eyes and mouth, but everything about him was relaxed and open. He was a man at peace.

"When did you leave the priesthood?" Noah risked asking.

"Fifteen years ago." The answer came short and quick.

"Do you mind telling me why you did it?"

John's weighty sigh disclosed a heavy heart. "Let's just say I grew disillusioned. I'm down with Jesus, and I consider myself a man of faith, but the Church, the institution of the Church, well, they betrayed my trust."

"That must've been hard for you."

John smiled and leaned back in the pew. "Nah." When he glanced at Noah, his eyes shone. "Someone inspired me."

"Had a religious experience, did ya?"

"Not so much as that, no. Just a punk-ass kid who forced me to have a long, hard think on things."

Noah's sharp bite of laughter echoed through the nave. "A kid, huh? Sounds like a good story."

"A punk-ass kid," John clarified.

"Yeah, I caught that. What'd he do?"

"A lot of noise followed this kid around, and some hard choices were put before him. He could've taken the simple route, done nothing, and let us all go on about our lives. Instead, he did the right thing, but at great personal cost to himself and his family. For no other reason than because it was the right thing to do." John regarded Noah with serious eyes. "He stood up for truth and goodness. The world be damned."

Noah's throat squeezed as his uncle's words rattled him. With the vibrations, his hands shook. First Mina, and now John, would force him to look back and reconsider his actions. It was almost too much to take, but his thoughts had already tumbled down the dangerous path.

For all that'd happened after that fateful day, he *had* paid a price. John was right about that. It'd cost Noah his dad, his home, and eventually, his brothers. But it'd cost him something else, too. Something more.

It'd cost him pieces of himself.

After the bombing and the fallout, something inside him had changed. He'd hardened. He'd no longer cried or showed emotion, and he sure as shit intended never to fall in love with some woman that could rip out his heart and turn him into a weak, cruel man like his dad.

Even now, he was paying back the debts incurred that day, from tense or non-existent relationships with his brothers to the fact he had never loved any of the woman he'd been with.

The memory flickered through his mind of Mina with her head thrown back and those incredible words falling from her lips as her body milked the orgasm from him.

Could it be true what she'd said? Did she really love him?

It seemed impossible that someone as strong and true as Mina could love someone like him, a man whose own father despised him.

That disbelief played a big part in his inability to say the words back to her. What the hell did he know about love? Other than what it felt like to have it ripped away.

With a thick swallow, he forced a reply from his throat. "Yep, sounds like a punk-ass, all right."

"That he was," John said, smiling. "That he was." Then he hoisted his tall frame off the pew bench and pulled a ring of keys from his pocket. "Want me to open the records room? That's why you're here, isn't it?"

Now that he'd finished the excavation work, his research moved indoors, where he hoped to hunt down clues about the person or persons who might've lived on the land of Mina's ancestors. It was probably a long shot, but he wanted to check out the old church tomes in case they might provide a name or nugget of information about the identities of the treasure keepers.

"You know me well," Noah said, standing. Then he followed John up the aisle. "They let you keep the key?"

A mischievous smile turned up the corners of John's mouth. "Father Michael thinks I'm trustworthy." They passed through the vestibule and moved down a short hallway. At one of several closed doors, John stopped, worked the lock, then pushed open the barrier to a small storage space filled with worn, leather-bound books and ledgers. "Enjoy."

With the prickle of adrenaline crackling through his veins, Noah stepped inside the room. In short order, he became lost in stacks of dusty, cracked spine books. As he combed through their yellowed pages, he jotted down notes and questions to follow up on later.

Nothing game-changing revealed itself over the next two

hours, and when dusk settled over the island, he set his pile aside with plans to return and finish his review throughout the coming weeks.

Outside, the wind had kicked up to whip off the lake and lash spiky water pellets at his skin. Ducking his chin, he darted to his truck and fell into the cab. He cranked the engine and turned the heat on full-blast.

While he waited for the fog to clear from the windshield, he fished his cell phone out of his coat pocket to text Mina and let her know he was on his way. But when he turned on the device, he found a voice mail waiting for him and tapped the screen to play the recorded message.

Through the phone's tiny speakers, it was difficult to hear Shea's deep voice over Maisie's cries of distress in the background. Something about Mr. Whiskers and whether the stuffed animal might be in Noah's truck since the day before, Noah had collected Maisie and Connor from daycare and delivered them to Shea at the pub.

Still listening to the garbled recording, Noah twisted his arm around behind the car's seat and cast about the floorboards with one hand.

Bingo.

With a quick stab of the button, he ended the call, then placed Mr. Whiskers in the passenger seat and drove from the church's parking lot, aiming the vehicle toward his dad's old place.

At the house, he entered through the side door and found Shea washing dishes at the kitchen sink.

Seeing Mr. Whiskers in Noah's hand, Shea's broad shoulders relaxed. "You saved my night."

Noah set the toy on the kitchen table and turned to leave.

"Haven't seen you around much lately."

Noah gritted his jaw. "I've been working a lot. Long hours."

Wiping his hands on a dishtowel, Shea twisted away from the sink. "What is it you do exactly?"

"I'm an archaeologist," he said. "And I teach."

At that, Shea's expression brightened. "You're a teacher? What grade?"

"College."

A soft chuckle rumbled in his chest. "Well, that makes sense."

Helpless to the disbelief, Noah's mouth slackened. He was a high school dropout. In what way did it make sense?

"How do you figure?" Noah ground out.

"You're the smartest guy in the room. It makes sense you'd be the one to explain things to the rest of us."

"That is not true."

Shea smiled. "Okay," he said, the word loaded with teasing disregard. Then his features pinched, as if he'd bitten into something sour or felt constipated. "You know…you're, uh, welcome to crash here anytime you want. Especially if the lake ices over in a few weeks and the ferry stops running."

Noah didn't see any reason to lie. "I've been staying at Mina's."

Shea tossed the towel to the countertop and folded his arms across his chest. "I didn't realize you two were that close."

The accusation in Shea's tone rankled. "I didn't realize I needed your permission."

Shea bristled, and Noah thought he might engage, but in the end, he turned away, a disappointed sigh his only reply.

"If you have something to say, just say it," Noah snapped.

Shea twisted back around. He leaned a hip against the counter and placed his palms on the ledge behind him. "She's a good girl."

"And you think I'm not good enough for her?" Noah

knew he wasn't good enough for her, but he wasn't about to admit that to Shea.

"That's not what I was saying." Weariness dragged at Shea's shoulders. "She's been through a lot, and I'd hate for her to get hurt, or humiliated, again. She doesn't deserve it."

A jolt of surprise straightened Noah's spine. "What do you mean, humiliated? Are you talking about her engagement?"

"I only witnessed it from an outsider's perspective." Shea gave his head a shake. "But man, it must've been brutal."

Noah's stomach lurched, and he swallowed with difficulty. "Brutal how?"

Shea crossed one ankle over the other. "A national tabloid set up camp in town for a while. They printed some pretty disgusting stuff."

The niggling, persistent unease that'd been hovering in the back of Noah's mind for weeks suddenly rushed to the forefront. What he'd at first chalked up to her shyness or a lack of good relationships with men, he'd started to think was something else altogether.

It's true she was shy and didn't have a long list of lovers to draw on for experience, but something else seemed to hold her back. Something closer to caution, bordering on fear.

The sex was amazing, hot and heartfelt, but she remained elusive somehow, just out of his reach.

He'd shrugged off his misgivings, telling himself it was understandable, given Drew's infidelity and general stupidity. Not to mention, they were only having an affair. So what if she wanted to hold something of herself back? He wasn't about to fling open the closet door and march out his demons and skeletons, either.

But knowing how her breakup had been fodder for the gossip rags went a long way to explaining her reticence.

"Just…be cool, okay?" Shea said. "I like her."

Noah liked her, too. A lot.

Rather than put his fist through a wall, he pulled his car keys from his pocket and turned toward the door.

"How's she doing, by the way?" Shea asked. "I feel terrible about what happened."

"Don't feel bad." Smug satisfaction curled through Noah. "She's over her idiot ex."

"Not that. I meant what happened at the pub."

Noah stilled with his hand on the doorknob. *What happened at the pub?* He fumbled to recall Mina mentioning anything about work for the past several weeks. Nothing came to his mind.

"I can't believe she thought I would fire her because some creep thought he had the right to put his hands on her."

Hot fury flashed behind Noah's eyes. Slowly, he released the doorknob and faced his brother. "She was a little fuzzy on the details," he lied. "What exactly happened with that creep, anyway?"

"Some drunk asshole got grabby with her. We bounced him, but I think he rattled her pretty good." Sincere worry ruffled Shea's smooth features. "She doing all right?"

Noah made a noncommittal noise while his heart tried to pound its way out of his chest. "She will be. In time. It's only been, what, a week?"

"Closer to a month now."

Noah swallowed, the sand filling his mouth. A month ago, an intoxicated creep put his hands on Mina.

He'd touched her with rough hands.

Hands rough enough to upset her.

Some asshole had hurt Mina.

His Mina.

An entire month had passed since then, and she'd never said a word about it to him.

CHAPTER 26

The noxious glow emanating from the laptop churned Mina's stomach.

She'd spent the last four weeks setting up an accounting system for Shea and entering three months' worth of data from his handwritten ledgers into the new software in her new position at the pub. In the numbers, she searched to escape the constant upheaval around her, to quiet the noise and still the frenzy.

Ever since that creep had copped a feel, she'd craved peace, but could find none, not even in the methodical logic of someone else's spreadsheet. Rather than being an external menace, she'd suspected the chaos was originating from some place inside her.

Lost in the numbers, she didn't hear Noah until he stepped through the door. A mouth-watering aroma emanated from a white bag tucked under his arm.

She offered him a smile. "Hey."

His expression warmed. "Hey. You hungry? I brought dinner."

A soft groan leaked from her. "Those aren't nachos, are they?"

"They might be." With a smile, he placed the bag on the table and shucked his winter coat.

A number jumped out at her from the spreadsheet, and she squinted at the computer screen. While Noah moved into the kitchen and rummaged around, she fiddled with the numbers.

When he sat across from her, his gaze shifted from her to the computer and back. "How are things going? Everything on schedule?"

For a moment, she was confused, but then she realized he assumed she was working on the spreadsheet for her renovation. She didn't know why she hadn't told him she wasn't waitressing anymore but was working as Shea's bookkeeper instead.

Probably because then she'd have to explain why, and that conversation danced too close to the topic of the groper.

The groper she'd also failed to mention to him. Not because she worried about how he'd react or what he'd say, but because she desperately wanted to forget the whole thing had ever happened.

"I won't bore you with the details," she said.

He tore open the bag from Lucky's. "What happened to the million-dollar trust fund?"

She rolled her eyes. "There was never a trust fund."

The bag rustled as he removed a takeout container. "I thought every Winslow got one of those at birth."

The numbers still weren't adding up. Mina tabbed to another column. "Rose set me up with a college fund, but I used it as a down payment on the house."

"An Ivy League education isn't cheap." With more crinkling noises, he rescued the other carton of food from the bag. "Did you get a scholarship?"

She deleted the data in the last cell and corrected a transposed figure. "I didn't go to college."

A heavy silence pulled her attention away from the computer.

Confusion furrowed his brow. "When I left town, I thought you were planning to go to Columbia."

Her mind stuttered. "I didn't get in to Columbia."

"How is that possible?" he asked, indignant. "You were an excellent student."

"Oh, uh…" She gulped down the slow rise of panic in her throat. "Well, senior year, my grades slipped a little."

"What?" He gaped at her as though he had no idea who she was. "What happened?"

"Nothing happened." Her heart thrashed inside her chest. "They slipped, and I didn't get into Columbia."

"There are plenty of good schools that aren't so difficult to get in to. Did you apply to any others?"

"Is this a quiz?" She slammed the laptop shut. "'Cause I didn't study."

He bristled with his shock, then eased back in his chair. "Not a quiz. Just a question."

Regret seared through her. "I'm sorry." She stabbed at her temples and rubbed. "I didn't mean to snap at you. You don't deserve that."

His features softened. "I might've deserved it a little."

The tension drained from her body, but she managed a weak smile. "I don't want to fight."

A teasing light danced in his dark eyes. "Were we fighting?"

"Yes. You were pointing out my flaws."

With the swiftness of a storm cloud racing ashore, he grew serious. "Then I'm sorry. That was not my intention. Please forgive me."

"Well, that depends. Do either of those boxes contain nachos?"

Soft laughter emanated from him when he shook his head. "An Irish pub known for its Mexican food. I can't say I saw that coming."

He flipped open the lid to one box and heaped a gooey pile of chips smothered in beans and cheese onto a plate. When he'd loaded it down, he passed the plate across the table to her, then filed another for himself.

"How is the waitressing going?" he asked, a nacho poised between his fingers. "Any easier?"

A chip lodged in her throat. "A little," she croaked.

He pointed toward the laptop. "Does it provide enough to help with the bills?"

She stared down at her plate. "More would be nice."

"It was the same way with bartending. After I memorized the drinks and got my speed up, I increased my tips enough to make up for the pitiful pay." He paused, as though considering his next words. "The hard part was the idiot clientele. Alcohol can turn some people into real creeps, you know what I mean?"

Terror ricocheted through her. She finished chewing a tasteless nacho and swallowed it with an audible gulp.

"Have you had to deal with any of that?" His casual tone seemed at odds with his steady gaze.

She stared hard at her plate while she fumbled for the words to tell him about the pervert. He'd given her the perfect opening. All she had to do was step through it.

But she couldn't.

Unable to speak, she shook her head, and the slight movement plunged them into an awkward silence.

He pushed his plate away. "I was talking to Shea earlier and—"

Her head snapped up. "What? When?"

"I just came from his place." His dark eyes shimmered with knowledge. "I don't think he likes the idea of you and me together."

Her heart dropped to her stomach. "I didn't tell him about us, I swear. I haven't told anyone."

His eyebrows slammed together. "Are we hiding it?"

"I assumed you didn't want people to know... to think..."

"I don't give a fuck what people think." His hard scowl softened a little. "Why wouldn't I want people to know I'm sleeping with a smart, smoking-hot woman?"

Because she was a fraud. She was a liar and a wreck, and he deserved so much better than someone like her.

The shrill ring of a cell phone punctured her stunned silence. Instinctively, she reached for her phone, tipping the device so she could read the new text message displayed on the screen.

"Emily's planning another visit." She pushed up from her chair. "I need to give her a quick call. Do you mind?"

His eyes told her he did. "Not at all."

Mina scurried away, and with trembling fingers, hammered out Emily's number. As she raised the phone to her ear, she slipped through her bedroom door, moving to close it behind her.

Through the last sliver of the door's opening, she risked a peek at Noah, who stood beside the kitchen table, watching her while a deep frown bothered his handsome face.

She eased the door shut on his too-perceptive gaze.

With a frustrated sigh, Noah tried to force his attention back to the stack of essays on his desk.

It was useless. All he could think about was Mina. Each day that passed seemed to carry her a little farther away from him. She was on edge. Jumpy and filled with a growing worry about…something.

Was it the renovation? Her work at the pub?

Was it him?

As someone trained to dig up and follow the facts, he had to admit all the evidence pointed back to him. Even as she threw herself into her other jobs, she was pulling away from him.

His chest ached with the realization. He wasn't ready to lose her. To leave her.

He didn't know how, or when, it'd happened, but he could no longer deny he cared about her. Like the Trojan horse, she'd slipped past his defenses and laid waste to his poor, defenseless heart.

He read an entire essay without registering a single word while his mind worked on the puzzle of Mina Winslow. Needing more data, he dug through old memories, and soon, a vivid one knocked loose.

It was one of the last times he'd seen her before he'd left school. They'd returned from winter break, and he'd realized right away that something was different about her. Her shy smile when she saw him hadn't materialized. The dark circles under her eyes had matched her dark clothing. All her color was gone, and it was as though in those days away from school, the light had flickered out inside her.

For two weeks, she'd ignored him. To get a reaction out of her, he'd snatched her notebook off her desk to copy her notes, as he always did, but when he'd peered down at the page, only nonsensical markings and scribbles had blanketed the paper.

Page after page of her notebook filled with nothing more than doodles. She'd written no words at all.

When he'd wordlessly handed the notebook back, she wouldn't meet his gaze.

After that, he'd watched her closely. She'd smiled and laughed with the rest of their classmates, but whenever she'd thought no one was looking, her eyes had filled with a deep, wounding sorrow.

The hair, the clothes, that notebook. Unease had settled in Noah's gut. Something was wrong, he remembered thinking. Terribly wrong.

Then his life had derailed, and he hadn't thought about Mina again for some time. When he had, he'd only recalled her with anger and bitterness.

A knock sounded on his office door and, jolting from the past, he glanced up to find one of his students hovering in the doorway.

He pushed away thoughts of Mina and offered the kid a smile. "Hey, Damion. C'mon in."

Halfway through fall semester, the kid was on course to fail the class. He skipped more often than he showed up, and on exam day, Noah could count on Damion to be absent.

So one day, when Damion had deigned to make an appearance, Noah had given a pop quiz.

That quiz had revealed two things.

One, Damion was bright, and contrary to appearances, had been paying attention to everything Noah had taught.

And two, he most likely had a learning disability.

Noah had quickly tweaked the class structure in a way that allowed him to record his live lectures and post them online for later, or multiple viewings, and to offer students the choice of oral, essay, or multiple-choice assignments and exams.

Damion took a cautious step inside Noah's office. "Hey."

"What's up?"

Damion pulled a rumpled note from his back pocket and held it up. "They was hungry."

Noah frowned at the note. "Who was hungry?"

In a meandering sort of way, Damion approached Noah's desk and dropped the note onto the surface.

Reaching across the desktop, Noah plucked up the sheet and smoothed out the wrinkles. He peered at the photocopied image of an old text and squinted to read small typeface.

Written in and an outdated narrative tone, the article discussed a small settlement of immigrants on a remote island in a "heretofore uninhabited" (for obvious, logical reasons) territory of northern Michigan.

Noah's heart pounded. He scanned the rest of the text, which detailed the settlers' struggles for food and shelter in the inhospitable locale and concluded with an ominous tone.

"Starving and banished from their homeland, they invited the devil into their midst."

Noah looked up into Damion's youthful face. "Where did you find this?"

"At the old courthouse. My mom was cleaning out the basement. She says they got all kinds of old books and stuff down there."

Noah's gaze sharpened on the skinny teen. "There are other books?"

Damion nodded.

A broad smile overtook Noah's face. "Can you show me?"

CHAPTER 27

The large snowflakes swirling in the wind mirrored the chaos tumbling through Mina's chest as she scurried up the walkway to the bank's front entrance. It was the same chaos the handsy creep at the pub had set off inside her weeks ago. And with every one of the assessing glances Noah was increasingly casting her way, it had only grown more frenzied, to the point she struggled to get through her days without forgetting to do even the most simple tasks. Such as remembering to breathe.

Or to deposit her paycheck into her bank account before the plumbers cashed the payment she'd written them.

She bustled through the bank's front doors and stomped the snow from her boots before plucking her paycheck from the back pocket of her blue jeans and approaching the ATM.

Once finished with her banking, she made a mental note to talk to Shea about automatic payroll deposit software, then scrambled through the lobby, past a faceless sculpture and disorderly wall mural, and ducked into the ladies' room.

In her perpetual chaotic state, she'd mindlessly sucked down too many cups of coffee that morning and urgently needed to use the restroom before heading on to her next errand.

She picked the stall at the far end and wriggled out of her voluminous winter coat, an awkward undertaking in the tight space. Once done, she wrestled on the heavy coat, but when she dragged the zipper up, the delicate lining caught between the metal teeth.

As she fiddled with the snag, taking care not to rip the fabric, the restroom door opened and voices filled the small space.

At first, she thought nothing of it. Then she picked up on the heavy, hushed tones of their voices. The woman's husky laugh.

And a man's deep baritone.

She peeked through a crack between the stall door and wall and glimpsed bare flesh. Her gaze traveled up a woman's leg, past the hem of a red skirt riding high on her exposed thigh, and she watched as the man's hand moved to cover the woman's thigh.

The hand inched higher, and the gold band on his ring finger winked under the fluorescent lighting.

Mina clamped a hand over her mouth to stifle her giggle. Were they newlyweds stealing a kiss on their lunch break? Or an older couple with children at home using their lunch hour to sneak in a quick, semi-private moment together?

The woman uncrossed her legs, and the man stepped between them. Then the distinct sound of a zipper coming down echoed in the small restroom.

Oh, no. They were stealing more than a kiss, and unless Mina made her presence known soon, she'd be trapped until they'd finished.

The man slurped on the woman's neck. "You're a dirty girl, you know that?"

At the sound of his voice, Mina froze in place. She knew that voice.

With one eye pinned shut, she peered through the small crack. Sure enough. That was Drew's dirty-blond hair, and the woman spread out on the countertop? She had long, slender legs, a trim waist, and no one, not even Vivian, could possibly call her chubby.

Which meant she wasn't Drew's "not very attractive," "even heavier than" Mina fiancée, Francine Howard.

She was not his new *wife*.

Did Francine have any idea her new husband was getting it on with Phoebe Taylor in a public restroom?

Fury rushed through Mina, straightening her spine. She unhooked the door latch and strode from her stall. While Drew stumbled out from between Phoebe's legs, she marched up to the sink and turned on the faucet.

She might've laughed at their twin expressions of shock, except it just wasn't funny.

"Are you getting déjà vu, too?" Mina asked.

Phoebe slid off the counter and began buttoning her blouse.

"Wh-what are you doing here?" Anger and alarm warred for dominance over Drew's features.

"It's a public restroom, Drew. What do you think I'm doing?" Finished washing her hands, Mina pulled a paper towel from the dispenser. She waggled a finger at Drew's open fly. "You might wanna…"

Drew yanked up his zipper while Phoebe smothered a laugh. The gleam of cruel delight in her eyes turned Mina's stomach.

"You're ridiculous. Both of you." Flinging the paper towel in the trash, Mina headed for the door.

"Be careful you don't hurt yourself climbing up on that high horse," Drew called after her.

Halfway through the open door, Mina tossed a fake smile over her shoulder. "Sorry I can't stay and chat. I'm off to lunch with my good friend, Frannie Howard. I can't wait to catch her up on the all the latest gossip."

With that, she turned her back, then let the door fall shut on the worst mistake of her life.

Eager to be away, she hurried down the hall toward the lobby. Behind her, the restroom door crashed open and struck the concrete wall with a thunderous crack. When she glanced back, Drew barreled toward her.

A ripple of fear, unreasonable fear, slithered down her spine. She tamped down the instinct to run and whipped around to face him.

His long strides ate up the ground until he stood over her. "Listen to me. This needs to stay quiet. Do you understand?"

"Do you understand the purpose of a *public* restroom?"

A muscle ticked in his jawbone. "If this comes out, my campaign is over."

"Your campaign?" Disgust rippled through her. Disgust with Drew, but more so with herself. How could she have been so wrong about him? "That's what you're worried about? What about your *marriage?*"

His hands balled into fists, and he leaned close. Too close. The hairs rose on her neck and arms.

"I kept your secrets, Mina. Now you can keep mine."

The world stopped.

Her heart did not beat. Her lungs refused to draw air. Her mind replayed his words but failed to grasp their meaning. Nothing made sense, so absolute was the horror that gripped her.

Before her eyes, Drew's cool demeanor returned. "Good. I'm glad we understand each other."

He stepped past her, and the sound of his footsteps slowly faded away.

She didn't know how long she remained frozen to the spot, panic squeezing her chest.

Around her, people went about their bank business while the chaos devoured her. Voices reached her through a tunnel of echoes until the screech of a small child pierced the drone of noises. Mina startled, and then her feet started to move, slowly at first, then faster.

Freed from her paralysis, she charged through the lobby. She launched herself past the congregating bodies and hurtled toward the exit. Heedless of the curious stares and the sting of winter air, she charged down the concrete path toward her car, her feet pounding in time to the frantic rhythm of her heart.

Footsteps thundered behind her, hounding her, and a sob wrenched from her throat. She grasped for her car keys as she ran, but they remained buried in the bottom of her purse.

Frustration and fear choked her. She couldn't breathe.

When her grip slipped, her purse dropped to the ground, and the contents spilled across the parking lot at her feet. With another helpless cry, she sank to her hands and knees and grabbed at her scattered things while snow and slush soaked through her blue jeans.

The panic stalked her, and she whirled, ready to confront her attacker.

But no one pursued her. She was losing her mind.

Her cheeks wet, she crawled behind the wheel of her car. She inhaled deep breaths, but her lungs had shrunk to half their usual size and she couldn't hold enough oxygen. Dizziness circled.

Though she had no recollection of making the drive, she reached the carriage house just in time to throw up in the shrubbery.

~

WITH SHAKING HANDS, Mina fumbled with the packaging of a new paintbrush. Restless, she wandered the carriage house in search of scissors but kept forgetting what she was looking for, only to return to the package of paintbrushes and recall.

Outdoors, storm clouds clashed and grumbled. Like the clouds gathering over the lake, feelings so strong and so dark hovered nearby, ready to unleash their wrath, and she knew with a certainty that if she didn't push them down, they would rip her to shreds.

Indeed, it'd already begun.

She tried to overpower them. To forget or ignore them. To move past them. Around them. Over. Under. Anywhere but through.

That path led to darkness.

But no matter how she tried, she couldn't outrun those dangerous feelings. They lived inside her. There was no escape.

At any moment, Noah would arrive. She had to calm down or else he'd notice her distress and ask questions. He'd want to know why she was upset. He'd want her to tell him what had caused her panic.

She tried to think about what she might say. What words could explain what she didn't understand?

In the kitchen, she pulled a knife from the drawer and attacked the plastic casing.

Then Noah was there. He was close. Close enough to touch her.

He did, and she jerked. The knife missed its mark and sliced into the flesh on her finger.

Pain snatched the air from her lungs, and she whirled. "Don't—" Her voice broke over the word. "Don't touch me."

He froze, his eyes going wide, his mouth open but unmoving. He must've felt as shocked by her outburst as she did.

But his expression soon softened, and without missing a beat, he reached for a towel. "Let me see your hand."

She clenched her hand into a tight fist and squeezed it to her chest. The walls of her small apartment inched closer, like a menacing beast. Her breathing became fast, too fast, and each pull of air burned through her lungs.

He was looking at her with those damn dark eyes, and she couldn't think of anything to say to make him understand—except the one thing she absolutely *could not* say.

Noah's mouth moved as he spoke, but she couldn't make out his words. She could hear nothing except the sickening thud of her own heartbeat hammering inside her skull. Nausea rose to the back of her throat.

"Mina!" Her name flew sharply off his tongue and broke through the fog of panic enclosing her.

She blinked several times until his face snapped into focus.

"Give me your hand," he repeated.

She obeyed, and he reached for her with slow, precise movements.

God, she hated herself for being so weak. When he pried open her fingers and pressed a towel to the bleeding wound, tears blurred her vision.

She sensed his too-clever gaze on her face now and then, making covert assessments. As if she were one of his artifacts, withholding secrets he was determined to uncover. Her stomach wrenched with terror, but not of him. Rather, she feared what he would see when he looked at her.

The real her.

She had to get away.

Her practiced lines tumbled out. "I think this renovation is getting to me."

"You've been working hard." He smoothed a hank of hair off her forehead. "You must be tired."

"I am." The exhaustion was so wide and so deep she feared it might drown her.

"Why don't you try to get some rest?" Tension corded his neck and shoulders. "I'll wake you after a bit."

She fled to the bedroom and fastened the door shut behind her, blocking out Noah and the small anguish marring his beautiful face.

In truth, she wanted to talk to him. She wanted to tell him it had nothing to do with him. That it was something else. Something inside her. Something that was ugly and fierce, and she feared if she let it loose, it would consume her.

She struggled to find the words, but no words could change what she was.

Alone in her darkening bedroom, she prayed for courage, but found none existed in her.

For that, she punished herself. It wasn't rational, but logic had nothing to do with the madness unfurling inside her.

Her throat closed with the sob that threatened to strangle her.

The dying light threw shadows across the still room. She trudged to the bed and collapsed on the mattress.

Unable to bear the nightmarish images that appeared when she closed her eyes, she stared at the bedroom ceiling, screaming inside, as fragmented memories of a past she'd long forgotten rushed to the surface.

She caught sight of him through the window and smiled at his familiar, well-loved face. He was like a big brother to her. She adored him and shamelessly sought his attention and affection.

She hurried inside.

To him.

Icy rain pelted her bedroom window, and the wind lashed the carriage house.

As she approached, his smile faded. She looked into his soft gray eyes, and what she saw there sent a ripple of fear chasing through her.

Resentment. Cruelty. Intent.

A crack of lightning lit up her bedroom and then dashed her back into darkness.

Painful, grasping hands... the stench of his panting breath on her face... the ache in her throat from screaming, though she knew there was no one to hear her cries.

In her bedroom surrounded by the things that she, the woman, possessed, she felt again the terror of the young girl she'd been. The nauseating dread that he would return.

The helplessness and crippling fear when he did.

The images hounded her. Like a nightmare.

Except they were not the harmless imaginings of a dream. They were a waking nightmare. They were memories. Memories buried so deep as to be nearly forgotten.

The truth took root inside her, expanding, twisting, filling all space and pushing out all that got in its way. Like weeds through cracks in the pavement, the truth scratched and clawed, tearing flesh from bone.

The menacing truth had always been there. Pursuing her, driving her, compelling her in every minute of every day to hide it, deny it, destroy it, defeat it, despise it. All in the futile attempt to change it and make it not true.

She didn't want the waking nightmare to be real, but it was.

She didn't want to be *that* girl.

But she was.

CHAPTER 28

$\mathcal{N}$oah's mood darkened with the bleak winter day. The north winds battered the exposed shoreline of Lake Michigan, and large, wet snowflakes fell lazily from the sky as he rolled into the parking lot of the local ice arena. He grabbed the oversized hockey bag from the bed of his truck and made for the locker rooms.

She was avoiding him. He hadn't laid eyes on her in days now, and the separation ate at his insides.

Helplessness squeezed his chest cavity as he tossed his bag to the locker room floor and dug out his gear.

Consumed by his churning thoughts, Noah missed Shea sitting at the end of the bench until he nearly tripped over him. With a grunt, Noah sidestepped his older brother.

Shea released a heavy sigh full of impatience. "I'm tired of this."

Noah dragged on his shoulder pads. "Tired of what?"

"Tired of us dancing on eggshells around each other. Let's just have it out and be done with it."

The familiar resentment twisted Noah's gut. "Let's not."

"You've obviously got something you want to say."

"I really don't." Noah yanked his jersey over his head.

"Bullshit."

All the self-doubts and bitterness amassed in a lifetime rushed to the surface, the ones that'd formed early and lived deep in his heart. No matter how fast or how far he ran, he couldn't escape them.

He couldn't escape his family's view of him.

That he was expendable. Disposable.

Anger rattled through him, choking him to silence. Without a word, or even a flinch to acknowledge Shea, he laced up his skates and left the locker room.

In the arena, he took laps around the ice while he sized up their opponent. The Fighting Nolans had defeated the Mighty Drunks in last week's game to move into first place in the six-team league. A win today against the Mother Puckers secured them a spot in the playoffs.

Jack skated by. "Your man's the lumberjack."

Noah looked to the men in casual conversation at the opposite end of the ice and pinpointed the broad-shouldered one with a bushy beard and red plaid flannel pants cut off at the knees to accommodate his shin guards.

"He's slow, but if he catches you, he'll make you pay," Jack said. "He likes to hit."

A slow, predatory smile curled Noah's lips. "Then it's his lucky day."

Jack's maniacal laugh carried around the arena as he skated toward Luke, who'd finished stretching and had taken his place in goal.

A few minutes later, Noah glided to center ice and took his position for the face-off.

The puck dropped, and Noah attacked. He flattened the lumberjack on the first play. After that, it was *on*. The two men battled for the next twenty minutes, even abandoning their pursuit of the puck in favor of delivering the cross-check.

With time running out on the first period, Noah slapped the puck toward the net. Planted in the crease like an oak tree, Shea deflected the shot into the back of the goal.

Intermission pissed Noah off because it gave him time to think about Mina. Though he'd agreed to keep things casual between them, he deeply regretted that decision now. He wanted to know what was happening with her. Why was she pushing him away?

He wasn't ready for their relationship to end. He didn't want to stop being with her, but neither did he want to be her plaything. A friend and a fuck, he thought bitterly. He'd had his lifetime full of being expendable to people, and just once, he wanted someone to want him to stay.

The second period began with the lumberjack sending Noah into the boards. It felt good to get hit, and Noah repaid the favor on the next play, skating casually away as the poor sap crumpled to the ice.

He decided it felt better to do the hitting.

In the end, the Fighting Nolans sent the Mother Puckers packing six goals to none, and Noah and the lumberjack shared a robust post-game handshake.

In the locker room afterward, Jack grinned at Noah. "I like you in beast mode. Bring that the rest of the way and we win this thing."

It's not as if there was ever any doubt that they'd defeat the other teams in the league of middle-aged, beer-drinking men with a pro on their side. Jack by himself could've beaten half of them.

Luke's cell was blowing up, and with the phone attached to his ear, he ducked out with a wave to the others. Jack made for the exit while Noah crammed gear into his bag.

Shea straddled the bench, facing him. Expectant.

Noah hurled a skate into an empty locker, and the clamor echoed through the vast room. "What do you want me to say?"

"I want to hear the truth." Shea folded his arms across his broad chest. "For once."

With a lash of anger, Noah whipped toward him. "Why did you do it?"

"It was the only way."

Bitter laughter grated like broken glass in Noah's throat. "Fuck you."

"He was going to kill you." Shea's eyes blazed bright. "I had to send you away."

Noah hauled his hockey bag over his shoulder and turned.

Shea shot to his feet. "God damn it, Noah, listen to me. He wasn't right in the head, and he was focused on you. I don't know why, but he was. He was killing you. We all were."

Noah held his body still while, inside, he cracked apart. The memory of that fateful night, so vivid it might as well have happened yesterday and not half a lifetime ago, carried him away against his will.

The telephone's shrill ring had awakened him. He'd fumbled to answer it before the noise disturbed the baby or the baby's exhausted parents.

It was Terry, the owner of Daniel's favorite bar. Their dad was drunk again, and there'd been a fight. Someone needed to come get him before the cops arrived.

Noah arrived a few minutes later to find Daniel slumped over the bar. Noah shook him awake. When Daniel lifted his head, he regarded Noah through red-rimmed eyes glazed by drunkenness.

"Take your hands off me." Daniel's speech was heavily slurred.

Unease prickled along Noah's spine. "Let's go home, Dad."

Daniel climbed off the barstool, but stumbled, and Noah reached to steady him.

His dad exploded. "Get your fucking hands off me!"

Noah backed off right away and showed his hands at his sides in a sign of surrender. But Daniel's course was set. He glared at Noah for many moments, a slight sway to his stance. Then he lunged.

Noah dodged the charge and executed a small deflection. Nothing more than a slight slap to redirect Daniel's advance. But the move was enough to drop the inebriated man.

Cursing, Daniel struggled to his knees as he fumbled through his coat pocket with frantic, jerky movements. Noah bent to help him up when a final violent tug freed the object Daniel sought.

Noah froze with the flash of metal, his body understanding the danger before his mind could grasp it. Hard steel pressed to his sternum.

"Dad—?"

"Why did you come back?" Spittle shot from Daniel's mouth with his anguished words. "When you're gone, at least I can pretend you're not my son."

Through the roaring in his ears, Noah heard the ominous click of the Glock turning over. A surreal stillness settled over him as he accepted what was to come.

"Danny!"

The thunderous bellow startled Daniel, who flinched but held the gun steady at Noah's chest.

With a flash of movement, Father John detached from the shadows and snatched the gun from Daniel's shaky hand.

Daniel blinked up at his brother-in-law as if waking from a deep slumber.

Then his face crumpled, and he slumped to the floor. "God damn him," he sobbed. "Why is he here?"

John's fierce blue eyes landed on Noah's face. "Go," he said. "Go now." He bent over Daniel's defeated form. "It's over now," John soothed.

As though mired in quicksand, Noah stumbled backward with slow, plodding steps, then turned and fled.

At the door, he slid to a stop. In the shadows, a dark figure lurked. Noah peered closer.

"Go." Shea's clipped command lashed at him. "Don't come back."

Swallowing back acid, Noah had fled town that night, an exile.

No matter how far he'd roamed, the pain of that night had stayed with him always. Each morning when he'd awaken and remember, he'd relive the heartbreak, and again a million times throughout the day, every day, whenever he thought of them and wondered how they were, who'd they become. Like a thousand tiny cuts draining the life from him, slowly and with excruciating agony, he remembered.

"You were eighteen." Shea's quiet voice pulled Noah back to the present. "Just a kid."

"We didn't have the luxury of being kids," Noah said.

"I couldn't save all of you," Shea said. "Not then. But I could save *you* that night."

Noah stood with fists clenched at his sides. Air rattled through his lungs with a fractured wheeze.

"You deserved more than this shithole town could give you. I saw a chance to get you out, and I took it." The edge was back in Shea's tone. "Leo was thirteen years old. He didn't understand. None of them did. I broke their hearts when I sent you away. It was the hardest thing I've ever had to do."

"Why didn't you tell me that?" Noah's hands curled into fists at his sides. "I thought you hated me as much as he did. Jesus, Shea."

"Would you have gone if I did?"

"It was my choice to make!" At the ring of anguish in his voice, Noah cursed.

"I know that. I do." The color heightened on Shea's cheeks. "But the thing is, I can't look at you now and regret what I did. I'm sorry if that pisses you off. I won't regret it, Noah, but I am sorry."

Noah couldn't still the quivering in him. "Don't you ever fucking do something like that to me again."

With that, he bolted for the locker room door, unable to put distance between himself and the past fast enough.

CHAPTER 29

$\mathcal{M}$isery destroyed her appetite and stole her sleep.

The waking nightmares continued to stalk her. Earlier that day, while working with Sam to configure the kitchen layout, another memory had flashed through her mind and left her shaken and ill.

She recalled coming to in math class, as though she'd been asleep or unconscious for some time. Not knowing how she'd gotten there, or how to work the math problems written in the textbook laid open in front of her, terror had overwhelmed her. With a sickening sensation, she realized she had no memory of the prior weeks at all.

Terrified the teacher would call on her, she'd buried her head in the pages of the textbook and beaten back the panic until class had ended. Then she'd run to the restroom and gotten sick in the last stall.

She'd remained locked in that stall for the rest of the day, overwhelmed with fear and shame.

Now, from the living room, the antique clock struck the hour, chiming twice to proclaim the late hour.

Mina burrowed deeper beneath the quilts piled on top of the bed. She could hear Noah in the other room, straightening his files, then closing his laptop.

A moment later, he came into the bedroom.

To her.

She pretended to sleep.

Shame at her deception washed over her, but she couldn't bring herself to open her eyes. To open her arms and her heart to him.

The memories had stolen her hunger, her peace, and now, her desire for intimacy. Even with Noah.

Noah.

Her heart screamed while a silent tear leaked from the corner of one eye. The bathroom door closed, followed by the sound of running water. A sob built in her throat and she buried her face in the pillow.

Cold seeped into her bones, but she didn't bother putting another quilt on the bed. Nothing could chase away the chill or the profound devastation that Noah wasn't able to fix her broken parts. He might've cured her damaged libido for a time, but it wasn't her sex drive that'd been ruined. It was her soul.

With that truth exposed, she knew she might never be the woman he'd want to be with forever. The woman he deserved. The woman she didn't have it in her to be.

She should let him go. Set him free to find another woman who was worthy of him.

A real woman.

The jarring jingle of a cell phone punctured the quiet in the room. Mina tracked the sound to Noah's phone laying on top of her dresser.

She tossed back the covers. Her bare feet smacked against the cold hardwood floors as she scurried to reach his phone before the call ended. The small display screen flashed with a sequence of numbers when she picked up the phone and moved toward the bathroom.

She stuck her head inside. "Noah?"

"Yeah?" he called over the sound of the shower's spray.

"Your phone's ringing. Do you want me to hand it to you?"

"Can you answer it? Take a message and I'll call 'em right back."

She shut the bathroom door and accepted the call. "Hello?"

"May I speak with Noah Nolan, please?" The woman spoke with a thick Irish accent, and it took Mina a moment to adjust to her lyrical cadence.

"He, uh, stepped out for a minute," Mina hedged. "Can I take a message?"

"Please. Tell him Anna called and the new project is a go," she said. "We can't wait to have him home in a few weeks."

Mina disconnected the call and clutched the phone to her chest, over her wildly thumping heart.

Understanding reached her in stages.

New project.

Home.

A few weeks.

She experienced the knowledge like an icy touch winding its way through her body to her chest, where it squeezed mercilessly.

Her heart gave an awful wrench.

The water had stopped, and she turned dazedly as Noah stepped through the bathroom door. A cloud of steam and the scent of her shampoo wafted into the bedroom with him. He wore a towel tucked around his lean waist, and his wet hair, which stuck out in all directions, curled at the ends.

"Have you eaten?" he asked. "I'm starving."

Mina made no response as he pulled on a pair of loose-fitting running pants. The St. Nicholas pendant glinted on his bare chest.

He stilled when he saw her face. His brow furrowed in silent question.

She held out the phone. "It was Anna." Her voice sounded faint to her own ears. She caught the flicker of surprise that flashed across his face before he concealed it. "She said to tell you the project is all set." Mina swallowed with difficulty. "She's excited for you to come home."

Color rose high on his cheekbones.

On suddenly unsteady legs, she sagged back against the exposed brick wall. "You're leaving?"

The outrageous copper of his eyes speared her. "The excavation is done. My appointment at ESU is over at the end of this semester."

A week, maybe two.

The Celtic cross tattooed on his right biceps stood as a testament to his wild youth. She blinked back tears.

"I always planned to go back to Ireland," he said.

She swallowed the tight knot clogging her throat. "When do you leave?"

"The end of this month."

Silence dropped like a sledgehammer between them.

He didn't quite meet her eyes when he spoke. "Or... I could stay."

The answer nearly flew from her heart. *Yes! Don't leave me. Never leave me.* Except, she'd promised him that when the time came, she wouldn't beg.

Her cheeks warmed, and she ducked her chin. "You should go. Of course you should go."

His soft footfalls echoed in the silent room as he crossed to her. Her heart thrashed in her chest.

Her nerves grew taut under his relentless gaze.

"If you want me to stay—"

"I'd never ask that of you." She injected as much strength into her voice as she could manage. It was all she could do to reassure him she wouldn't fall to pieces at his feet.

He pulled up abruptly.

She kept talking, only faster now. "You're right. You've been nothing but honest with me."

He rammed a hand through his hair. He might have cursed. Then he jerked back around. The movement, swift and severe, triggered an instinct born of betrayal, and Mina flinched.

The tell was slight but suppressed too late. Noah saw it and stilled.

When she witnessed what lay naked in his eyes, the acrid tang of fear flooded her mouth.

He spoke in a low, lethal tone. "Mina, what is going on?"

"Nothing." Her quick reply was toneless.

"Don't lie to me. Not about this."

The cool admonishment stung. Her stomach churned.

"That pervert at the pub—" His words cut off when she gasped.

Terror stole her breath. He meant to draw her pain into the light. "How did you...?"

"Did he hurt you?"

Recoiling, she sputtered words, hoping to hit upon the ones that'd make it all go away. "It wasn't him."

She realized her mistake almost immediately.

Time slowed as the warm molasses in his eyes cooled with anger and fear.

And knowledge.

He *knew*. Simply reached out and touched the truth, as if he, too, bore witness to the waking nightmares.

Her field of vision narrowed. There were no words. No thoughts. Nothing. Only panic and shame.

"Someone else hurt you? Who? When?"

His words reverberated through her like a hundred tiny earthquakes. Walls crumbled and fell away, and the memories flooded in, vivid and real.

Denials fell from her lips. "No one. Nothing happened."

Deep in her heart, she knew Noah wouldn't blame her for what had happened all those years ago. But he was right. She was afraid. Mostly, she feared the way he'd look at her if he knew the truth. That the tenderness she sometimes glimpsed in his eyes would change, or be replaced by something else. Something closer to disgust or pity, and in his seeing her differently, she'd be forced to see herself differently, too.

Then she'd *be* different.

"You can tell me anything. You know that, don't you?"

She almost hated him for seeing what she really was, except it was her own weakness that revolted her.

Someone hadn't hurt her.

Someone had ruined her.

"No." She forced the word through jagged breaths.

Noah cursed and slipped a hand beneath the curtain of her hair. He kneaded her nape until she relaxed. Her breathing slowed.

His voice deepened with emotion. "Don't shut me out, *a mhuirnin*. Please."

Icy terror snapped and snarled through her. Shaking her head, she reared back.

"If you're so sure I'm hiding something, why even ask me?" A nasty edge crept into her voice, which didn't match the anguish in her heart.

His hand on her neck stilled. "I'm not sure of anything. If you'd just talk to me, help me understand. You've been distant—"

She gasped and jerked away from his touch. "I warned you about that, didn't I?"

"That's not what I meant."

"You should go," she said.

"Mina, don't do this. Let me in. Let me help you."

"I don't want your help. I want you to leave."

His face hardened, obscuring all the soft contours she loved so well.

"You said you loved me. Was that a lie?"

Tears streamed silently down her cheeks. "No."

His features softened. "Then talk to me. Tell me—"

"No." Fear grabbed hold of her heart and lungs and squeezed. She gasped for air. "Never."

He flinched as though she'd struck him. She glimpsed a moment of troubled anguish before he blanked his features. His hand dropped away.

"So, that's it?"

Her silence was deafening, damning.

Decisive.

Through the haze of panic, she was aware that he moved through the carriage house. He gathered his belongings, rapidly and without care, removing his presence from her home and from her life in only a few brief minutes. He left her there, back flat to the wall, when he slammed out of the house.

The crash of the door released Mina from her paralysis and she sank to the floor.

There, she let the darkness take her.

CHAPTER 30

*H*e'd been drunk for days, but all the liquor in Shea's bar couldn't make him forget her. Not this time.

Noah flopped onto the couch at his dad's old place and shoved the heels of his hands into his eye sockets.

"You look like shit," Shea observed.

Noah laid his head on the couch back and closed his eyes. "I feel like shit."

He hadn't been hungover in years. The fact he was stuck in this town, near her, but not able to touch her, or talk to her, or tease her until the sound of her light laughter filled a room only made the agony worse.

The soft leather groaned as Shea lowered himself into an armchair. "Everything all right?"

"Everything's fucking fine."

A beat of hesitation followed, then Shea said, "You don't sound fine."

Noah rolled his head upright. "Is this why you called me here? To talk about my feelings?"

"We're doing family dinner at the pub on Friday night." Unease packed Shea's shoulders. "You should come by."

"Can't." Noah let his head fall back. "I need to wrap things up before I leave."

A charged silence infused the air.

Noah cracked open one eye. "What?"

"Does Mina know you're leaving?"

Noah closed his eye. "She knows."

Another damnable silence followed.

"When do you leave?" A chill snuck into Shea's tone.

"Day after classes end."

"Which is when?"

With the wave of nausea that hit him, Noah swallowed thickly. "Friday."

Shea's sour chuckle gave way to a sigh, heavy with bitterness.

Noah fixed him with a stony glare. "I need to work."

"Whatever you say." Shea shoved to his feet.

Devil take him, Noah took the bait. "You think I'm running away?"

"No, not running." He balled his hands into fists, but rather than explode, he clenched his mouth shut with ruthless resolve, as if swallowing back angry words.

"Christ, Shea, just say it. I can tell you're dying to."

On his brother's face, a war waged between anger and sorrow, hope and regret. "I don't think you're running away. I think you're deserting us."

Noah's bitter laugh was part pained sob. "Are you being serious right now?"

The ire seemed to drain out of Shea. "I'm not mad that you left. Or that you stayed away. I think you did what you thought you had to do, and for the record, I honestly believe you made the right decision. Noah, I don't begrudge you your choices. I admire you for them."

The shaking started in Noah's hands and soon spread through his entire body.

"But none of that matters now." The hard edge in Shea's tone melted away. "You were only a kid then. You're not a kid anymore."

Exhaustion dragged on Noah, and he held out his hands. "What do you want from me?"

"I want you to do what's best for you this time."

The words knocked into Noah with the weight of a freight train. Beneath his breastbone, his heart thrashed, and he laid a hand over the battered organ, as if to stop it from beating its way out of his chest. What was best for him?

Meaning what, exactly? What did he want? What did he need?

His heart stuttered its answer.

But his mind swiftly countered. If he stayed, and they rebuffed or discarded him again…

He forced words through his throat's suddenly tight passageway. "It's better if I go."

"Better for who?"

Shea's question hung in the air and left Noah staring, dumb and mute, as Shea turned to leave.

Except, he didn't leave.

At the desk in the corner by the door, he stopped. He slid open the top drawer, but his body blocked Noah from seeing the item he retrieved. The teardrop knob clattered against wood when he slammed the drawer shut. With sharp movements, he twisted around and strode across the room.

"Here." He thrust a small green box at Noah.

Noah blinked stupidly at the box. "What's this?"

"Mom's wedding ring. I found it going through Dad's things."

Noah staggered to his feet. "I don't want to see it."

Shea shoved the box in Noah's direction. "I'm not showing it to you. I want you to have it."

"*What?*" Shock ripped through him. "Why?"

"It's a family heirloom," Shea growled.

"Then you keep it," Noah bit off, incredulous.

"I bought Isobel a ring twenty years ago. I won't be needing another one."

"Then…give it to Luke or Jack." Noah's arms moved wildly as he spoke. "Leo was too young when she died. He should have it."

A frown touched Shea's features when he looked down at the box. He smoothed one thumb over the lid's glossy surface. "She'd want you to have it."

Noah's desperation bordered on panic. "How do you know that?"

"I just do." His arm shot out, and he let go.

Noah lunged to catch the box before it tumbled to the floor.

"You should come Friday, before you go," Shea tossed over his shoulder on his way out of the room.

"I need to work," Noah called after him.

But he was already alone, in a suddenly haunted room.

MINA STARED open-mouthed at the bounteous variety of toilet tissue. Standing in the aisle at Mike's, the necessity that forced her to get out of bed now overwhelmed her.

"Mina?"

Mina turned at the sound of a woman's voice.

"Omigod, you look amazing." Abbie let out a delighted squeal as she bore down on Mina. "How much weight have you lost?"

Mina managed a wooden smile. Had she lost weight? "I… I

don't know…." she trailed off as she recalled her reflection in the mirror before she left the house. Red, bruised eyes, sallow skin, limp, dirty hair. She looked sick.

She *was* sick.

"Are you starving?" Abbie asked. "My New Year's resolution is to lose ten pounds. How did you do it?"

Mina stared into Abbie's openly curious face while her mind grappled with the information coming at her.

All her life, Mina had been chubby, and after that winter break, she'd cloaked herself in dark, baggy clothing to hide herself away from the interested gazes of the boys her age, preferring her mom's incessant criticisms to their attention.

But now, when despair and helplessness ate away at her, she received compliments for her appearance.

Seriously?

A seed of anger sprouted in the pit of her stomach. "I've got the flu," she lied.

"Oh, well, that's one way to do it, I suppose." Abbie's laughter faded, and, growing serious, she darted quick glances to her left and right. "I cannot believe that rat ex of yours. What a jerk, huh?"

They blinked at each other.

"I'm sorry, who?" Mina asked.

"Drew."

"Drew," Mina repeated as her brain tripped to catch up. "What about him?"

Delight tinged Abbie's scandalous gasp. "You haven't heard?"

"Heard what?" Dread formed around Mina's words.

"His wife filed for an annulment after only one month." Abbie's cheeks flushed pink with excitement. "She found out he was doing some creative accounting with his office assistant and showed up at City Hall with a baseball bat. Can you believe it?"

"I think I might," Mina muttered.

"Oh, I wish I could've seen it. No one was hurt," Abbie was quick to add. "But she trashed his Porsche. About wrecked him, too, from what I hear."

Bile rose in Mina's throat and stopped her from assuring Abbie Drew's behavior had, in fact, hurt many people. He was like a bomb detonating in their midst. Everyone suffered the collateral damage. His family, Frannie Howard, his employees, even the citizens of Thief Island, who'd put their trust in him and voted him into office. They deserved better than him.

Mina plucked a random pack of tissue from the shelf and aimed for the checkouts.

"Let's get together for lunch sometime soon," Abbie called out.

Mina lifted a hand in a half wave and kept walking.

As she drove home, a haze of fury churned inside her. She'd tried so hard for so long to change who she was. To twist and bend herself into the woman she thought they wanted her to be. To hide a truth so dark and ugly, it would destroy them all if they found out.

Disgust at her warped and pathetic need filled her.

Then came the anger. Fury unfurled inside her. Layer upon layer, it unfolded, until a lifetime of denials burned away, leaving only the red-hot heat of her rage.

Suddenly, the veil was lifted.

Why had she tried so hard to become someone else? Why was she so convinced the defect lay inside her? She'd been seventeen when it happened. A child, full of sincerity and affection. Her desire to please, to appease, so strong it'd outweighed even her instinct for self-protection.

He'd taken advantage of that. Preyed upon it.

Afraid she would be sick, Mina raced up the rickety porch stairs and darted to the bathroom, barring the door behind her. At the sink, she splashed cold water on her face and forced air through her lungs with long, painful breaths.

When the nausea passed, she crawled to her bed and hid beneath the covers. She craved sleep, for it offered the only escape from the torment of her own mind.

She awoke sometime later to darkness and a pillow wet with tears. Grief pressed down on her, and she feared it would never ease. How could it? Nothing could give her back what she'd lost.

Like the anger, grief rolled through in increasingly painful stages. The agony consumed her as she grieved all that'd been taken from her. Her innocence, her hope, her dreams for a future filled with love and intimacy.

Mostly, she mourned the loss of the tenderhearted person she'd been before he violated her. Before she'd become fearful and untrusting, and her heart had hardened to others. To men, all of whom she regarded with accusation in her eyes.

Good men, like Noah, who didn't deserve her condemnation.

She recalled the anguish that had slashed across his face when she'd flinched away from him.

He'd extended a hand, offering to help pull her out of the darkness, and she'd slapped it away.

She was a coward, spending all her damn time trying to be liked by others when the problem was she didn't like herself.

When next she opened her eyes, daylight streamed through the cracks in her window coverings.

A pounding took up inside her skull while nausea roiled her stomach. She rubbed her temples, waiting for the sickness to pass, but the pounding in her head only grew louder.

No, not in her head. Another sequence of sharp knocks rattled through her.

The door. Someone was at the door.

The drumming in her head moved to her heart and became a throb. What if it was Noah? What if he'd come back? What if, after everything she'd said and done, he still wanted to be her friend? She desperately needed a friend.

On heavy legs, she slogged through the carriage house, but the hope in heart spurred her on. She unbolted the lock and swung open the front door.

Bright sunlight poured inside, and she raised a hand to shelter her eyes from the harsh glare. Squinting into the light, she made out Emily's form hovering hesitantly in the doorway.

"Emily? What are you doing here?" Mina tried to banish the apathy of despair from her voice.

Uncertainty shimmered in Emily's toffee-colored eyes. "I thought—We talked about a visit—" She gnawed her bottom lip. "Did you forget I was coming?"

Shock seized the gears of Mina's mind.

"Oh, gosh. I sh-sh-should've c-called or texted." At the sudden appearance of Emily's stutter, Mina fought through the cobwebs.

"No." Her throat was dry and her voice cracked. She swallowed painfully and restarted. "I did, I forgot. Em, I'm sorry."

"It's okay." Soulful brown eyes swept over Mina. "Are you okay?"

Mina's face heated with shame. "I... I've been sick."

Calm determination wiped all doubt from Emily's face. "Then it's a good thing I'm here."

With a weak smile, Mina welcomed her cousin inside even as a fresh wave of anguish washed over her, knowing that Noah was likely never coming back for her.

CHAPTER 31

The pub reeked of beer and grease, and music blared from the speakers to rattle around inside Noah's skull. His mind was a mess. He couldn't make sense of anything, which was the only thing that might explain how he wound up at Shea's family fucking dinner.

It was his last stop before heading to the airport, where he'd booked a hotel room and planned to stay overnight ahead of his international flight the following day. Originally, he'd planned to depart a week later, but that morning he'd called and changed his ticket to the earliest available flight. The sooner he got away from this place and the people that didn't need or want him around, the better.

In his hand, he gripped a tumbler of whiskey. If all went according to plan, he'd stay drunk straight through from now until tomorrow night when he was wheels up. He didn't know how else he'd get through the next several hours. Although, so far, the smooth alcohol had done little to calm the turbulent storm inside him.

He'd already checked out of his motel room and returned his rental vehicle, so tonight, he'd crash on the couch in

Shea's office where he'd tossed his luggage, then catch the first ferry out in the morning to meet up with the driver he'd hired to shuttle him to the airport. Soon, this island would be nothing but a distant memory once more.

Then, he'd need only to forget her.

Emotions battered him, and his hand tightened around the sleek glass. The grief and anger were agonizing. How in the hell was he supposed to forget her? How was he supposed to exist outside her heart and her heat and the sound of her voice? He downed the contents of the glass.

He knew how. He'd done it before—he had only to repeat the steps.

Get away.

Stay away.

Bury himself in work, and whiskey, and if need be, women.

Repeat, over and over, with added urgency and determination if the pain returned.

When the pain returned.

The pain *always* returned. But if he stuck to the plan, eventually, it wouldn't hurt so much.

"She isn't worth it, you know." The unfamiliar woman's voice came from the barstool beside him.

He turned his head toward the sound. She was beautiful. Tall and long-limbed, with a porn-star chest.

He shook his head to clear it. "Who?"

Her husky laugh irritated him. "You're right, let's not talk about her." She smiled a smile any man would recognize and touched his forearm. "What shall we talk about instead?"

Noah looked pointedly at her hand on his arm before dragging his gaze back to her face. Like so many others, she looked familiar, but he couldn't place her. Truth was, he didn't care.

"Who the fuck are you and what do you want?" he demanded.

Shrewd calculation swirled in her cold eyes. "The best sex of your life and to make you forget all about Mina Winslow."

For one brief, insanity-fueled moment, he was tempted. If he kept his eyes closed, he might be able to imagine a face with a smaller, straighter nose. A mouth that was plump and sensual, not wide and thin. Curves that filled his hands and hardened his cock, not flat, uninteresting plains that left him soft and indifferent.

After a while, it might not matter that her eyes weren't the deepest shade of blue, or brimming with a grave sincerity that caused his heart to constrict.

The bartender happened by and Noah raised his empty glass to order another.

"Tsk, tsk," the woman clucked near his ear, her hand moving to his thigh. "You let her get to you."

When her fingertips inched higher, he clamped down hard on her hand.

Her eyes flashed with the unmistakable spark of arousal.

He didn't bother repressing his bored sigh. Great. She was a pain junky.

"Look," he said, "this is not gonna happen."

Her hand beneath his explored, squeezing and massaging. "I'm offering you the best sex of your life, no strings attached. Anything goes. It's what every man wants and most never gets. And for you, I bring the added pleasure of knowing you got back at the little bitch."

Her scent, thick and sweet, enveloped him. Cloying. He was losing patience.

Music blared overhead, and he leaned close so that his mouth nearly touched her ear. "Contrary to popular belief, not every man wants meaningless sex."

She yanked her hand out from under his grip. "You're not the only man she's left unsatisfied."

Through the growing haze of his intoxication, he studied her pointy profile. Realization struck. "You were the one fucking the fiancé."

Annoyance pinched her features and when she shot him a dark scowl, he saw that the fire in her eyes had shifted to something almost like fury. "You make it sound so naughty."

"I was thinking desperate."

Definitely fury.

"Don't misunderstand me," he continued. "I'm glad you did it. That little prick didn't deserve her."

She lifted her sharp chin and looked down her long nose at him. "You can't steal a man who isn't willing to be stolen."

"Can we really call Drew Alexander a man? I thought testicles were required for that."

"Convinced you she's a saint, has she? Well, let me save you the suspense. She's not." The woman signaled for the bartender. "You don't know her."

Funny, Mina had tried to tell him the same thing.

The woman wouldn't stop talking. "She's a spoiled brat who's never had to work for anything."

That "spoiled brat" was one of the hardest workers he'd ever met. "Obsessed much?"

Her eyes narrowed to slits. "She doesn't know what it's like for people like us."

The bartender set drinks in front of them, and Noah plucked his glass off the counter. "People like us?"

"People who haven't been given everything. If we want it, we have to go out and earn it."

"Oh, that's a relief. For a minute there, I thought you were lumping me in with trailer-park trash."

By the flash of anger across her face, he'd placed his shot well.

"Just wait," she said. "She'll get what's coming to her."

He struggled to keep the mask of boredom in place when the alarm bells sounded in his head. "Sounds ominous. Are you going to write a naughty word on her locker between classes?"

A viper's smile curved her lips.

The storm that'd been building inside him suddenly exploded through his veins. "You know something, don't you?"

Abruptly, she stood.

He swiveled on the barstool and trapped her between his thighs before she could escape. "Talk."

Triumph flared in her eyes. She reached out and raked her fingernails lightly down the side of his cheek. The urge to slap her hand away nearly won out, but her apparent desire to incite his passion stayed him.

"We could be so good together." She trailed her fingers down his neck to the exposed skin over his collarbone. "Let me prove it to you. Afterwards, we'll talk."

With great care, he drew her hand away from his body, clamping his fingers around hers in a lingering touch, if only to keep her from touching him for a few moments. "Tell me now."

One of her overdrawn eyebrows arched, and the smile turned triumphant. "Your body for my cooperation? How kinky."

He bared his teeth. "Unless your boyfriend has a problem with that?"

She hitched one small shoulder. "Fidelity between us isn't essential."

"How convenient for you," he ground out.

"And for you." She pulled her hand free from his and explored the folds of his Henley above his abdomen.

A boisterous song kicked on overhead and he gritted his jaw.

He pinched a lock of hair from her shoulder between two fingers and rubbed the dark strands together. The color appeared dull, lacking the fascinating variations of browns and reds in Mina's hair.

"Tell me what you've done," he said.

"I don't have to do anything. She'll do it to herself." The cold, cruel curl of her lips could hardly be called a smile. "It's karma."

He dropped the listless hank of her hair. "You hate her."

Her smile vanished. "She's a stuck-up bitch who thinks she's better than everyone else."

With a grimace, he leaned close. "You try too hard. She's everything you're not, and that makes you sick with jealousy."

The woman scoffed, but she couldn't hide her furious envy.

"Unfortunately for you, you'll never compare to her." He spoke low next to her ear. "No matter how many of her boyfriends you fuck."

Pure hatred contorted her features, which sent a jolt of satisfaction shooting through him. The pleasant sensation, though dampened somewhat by the effects of the alcohol, was shallow and mean.

And short-lived.

When he twisted on the barstool to allow her to step out from between his legs, the image that greeted him landed like a blow to his sternum.

Merely a few feet away, Mina stood watching them with large, round eyes.

$\mathcal{M}$ ina's heart clamped like a vise and she couldn't stem the gasp of pain. Unable to hear the words they spoke to each other over the loud music, her eyes fastened on each point of contact—his hand clasping hers, his mouth a whisper from her ear, his thighs encasing her hips.

She clutched Shea's ledgers to her chest, a useless shield against the knife already plunged into her heart.

The music overhead switched and the sudden quiet jarred her from the haze of anguish engulfing her. Slowly, his beautiful face came into focus. Unshaven and disheveled, dark circles ringed his eyes while shadows haunted his features. He looked tired, ragged even.

She didn't want to contemplate why he wasn't getting enough sleep.

"Your timing is incredible," Phoebe drawled, a viper's smile curving her mouth.

"And yours is predictable." Mina wished to get away, but Noah's dark eyes captured hers.

"It's not what you think," he said.

She didn't know what she thought about anything anymore, but the anguish pummeling her felt like betrayal. Which made little sense.

Noah hadn't betrayed her. He'd moved on without her. Just as she'd told him to.

Inevitably, there'd be other women. Another woman. She'd resigned herself to that when she'd sent him away. Even though the thought of him with someone else turned her stomach, she'd known it would happen. Eventually.

But not this soon.

And not with *her.*

With the sinuous bearing of a snake, Phoebe slid onto the barstool beside Noah and watched them while she sipped her drink.

You did this. You sent him away. Did you think he would wait for you?

"It doesn't matter what I think." Mina's throat ached with the effort to hold herself together and not break wide open in front of them. "You don't owe me any explanations."

She expected his anger. With an aching sorrow, she braced for his hatred. But the severe slash of anguish that cut across his face stunned her. She blinked several times, baffled by it, but he was already in motion, pushing off his barstool and stalking around behind the bar, taking with him any chance she had to scrutinize what lay behind the hurt she'd glimpsed.

Impulse carried her a few steps toward him, but right then, Luke slipped onto a barstool beside the one Noah had vacated and she stumbled to a stop.

"Hey, kids," he said. "What's happening?"

In reply, Noah snatched a tumbler off the bar top and tossed its contents into the sink basin. He overturned a coffee mug and reached for the coffeepot.

Luke's gaze bounced from his brother to Mina and back

again. Noah stirred a heaping spoonful of sugar into the black liquid, then raised the coffee mug to his lips.

Over the brim of his cup, he glared dark, piercing daggers at her as he drank. The cold lash of his fury was clear even across the space of between them. He appeared much as he did that day, several months ago now, when he'd suddenly appeared in the ballroom after years away, full of anger and hatred.

For her.

Luke stood. "I can see I've interrupted something here…"

"Sit," Noah commanded. "Mina and I are finished."

The words, delivered with a sharp bite, twisted the knife lodged in her chest. It was the fatal puncture.

She shattered.

Blindly, she turned and fled.

As she careened toward the exit, she caught sight of Emily slipping in through the back door and ran toward her cousin's familiar face.

But just when she neared the door, a large, lumbering body staggered into her path.

She skidded to a stop, then reared back when she glimpsed Drew's face, flushed red and contorted with rage.

"How could you?" he seethed. His fingers bit into her flesh when he gripped her arm. "After everything I've done for you, you would pull something like this?"

"Drew, that hurts." She tried to tug free of his painful grasp. "Let me go."

He squeezed tighter. "All you had to do was keep your mouth shut, but you couldn't do it."

"I don't know what you're talking about?" Her fingers pried at his large hand, trying to loosen his constricting grip.

"You think you're the only one he hurt?"

The warmth leeched from her body, and she froze with the terror that seized her.

"You weren't the only one he fucked over." With a hard shove, he released her. "He wasn't our friend. He was a fraud."

Her gaze darted left and right. "Drew, people are looking."

"Screw them. I'm ruined. All because of you." His arms flailed as he ranted at Mina for the unforgivable crime of telling his wife what had happened in the bank restroom.

She backed away, but his gestures only grew more wild and sweeping.

Until, as if in slow motion, his arm shot out and the back of his hand struck her cheek with a crack of sound. Her head snapped around as pain exploded behind her eyes.

Behind her, a savage cry rent the air.

"Oh, shit," Drew sputtered. "Mina, I didn't mean—"

Tears flooded her vision when she recoiled from his touch and turned toward the sound of that ferocious howl.

People seated nearby scattered in all directions as Noah bore down on them.

Drew's eyes grew wide. "I didn't mean—"

A roar erupted from Noah when he slammed Drew into the wall. He closed his hand around Drew's throat and pinned him to the exposed brick. "You son of a bitch."

Luke burst into view. "Well, that escalated quickly." He grunted as he angled his body between the men.

"Let me go," Noah hissed. "I'm going to kill him."

"You made your point," Luke said.

"Not by a longshot." Beneath Noah's death grip, Drew squirmed.

Luke tipped his head to one side. "Oh, look, he's turning purple."

"I didn't mean to hit her," Drew croaked. "Look at her. She's fine."

With an abruptness that shocked, Noah released Drew,

who collapsed against the wall while choking coughs racked his body, and rounded on Mina.

Suddenly the focus of his fierce regard, her breath snagged in her throat.

Then he was in motion, his dark eyes burning like hot coals as he stalked toward her.

She stumbled back, a step for every one of his, but he pursued her to the last, until her back came up hard against the wall and a whoosh of air knocked from her lungs.

He peered down at her for a moment. Then slowly, he lifted his hand to hook his finger beneath her chin and, with a gentleness that grabbed at her insides, tilt her face toward the light. Anguish touched his features as his fingertips floated across her stinging cheek.

An aching breath shuddered through her.

Then his face darkened. "Luke!"

At his bellow, she jolted.

"Right here," came Luke's dry reply.

Noah glowered back at his brother. "I want Drew Alexander arrested."

Mina grasped his wrist. "Noah—"

His head whipped back around. "He hit you."

"I didn't mean it," Drew argued.

"Arrest him," Noah ordered Luke. "Before I kill him."

"You're really committed to this outcome," Luke observed. "It's a little caveman, don't you think?"

Mina tried again. "Noah—"

Noah's head whipped around. "What?"

"I'm okay," she soothed. "He's drunk and—"

"He hit you," Noah ground out.

Luke unwrapped a sucker and the red ball disappeared between his lips. "Let the woman speak, Noah."

"He was upset," she began.

"What was he upset about?" The sucker's white stick bobbed with Luke's question.

"He thinks I exposed his affair."

A small gasp slipped from Emily, who had just returned from the bar with a towel filled with ice cradled in her hands.

Noah reached for the towel.

"Did you?" Luke said around the sucker.

When Noah pressed the cold towel to her cheek, Mina sucked in a hiss of air. She shook her head. "No."

Luke pulled the sucker from his mouth. "I take it he didn't believe you?"

"He didn't give me a chance to say anything. He's drunk and careless... It was an accident."

"Told you," Drew said.

A growl vibrated in Noah's throat.

"Hush." Luke made a quick sweep of the small crowd gathered around them. He nudged his chin at Phoebe. "You just spectating with the rest, or do you have some part to play in this little drama?"

Phoebe's cruel smile made an appearance. "I'm just enjoying the show."

For a moment, Luke regarded her through narrowed eyes. Then his expression cleared. "Ah, I get it."

"Get what?"

"You're the other woman."

A dangerous light flashed in Phoebe's eyes, but she lifted her chin. "That's not a crime, is it, Officer?"

"Not in the legal sense, no." Luke aimed the red ball of his sucker at Drew. "So now that the fun with this one is over," the red ball shifted toward Noah, "you're onto your next good time. Do I have that right?"

Phoebe's eyes blazed with anger. "You have no idea what you're talking about."

With a knowing smile, Luke popped the sucker between his lips once more. "If you say so." He started to turn from her, but then twisted back. "Oh, you can go now." He waggled his fingers at her. "We won't be needing any more of your help."

There was a split second where Mina thought Phoebe might combat Luke, but in the end, she squared her shoulders and marched toward the exit, disappearing through the door.

Luke's bright green gaze swung to Emily. "Don't tell me you're the wife."

Emily's bright strawberry blonde hair shimmered when she shook her head.

"Well, that's a relief." Luke yanked the sucker from his mouth, which painted his lips red. "So what's your story?"

A frown tugged at Emily's features. "M-m-my story?"

"Where do you fit in to this soap opera?"

"I don't," Emily said. "I'm n-nobody."

For a moment, Luke studied her with intense interest. Beneath his scrutiny, her pale skin flushed bright pink, which somehow enhanced the smattering of freckles across the bridge of her small nose.

When Luke finally spoke, his voice was heavy with his gravity. "It's the nobodies you have to keep your eye on."

At that, the color leeched from Emily's cheeks.

A wicked smile curved Luke's red-stained mouth.

"I don't give a shit what the mayor thinks Mina did or didn't do to him." Fury lashed with Noah's words. "He's dangerous, and I don't want him anywhere near her."

Clumsily, Drew staggered to his feet. "You're acting like her bodyguard or her boyfriend or something. Why don't you get lost, Nolan?"

Noah's muscles bunched.

"Don't talk to him like that." The command shot from

Mina with a strength that surprised her as much as it appeared to shock both Drew and Noah.

"Why not?" Drew shuffled over to the nearest table and collapsed into a chair. "Is he a registered voter?"

"Because I asked you not to." Her skin aching with cold, she pulled the towel away from her cheek and moved toward the table. "He's my friend, and he doesn't deserve your abuse."

Drew grunted his derision.

She dragged a chair around so that it faced him and lowered herself down.

His glassy-eyed gaze struggled to find her face. "You talk like you're in love with him or something." A severe scowl twisted his features. "Are you in love with him?"

"Yes, I am."

He made another scoffing noise.

"Drew, you have to stop. You're self-destructing."

He regarded her with wild, troubled eyes. "What the fuck do you know about it?"

"I know enough," she said. "I know you."

"That doesn't give you the right to ruin my life."

"I didn't tell anyone what I saw."

He tried to stare her down, but struggled to do so with his unfocused gaze.

Droplets of water leaked through the towel and dripped onto her lap. How long ago it seemed now since he'd been good to her.

"Stop it." His soft command lashed. "Stop looking at me like I'm *him*."

Her heart thrashed against her rib cage.

"I am not him." Though he spoke quietly, his words bounded at her like a snarling dog.

"I know you're not," she whispered.

By unhurried, heart-stopping increments, he sat forward

in the chair. As she watched, a lifetime of pain and shame tormented his features.

Her lungs spasmed, and she struggled to draw breath.

Then, with a gasp of pain, he dropped his head. "I tried to stop him."

She squeezed her eyes shut. "I know you did."

"But I was too late, wasn't I?"

Over her shoulder, Noah murmured her name.

"He was my best friend."

"Drew, please...."

When his head came up, his eyes glowed. "I should've killed him myself."

"Don't say that." Mina swallowed back a surge of nausea. "You were the only one who tried to help me, and I will always be grateful to you for that."

He blinked at her with bloodshot eyes.

"But, Drew, you're hurting people. I know that's not what you want."

A heavy sigh leaked from Drew, and he fell back in the chair. He wiped his nose with the sleeve of his dress shirt. "I didn't mean to hit you."

"I know," she said. "It better not happen ever again."

He dragged a hand over his face, and his demeanor changed, as though he'd pulled a mask into place.

Craning his neck, his blurry gaze found Luke. "Are you going to arrest me?"

"I don't think that's necessary," Luke said. "Do you?"

With a hiccup, Drew shook his head. "I could use a ride home, though. I'm wasted."

"In that case, I'd be honored to escort you, Mr. Mayor."

Drew hoisted himself to his feet and shuffled toward the exit. "You're a real smooth guy, Officer Nolan."

Chuckling, Luke fell in step behind him. "I try."

Suddenly, Drew pulled up. "You know, I'm looking for a new campaign manager—"

Luke slapped a hand on Drew's shoulder and gave him a light push toward the door. "With all due respect, there's not a chance in hell I'm interested."

While Drew disappeared outside, Luke turned back.

His intense green gaze fixed on Emily. "Can I walk you out?"

Hectic color whipped into Emily's cheeks, and she gave her head a firm shake. "I'm good on m-m-my own."

Two boyish dimples appeared in Luke's cheek, though he didn't smile. "But I insist."

Her shoulders held high and tight, Emily crossed to him, and together they disappeared through the door.

Around them, the pub goers had resumed their revelries while overhead, an energetic Irish tune played. For a moment, she could almost pretend everything was normal.

Except Noah stood at her shoulder, exactly where he'd been when, for the first time, Drew spoke to her of the awful past. Noah would've heard their words. Had he understood their meaning?

Stop looking at me like I'm him. Drew's desperate demand pierced her. *I'm not him.*

Of that crime, she was guilty. Likely, she'd perpetrated the same offense against every man she'd ever known.

Including Noah.

She'd hurt him the most when she'd closed herself off.

He deserved better. He deserved to know she wasn't afraid of him. Never him.

Her hands shook, and she abandoned the soaked towel on the table, then pushed to her feet. Slowly, she turned.

He watched her closely, the tension in his body reflected in his face. He appeared pale, stricken, and the hard set of his features obscured all the soft contours of his beautiful face. A face she loved so well. Her heart gave a painful wrench.

"There is something I should tell you."

A small crack in his expression echoed through her, like a pulse of pain. Fear seized her chest and squeezed. The tightness grew unbearable. When she told him the whole truth, what would he think of her? Would her ugly past repulse him? Would he wish to stay away from her? Would another decade pass before she ever laid eyes on him again?

A flash of longing sliced through her, a sharp yearning to be away from this moment. But it was no use.

Her time for hiding was at an end.

CHAPTER 33

*W*ords formed, dried, and turned to ash in her mouth. Her hands trembled, so she balled them into fists.

"I broke your rule."

He blinked several times. "You broke my…?" He repeated her words as though he struggled to grasp their meaning.

"I did." She lifted her shoulders and dropped them helplessly. "I promised not to fall in love with you, but…I couldn't stop myself. Although technically, I didn't do any falling. I'm pretty sure I was already in love with you."

He stared, glassy-eyed.

"I'm sorry. F-for everything…for the way I acted and the things I said. For Drew, and Phoebe."

A flash of alarm chased across his face, and her heart ached at seeing it.

"Don't worry." She held up her hands. "I will not freak out about you two."

He cursed, then grasped one of her hands, whisked her through the pub, and down the narrow hallway to Shea's office.

He flung open the door, then barred them inside the small space.

When he turned to face her, his presence overpowered the tiny room. "What you saw was the entirety of my one-sided relationship with that woman. Entirely on her part, by the way."

The suffocating despair tightening her chest eased a bit.

But the office walls appeared to wobble, and his tension-filled body seemed to vibrate with the tempest of emotions coursing through him.

Instinctively, she retreated, but tripped over a something big and solid.

She looked down, and her racing heart stopped.

A suitcase.

Her heart gave a painful throb as she realized the pile of luggage at her feet belonged to Noah.

"You're leaving." The words sounded hollow and a not a little dumb.

When she met his gaze, his dark eyes searched her face, and she saw in them the emotion his body cried out. Reflected beneath the shimmering copper glints was raw, naked fear.

Any moment now, he would get on a plane and fly away from here. If she never said another word to him, he would leave, not knowing the truth about what happened all those years ago. He would go on believing that she'd discarded him and continue hating her for her awfulness.

He might never know how hard and how long she'd pined for him, wishing to see his face from time to time, when her world had collapsed in on her.

"Before you go, I wondered if I might talk to you." Her voice sounded faint over the sound of her heart thundering in her skull. "To t-tell you something that might help you understand why I... why I'm...." Her voice broke with her misery. "I want you to understand."

The fear in his eyes grew with her own.

"The other night, when you asked me to talk to you—" The words jammed in her throat and she lifted her shoulders. "I panicked."

"I know."

"I'm sorry if I hurt you—"

"It's okay."

"It's not okay," she burst out, then yanked her bottom lip between her teeth. "I don't want to hurt you, Noah. I never meant to. Not now, and not back in high school."

He grew still, unnaturally so, and she considered the possibility that he already knew what she'd say next.

"You said I mistreated you back then, after our first time together. Do you remember you said that?"

"I remember." The words rasped in his throat.

"Well, I didn't remember. Until a few weeks ago, everything that'd happened after that Halloween party was just..." Her hand moved through the air as if she might capture the words. "...lost to me. It's like the memories were misplaced or stolen. I didn't understand what had happened to them."

A deep, shuddering breath rattled through her when she steeled herself against the fear. Then she started talking.

With broken sentences and an uncontrollable tremor to her voice, she stumbled over the terrible words. She told him what had happened to her during that school break, and how it'd taken her years to trust anyone or to let anyone touch her.

She told him how she'd spent her twenties trying desperately to fill the hole inside her with other men and food and sometimes even alcohol. Anything to make her forget what she'd lost. To make her numb to the pain.

She told him how, before he'd returned, she couldn't

recall a time when sex wasn't lonely or sad or fearful, and how it made her stomach sick to think about.

He showed no condemnation as she spoke, only a sorrow that threatened to set loose the tears she choked back.

When finally, there were no more words, the room fell quiet. Her head ached, and her muscles screamed with the tension of holding back the torrent of shame and tears.

In his pale face, his dark eyes gleamed as someone who'd suffered a severe shock.

"Noah?"

He startled and blinked.

Her heart tried to pound its way out of her chest. "Say something," she whispered. "*Please.*"

A smothered sound, like a curse or a sob, tore from him. Then, with a flash of movement, his arms were pressing her face to the soft fleece of his jacket. "I'm so sorry. *A chuisle mo chroí.*" His voice was ragged, shredded with emotion. "So goddamned sorry."

"I wasn't trying to keep secrets from you." She tried to pull back, but he held onto her. "Some things I remember and some things... I'm not sure if they really happened or not. Maybe they're memories, or it's possible they're only nightmares." She buried her face in his chest. "The truth is, I don't want to remember."

He slipped a hand beneath her hair and massaged the tight muscles of her neck. His jacket smelled of laundry detergent and wood smoke from the fire, and she closed her eyes, feeling the rigid tension drain from her body beneath his touch.

"I've been so afraid." Her words were muffled by his fleece. "I was afraid if you knew—"

"I know—"

"That it'd change things—"

"I know—"

"But I wanted to tell you in case..." She lifted her head and his hand slid to her cheek. She wrapped her fingers around his wrist. "In case... possibly... you might forgive me."

"There's nothing to forgive."

"There is. I need you to know it's not that I didn't trust you, or that I don't want to be with you. It's just...I had no clue how to..."

"Hush now, *mo chroí*. You don't need to explain." He pressed his lips to her forehead. "Thank you for telling me."

Adrenaline leached from her body, and she sagged against him. "I never told anyone."

A broken curse fell from his lips. "No one? All these years...?"

"I tried to tell my mom once, but I couldn't get the words out. Not long after that, she sent me to live with Rose. I want to believe she was trying to protect me..."

His thumb rubbed the spot at the base of her ear. "But you told Drew."

She shook her head. "He found out when..." Her stomach pitched with the memory and she trailed off.

Noah's thumb stilled.

Reaching up, she tugged on the earlobe of her injured ear. "That's why they were fighting."

Confusion clouded his eyes, but then, with his understanding, came the agony. "When you lost your hearing... your cousin... He hit you."

"It was him." She couldn't bring herself to say his name. "He's the one who...hurt me."

A hiss of air leaked from Noah.

"After the fight, Drew drove me to the hospital. My ear hurt so badly, and I was scared and sick to my stomach." Her voice trembled, but she rushed on. "He cracked jokes the whole way. I never would've gotten through it if he wasn't there, trying to make me laugh."

"Then I'm glad he was there for you," Noah said softly, sincerely. "And your cousin?" A hard edge chased the softness from his voice. "How did he die?"

"He became self-destructive. Even before he... hurt me, he drank and did hard drugs. But afterwards, he was out of control. He was reckless. Careless in everything he did. He'd drink and drive, get high and take stupid risks. He liked to play with guns. Once, he overdosed." Moments ticked by while she picked and discarded words. Finally, she settled on the naked facts. "He killed himself."

Noah squeezed his eyes shut.

"It devastated our family." Her courage failing, she studied the floorboards. "He was their golden boy."

"Mina, you are not responsible for anything that happened. He was sick."

"I know that. I do." She risked looking at him. "But it *feels* like I did something wrong."

"Don't say that." He nuzzled her ear to soothe the bite of his tone. "Don't you dare say that, *a mhuirnín.*"

She wanted to argue, but exhaustion overwhelmed her. With her knuckles, he rubbed her eyes.

He pulled her snug against his chest. "I'm so proud of you. You're so strong and so brave."

She wished to hear him repeat the words, over and over, until a new truth replaced years of shame and self-doubt.

But there wasn't enough time.

With her ear pressed over his pounding heart, his suitcase lay in the path of her gaze. It was time for him to go, but she'd take the gift he'd given her, accepting his words inside her heart. She'd tuck them away there, and after he'd gone, she'd take them out from time to time and remember and smile.

And occasionally, she might even let herself believe what he'd said was true.

He rode with her back to the carriage house and kept her hand wrapped in his as they stumbled across the dark lawn and up the rickety staircase. Inside, they kept the lights low and made their way to her bedroom.

She crawled beneath the quilts, and he stretched out beside her, wrapping his body around hers. They lay together in the dark quiet and she listened to the sound of their breathing slow and deepen together.

Sometime later, she cracked open her eyes. A warm, heavy sleep wanted to pull her under, but she fought her way to the surface to see Noah crouched before the fireplace, placing a log on the flame. The fire's soft glow washed over his face and hair.

Watching him, she became aware of a tiny pulse of feeling in her chest. She waited while it strengthened and bloomed into something she could name. Relief? No, something more. Like hope, but not as strong.

Almost-hope.

Almost-but-not-quite hope that she'd spoken the truth aloud, and the world hadn't caved in around her.

She couldn't help but wonder if life might go on after all. If, in fact, it was possible to pick up all the scattered pieces of herself and fit them back together again. Not in the same way, but in an entirely new way that was different and unfamiliar but whole, nonetheless.

One word whispered from a place deep inside her. One word that meant nothing and everything. The sliver of shame extracted, perhaps the wounds of her past might begin to heal.

Maybe.

∾

Denials screamed inside his head.

NO! Not this. Not her.

From the bed, she regarded him with solemn eyes. He stood and returned to her.

The mattress dipped beneath his weight as he sat beside her and closed a hand around her ankle.

He traced small circles with his thumb. "I need to go out for a little while."

Her gaze sharpened on his face. "Okay."

"I won't be long." He dropped a kiss on her forehead. "Sleep. I'll be back as soon as I can."

"It's okay if you have to go…"

With a soft sound, he shushed her. "Rest now, *mo chroí*. I'll be back before you wake."

He rubbed her ankle until her breathing changed, deepened. When her soft snores carried over to him, he pushed up slowly from the bed and stole silently from the room.

When he slipped through her door and into the dark night, he barely noticed how a black sky heavy with clouds blocked out the moon and stars. His feet gained speed as he staggered to the rusty old truck parked in the driveway and climbed behind the wheel.

As he drove along the darkened lakeshore, his mind descended further into chaos. Outside Lucky's Pub, he whipped her truck into an empty parking spot.

He glimpsed the wild-eyed man in the glass-paned window before he hauled open the pub door and stepped inside. At the late hour, the place was mostly empty, but the lingering scents of warm bread and pub food made his stomach roil.

One by one, he picked them out of the sparse crowd.

Jack poised before a dartboard, about to let loose a flying dart.

Luke reclined in a booth near the front, a beautiful blonde snuggled into his side.

Shea stood behind the bar, chatting it up with the line of older men seated on barstools.

Noah's feet moved under him, carrying him across the room as though he treaded through waist-deep water.

Dimly, he noted Jack's head turn and his arm drop harmlessly to his side.

The charmer's smile fell from Luke's lips.

Shea's raspy voice tossed a throwaway comment toward the men, and then his bright eyes appeared directly in Noah's field of view as he claimed an empty barstool.

"What can I do?" He placed a Guinness on the bar before Noah.

Noah's throat closed. He dragged the back of his hand across his mouth, saw how it trembled, and curled his fingers into a tight ball. "You'd help me?"

"Anything," Shea said. "Name it."

Tell me how to do battle with ghosts.

Nothing could erase what had happened to her. Nothing could restore what she'd lost. What was taken from her. Noah shook his head and raised the glass to his lips.

Luke and Jack slid onto stools on either side of him. When he refused to fill their silence, their voices swirled around him while he stared unseeing at a spot on the wall. Jack razzed Luke about the third woman he'd brought to the pub inside a two-week period, and Shea questioned Jack about the finer points of the NHL lockout, over which they'd now canceled the entire season.

Voices still unfamiliar to Noah somehow comforted, and as he sat among them, listening, something inside him shifted. He couldn't make sense of it, not in those moments, but one simple, disturbing truth crystallized in his mind.

He belonged to them.

He belonged to this cold, turbulent place.

To this woman.

Mina.

The realization might've dawned too late.

Or perhaps it was only an impulse born of shock and despair. Of his desire for her. The desire of a man for a woman.

It wasn't only that. He knew it in his bones.

It was more. It was everything.

But was it too late?

He needed to accept the possibility she might never belong to him. To any man. His heart recoiled at the thought, even as his mind understood the truth of it.

Her pale, stricken face swam before his eyes. He'd never born witness to so much pain, and he didn't know whether he could bear it.

God dammit, but it hurt.

Had he done this to her? He'd pushed her. Past the point she wished to go. Faster than she was willing. In doing so, he'd brought back the horrific memories. He'd poked and prodded to get what he wanted, as he too often did.

He'd hurt her. The same way he'd hurt everyone he'd ever cared about.

As he listened to his brothers talking around him, his chest ached with an excruciating tightness.

He couldn't take back what he'd done. He didn't know how to fix what he'd broken.

How could he help her?

He feared there was only one thing he might do to ease her suffering.

He should leave and let her forget.

CHAPTER 34

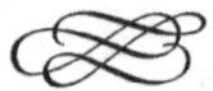

The clock on the mantel drummed out the relentless rhythm of each second ticking by. At Mina's kitchen table, Noah tried to focus on grading the stack of final exams in front of him and not the minutes slipping away.

With every swing of the clock's pendulum, his time with her drew nearer to the end.

He'd planned to score the exams on the flight and log his students' final grades remotely from Ireland, but he needed the distraction now. Anything to escape the turmoil churning inside him. How would he do it? How in the hell was he going to make himself get on that plane and leave her?

While he waited for her to wake up, he worked his way through the pile of essays. Near the bottom, he came across a test with barely legible handwriting and he paused over the paper a moment.

Without having to check the student's name at the top, the poorly spaced, oddly shaped letters told him the exam belonged to Damion. Noah's hands grew clammy, and he smoothed his palms down his thighs.

Then, slowly, he reached for the pages and started to read.

Damion's poor penmanship made scoring his answers slow going, but soon enough, a bloom of pride unfurled in Noah's chest. He reread Damion's answers with a more critical eye, then turned to his laptop where he'd pulled up the class register. With clumsy fingers, he input the score and tabulated Damion's final grade.

The number leapt off the computer screen. The kid had done it. After almost failing the first half of the semester, he'd aced the second half and pulled a B in the course.

A slow smile curved Noah's mouth. Lacing his fingers together behind his head, he sat back and marveled at the data displayed on his laptop's screen.

Of all the career successes he'd amassed over the years, this one was the sweetest. The truest.

Just then, his computer chirped, and the invitation to an online chat popped open. Noah accepted the request, and the face of his graduate student, Caleb, filled the screen.

The prior week, Caleb had arrived on site to begin setting up Noah's next excavation. Reading from his notebook, Caleb provided a quick update on the team's progress. Every locale possessed a unique set of peculiarities that had to be managed, and this site was no different, so they spent some time hashing out a plan to deal with the issues that had surfaced already.

A half hour later, they were wrapping up their conversation when the bedroom door creaked open. Noah turned his head at the sound just as Mina emerged.

He drank in the sight of her. Her fascinating auburn-brown hair lay in sexy disarray about her head and shoulders and her small bare feet peeked out from the bottoms of her loose-fitting pajama pants. Soft, sad eyes touched over his face.

His heart throbbed, and he rubbed his chest with the heel of his hand.

"So, we'll see you tomorrow?" Caleb asked.

Noah's head snapped back around to the computer screen. "Oh, uh…hey, Caleb, I gotta go. I'll talk to you soon."

Over the grainy feed, Caleb's forehead creased when he squinted into the camera. "Wait, why aren't you at the airport?" His head bent and he checked his wristwatch. "What time is your flight?"

"I'll call ya soon." Noah reached for the laptop lid.

"Don't forget you're meeting with the consulate on Monday—"

The rest of Caleb's sentence was cut short when Noah clicked the laptop shut.

Mina tugged the cuff of her long sleeve cotton T-shirt over one hand. "I didn't mean to interrupt."

"You didn't." With a soft nudge, he kicked out the leg of the chair next to his so that the seat faced him.

He tracked her movements as she crossed to him and settled in the chair.

"How are you?" he asked, peering into her pale face.

"I'm okay." She tortured the sleeve of her shirt with trembling fingers. "I feel like I could sleep for days."

"Then you should."

"How about you?" She probed him with haunted eyes. "Are you okay? I kind of dropped a lot on you last night…"

He couldn't lie and tell her what she'd shared had devastated him, but neither could he bring himself to add to her distress with the truth. That he was not okay. That he would never be okay again. "Don't worry about me."

"Too late." Her soft smile was fleeting. "Noah, I'm sorry…"

He shifted forward in the chair and, resting his forearms

on his knees, gripped her hand in both of his. "Please don't apologize to me. You have nothing to be sorry about. I hate what happened to you, and I'm so sorry for all that you've been through, but I'm honored and humbled that you found the courage to tell me." He lifted her hand to his mouth and brushed his lips across her skin. "You amaze me."

She uncurled her fingers and lightly stroked the side of his face. "Thank you for saying that."

"I mean it."

Pink touched her cheeks and her gaze bounced over the table, as if searching for an anchor amidst the wild storm inside her.

"What's this?" She pulled her hand from his and reached for the envelope on the table with her name on it.

A slither of dread snaked through him. "I wanted to talk to you about that…" He straightened in his chair. "It's my write up about the excavation."

"Can I open it?"

"There are a couple of things in there…that I want to talk to you about." His eyes found hers. "Things that may be diffi-cult for you to hear."

The color touching her cheeks faded, and she set the report aside. "All right…"

"We don't have to do this now—"

"It's okay. I'm okay." The haunted shadows in her eyes spread to her features. "Tell me. Please."

"A lot of what I'm about to tell you is only my best guess." He pressed his fingertips to the file folder, as if recalling the contents. "It's an educated guess built around a sprinkling of facts."

She studied him for a moment. "You think you know who the treasure belonged to?"

"Yeah, I think I do." He shifted in his chair. "It starts with your four-times-great-grandmother, Rachel. She grew up in

Virginia, and when she was about fourteen years old, Indians raided her family's home. She was captured and taken."

At her small gasp, his heart lurched.

"I have found no sources referencing her time in captivity." He watched her closely, gauging her response. "But she turns up again ten years later in Detroit, where she was ransomed from the Indians by a trader named Adam Winslow."

She gave a small shake of the head. "Ransomed?"

"Bought."

Her hand shot to her mouth.

"Rachel's father had hired Adam to find her, but by the time they returned to Virginia, her father was dead." Noah forged on, eager to reach the end. "Three years later, Adam shows up in the census records, living here on the island."

"That's what you found out back?" She bent over the drawing. "Their home?"

Noah pulled a paper from his stack of working files and laid it on the table between them.

"Here's a rendering of the layout of the buildings. It's a typical early American dwelling, and there's some evidence that Adam ran a shipping operation from here." Noah licked his dry lips. "But he became notorious for his other activities."

"The Winslows were loggers. Did he own a logging business?"

"Sort of. He was a timber pirate."

She blinked at him. "A pirate?"

"He intercepted ships stocked with lumber—stole them, actually—and sold the cargo himself. Apparently, he excelled at his chosen profession."

"He was a thief."

"It appears so, though his pirating activities weren't limited to timber." Noah stared at his hands, searching for the right words. "There is at least one account—" His voice faltered and he cleared his throat. "That claims Adam kidnapped women and transported them to Chicago."

The color seeped from Mina's complexion.

Noah gulped. "Where he sold them."

She stared at him with huge, round eyes, her hand clamped over her mouth as if to stem the shock and dismay from pouring out of her.

He leaned forward and grasped her hand lying limp in her lap. "Are you okay?"

Slowly, she pulled her hand away from her face and smoothed her fingers over his knuckles. "What happened to them?"

His long silence as he weighed his words grew heavy. "I don't know for sure. They disappear from the records."

The column of her throat spasmed when she swallowed. "And Rachel? What happened to her?"

"She brings us back to the treasure."

"Was it hers?"

"I believe so, based on the contents of the box. There was a silver hair comb commonly worn by Native Americans at the time as a status symbol and a gold-plated brooch engraved with the Welsh dragon, which also appears to be authentic."

"A Welsh dragon…?"

"Rachel's family name was Pryce. A Welsh surname." "And the maker's mark on the chest traces it to a well-known furniture craftsman in Virginia."

"Where she grew up," Mina said.

"That's right. Given these facts, I suspect she amassed the hoard. It's possible she and Adam built it together, or maybe she kept it hidden from him. Either way, I suspect she played a key role in its existence."

"Are you saying my four-times-great-grandmother was a pirate, too?"

"Maybe." With a smile, he shrugged. "Why not?"

She made a sound that might've been a laugh or a sob and rubbed her forehead.

He grew serious again. "She was a survivor. That much I do know."

From beneath the heel of her palm, she peeked at him. "She sounds like she was kind of badass."

"That she was. And you'll be relieved to hear Adam cleaned up his act. He went to work for the U.S. Marshals—fighting piracy on the Great Lakes, of all things."

An incredulous laugh slipped from her. "You're kidding."

Despite himself, he chuckled. "Not even a little. After that, the Winslows went legit. Adam's son turned the family operation into a lawful shipping company. His grandson built a logging empire, and your house."

For a moment, she stared at the envelope on the table, a mix of wonder and sorrow and mirth playing across her features.

"I'm sorry to spring all this on you right now," he said. "But I wanted to be the one to tell you."

Her cheeks flushed a dusty rose and brightened her eyes to cornflower blue. "Thank you for this. It's incredible what you've done."

Warmth from her smile curled through him. "You're welcome."

Her hand in his was small and cool, and he brushed the pad of his thumb across the soft skin over her knuckles.

The clock's steady pulse filled the silence. In his chest, his heart pounded to the beat and pushed the desperate aching through his veins to every part of his body.

He wanted to stay. He wanted to beg her to allow him to remain close enough to touch her and to share her pain. To carry some of the burden for her, if only for a little while. He wanted her to need him, or even just wish him to remain by her side, but he feared she would not. He feared she could not.

"What time is your flight?" she asked.

Against the slash of pain, he squeezed his eyes shut.

"You have to go." A soft smile touched her lips. "It's okay."

"I can…stay…if you want…?"

She was already shaking her head. "I can't ask you to do that."

"You can. If you want me to, I will."

Her eyes searched his for many long moments. Then she shook her head. "You need to go. They need you."

He hung his head. He knew in his mind her reasons had less to do with him than with everything else, but logic and fact did not persuade his battered heart. To it, she didn't want him.

She placed both her hands on his head and kissed the top of his hair. "You need to work. You love your work. It's important, and you're so good at it."

His work wasn't the only thing he loved. He opened his mouth to tell her that, but at the last, he pulled back the words. He didn't want to add any more to her plate. Already, he'd done enough to overwhelm and overburden her.

He laced his fingers through hers.

She squeezed his hand. "I think…I need a little time. I need to…process some things and…figure out some stuff. Go, please. I'll be fine."

He lifted her other hand to his mouth and pressed his lips into the heart of her palm. As much as it hurt, he understood. Though he wanted to curse with the frustration of not being able to take away her pain.

Her fingertips brushed his face. "I'll miss you."

His throat closed at her easy declaration. He tried to swallow but couldn't. "I'll miss you too."

"I'm going to talk to someone," she said in a small, hesitant voice. "I think it will help—I hope it will—I don't know…"

"I'm so proud of you." He brought her fingers to his lips. "You're the strongest person I know."

With a soft groan, she rolled her eyes.

"I'm serious."

Doubt-filled eyes searched his. "I don't feel strong."

"I know you don't, but trust me on this one."

He willed her to trust that what he said was true. Just as he'd trust her to make her way through the darkness, alone.

And he'd pray that her path might one day lead back to him.

CHAPTER 35

The day of her first therapy appointment, Mina threw up twice before she left the carriage house and once in the restroom at Dr. Smallwood's office. When she returned to the waiting room, an attractive woman with a warm smile and calming demeanor greeted her.

Probably in her thirties, Dr. Smallwood insisted Mina call her Chloe. Mina liked her almost immediately.

Chloe led Mina to a cozy office awash in neutral tones and textured fabrics and gestured Mina to an overstuffed armchair before lowering herself into an adjacent chair. She placed a bottle of water in Mina's hand and eased back in the chair.

"So, Mina, tell me why you've come to see me today."

The first minutes of that first session were torturous. She struggled to string together even two or three sentences on her reasons for making the appointment, stammering and stuttering, until Chloe leaned forward in her chair and grasped Mina's hand. She didn't speak, but just curled her fingers over Mina's knuckles and held on.

Until the tears came.

They streamed down Mina's cheeks while Chloe explained that she, too, was a survivor of sexual assault, and that her abuse was the reason she made it her life's work to help women like herself.

Women like Mina.

Dr. Smallwood described the grief process and explained post-traumatic stress disorder. Mostly, she talked about patience. Patience with the process. Patience with herself. Trauma to the soul, she explained, took time to heal. Whether the trauma had occurred recently or years before, as it had with Mina, the healing process was much the same. She didn't stop talking until the hour had ended.

All the while, Mina's tears flowed. She couldn't stop them. She emptied a box of Kleenex and muttered a humiliated "thank you" when Chloe handed her a fresh box.

Chloe scheduled Mina to meet with her three times a week. "Just for a little while," she said. "To get you through the next few weeks. Until you're ready to do more of the work on your own."

During those weeks, Mina suspected she'd descended into a certain kind of Hell.

She cried. She screamed. She despaired, then regrouped, only to start the shame spiral all over again.

Chloe helped Mina grapple with the darkest memories and the anguish that accompanied them, but even as they wrestled with the past, the future loomed before Mina like a menacing beast. She simply could not imagine a future where she might live with this truth. What did her recovered memories mean? Would she always feel so powerless to them? Would she ever be able to move past them? Would Noah?

"Noah?" Chloe asked. "He's someone special to you?"

"He is." Then Mina confessed her fear. "I'm afraid I'll let him down."

"How so?"

"Sometimes I don't want to... I don't like... I have bad days, and the memories are so real. Some days, I don't want to be around anyone. I don't want to talk about it, and I don't want to be touched. I can see that hurts him." Mina's cheeks burned.

Chloe gave her a reassuring smile. "In time, and with love and trust, you'll seek intimacy, and when you're ready, you'll be able to communicate your needs to him."

Mina worried her bottom lip. "What if he gets tired of waiting for me to get over it? Or comes to resent me?"

The way Drew had.

Emotion swirled in Chloe's gray-blue eyes, but the warmth and gentleness Mina had come to rely on remained. "Our experiences are part of who we are, but they aren't all that we are. We can move past trauma. I'm proof of that, and so are you."

"I don't want to disappoint him," Mina whispered.

"You won't disappoint him beyond the normal disappointments every couple experiences in each other. You're growing stronger every day, and soon you'll be able to articulate to him what you need, when you want intimacy, and how, and when you just need to be by yourself." Chloe handed Mina another tissue. "If you think it would help, and when you're ready, we can invite him to join us."

"He's not here. He's in Ireland, working."

"When he returns, we'll invite him to join us."

What if he didn't return? He was back in his home country, doing the thing he loved most. What if, once he'd gotten away from her and her awful baggage, he didn't wish to rush back to be with her?

She could hardly blame him if he stayed away.

In between counseling sessions and crying jags, Mina kept Shea's accounts up to date and worked on the house.

Done with the heavy construction and repairs, they moved into the final stages of the renovation.

Mina painted every inch of every room, including untold miles of trim and molding, while Sam and his men installed cabinetry and fixtures and laid tile in the kitchen and in all seven bathrooms.

Maybe it was the long winter slog, or a growing impatience with her gloomy thoughts and moods, but Mina couldn't bring herself to select the darker, more traditional decor in keeping with the home's history and instead chose light and airy color schemes, including warm creams and beiges for the walls, white cabinetry, and bright tile. So even as she worked to preserve the home's original look and feel, every day the house appeared more and more like a beach-side resort.

Finally, in late-February, winter showed the first signs of relenting. Mina fled the cramped confines of the carriage house and plunged toward the beach. But after only a few minutes, she retreated indoors and out of the harsh, biting winds whipping off the lake.

Over the next weeks, temperatures climbed steadily, and soon the large sheets of ice covering Lake Michigan began breaking apart with sharp, thunder-like cracks and deep rumbles. The lake raged, roaring back from its winter slumber as it swallowed the melting snow.

Whenever she had the chance, she escaped outdoors. On one such day, she ventured out with the hood of her coat drawn tight over her head and her rubber boots squishing in the slushy mud.

She aimed for the shelter of the tree grove. As she hiked across the yard, her breathing increased with the exertion, but she pushed on, relishing the burn of fresh air in her lungs and the rich, loamy scent of earth, so thick she could almost taste it on her tongue.

At the far edge of the woods, she spotted a lone crocus pushing up through the snow. She stopped and stared down at the tiny flower with its deep violet color, stark and brilliant against a backdrop of snow and mud.

Just a stumpy little thing, the flower stood only a few inches off the ground. She pulled the glove off one hand and crouched down to stroke a soft petal.

A smile teased across her lips at the small bud's stubborn persistence, sprouting with life in defiance of decay and death.

She continued her walk through the woods and then rounded back to the north edge of her property, where the remains of Adam and Rachel's home sat overlooking the expanse of Lake Michigan.

With Noah's guidance, she'd applied for a historical marker. Someday soon, she hoped to find the funding for a memorial or an exhibition to allow visitors to view the ruins and learn about life on the island for the early settlers.

Wandering through the site always made her feel closer to Noah. Though he was never far from her mind, here, his presence was strongest, as if he'd left a part of himself behind to protect and defend that which was irreplaceable and precious to him.

In the weeks since he'd been gone, their packed, erratic schedules, rural locations, and differing time-zones all conspired to make regular communications between them a challenge.

Three days ago, he'd called her in the afternoon, but she'd missed her phone's ringing to the wail of the wet saw the crew used to cut tile for the kitchen backsplash. He'd called her again just after midnight, which was five o'clock in the morning in Ireland, but after a grueling session with Chloe, Mina had crawled into bed, seeking sanctuary in sleep, and slept through her phone's ringing.

When she awakened to find the missed call, she dialed him back right away. But she got the automated message telling her he was out of the service area, which meant he was at his new site somewhere in the Irish countryside that lacked reliable cell phone service.

She then tried sending him a text. *How are you?*

His reply didn't come through until later that night. *I miss you. Tell me you're okay.*

I'm okay. I wish you were here.

Over twenty-four hours had passed since then.

After her morning walk, she changed into her paint clothes and set up in the ballroom with her drop-cloth, can of paint, and brushes. She worked for a few hours until the end of Noah's workday neared, then she put down her paintbrush and pulled her cell phone from the back pocket of her jeans.

With shaking hands, she scrolled through her contact list and selected his name. She sat cross-legged on the floor while the first ring sounded in her ear.

From her vantage point, she inspected her handiwork with satisfaction. The fresh, light paint color brightened the massive room, and the neutral palette enhanced the opulent mural on the ceiling.

As the second ring sounded in her ear, a memory came to her of that rainy day last summer when she'd stood alone in this darkened room, feeling lost and lonely.

The day Noah had walked back into her life.

On the third ring, her call went to his voicemail. A computer-generated voice rattled off instructions, and at the beep, Mina started talking. She left a rambling message full of awkward missteps, restarts, and prolonged silences. She even dropped the "I love you" bomb before panicking and disconnecting mid-sentence.

Her groan of mortification echoed around the empty

ballroom. She smacked the cell phone to her forehead and then let her head fall back against the wall with a soft thud.

That was probably going to freak him out, she thought as she gazed up at the meticulously restored cherubs floating overhead.

While she kept repeating her clumsy declarations of love to him, she didn't know if he loved her back. He hadn't said so.

If pressed, she'd believe that he cared about her. But what if, now that he was away from the island and away from her, he was happier? What if the darkness inside her was too much for him?

If the choice were hers, would she choose to stay away? Once free from the cloud of sorrow, it would be difficult to return.

An elfin cherub smiled down at her with a glint of mockery in his baby-blue eyes.

Silly, stupid girl, he seemed to say.

"I know, I know."

~

NOAH HAD DONE IT AGAIN.

Caleb stared at him, wide-eyed. "I can't believe it. Another royal. That's two in five years. It's insane."

It was like winning the lottery twice. Three times, if you counted the Thief Island treasure hoard.

"You have the most amazing luck." Caleb's triumphant laughter rang in Noah's ears. "You're going to win Archaeologist of the Year again."

There were worse things that could happen for his career, though the possibility of receiving the field's top honor didn't particularly appeal to Noah. His goals had shifted.

More accurately, they'd been turned upside down and jumbled all out of order.

Rather than accolades, he craved the satisfaction of turning on a young mind.

The friendship of a brother.

The love of a good woman.

When had it happened? He couldn't say exactly. Probably about the time he'd fallen in love with a sad, sweet woman.

Mina.

Noah shook himself. He kept doing that, thinking of them when he should be focused on work.

He arranged his features into the semblance of a smile. In the last twelve weeks, he'd perfected the fake curvature of the mouth. It was a useful tool. One that masked the constant ache in his chest where his heart gasped and strained without them.

Dammit, but it hurt.

"Don't go booking your airfare just yet," Noah said. "There's a lot of work left to do."

"Not tonight, though." Caleb closed his laptop and slid it into a black leather case. "Catch you at the pub later?"

Noah didn't want to go to the local tavern with Caleb and the rest of the research team. He wasn't in the mood.

He was never in the mood. "Sure."

With a parting nod, Caleb ducked his head and slipped through the tent flap.

Noah stared down at the sixth-century artifact and tried to turn his mind back to his work.

He'd been right to leave, he reminded himself. She was better off without him there.

The time away, alone, had been good for him, too. It'd given him a little distance. Some perspective.

He'd begun to remember his father without fear and anger. The dark memories had faded, and he even recalled some good times. For all his faults, Daniel had cared about his wife, and when fate took Fiona from them too soon, it might as well have taken Daniel with it. A tragedy within a tragedy.

Noah might never fully forgive his father for his weaknesses, for being unable to love a child the way a parent should, but he understood a bit more clearly now the devastation that had warped Daniel's mind and corrupted his heart.

If he lost Mina forever, could he honestly say he'd survive it any better than Daniel had?

Who knew? Sometimes life's sadness broke people. The way it'd broken Daniel.

What if tragedy had broken his Mina, too?

Weariness tugged at him, and for the first time, Noah considered that, though his anger at Daniel was justified, it might be all right to let it go. Lord knew he was tired of carrying it around all the time.

With a sigh of surrender, he packed up his gear. He headed back to his hotel room. Maybe he'd sleep before heading out to the tavern, where he'd fake his way through another night of socializing and pretending everything was fine.

It was exhausting, the pretending. He pretended a lot.

He pretended he wasn't destroyed, and that this separation from Mina wasn't a tear that'd hang inside his soul forever.

He pretended to move on, like all the other times.

In reality, he was a mess.

Away from them, he was bereft.

Away from her, he was lost.

He was homesick.

Fuck.

CHAPTER 36

Sunlight streamed through the oversized windows and spilled across the gleaming black-and-white marble tiles of the foyer floor.

"So, this is it." A hint of wonder lightened Sam's voice.

Mina held her arms out wide. "This is it."

Their gazes soaked in the transformation, from the smooth, ivory walls to the rebuilt twin staircases and antique crystal chandelier Mina had found at a flea market and rewired.

It'd taken eleven months, hundreds of gallons of paint and stain, and her life savings.

But it was done, and it was beautiful.

No longer a hopeless ruin.

Sam bent and plucked his contractor belt off the floor. He slung the heavy tool belt over his shoulder and pulled open the front door.

"On to the next job?"

Sam turned from the archway, a gleam in his brown eyes. "We're finishing the basement on a 1970s ranch. Place feels like a shack after this."

Her laugh sounded rusty from lack of use.

"Welcome home." He tipped his head in parting, then ambled down the front stairs and climbed into his truck.

The vehicle awakened with a growl. Beneath its tires, gravel crunched and popped as Sam rolled down the long drive for the last time.

Alone with her nearly seven thousand square feet, Mina released a deep, drawn-out breath.

Home?

She listened and waited.

Nothing. Except the solitude of a cavernous estate. In the distance, the soft sway of the lake.

And an empty hole next to her heart. Because he wasn't there.

Mina reached for the door to shut it when a blue sedan pulled into the drive. She didn't recognize the vehicle and stepped out onto the front porch as it maneuvered the winding driveway and pulled to a stop at the bottom of the porch stairs.

Mina's heart thrummed as her mind raced with the possibilities of who might drop in on her unexpectedly.

Emily stepped from the sedan. "Surprise."

Mina's shoulders sagged. "Oh, no. Did I forget you were coming again?"

With a laugh, Emily shook her head and climbed the stairs. "I decided to make the trip last minute."

"How come?"

Emily shoved both hands into the back pockets of her blue jeans. "I was bored, and I like it here."

When Emily joined Mina at the front door, Mina saw some emotion disturbing the calm depths of her brown eyes. A pinch of affection struck her in the rib cage.

"Is that all?" Mina prodded.

After a beat, Emily flung a heavy sigh into the air. "I was

m-my m-mom's full-time caretaker for nine years." Her voice grew watery. "And now I have nothing to do. And nowhere to be."

Mina's heart squeezed. "I'm glad you're here." She slipped an arm around Emily's shoulders and led her inside. "You can be my first guest."

"Oh, wow," Emily breathed, her gaze traveling around the foyer. "This is amazing."

Pride bloomed in Mina's chest.

Emily turned toffee-colored eyes on Mina. "It's done?"

"It's done."

"So what's the plan?"

With a jolt, Mina realized she didn't have a one.

Mired in the darkness and despair of her past all those long months, she'd struggled even to remember to eat and to get out of bed each morning. The renovation had pressed on, but only because a crew of five to fifteen men had showed up at the house every day.

The time to fill the house with summer tourists was nearly upon her, and she lacked a viable business plan for operating a bed and breakfast.

The pang of disappointment wrenched in her chest. At the goal line, she'd stubbed her toe and tripped, a yard shy of the finish.

"I tried to start a website a few months ago," Mina began. "You know, for the business. But it crashed, and I can't figure out how to fix it."

Light from the chandelier caught the flicker of alarm that stole over Emily's face.

Mina poked the toe of one sneaker at an imaginary speck on the floor. "I posted a free ad on a travel website online," she mumbled.

Emily worried her bottom lip. "Has anyone called to m-make a reservation?"

Mina shook her head.

"Oh. Okay." Emily's gaze swept from one side of the house to the other. "M-maybe we could hang some curtains?"

Mina suppressed a groan. "I'm kind of out of money right now, but maybe in a few weeks—"

Emily lit up. "Let's go shopping. It'll be my housewarming gift to you."

"Buy me a plant or something. There are fifty-nine windows in this place. Curtain will cost way too much."

"I'm rich." Like a criminal's confession, Emily's declaration burst into the air between them.

Mina blinked at her.

Emily's mouth pulled down into a fierce scowl. "I hate it. It was my m-m-mom's money, and now it's m-mine b-because she's dead. I'd give it all away if it meant I could spend one more day with her. But I can't. So…help me get rid of some of it."

"Oh, Em, I'm so sorry."

"Help me spend the money." Her dark eyes glistened. "I don't—I don't want it."

Mina wanted to protest, but she wanted to help her cousin, too. "I don't know. We'll see. Why don't you come pick out a bedroom?"

Mina turned toward the stairs.

While Mina took the staircase to the right, Emily moved toward its twin on the left side of the foyer. "You know what else we should buy?"

"What's that?"

"Some furniture."

Mina tripped on the stair step, but quickly recovered. "I have furniture. Lots of furniture."

"Really?" Emily's smile beamed across the gulf between them. "Then all we need is some people."

~

AROUND NOON THE NEXT DAY, Mina and Emily pulled into Vivian's driveway to retrieve Mina's dumpster-rescued treasure trove of furniture. The house appeared closed, and Mina hoped Jake and Vivian were still at their Florida home, waiting out the last remnants of winter weather.

But when Mina unlocked the front door, the sound of the TV playing carried from the other room. She and Emily slipped inside the house?

"Hello?" Mina called. "Mom?"

There was no response.

With a frown, Mina crept toward the living room, where the theme music of a daytime soap opera blared from the flat-screen TV hanging above the fireplace. Had they left the TV on for the cat again?

Just then, Vivian's head popped up from behind the sofa.

Mina gasped with her shock. Her surprise had less to do with her mom's sudden presence and more to do with her appearance. Every day, her mother woke up early and dressed in one of her stylish outfits. But now, she wore no makeup, and gray hairs streaked her temples and crown. The sun streamed in through the large windows and cruelly bared the lines of age on her face and neck.

"I didn't know you were home."

As Mina came around the end of the couch, she saw a throng of faded Polaroid pictures littered the coffee table.

Vivian dug out from under a pile of blankets and tugged on her twisted-up nightgown. "I'm moving a little slow this morning." She sniffled and ran a hand through her uncombed hair.

"You don't have to get up. Emily and I are here to get that stuff from your garage."

Vivian's gaze landed on Emily. "Oh, very good. Take

anything you need." She sank back down into the sofa cushions.

Mina hesitated, uncertain. "Uh, where's Jake?"

"He's still in Florida. I think he'll be home in a few days."

"Did you stay in Michigan all winter?"

Vivian nodded. "A lot of it. I grew tired of the sunshine. It gets obnoxious after a little while."

Mina gaped. "Mom, are you okay?"

"I'm fine." Vivian's attention riveted on the TV, where the soap had resumed after a commercial break. "You girls have fun."

Mina led Emily through the kitchen and into the garage. It took them more than an hour to load Mina's truck and figure out a way to tie everything down securely. Mina estimated it'd take at least two more trips to collect all the items she'd stashed in her mom's garage.

On the ride back to Thief Island, Emily stared out the passenger window. "I cannot believe how b-beautiful it is here. It's like the exact opposite of the desert."

"You live in Phoenix?"

"Tucson." She laughed and added, "Unless I decide to stay here forever."

"I'll put a permanent hold on your bedroom, just in case."

A dimple formed high in Emily's right cheek when she smiled.

Prompted by the look of wonder on Emily's pretty face, Mina spent the next several miles catching glimpses of the view with fresh eyes. Rolling hills and sloping sand dunes gave way to the sweeping expanse of water, with diamond chips sparkling across the surface.

"What do you think about having a party?" Emily asked.

At their exit, Mina switched on her turn signal and eased onto the off-ramp. "What kind of party?"

"I think you should have a grand opening."

Mina frowned. "Do you think anyone would come?"

"People will come," Emily said. "They're curious."

"They are?"

"Okay, it's possible they're just nosy, but if w-we can get them to come tour the house, they might recommend us to their friends and family when they visit. Anything to help you fill those empty guest rooms."

Mina considered that. "But how do we get them to come to the grand opening?"

Emily shrugged. "Free food and alcohol." Her smile turned mischievous. "W-works like a charm."

MINA AND EMILY spent the next few weeks in a constant state of feverish activity to prepare for the Winslow House Inn grand opening.

They mailed invitations, contacted vendors, and under Emily's tutelage, launched a full-blown marketing campaign to lure guests to Thief Island and the inn.

Then they shopped. They bought rugs and window treatments, cookware and place settings. They kept on shopping until the mere sight of the department store parking lot brought tears to Mina's eyes.

One afternoon, they returned with bedding for each of the seven guest bedrooms and set about outfitting the second floor. With her arms full of white linens and a queen-sized patchwork quilt, Mina headed for the bedroom at the end of the hall. When she stepped into the room, a fragrant perfume wafted in the air.

A kaleidoscope of memories crashed into her.

She tripped to a stop while a barrage of emotions assailed her. The choking fear. The nauseating shame. She recalled the day she'd arrived at the house, having been sent to live here with her grandmother. She remembered the bone-deep relief she'd felt at knowing she wouldn't see Jeremy that afternoon when she returned home from school, before any adults arrived home from work.

With the pain, she dropped the quilt onto the bed and pressed a fist to her abdomen, as if she might hold back the nausea.

She'd watched her mom drive away, and when Rose had disappeared into the kitchen to fix them a snack, Mina had set off to search the house, seeking the most isolated, secret spot she could find.

A hiding place.

There'd been nowhere to hide in her uncle's home, and she'd prayed this house offered her that much, at least.

That day, she'd discovered the widow's walk, and it'd become her hiding place ever after.

Mina blinked back the tears.

Slowly, she became aware of the white pitcher perched atop the dresser, stuffed with a bouquet of tulips and daffodils. Their familiar but long-forgotten scent had brought the memories hurtling back. When Rose was alive, she loved to fill the house with flowers from her garden. Emily must have discovered Rose's garden and gathered the flowers.

Mina squeezed her eyes shut and focused on her breathing. The recovered memories had a way of sneaking up on her at unexpected times. She and Chloe had talked about them. They'd talked, too, about faith. Faith in the process and in herself. They'd devoted an entire session to that one thing.

Mina's knees buckled, and she sank down onto the edge of the bed.

And she waited.

She didn't fight the dread and terror that spiraled through her. She didn't cry or cry out, but only waited as the tumult whipped through her with the wrath of a raging storm.

Moisture clung to her forehead, and she wiped a trembling hand across her clammy skin. In time, the grip of the past would release her. She knew now that it would.

She needed only to wait it out.

Through the dark tunnel of grief and chaos, a memory of another time touched the edges of her mind. Of Jeremy, as a young boy about seven or eight years old. He'd run to his dad, overjoyed with the wonder of finding a toad in the back yard.

But Jeremy had found this miracle moments before Senator Winslow was about to give a press conference. Heartbroken by his dad's cool admonishment, Jeremy had let the door bang shut when he left to return the toad outside.

Later that night, Uncle Preston had taken a leather belt to Jeremy for his disrespectful behavior.

Mina had cried when she heard the leather strap crack against the bare flesh on Jeremy's back. She recalled the agonized cry of a child and the angry welts that had wept with blood and morphed into gruesome bruises in the days after the abuse.

Mostly, she remembered the fear and confusion in her cousin's eyes.

With the memory, pity for that little boy flowed through Mina. On a broken sob, a dam of tears burst from her and streamed down her cheeks. The tears poured out of her. Powerful and relentless, they washed away all that stood in their path. They purged, and they cleansed.

The grip of shame and fear released her.

Her moment of grace had arrived.

CHAPTER 37

The night of the grand opening, Mina took the time to curl her hair. She pinned it atop her head, pulling a few curls loose to frame her face. A face that was pale, but not gaunt. Sad, but no longer haunted. The shadows under her eyes had faded.

She moved to her still-half-empty closet and retrieved her dark-wash blue jeans. She paired them with an ivory blazer, added brown ankle boots and Rose's pearls.

In the mirror, Emily popped into view wearing a flowy black blouse and black slacks, the same outfit she'd worn the day they'd buried her mom. "Ready?"

It surprised Mina to realize that she was ready. At one time, she would've avoided the spotlight the way a vampire avoided sunlight. But now, she was proud of the work she'd done to restore one of the island's oldest structures, and she was eager to share the majestic home with her neighbors.

Her past was still her past. That hadn't changed. But all appeared different to her now. Sharper, clearer. Full of sound and color. After a lifetime in the shadows, she'd awakened, and she no longer viewed the world through sleep-veiled eyes.

Downstairs, they'd propped open the front door to allow guests inside with the warm westerly breeze.

At the bottom of the staircase, Sam smiled up at them. "You clean up nice."

Reaching the bottom step, she smacked him on the arm. "Gee, thanks."

His gaze swept the foyer. "The house is amazing. I think you're the only one who thought it could be."

She feigned shock. "I'm sorry, are you saying I was right?"

Sam laughed. "You were right, I'll admit it."

As Sam ambled away to join some of the other guys from the crew, Eddie lifted his chin, giving her a curt nod in place of a verbal greeting. Then Tyler bumped his elbow and red punch sloshed onto the floor.

Eddie's face turned bright red, and he let loose with one of his salty tirades. Fortunately, Sam intervened before Tyler retaliated.

The thought struck her then that she no longer feared these men, but felt a kinship toward them instead.

En route to the ballroom, Mina and Emily stopped to chat with Abbie and her dad, Mike, and Heather, and a few others from the pub.

In the ballroom, a swift beat of pride drummed in Mina's chest. Two large chandeliers and the many wall sconces cast a warm glow over the room and spilled outside onto the patio.

Guests, enticed by the light and the warm night air, trickled outdoors where torches on the patio's perimeter kept the darkness at bay. The low din of partygoers carried above the rhythmic sound of waves lapping toward the shore.

Just then, the sight of a form hunched over the hors d'oeuvres table caught Mina's attention.

She squinted in the dim lighting. "Mom?"

Vivian jerked around, a nacho poised at her lips.

The surprise of seeing her mother didn't compare to the shock of watching a nacho disappear into Vivian's mouth. Her mother never ate anything so decadent as nachos.

Never.

Ever.

"What are you doing here?" Mina asked.

"I was invited." Vivian sniffed. Her gaze skittered over Emily before returning to Mina. "Though I didn't get my invitation until Thursday."

"Sorry. The whole thing was kind of last-minute." Mina continued on her trek through the crowd, unwilling to let Vivian's negativity affect her evening.

"Thankfully, Drew called—"

Mina lifted a hand. "If you're going to tell me Drew's single again, I heard. I'm not interested."

Vivian waved off her words. "Don't be silly. You two would never suit. He called to make sure your invitation reached us. Which it hadn't, so it's a good thing he called." Vivian scanned the crowd. "Where's that doctor of yours?"

"The doctor...?" Mina blinked. "Noah? He, uh, he's over-seas. Working."

Vivian refocused on her daughter, and Mina braced for whatever criticism her mom would choose to highlight.

Instead, a wicked gleam glinted in Vivian's bright eyes. "Not for long, I'll bet. He'll want to be back at your side as soon as possible."

The shock slackened Mina's mouth.

"Trust me, darling. I know men, and that man sees only you."

"Mom, are you okay?"

"I'm fine." Vivian swiped a splotch of sour cream from the corner of her mouth with her index finger. And licked it.

Mina gasped.

"What?" Vivian asked.

"Nothing." Mina ate the smile from her lips. "I didn't realize you liked nachos."

"Have you tried these?" Vivian groaned. "They're divine." Another nacho bite of disappeared between her mom's lips. While she chewed, she reached for Mina's hand and squeezed. "You've done a good thing here," she said when she'd swallowed. "I'm proud of you."

When Mina realized Vivian wasn't talking about the nachos, the swell of emotion caused tears to prick the backs of her eyes.

Then Vivian's face twisted into a scowl, and she hauled Mina's hand beneath her critical gaze. "Honestly, Wilhelmina, you need a manicure. No man wants to be touched with these sandpaper hands."

Mina didn't bother to stifle the laughter that burst from her.

Vivian's attention fixated on someone over Mina's shoulder, and she wiggled her fingers through an immobile smile. "There's Lydia Russell. The last time I talked to her, she tried to tell me this little project of yours was doomed. I can't wait to gloat."

With that, Vivian tossed Mina an air-kiss and floated away.

But after only a few steps, Vivian turned abruptly, and her shrewd gaze alighted on Emily. "You have your mother's smile. Audrey always had the prettiest smile."

Then she was gone.

Two pink spots stained Emily's cheeks when she surveyed the table. "Do you think we need more..." Her sentence trailed off, but the last word leaked out. "Ice?"

Mina turned to see what had captivated Emily and found Luke standing at the ballroom entrance. He looked so like Noah that Mina's heart stuttered and fell into a thundering gallop.

A roguish smile teased Luke's lips as he leaned down to speak into the ear of the gorgeous woman on his arm.

Mina didn't recognize the woman. Her blonde, over-styled hair framed her perfectly symmetrical face, and large, jutting breasts capped off a narrow waist and long, lithe legs. Whether the luminous glow surrounding her was the consequence of her own beauty or a reflection of Luke's carnal smile and unbroken attention, Mina couldn't be sure.

Turning back, Mina glimpsed the misery in Emily's soft brown eyes as she watched the striking couple.

A stab of sympathy struck Mina in the breastbone. She, of all people, knew what it was like to pine for one of the Nolan brothers.

"There's plenty of ice." Mina looped her arm through Emily's and led her cousin from the ballroom.

MINA FOUND an empty table on the patio and sank into a chair. Her feet screamed to be let out of the confining heels, but the mellow breeze and soft drone of contented party-goers went a long way to soothing her body's aches.

When a shadow fell across the table, Mina peered up to find Shea filling the space in front of her, his shoulders blocking out the firelight from the tiki torches.

"The house is awesome. It's like I stepped back in time." A grin split his handsome face. "A very rich, luxurious time."

It was probably the nicest thing he could've said to her. Mina's cheeks warmed with pleasure.

"Thanks for fitting us in at the last minute for catering.

Your nachos are a universal favorite, by the way. I should've ordered twice the amount."

Shea's gentle laugh made him seem ten years younger. "I'm pretty sure they're the perfect food. After pizza, of course."

Their laughter died down, but he didn't immediately turn to leave.

Awkwardly, she cleared her throat.

"Have you talked to him?"

Mina didn't have to ask who "he" was.

"Only twice. We text, mostly. It's hard to get through, and with the time difference...." She stopped, knowing how lame her excuses sounded. "You?"

Shea shook his head, then sniffed. "Nah."

In the silence that followed, Mina's stomach churned. "Do you think he'll come back?"

Shea scratched at the bristle covering his square jaw. "I don't know."

Twin sighs drifted into the air between them.

"I was thinking," Shea began. "Maybe we shouldn't expect him to come back."

Her heart stopped.

"Maybe," Shea continued, "someone should go get him this time."

The words struck her like a match to tinder. Her spine snapped straight, and her heart thumped painfully against her breastbone.

Maybe someone should go get him.

Yes.

No one had tried to stop him. Not fifteen years ago, and not in the last several weeks.

No one had followed him. Not once, in all the years he'd been away, had anyone gone after him. No one had tried to find him and bring him home.

But she could. She could find him. She could tell him she loved him—they all did—and they needed him to come home.

Yes. Yes! YES!

Her heart whirred with longing. *Noah.* He was the only one who'd ever truly known her—who she was, who she wasn't, and who she wanted to be. She owed him this much, at least.

Doubt doused the flare of hope, and she deflated a little. What if he said no? What if he didn't want to come back? Or had decided he didn't want to deal with her and all her baggage? What if—

Shea held out a slip of paper.

With a curious glance, Mina took it and tilted it toward the light to peer down at the untidy, slanted handwriting. There was a phone number, and the name of a business. No, it was a hotel, with an address.

She squinted in the dim lighting. "Clonbur?"

"Fly into Shannon airport if you can, not Dublin," Shea said. "From there, you'll need to rent a car or catch the bus. The bus will take you from the airport into Galway. There, you'll have to catch another bus from Galway to Cong. That bus only runs once per day, so you'll need to time your arrival."

Mina stared up at him.

"In Cong, you'll need to get a cab to take you to Clonbur." He fell quiet. "What?"

"You sure know a lot about the geography of Ireland. Do you get back there often?"

"I've never been back." He scratched the underside of his chin. "I, uh, did a little research."

A warm tenderness squeezed her chest. "You were going to go get him, weren't you?"

Shea rolled his shoulders. "I'm not the one he wants to see."

She lurched to her feet and started toward the carriage house, her mind racing with logistical details—Shannon not Dublin, to Clonbur, no, Cong then Clonbur. When could she leave? Would it be possible to catch a flight tomorrow? Had she reached the limit on her credit card this month? Where was her passport? She hadn't used it in over five years, not since traveling to St. Bart's the year Vivian had decided to vacation there for Christmas.

She pivoted on her heel and headed in the opposite direction. First, she needed to talk to Emily and ask her if she'd house-sit. How long would she be gone? Would Noah want her to stay with him?

What if he didn't?

With a mental shake, she cast aside the questions. Whatever Noah decided, whether or not he wanted her, it was worth the risk of having her heartbroken to find out. *He* was worth the risk. She knew that, and so did his brothers.

She stumbled to a stop and spun around.

Shea stood alone in the center of the patio. He took a slow drink from his champagne flute and lowered the glass.

Mina pressed the note to her heart. "Thank you."

A satisfied smile transformed his face. "Bring him home."

CHAPTER 38

oments before boarding a flight the next afternoon, Mina called Noah's cell phone, but he didn't pick up and her call went straight to his voicemail.

In Chicago for a layover, she would've tried him again, except it was three a.m. in Ireland. When she arrived in London, she had only forty minutes to trek across the airport to catch her connecting flight to Shannon, which left her without a spare moment to try him again.

Nineteen hours after departing Thief Island, she set foot on Irish soil.

From the airport in Dublin, she took a train to Galway, boarded a bus that took her to Cong, and then caught a cab that carried her the rest of the way into Clonbur. By the time the cab deposited Mina outside the inn where Noah was staying, it was well past dinner and hunger warred with exhaustion for control over her mood.

A light mist dusted her hair and clothing as she rolled her suitcase to the inn's front door and ducked inside the lobby.

Warm heat and the scent of peat smoke crowded the

small cottage and clung to her as she crossed to the reception desk.

A young woman with dark hair and eyes smiled at her as she approached.

With one last obsessive glance at her cell phone to confirm Noah still hadn't returned her call, Mina mimicked the woman's smile. "I'm here to visit a guest. His name is Noah Nolan."

The woman consulted her computer and reached for the desk phone. "I'll ring the room. Your name, please?"

Her heart lodged in her throat, so Mina squeaked out her name.

Through the phone's receiver, the muffled sound of ringing carried over the line. A gang of butterflies banged with furious flutters in her empty stomach.

The woman replaced the receiver in the phone's cradle. "I'm sorry, no one's answering."

As the butterflies quieted, the adrenaline that'd brought Mina halfway around the world suddenly threatened to abandon her. "Is it okay if I wait here for him?"

"Be our guest." The woman gestured toward the loveseat and armchairs bracketing the fireplace.

Beside the fireplace, Mina propped her suitcase against the stone hearth and collapsed into an armchair. She laid her head on seatback and stared up at chunky wood beams that ran the length of the low-slung ceilings.

Now what? When would Noah return? What would he think about finding her here?

Through the row of recessed windows across the front wall, rain struck the glass, and a steady wind rattled the panes. The fire crackling in the stone fireplace chased the chill from her body even as unease rushed in.

She was in a foreign country, with nowhere to go, or

sleep, and the one person she knew on the entire island—hell, on the entire continent—wasn't returning her calls.

NOAH WAITED until his research team was well into their cups before he slipped off his barstool and made for the exit. At the door, he waved, and the group sent up a raucous cheer for no particular reason other than they were drunk and it was the end of another long workday.

The misty rain had turned into a steady drizzle, and the cool night air wrapped its chill around him as he made the short walk back to the inn.

With a quick glance in either direction, Noah crossed the darkened street at a clipped pace. Tonight, he was more anxious than usual to get away from the revelry and return to his room.

Return to his room, and to his cell phone.

He'd left it charging on the nightstand, and now his anxiety threatened to destroy his composure. He didn't wish to be without it, even for short periods. What if she tried to call? What if she needed, or wanted, him?

At the intersection near the inn, he stopped and waited for the traffic to clear before crossing the street.

He never should have left her. Every day his certainty in that grew.

He should've stayed. There was no doubt in his heart that he could have given her the space she needed while remaining physically close.

As it was, with him halfway around the world, he couldn't talk to her regularly. She couldn't reach him reliably.

He needed to go home.

The thought struck him like a lightning bolt and left him standing in the rain on the street corner, unmoving.

That was it. He needed to go home. Now. If not to be with her, then to at least be near her. Wherever she was, that's where he belonged.

She was home.

He burst into motion, darting through the rain and the rest of the way to the inn. He needed to pack and check the web for the earliest flight back to the States. Then he needed to let Caleb know he'd be in charge until Noah could return.

If he returned.

He yanked open the glass-paned door and shot across the quiet lobby toward the guest suites. This late, the staff had gone home for the night and the place was deserted. Only one small table lamp remained lit, and in the dim light he didn't see the black suitcase propped against the hearth until his toe caught its edge and he stumbled.

He bit out a curse and bent to right the compact suitcase that had fallen across his path when his foot had knocked into it. Who had left the blasted thing—?

Just then, he noticed the woman lying curled up on the loveseat. Her back was to him, and her hair spilled over the settee. Rich gold and deep ginger shimmered amidst chestnut brown in the firelight.

His insides clenched. He blinked several times to make sure she was real.

She was.

His heart gave a painful wrench. Could it be…?

It'd been twelve weeks since he'd seen her last. The longest twelve weeks of his life.

Twelve weeks, two days, and eleven hours.

Was his overtired, overstressed mind playing tricks on him, bringing to life that which he most wanted and could not have? Was it really her? Was she really here?

With a soft sigh, she rolled toward him. Her eyes fluttered

open and when her gaze landed on him, she bolted upright, scrambling to her feet with a sputtering of shocked noises.

Then she stood before him.

While his pulse pounded in his ears, he stared. The color had returned to her cheeks, and the fullness of her curves were restored. A faint, almost tentative curvature upturned her plump mouth.

With it, his heart beats doubled up, and air wheezed through his lungs. He accepted it all as the soundtrack of her smile.

Her genuine smile.

She whispered his name.

The breath left his body in a rush. God, how he'd longed to hear her say his name again.

He put down the urge to snatch her to him.

Fists clenched at his sides, he gulped. "You're here."

"I'm here."

In the silence that followed, the smile fell from her face and uncertainty filled her sapphire eyes.

Alarm trilled inside his skull and he shot several feet across the space between them before sliding to a stop. "Is something wrong? Did something happen? Are you okay?"

"I'm fine. Nothing is wrong." She tugged on the sleeve of her blouse. "I came for you."

"For me?" Her words knocked around inside his head but refused to line up in a way that made sense. "Did something happen to me?"

Her light laugh ricocheted through him. "I miss you. Your brothers miss you. They want you to come home as soon as you can."

Each word poured over him as a balm, healing the wounds from his past.

"I want you to come home, too." She tugged on the hem of her sleeve. "Forever."

He stood rooted to the spot, paralyzed by her light and love. Afraid that if he moved, the dream he found himself inside would suddenly shatter. If it meant he had to spend the rest of his days asleep, he never wanted it to end.

"You don't have to go back to Michigan." A nervous quiver infected her voice. "We could go wherever you want to go." She swallowed with an audible gulp. "I'm sorry if I s-surprised you by just showing up here. I tried to call…"

It was the sweetest dream he'd ever lived. But only a dream.

Reality awaited.

"Noah…?"

CHAPTER 39

He remained standing at a distance, his dark brown eyes glittering behind thick black lashes. He'd cut his hair, and the sun had recently kissed his cheekbones and the bridge of his nose.

No smile touched his mouth.

No words fell from his lips.

He didn't reach for her, nor did he display any sign how her sudden appearance after so many weeks apart affected him, or whether it affected him at all.

Sorrow clung to him.

Her heart sank with the tangle of self-doubt and insecurity pulling her down.

She pushed aside the fear that kicked in her chest and took a small, tentative step closer to him. "I'm sorry it took me so long. I should've come weeks ago."

His throat worked, as though he would speak. But just then, the inn door burst open, and a couple stumbled into the small lobby on a rush of laughter and cool air.

She jolted, and a soft curse slipped from Noah. Then he stooped to haul her suitcase off the floor.

Her heart thrashed against her ribcage as he clasped his hand around hers and led her down a dimly lit hallway to a door at the far end.

With the hotel card key he filched from his back pocket, he gained access to the room and shoved open the door. He placed his hand on the small of her back and she slipped into the dark room ahead of him.

The door shut and plunged them into darkness.

A chill touched her skin when he left her side, then with a soft click, dim lighting from a desk lamp trickled across the cozy bedroom.

He stood in a ribbon of shadow.

She sidled closer until a strand of light fell over his face. His features remained set, inscrutable. Slowly, she closed the gulf between them. When she stood before him, she reached up and trailed her fingertips through the prickly stubble along his jawline. He held his body rigid, and she could feel the tension vibrating off him.

"Noah," she whispered. "What is it? What's wrong?"

His chest rattled when he dragged in a shaky breath. "I don't want to hurt you."

Unsure what his words meant, she searched his face. Was he apologizing for some hurt he believed he had caused her? Or was the hurt he alluded to forthcoming? Was he about to break her heart by refusing her?

Then her eyes found his, and behind the deep brown flecks, she discovered a stark, heart-wrenching fear.

He was afraid. Not for his sake, but for hers.

A smile brushed her heart. "You couldn't hurt me. It isn't possible."

Doubt battled with hope in his eyes.

She willed herself to be as vulnerable as he was.

Reaching up, she cupped his cheek. "Noah, do you think I'd cross an ocean to find you if I thought it possible you could hurt me?"

Air whistled through his clenched teeth. "I don't know…"

"I love you," she whispered. "I want to be with you, and if you say you want to be with me too—"

On a smothered curse or a sob, she couldn't tell which, he snatched her to him and buried his face in her hair. "I want you, too."

Joy erupted in her heart, and a watery sound escaped her. "When I asked you to leave, it's not because I didn't love you. I was afraid."

"I know."

"I'm still afraid."

When he pulled back, she saw that the pain in his eyes burned brighter.

"I'm afraid I'm going to hurt you, too," she confessed. "Or disappoint you."

"Ah, Mina." He slipped his hand beneath the curtain of her hair and gripped her nape.

"I'm afraid…" She grasped his wrist and held on, as though his strength might steady her. "I'm afraid I'm broken."

"You're not broken." He held her tight to him. "You're human."

She prayed that was true. She believed it was. With her ear pressed over his heart, the thundering refrain inside his chest pumped through her. To him, the man that she loved, and to herself, she wanted to prove it.

She rose on her tiptoes and, placing her hands flat against his broad chest, touched her lips to his beautiful mouth.

He allowed her exploration, so she relished the feel of his heat and the delicious smell of his scent without hurry. When she tasted him with a tiny, tentative lick of her tongue, the warm, buttery kiss fluttered low in her belly, and lower still, like soft fingers between her legs.

With it, the old fear surged.

They hadn't been intimate since she'd recovered her memory. What if she froze? What if he saw her fear and misunderstood its source? What if he blamed himself? What if he blamed her? What if—

No!

She took control of her racing thoughts.

Her muscles had tensed, a reaction born of instinct rather than reality, and he had noticed the fearful response.

He peered down into her face. Lines bracketed his mouth, and his dark eyes shimmered with a pained hesitancy, as though the effort to hold back cost him greatly.

But hold back, he did.

I don't want to hurt you.

She realized then that he was waiting for her. He needed to know she wanted this as much as he did. He needed her permission, and the fear he wouldn't receive it showed on his face, naked and raw.

Her heart contracted. That he worried about her made her feel cherished. Loved.

The fear vanished like the stars at dawn.

"I love you." She kissed him, then lingered with lips barely touching. "I trust you."

Warm molasses sparked with heat.

Her eyes held his when she lifted her hand and brushed her fingers across the spot on the inside of her wrist where her pulse throbbed.

He dipped his head and pressed his mouth to her sensitive skin.

While his thumb swept over the mark of his kiss, she trailed the fingers of her other hand over the hollow at the base of her throat.

His mouth covered the place where she touched.

Her hand slipped lower to pop the buttons on her blouse.

She drew the fabric apart with a soft sweep of her fingers over the rounded swells of her breasts.

A look of secret wonder stole across his face, and his mouth followed the path her fingers forged.

Working together with hands made clumsy by the emotions surging through and between them, they removed their clothing, taking time to stop and explore with each revelation of newly bared flesh.

When she eased onto the bed, Noah stretched out beside her, but on his face, his struggle played out for her to see. Passion warred with worry. Arousal with restraint.

And in that moment, Mina discovered a place deep within her that had remained untouched by the pain and betrayal of her past. A tiny corner of her soul that couldn't be reached without her permission. It was to that place she went when the memories returned.

It was love, and Noah lived there, inside her heart.

For him, she parted her thighs.

He settled in the cradle between her legs and sank into her wet heat. She took him deep, gasping in sweet agony as the fire in her heart spread to the spot where their bodies joined.

Together they moved, seeking, and finding, that exquisite rhythm. With each delicious push, her heart expanded. He filled her, again and again, and she stretched to take him fully. Completely.

Until he became a part of her. Inseparable. Whole.

Wholesome.

When the first ripples of an orgasm shuddered through her, he took her face between his hands and stared into her eyes. He pumped into her with long, unhurried strokes until, finally, the ecstasy crashed over him, too.

In time, the sounds of their heavy breathing faded. Their heated skin cooled.

Still inside her, his dark, compelling gaze touched her face. "You're not alone, *a mhuirnín*. Not anymore."

With his words, a frisson of alarm rattled through her.

He dropped a kiss on her nose. "Don't fret. I only wanted you to know you don't have to carry it alone. I'm here for you if you need me, and I love you."

With the soft gasp of her surprise, he cocked his head to one side. "What? That surprises you?"

"It's just... you never said that to me before."

"Said what? That I love you?" Cupping her face, he stroked her cheek with the pad of his thumb. "I'm sure I did. You probably just forgot."

"I don't think I'd forget something like that." A frown tweaked her features. "Although I can't understand what you're saying half the time."

"See, there you go." He toyed with the hair at her temple. "I told you it couldn't be true."

She closed her eyes and tilted her head toward the soft brush of his fingertips against her cheek.

"Marry me," he said.

Her eyes flew open. The cocky grin might've fooled her, but the glimmer of vulnerability in his eyes told her his aim was not to tease.

She nearly blurted out her answer, but a ripple of uncertainty stopped her. "Are you sure?"

He gave her a disapproving scowl. "Have you ever known me to be unsure of what I want?"

"Well, no, but... this is a little different..."

"I can't risk us being separated ever again," he said. "Marry me."

"Even though I...? Even though I'm...?"

He nuzzled the spot below her ear. "Marry me, Mina."

She moistened her dry lips. "Even after...?"

The ugly words died on her tongue when he lifted his head.

His features softened with a heartbreaking tenderness and he tucked a strand of hair behind her damaged ear. "Even after all the years we spent apart, I never stopped thinking about you. Wanting you. No matter how much distance I put between us, I couldn't let you go."

Tears blurred her vision, and she inhaled a sharp, shuddering breath.

"I hate that someone hurt you," he said. "But I love you. All of you, and there isn't a single thing about you I would want changed."

Her watery laughter bubbled up. "Now I know you're lying."

"I want to call you my wife." He captured her hand in his and laced their fingers together. "Say yes."

"Of course I'll marry you."

A whoosh of air escaped him, and he dropped his forehead to her shoulder. "Geez, you had me worried there for a second. I thought I was going to have to resort to the nuclear option."

"What's the nuclear option?"

"I was going to promise to live on that god-forsaken island, if that's what you wanted. Lucky for me, you caved first."

"We don't have to live on Thief Island. I'll go anywhere you want to go."

He rolled to lie beside her on the bed. "It's okay. I've resigned myself to it. It's a ridiculously big house, though. You don't expect me to clean, do you?"

"Well, actually...."

He turned his head on the pillow and hitched an eyebrow at her.

"I was, uh, thinking perhaps I might...."

"Out with it, Winslow."

"I want to sell the house."

"*What?*" He propped up on one elbow and glared down at her. "Why? That house means everything to you."

Her smile tasted bittersweet, flavored with a twinge of fear at what she'd almost lost. "No, not everything."

The light in his eyes softened. "But I don't understand. You love that old place."

Yet she felt nothing remotely like sadness at the thought of selling it.

"I do, but I love you more. You're my home now, and I want to be with you, wherever that may be." She flung her arms out wide on the bed. "And I'm tired."

A smile twitched near the corners of his mouth. "If you're sure about this…"

"I am. I'm going to sell it to Emily. That way, I can visit whenever I want. But she'll have to figure out how to earn an income off that blasted money pit."

He scratched the back of his head. "Well, this is certainly interesting."

"Interesting?" She turned her head on the pillow to better see his expression. "How so?"

"I talked to the couple subletting my flat in Dublin. They want to take over the lease. Permanently. I told them they could."

She gaped at him. "Why did you do that?"

"I planned on moving to the States." With his shrug, a smile broke loose. "We're homeless."

A moment of stunned silence hung in the air, then their laughter filled the room.

He dropped his hand onto his bare torso as his laughter died down. "I wonder if Emily will let us rent a room for a while?"

"I don't care where I sleep." Mina rolled up against his side and laid her hand over his. "As long as I'm with you."

Plucking up her hand, he pressed his mouth to the center of her palm, and his wicked smile flashed. "Because you love me."

"You and no other."

"Say it again."

"I love you, Noah."

He studied her with serious, heavy-lidded eyes, as though he might find a different answer if he peered closely.

She allowed him to see the words she couldn't yet speak. That before he'd come back into her life, her world had been dark and cold. That the violence and the chaos of her past had eaten away at her soul all those long years, and when he'd cracked open her heart again, the anguish had come pouring out. It'd nearly drowned her, but through the darkness, his love had found her and pulled her from the black pit of despair.

Their love had saved her.

The smile that touched his lips filled her heart. "How long have you loved me?"

"Oh, I don't know…" She raised her arms over her head and his hand slid to her waist. "A week. Possibly two."

She gasped at the first tickle.

"How long?"

"It's hard to say—Noah!"

He soothed her with kisses until she was soft and liquid in his arms.

Above her head, his hand found hers, and he entwined their fingers. "How long?"

At the hitch in his voice, she whispered, "All of my life."

Sorrow shadowed his expression. "I'm sorry it took me so long to figure it out. Can you ever forgive me?"

"Never."

He closed his eyes.

Her fingers traced a lazy path from his cheek to his jawline. "You know, for supposedly being a genius, you're surprisingly dense."

"So I've been told."

"Lucky for you, you have the rest of your life to make it up to me."

"Then I better get started." He bent his head and nuzzled the side of her neck.

It had taken them more than a decade to find their way back to each other. But she couldn't muster any anger or resentment over their separation. Maybe all was as it should be.

If he'd stayed, maybe the memories would have lain dormant inside her, a silent haunt. Or maybe the past would've poisoned their love and separated her from him long ago.

If he'd never returned, it's possible she'd have come to this place of fragile peace without him, and her life would be much the same as it was now.

Perhaps.

Except she wouldn't be about to marry the Rock Star of Academia.

Want more Nolan brothers? Next up in The Nolan Brothers series is Luke and Emily's story, SWEETEST MISTAKE.

Snag your copy now.

ALSO BY AMY OLLE

THE NOLAN BROTHERS

Beautiful Ruin

Sweetest Mistake

Dirty Play

Mad Love

Last Heartbreak

THE NOLAN BASTARDS

Her Wicked Stepbrother

Saint

Warrior

ABOUT THE AUTHOR

Amy Olle is a USA Today bestselling author of contemporary and new adult romance novels. She enjoys putting her psychology degrees to good use writing emotional, redemptive love stories filled with beautifully flawed characters, cozy settings, and deliciously erotic sexiness.

Amy is living happily ever after in Michigan with her college sweetheart, their brilliant son, and a turtle named George.

When she's not busy burning up the pages in her next novel, she loves to hear from her readers. You can email her at amy@amyolle.com or contact her on social media.